THE DAY MUST DAWN

By Agnes Sligh Turnbull

THE ROLLING YEARS

REMEMBER THE END

THE DAY MUST DAWN

DEAR ME: LEAVES FROM A DIARY

THE DAY MUST DAWN

By

AGNES SLIGH TURNBULL

NEW YORK

THE MACMILLAN COMPANY

1942

To the People
of
Old Westmoreland

"Many cities have risen and fallen to decay without leaving so glorious a record as this collection of mud-plastered huts scattered along the old military road among the trees of the primeval forest. Its name lives only in the history of Western Pennsylvania, and the site of those scenes of war and peace is now covered with clover blossoms and waving wheat.

"Its claim for remembrance is in this, that it was the first place in the United States west of the Appalachian mountain chain where justice in the legal forms, sacred to the traditions of the English-speaking people was dispensed; in this, that here the back woodsmen, descendants of a patriotic British ancestry, first raised their voice against ministerial tyranny; in this, that here dwelt the race which, standing a barrier, as a wall of fire between civilization and barbarism, defended their homes through years of an incessant war with the fiercest enemy ever opposed to the Whites. To one given to speculation, the destruction of this place is a subject for reflection."

GEORGE DALLAS ALBERT in his
"History of Westmoreland County"

When I was a small girl, driving with my parents from the village of New Alexandria in western Pennsylvania to Greensburg, the county seat, I always used to beg them to stop the horse at one spot in the road and tell me again about Hannastown-that-was-burned-by-the-Indians.

With the buggy-whip for a pointer, they would indicate a little valley beneath a hilltop. "There," they would say, "once lay Hannastown right on the old Forbes Road. There stood the fort and stockade; about there, probably, was the old plank bridge over which a few brave horsemen rode back and forth one night to fool the Indians into thinking great reenforcements were at hand. About there must have stood Robert Hanna's big cabin which housed both tavern and court. Over that hill you can still see Captain Brownlee's grave. His wife was taken captive. They were kin of ours." As we jogged on again through the summer dust the tales were told more fully.

Gone, long gone now, are the town, the court, and the tavern. Only the old spring bubbles still where the stockade once stood. But the ground is soaked with memories.

I have tried to evoke some of them in this story. The

plot is, of course, fictitious as are many of the characters, though I have used names which were a part of the town for sentiment's sake; but the details of the Indian engagements are all authentic—even to the buffalo and Sam Craig's singing!

It is impossible to record the names of all those who have helped me with this material: those who put old manuscripts into my hands; who lent me books now out of print; who told me old stories and who gave me wise advice and counsel. But though I cannot list them here. I acknowledge their help with deepest gratitude.

A. S. T.

MAPLEWOOD, NEW JERSEY

THE DAY MUST DAWN

The Fawn

That fall of 1777, winter had set in early in the Back Country. A hard frost had dropped upon the corn crop before September was gone; the first good hunting snow had come the last of October and now, since mid-November, the world had been buried deep in white.

Forbes Road, that thoroughfare conceived and born of military necessity, moving sharply, straight up and straight down the western Pennsylvania mountains, keeping to high ground whenever possible in order to avoid alike ambush and swamps, was now discernible only by blurred, low running drifts. Travelers and express riders from the east were wont to pause for a little in the summertime when they reached the crest of the Laurel Ridge so that their eyes might envision the far-flung majesty of the rolling wilderness.

In winter, however, they only tightened the girth straps on their horses, pulled their own coats closer, gritted their teeth, and set themselves for the last leg of the journey: Ft. Ligonier, Hannastown, Pittsburgh—the edge of the frontier.

While the snow still lay deep everywhere in the Back

Country after the turn of the new year, it seemed to settle heaviest in the narrow valley, where the village of Hannastown sent up the blue smoke from its thirty-odd chimneys. There was indeed a strange bounty about the snow here; a free and careless surplus which contrasted ironically with the hard scarcity of the materials of daily living.

There was a beauty about it also as it covered the raw roofs of the log cabins with curving windrows, and topped the sharp posts of the stockade around the fort with tufts like tow. It softened over the bleak outlines of the whipping post and the pillory, and formed crystal walls on either side of the paths that led to the stables, the blacksmith shop, the tavern, and the spring.

But, to most of the dwellers in the town, this bounty and this beauty meant nothing. To them the snow had a much greater significance. It meant respite. It meant that for its duration the darkness of the small settlement's brief history was sealed over by the white. The men (those few who were left after the Eighth Pennsylvania had been recruited) could sit about Robert Hanna's tavern emptying their noggins of beer, or supping up their bowls of Continent, free to shout at the top of their lungs over a good lusty story, with the muscles of their faces relaxed from the eternal strain of watching and listening. They could go to the stables to feed a horse or fodder a cow without a rifle in one hand.

And the women? Oh, blessed, blessed snow! The women could go about their daily tasks these weeks with their hearts a bit eased from the iron hand of fear which usually gripped them. The tense network of lines around their eyes smoothed out a little, and something like peace—even though transient—touched them. For Indian summer with its last threat was now behind them for another year; and the powwowing days of February lay ahead. There would still be four weeks more, perhaps even five, before open weather.

And in this time of relaxing, this winter hiatus, there was always a chance to hope. Perhaps by another spring and summer things would be better. There might be more rangers on duty. The Eighth Pennsylvania might be sent back where it should have been all the time. Oh, perhaps, come this next spring, the Indians would all move on westward . . . Even this extravagant hope had place. Meanwhile, the snow.

In the last of the thirty log cabins, at the very edge of the village, on this January morning Martha Murray stood before the great fireplace, a long stick in her hand, stirring a kettle of tallow which hung, melting, on the crane. She was a tall spare woman with strong bones showing in her thin face. Her eyes were brown, and her complexion sallow. The only beauty that remained to her was an abundance of curly hair which, by some curious alchemy of the body, had turned darker through the years instead of gray. Her mouth was large and firm, and her smile set the whole face alight.

She was smiling now, as she stirred the tallow.

"I'd think you'd be tired hearing it. I've told it all so often."

The young girl sitting behind her on a rough wooden bench, her lap full of cotton yarn, looked up eagerly.

"But it all sounds new to me every time. It does, Mother. Please go on. It's like reading a book to hear you tell it. Or taking a journey even. Don't stop."

"Well, that was the way the garden was, good rich earth made up into beds with little paths between them. There were currant bushes and gooseberries to the one side and a long row of bee boxes along the back fence. My mother had such a knack with the bees. She hardly ever got stung. Once in a long time we'd see her come in from the garden holding an onion to her face or her arm, but that was all there ever was to it. She liked bees. I've always thought if only I could have them here it would seem more like home some way."

"And the lilacs?"

"Yes. They made a sort of hedge between the garden and the lawn. Big bushes they were, both white and purple, and when they were all out in the spring, if we had a warm, rainy spell you could smell them clear to the house."

The woman turned from the fireplace, the long stick with which she had been stirring the tallow still in her hand, and stood looking past the girl.

"And the summer nights back home were something wonderful. You could go out in broad moonlight with never a thought of a savage! A many a time I've slipped out to the garden when they thought I was asleep in my bed, and just stood there. In June maybe when the roses would be at their best, or at midsummer when the moon would be red and the stocks and the pinks would be blooming. It would nigh overcome me. The scent, you know, and the moon overhead, and everything clear and open so you might a'most think it was day."

"Yes. Yes, Mother . . ."

"And all the houses would be quiet and peaceful and people sleeping easy with no terror on them. And the watchman's voice coming faint and comfortable-like from the next street, 'Twelve o'clock and all's well.' I didn't realize what the peace of it meant then, but, mind, I've thought of it plenty since."

"Don't stop, Mother."

"And my father rented the little field just back of our house so my mother could raise her flax there. And there was never a fear of a rattlesnake, *never*. You could go out through it any hour of the day or night, and pick up the retted stalks in your arms and never a serpent to be seen or thought of!"

The girl sighed a little. "It don't seem possible any place could be as safe as that."

"That's the way it was, back east. And the house was all white and set back a ways from the street with two maple trees by the walk. There was a little porch to the front, and when you went in you were in a hall where the stairs went up from. Real stairs, they were, with a landing halfway up. And the rooms were all ceiled in and papered. In the dining room there was a big sideboard that my mother brought from the old country, and a corner cupboard with willowware like I've told you about—"

"To eat off flowered plates!" Violet mused. "If I could do that but once, I think I'd die happy."

"And in the parlor there were two side tables, polished to see your face in them, and my father's desk—"

She broke off suddenly and turned toward the kettle, sniffing sharply.

"If I've scorched this tallow, I'll never let my tongue get the best of me again! Sometimes I wonder if it's right of me to be bringing up the past like this . . ."

Violet rose from the bench, holding up the yarn she had been cutting in her linsey-woolsey skirt. Together they smelled the tallow.

"Is it scorched, think you?"

"I guess mebbe not. But I was scared there for a minute. That would have been glaiket of me and no mistake. It's melted now, so we can get to work."

The woman lifted the kettle carefully from the fire and poured the contents into a wide wooden firkin that stood waiting at her feet. Violet, meanwhile, was busy looping the last lengths of the white yarn she had cut over straight pieces of stick. When she had finished, there were fifteen of them, with six dangling strings spaced evenly on each

"I guess it all comes back to me every candle making," Martha said, "because there's nothing irks me more than to be still using tallow dips! I suppose it's wicked of me but I'd like so cruel well to have good pewter molds before I die!"

"You know we could borrow Mrs. Hanna's. She's often told us. I don't see what's to hinder."

"I'll be beholden to nobody," Martha said firmly. "If I can't afford my own molds, I'll do without. What if they would get dinged or out of shape when we had them

Then a pretty face we'd have returning them! Oh, well, you're young yet. Things are bound to be easier for you. If I thought *you'd* be dipping candles all your life I'd feel worse."

Violet laughed lightly. "I don't mind the work so much, but I do like the looks of the smooth round ones. Are you ready now?"

Holding the sticks carefully, they plunged the strings into the melted tallow, then rested the stick ends across an empty vessel near by so that the wicks might drip. When the last one was done, they began with the first again, repeating their motions over and over, and with each dipping a thicker coating of tallow formed upon the strings.

"It's strange the way I am," Martha said suddenly, as they worked. "When it comes to big troubles like sickness and death and serpents and Injuns I can keep my upper lip as stiff as the next one. But it's the little things that fash me. Like not having good candle molds now, or your father always standing in front of the fire when I'm cooking, or the cow kicking over the milk bucket! It's wrong to be so fretted over little things, and yet I guess maybe women are like that."

She looked across the firkin at her daughter. The girl was completely intent upon her work. She dipped and set to dry, dipped and set to dry, sometimes touching and shaping the soft, swaying tallow strings with careful fingers, her brown brows drawn lightly together, her rosy lips pursed.

Martha sighed as she watched her, and remained silent. Her thoughts, however, according to an old habit formed through years of stress and loneliness, had the articulated emphasis and rhythm of the spoken word, even though the sound of them echoed only in her brain!

Look at her! She can make a halfway dainty business even out of candle dipping. Oh, she's pretty! Even if she's flesh of my flesh it can't be a sin to think it! But she can't ever stand what I've stood. She's too tender made by far. . . .

The woman's face drained white, but she set her strong lips firmly together: *Even though she's all I've got left, even if I'd never lay eyes on her face again in this world I'd send her east tomorrow if I could. . . .*

There was a sudden quick knock at the door, and the two straightened from their task.

"Run, Violet," Martha said. "It'll be either Betsy or Peggy, I doubt."

It was both of them. Betsy was plump and blonde, with dimples in her cheeks and blue eyes that twinkled as she talked. There was in them, though, none of the still wonder which lay in Violet's. Peggy was tall for her thirteen years, with a womanly face and long brown braids.

Seeing the girls together, Martha felt the blood rush more quickly through her veins. The youth were never completely young in the Back Country; not with death and destruction upon them from their cradles. But they were still beautiful. A force stronger than the savages saw to that.

It was only for a little while, though, that the fresh loveliness lasted. Age would come early to these girls as i had come to her. The youth must bow under the mid-day heat and burden before the morning dew was spent. That was only one of the cruel laws of the wilderness.

"We came to tell you that the crust bears!" Betsy was announcing excitedly now. "The young ones have been out this morning with the dogs, and it holds right up. Last night's freeze was just enough after the little thaw. Will you go racing this afternoon, Violet? Can she, Mrs. Murray?"

"To be sure. It'll do you good. We'll hurry through with this candle mess as fast as we can. No word of the hunters back yet, I suppose, Peggy?"

"Oh, no. They'll stay on for a week, Father says. Mother still worries some about panthers, but Father says Dave and Hugh could give a panther the first bite and still lick him. I wish they'd get one. I'd like fine to have a skin for in front of my bed. But even if Dave got one he'd sell it, you may be sure. I'd never see hair of it!"

"Brother promised me one," Violet said eagerly. "He says he'll fix it up for me without the head. I hate to see the jaws. A bear's, I don't mind some way, but a pan-ther's! Ugh! He said he'd get one for me if he possibly could."

Martha's eyes rested tenderly upon her daughter's face.

He's just the same as a brother to her, she mused to herself while the girls went on chatting. *I doubt she's never had a thought about him different from Peggy here about their David. And Hugh's been a son to us, God knows, from the day we took him in. I couldn't fault him if I tried.*

The girls had finished making their plans now. They would pass the word along to the other young people, and by midafternoon, when the heaviest of the day's work in the cabins was completed and the older women were ready to settle to their spinning, they would begin upon the sport which the bleak necessity of their lives had helped them to invent. This was racing over the crust of the snow, made impervious by a slight thaw followed by a hard freeze. At such a time men, dogs, and wolves traversed the shiny surface with safety and ease. Only the tiny, sharp hoofs of the deer ever broke through.

"We'll be off, then," Peggy was saying. "I'll tell Mother you're getting a hundred new candles, Mrs. Murray. Now the long nights are come we'll have to be at the dippin' again ourselves."

"Your mother must come up of an evening and see how they burn, then," Martha answered with her ready smile. "It's time we women had a good crack round the fire to keep up with the menfolks at the tavern. Have you heard whether any late express has come with more news?"

"I don't know. Father's at the tavern now. That Irish man that came through last Saturday is still there. He thinks the roads are too drifted yet to go on to Fort Pitt. Father says he's a big blatherskite and he wouldn't trust him round a stump, but he's got such good stories to tell they hope he'll stay a few days longer."

Martha's face clouded.

"That minds me," she said, "you girls must not go too far when you're out on the crust and have some of th little boys along, since the big ones are away. I declare if it isn't Injuns you have to look out for in this county, it's some of these good-for-nothing stragglers. Mind you, now, what I say."

"Oh, we'll be careful," Peggy answered. "You see, I'll have Jamsey along, and that'll hold me back sure enough. It's Violet here that always outruns everybody else!"

"But I never go out of sight," Violet said eagerly. "I'll stop for you then, girls. Won't it be fine to have some racing? I only wish Hugh and Dave were here for it too!"

They settled again, mother and daughter, to their work, while the candles gradually took on more thickness and form. As it neared noon the last dipping was completed, and the sticks with their whitening pendants were carried carefully to the far end of the room where they were deposited across two light poles laid from one chair back to another. Here, away from the fire, they would harden gradually. It would remain then only to slip the looped ends of the wicks off the sticks and lay the new supply of candles in the long box on the shelf.

"Well, that's done, and a good job too," Martha said with satisfaction as she cleared away the vessels and set them in the corner. "Now we'll get a bite of dinner ready for your father, for there's no story big enough to hold him at the tavern when his stomach's empty! We'll fry a bit flitch, I think, and stir up some pone, for if he can borrow the Brisons' horse this afternoon he's going to finish getting those logs in, and that's a cold, hard business in the snow."

"Why doesn't he wait till Brother's back to help him?"
Violet asked.

"Oh, no telling when that'll be. And you know your
father! If there's a mean job to do, he'll be at it himself.
No matter how many dogs he kept, he'd still do his own
barkin'."

The interior of the Murray cabin in its general outlines was like all the others in the thirty dwellings of
Hannastown. The one room serving all purposes, the
chinked-in logs, the great fireplace with its array of iron
trammels, trivets, pots, and crane; the rifle hanging across
a couple of bucks' horns on the wall, the rude homemade
furniture, and the split log beds across the end—all this
followed the usual pioneer pattern.

But Martha Murray's native ingenuity, stimulated by
the warmth and intensity of her girlhood recollections,
had wrought some measure of transformation in the bare
room. First of all, there was a pervading air of cleanness
made possible only by superhuman efforts and, perhaps
even more, by an inborn nicety of movement and behavior which held in check some of the roughest details
of living.

Moreover there was a mellowness of browns in the
place which gave it a curious air of civilization. For
Martha by her unremitting industry had raised and spun
more flax than any of her neighbors. So she had linen left
over after the hunting shirts and waists and kerchiefs
were finished. This surplus, for which she had paid with
the very flesh from her bones, she had dyed a rich brown
with walnut hulls and made into cushion covers to be

filled with deer's hair and placed on the rude settle and the chairs. She had pieced together a sort of curtain too, to screen the beds from the rest of the cabin.

She had gone even further with the dark walnut hull brew. She had patiently stained the rough furniture itself, toning down the raw, new-hewn lightness to the tawny richness of autumn leaves.

Sam Murray, her husband, had laughed at her as she worked.

"What's the sense of fashin' yourself over that, now?" he had inquired. "This ain't Philadelphy, mind ye. This is the Back Country. This here, as the preacher says, is the frontier of the new world!"

"I'm not like to forget it," Martha had answered briefly. But she had continued her staining.

She had insisted upon shelves too, many of them. Sam grumbled a little but made them at various times by setting pegs between the logs and laying clapboards thereon, one above another. In the middle of the long wall was the most sacred of these. It held the three books which Martha had received from her father on her wedding day, and which she had managed to preserve through all the changing fortunes of her married life. They were the Bible, "Pilgrim's Progress," and Shakespeare. She read them over and over, snatching moments from her spinning, her scutching, her knitting, from the interminable warfare against the rough elements which constantly threatened to vanquish her. She had read them as an opiate back in the Cumberland Valley when her first babies had died and later when her two small boys were

slain by the Indians; she had read them as food for her
eager mind when the round of physical work all but
overmastered the spirit, as comfort for her soul when she
wrestled inwardly with bitterness, as stay for her reason
when memories would not let her rest.

Now Violet was reading them too, and they talked the
books over together, sometimes, of an evening. For them
especially, Martha had a way of pulling the big bearskin
in front of the fireplace, of sweeping up the hearth with
a wild turkey wing and then drawing settle and chair
nearer so that in the soft glow of the candles and the firelight this one corner of the room seemed in a measure
removed from the hard rigors of the wilderness.

She and Violet busied themselves now with preparations for the coming meal. Martha took down one of the
flitches that hung from the rafters and cut slices for the
skillet. Violet mixed the corn meal for the pone and laid
another log on the fire. Soon the heavy odors of the
cooking mingled with the smoke that filled the room.
The table setting was always a short business, for eating
utensils were scanty enough.

So everything was ready when the door opened at
noon, and Sam Murray entered with Watch, the big
shepherd dog, at his heels. He limped over to the fire and
stood in the center of the hearth, comfortably warming
his back while Violet and Martha dodged about him to
lift the flitch and the pone.

He was a big man, lean and rawboned like most of the
Scotch-Irish. His eyes were a cold, shrewd gray, his features strong and sharply cut. Forty years on the frontier

had weathered his naturally blond skin until it was wrinkled and swart as an Indian's. There was written all over him the hardy, invincible quality of his race. His grandfather, one of those Scotch Calvinists who had been transplanted to Ireland during the reign of James I, had shouted "No surrender!" at the siege of Londonderry and backed the words up with his life. Later his father, on his thrifty farm in Ulster, had shouted "Down with the Pope!" so often and so violently that discomforts multiplied as they did for many others like him, and the dangers of the yawning sea looked insignificant compared to the bitter thrall of persecution at home.

Moreover, the vast unexplored country beyond the stretch of waste waters whetted the appetite of the average Scotch-Irishman not only for religious liberty but for that sort of adventure for which he was by Heaven designed. It was because of this that Sam Murray at the age of five had found himself on one of the crude edges of the new world.

"Well," Martha was saying now cheerfully, "I suppose there were some big stories at the tavern this morning."

"Big enough, an' true ones this time," Sam replied, his bushy brows knitted. "There was an express come through from the east last night late, an' he says the war's goin' bad. The British are still holdin' Philadelphy, an' Washington's made camp at a place called Valley Forge, 'bout twenty mile to the north'ard, an' our troops are in' there like pizened rats. Freezin', starvin' they are, while the Commissary Department are sittin' on their fat hinds. May the devil pinch 'em!"

"Sam, mind your language now!"

"An' the Eighth Pennsylvany's there with the rest of 'em. There in Valley Forge. Damned if I didn't think better of Washington than that, so I did. 'Tain't as if he'd been sittin' round the east all his life twiddlin' his thumbs like some of them. *He's* been round these parts himself. He's had enough dealin's with the copper gentry, God knows, to reelize the dangers out here."

"He's maybe doing the best he can. He's got a big job on his hands, mind," Martha put in.

"I don't care if he has. He'd no need to order the regiment east. Wasn't we fair promised it when the Iroquoi went over to the British a year ago last July? Seven companies to be raised from Westmoreland County alone an' one from Bedford to protect us from the Tories an' the Injuns! That was the cry then. Every mother's son of 'em enlisted for frontier duty. An' look where they are now. Freezin' an' starvin' at Valley Forge. If they was ever fightin' there it wouldn't go again the grain so with me."

"We've just got to have patience and faith, Sam."

"Patience an' faith be damned! It's *works* we're needin' now, an' we're needin' 'em bad. There's crackin' warm fightin' to be done afore all these troubles is over. An' here I am beddin' down a cow! I tell ye, I've a good mind to start raisin' a new regiment myself, yet."

Martha from long experience let the first fury pass then added her arguments quietly.

"There's no use fashin' yourself like this, Sam. When the companies were forming you were flat on your back on that bed there, and none of us ever expected you to b off it. Look at your knee even now. Still stiff as a poker. A posy you'd have been to go marching over the mountains with the Eighth or off on Indian raids, either one. Besides, you've done enough of that already, dear knows."

Her face was grave, for she knew from the cold tension in Sam's gray eyes that he had not told all the news. She waited for it, the old familiar fears coming back to grip her heart as she placed the fried flitch on the table and Violet set down the pone.

"Was—was there anything else new?" she inquired hesitantly.

Sam limped to the table without replying. She could see that he was trying to envelop himself with some show of casualness. This was much more ominous than his outspoken anger. He ate now, heartily as usual but in silence. Violet too, Martha could see, was busy with her own thoughts: of the afternoon's play on the crust, no doubt. She was still at the age to savor the present without drawing fright from the future for long.

When Sam's appetite was appeased he spoke without looking up. His voice was lower.

"That feller Girty's at the Tavern. Come in from Pittsburgh last night. Simon Girty. He's been round here before. He brung some news."

"What was it?"

"Well, seems General Hand at Fort Pitt sent him out in November along the Allegheny to talk to the Senecas. The idee was for him to smooth the fur on 'em, especially old Guyasooter himself, an' keep the Six Nations quiet. Well, Girty was just tellin' us that it didn't work.

The blasted Injun's gone over to the British, an' he'
takin' the rest of them with him."

Martha's face was paler now. "Oh, Sam! That'll mak
things worse for us sometime, won't it?"

"Says they've been deceived by the whites, Guya
sooter does, an' they're goin' to join up with the King o
England." Sam's tone was bitter. "An' what else coul
you expect? Butler up at Niagara has been promisin' t
supply them an' their families with every needcessity
they'd just join up. An' old Hair-Buyer Hamilton out a
Detroit—may the devil pull every hair from his own pate
—offerin' them a bounty on every pioneer scalp the
bring in!"

Sam got up and limped across the floor.

"That fox of a Guyasooter!" he growled. "Standin' u
at Fort Pitt at the Injun conference, handin' out string
of wampum right an' left an' givin' his solemn promi
the Six Nations would stay neutral! An' now goin' rum
an' stump over to the British. I tell ye I wouldn't tak
the oath of a redskin if he swore on a stack of Bibles l
was a liar!"

He sat down by the fire and removed his shoe pack
putting a new layer of deer's hair in the sole of each sho
before he returned it to his foot.

"An' I don't care for the cut of this here Girty's ji
either," he went on. "Never have. He's got an Injun loo
in the eye to me. They say he growed up amongst ther
an' that ain't so wholesome. He was tried in court here
Hannastown once, don't ye mind, a few years back? M
demeanor or somethin'. True bill, anyhow. Yes, sir,

Hand only knowed it, I think it was givin' the wolf the wether to hold when he sent Girty out to smooth down Guyasooter."

He drew a long breath as he hitched himself to his feet.

"I'm borrowin' Brison's horse, so I'll be gettin' some logs hauled," he stated briefly.

"Watch out for your knee, then," Martha adjured him anxiously. "Mind, the sort of rheumatism you've got isn't to be trifled with. The girls are going to go out racing on the crust this afternoon," she added.

Sam's face relaxed as he looked over at Violet. She was the very apple of his eye. In a time when parents were not given to demonstrative affection, fathers least of all, Sam Murray's love for his daughter was a matter of comment and frequently of criticism.

"If the Lord had smitten four of my childer already," Mrs. Brison often remarked, "I'd be slow about makin' an idol of the last one! It's temptin' Providence."

"At least I wouldn't be fondlin' her in front of folks. It don't seem decent, some way, in a man," Mrs. Shaw would concur. "Not that it's seemed to spoil Violet, I must say, but still it don't look becoming."

So said the neighbors behind Sam's back. But if they had charged him with idolatry to his face it would not have altered his conduct. The qualities that had made him once a tempestuous and overpowering lover, now made him more than the sternly conscientious parent of the prevailing pattern. He delighted in his daughter. He teased her; he bandied her with gentle jokes; he drew her to his knee and curled her hair about his fingers; he caressed her. None of the other fathers in the town did that.

"So you're goin' to do a little racin' today, eh?" he said now. "Well, don't fall through the crust an' forget to come back. Pity Hugh ain't here to outstrip you runnin'. You can't beat that feller in a chase. I'll bet he could outfoot Guyasooter, himself. Well, I'll be gettin' to work."

He tweaked the girl's curls gently and, calling Watch, left the cabin.

Martha and Violet went on about their work with the new shadow across their faces. This word of the Indian defection did not alter the peace of the present, but the hand of Time could not be stayed. Spring would come. Summer would come.

"I'm afraid," the girl said quietly, "that the news is too bad not to be true."

The form of the statement struck her mother's heart but she tried to make her voice reassuring.

"Oh, there's no telling. This Girty man may not have it straight. Besides, we may get more militia or rangers before warm weather. And don't take to heart all your father says. He don't mean it the way it sounds. About faith now, for instance. We've all got to keep firm hold of that, mind. Faith in the providences of God."

Martha's quick smile suddenly lighted her face.

"Who knows but that some of these days . . ."

"The forest will be all cleared . . ."

"And there'll be no more rattlers and copperheads . . ."

"And no more Injuns . . ."

"And we'll all have candle molds . . ."

"And eat off flowered plates!"

They laughed together over the little game, which was an old one with them when spirits were low. The woman saw with relief that the girl's eyes were bright again.

By midafternoon Martha was ready to settle to her spinning and Violet was free to join the other girls. She said good-bye to her mother and set out eagerly in the cold crisp air. It was a small thing enough, this matter of running over the crust in company with a few of her friends. And yet Violet was tingling with anticipation. The least excitement, if it was pleasurable, was both welcome and rare. Of the other sort there was always enough.

Peggy was waiting in front of her door, holding little Jamsey by the hand. The child had become her special charge since an Indian raid a year ago had left him orphaned and homeless. The Shaws as a family had taken him with all kindliness into their home, but Peggy had taken him to her heart.

"Come on, Vi," she called. "Don't let's lose a minute. Betsy went ahead to get the Hanna girls and Mary Dunan. They're all going. Isn't that fine? There they are now with the little boys. Let's cut across and meet them."

They hurried along, Peggy finally picking Jamsey up in her arms, until they were all together on the open space to the south of the fort. Here the gently rolling hillocks of snow smoothed out to a hard, glassy sheet. The sun was sheathed in a thin cloud so there was no glare to stab the eye with tiny, fiery swords; only a blue-white brightness which lay upon the hills like the beginning of dawn. The hush of dawn was here also; for the few sounds of the village were soon behind them and the forest stretched, white-shrouded and still, beyond the cleared space. Only deep within it, Violet knew, were quick-moving forms and sharp bright eyes peering from log or limb; cruel claws and tearing teeth also. But all that was what Hugh and David had gone to seek, to match their young strength against! And they would be safe enough. Nothing could harm Hugh. He was too strong and quick.

"I'll keep Jamsey," Jenny Hanna was saying, "if you want to race fast, Peggy. I don't like to run the way you and Vi do."

"I'll stay back too," her sister Marian said. "I get a pain in my side when I race too hard. So be off, the rest of you!"

It was settled after some parrying, and the others started with much lighthearted laughter, running, sliding, racing over the frozen snow.

"You can't catch me! You can't catch me!" Violet called as she darted ahead.

The clean, sharp air struck her as she raised her face to meet it. A great exhilaration possessed her: a joyous lightness which came seldom. She felt altogether happy and secure.

There were dark things hidden far below the crust. Great trunks of fallen trees, rough stumps, sharp rocks, dens of rattlesnakes. These all had power over her in the summertime, she was thinking. Now she sailed high above them, triumphant.

She glanced over her shoulder. The little boys had struck off toward the forest, the Hanna girls were having their own games with the child, the others, smiling and rosy, were panting some distance behind her. She could always outrun all the girls. She felt so light, so effortless now. It was not her body that raced and ran; it was her spirit which met the frosty wind and fused with it as it flew faster and faster over the smooth stretches of the snow.

Suddenly in front of her she saw a white-tail fawn emerge from the forest and start across the open space. It was well grown, having long since lost its spotted coat. It ran now with a vigorous, springing beauty, its head up, its flag aloft.

Violet stopped, watching it as though she had never seen a creature of its kind before. And this she suddenly realized was the truth. Never before had she looked at a deer with eyes of understanding. Often enough she had seen in them skin for garments, hair for stuffing moccasins, and flesh for the pot. But never had she been conscious of a fawn, running lightly, fleetly, even as she herself was doing, over the frozen snow; warm with life and with the unfulfilled promise of its body; atremble with the sweetness of the cold air, and the joy of flight. A young, glad thing with slanting eyes edged in velvet, with little heaven-pointed ears and delicate, glistening legs.

But she saw this all now, and a wave of feeling for the fawn swept over her. She was sister to it. They were bound together by some vital affinity. Both so young, so eager for life if it was vouchsafed to them, and both, for this brittle moment of time at least, lifted above the dangers of earth, safe and free.

She herself was running again, but more slowly and still softly for her moccasins made no sound. The fawn was heading for the copse in the valley below. With a few more bounds it would be gone from her even as this moment. Would something of herself go with it, she wondered. This new sight, this inner eye which made her see the heart of the deer? Would a curtain fall then and she be again as she had been before?

All at once she stopped, her breath catching in her throat. The fawn had stumbled, plunged and sunk into the crust, its hindquarters caught, its front legs struggling. The sharp little hoofs that could surely and lightly carry it to safety in the wilderness or on rocky ground had been its undoing here.

Violet turned quickly toward her companions. They had paused to invent some new game apparently and were now a good way behind her.

"Girls," she called. "Come on. There's a deer caught."

Her breast still held the feeling of exaltation. She would release the fawn with the aid of the others. Her hands now would touch it, caress it, as they could not have done if it had bounded safely over the brow of the hill and been lost forever in the valley. All that she had just been feeling would be in her finger tips as she smoothed the brown silken coat and quieted the tumultuous beating of the frightened heart.

She had begun to move forward again when there was a shout behind her followed by a chorus of warning cries

She wheeled about. The girls were motioning violently. Violet's eyes followed their pointing arms. There, a dozen yards across from them, a man was kneeling on the snow, covering the fawn with his rifle. It was the Irishman who was staying at the tavern. He was drawing the sight now —coarsely, with an inexperienced hand, Violet could see at a glance. But even so he could hardly miss, with the fawn pinioned before him.

"Stop!" she cried, startled herself by the vehemence of her voice.

She ran back like an arrow, nearing the man yet keeping out of his range.

"Stop!" she called again. "The deer's caught!"

Her voice sounded thin on the wind, but the man heard her and glanced up with a leer. He did not lower his gun.

Violet looked over her shoulder for a second at the fawn, still struggling, its young pointed head straining forward, its proud white flag dim against the snow. She felt its eyes though she could not see them—soft, swimming eyes, filled with their first great terror.

"Don't shoot," she cried again frantically. "It's caught, I say!"

For answer there was a spurt of smoke and the sharp report of the gun. She was compelled to look again. She had to know, so she turned slowly. The Irishman's rough aim had not missed. The fawn was still, its beautiful, shining head, spent now of life, fallen slack upon the crust.

The man stood up, grinning.

"Caught was it, you're sayin'? Well, it's after bein' better caught now. Me first deer, young ladies, an' with as purty a gallery lookin' on as a man would wish to have at a shootin'. I'll be havin' a fine piece of news to write back to the old country, I will. An' as for you, me pretty," he added to Violet, "from all the stories I've been hearin' about the scalpin' that goes on in these here parts, it don't seem to me the killin' of a deer less or more would need to be excitin' ye so."

He laughed thickly as he started toward the fawn.

The other girls came hurrying closer. "Father says he's a blasted Tory," Betsy Kinkaid spoke. "And he can't shoot as well as a dead Injun, you could see that!"

"He couldn't bring down a deer on the run, yon one," Mary Duncan said with scorn. "If he was ever goin' to kill one it would have to be caught!"

They watched Violet curiously, for her face was pale.

"If Brother had been here," she said slowly, "he'd have stopped him. He'd have saved it."

"Well, it's done anyhow." Peggy was practical. "So let's get on with our fun. The sun's beginning to go down already. Come on, Vi, I'll race you over to the sugar hut."

But Violet shook her head. "I'm—I'm kind of tired," she said. "I don't think I'll race any more."

Peggy was anxious. "What's wrong? It was a low-down thing to do and he's a low-down Irisher, but, after all, the woods are full of deer. Are you sick?"

"No. But I think I'll go back to the house. You girls go on. It's fine racing today, but somehow I guess I'm a little tired."

"Why, this beats me!" Betsy's voice was mystified. "And you running like a killdeer just a minute ago so's none of us could get nigh you even! Well, if you're sure you're all right, we'll go on. Let's head over toward the sugar hut, girls."

They were off. Violet turned toward the town, her feet gone heavy like her heart. She kept away from the Hanna girls, for she did not want to explain. In fact she could not interpret even to herself the strange moods which had possessed her during the last hour: the exultation, the tender kinship with the fawn, and now this weight of sadness. If Hugh had only been here . . .

Suddenly she saw him as though he really were beside her, standing straight and strong in his fringed hunting shirt and breeches, his tomahawk hanging at the right of his belt, his hunting knife in its leathern sheath to the left, his coonskin cap with the pendent squirrel tail pulled down over his black hair.

Most clearly of all she could see his dark eyes smile as they always did when he looked at her.

"Well, Sister," he would say in his slow voice.

For so he had always named her ever since that first day they had taken him into their family to be one of them. That was ten years ago now. She had been six then, and Hugh eight. But no born brother could ever have been kinder. Surely no born brother could possibly be more dear to her.

She could hear him now as he always spoke when he came in from the winter hunting or the work around the place: "Where's Sister?" And in flax gathering time it was always: "Watch out, Sister. Mind there's like to be snakes there. Call me quick if you see one." Of an evening by the fire, too, it would be: "When I finish these moccasins I guess Sister can have them. She's about ready for a new pair."

Always looking out for her and taking care of her, he was. She wished he were safely back now. For all at once they were together, somehow, in this new sadness: the fawn and herself and Hugh, with the bright day commencing to die behind them, there where the first red embers of sunset smoked on the far hill. So many bright days she had known had been stained by death even as this one!

In the depths of the forest now, the dark and threatening night would already have begun.

Her mother was stirring a pot of corn-meal mush over the fire when Violet entered the cabin.

"Why, you're back in good time," Martha said. "How was the crust?"

"It was fine and hard. The rest are still racing. I—got tired."

Martha looked up in surprise, but Violet spoke quickly.

"There was a fawn, Mother—a young fawn. . . . I never noticed they were so pretty, before. . . . The way it ran and held its head—I don't know what there was about it but it was different from any other I've ever seen in all my life. And it was running across the open toward the valley when it went through the crust—"

"Aye, so they do often."

"—and the Irishman that's at the tavern shot it while it was caught! I called and shouted to him, but he wouldn't heed. I went up to him and—"

Violet's breast was heaving, and her eyes running over. Her mother's face had gone fearful.

"Did he touch you? Did he lay hand on you?" she asked quickly.

For answer Violet sank down on the settle and leaned her head on the wooden arm while sobs shook her.

"No, he never touched me, but he killed the fawn. It was there so pretty and frightened one minute, and the next it was lying on the snow, all the life gone out of it . . ."

Martha looked at her daughter in anxious bewilderment. True, it was against the frontier hunter's code to shoot a deer caught in the crust unless necessity demanded it; but even so, why had this incident affected Violet so deeply? A deer after all was a deer. She drew a sharp sigh. After seeing what she had seen, there were no tears left to waste on a fawn. The girl must not be well.

"You're just a bit overwrought, child. You worked too hard at the candles, I doubt. It's trying business, that it is. Dipping and dipping again and again. I'll fetch you a cup of bitters, and you can rest till your father comes home."

Martha drew the pot of mush to one side; then, going over to the shelf, she poured out a good dram of the whiskey and wild cherry mixture which she always kept there. Violet drank it obediently, but she still wept. Quiet tears now, with a shivering sigh now and then.

"Yes," Martha went on, "you've just got a bit of the vapors, and a good bowl of mush and milk will help clear them away. Then, when your father and I are in bed tonight, you can take a little wash-off. I'll put a pot of water on to heat, and you can cool it down with a pan of snow."

"I never somehow noticed a fawn, Mother, not like I did today. It was just as if I'd never *seen* one before. And it looked so . . ."

"I know. I know. They're pretty things, the young fawns. Mind tonight you keep close to the fire and get into bed right smart when you're done. There's nothing soothes me down like a little wash-off with warm water It'll do you good."

"But I felt so strange when I saw it lying dead. I can' *tell* you how I felt."

"Ah, well, death's never a pleasant thing to look upon And it's sometimes worse to remember. But we have to thole the thought as best we can. There, I think that' your father back. I'll dish up the mush."

Sam Murray was very lame as he came up to the fire but he smiled his twisted smile at sight of his daughter He eyed her keenly as he sat down and took off his sho packs.

"Well, well," he said stretching his feet toward th warmth. "Did you young ones have a squabble, or wh fur the greetin'?"

Martha spoke up quickly. "She's just got a touch of th vapors, I doubt. And then that Irishman at the taver shot a fawn in the crust right under the girl's eyes. It's upset her some way."

"Him! Ach, he's a windbag anyway. I s'pose he conceited if he got a deer he could send some braggin' word back to the old country. All these fellers fresh over is that away. Fur because on tother side if they killed a deer they'd get their necks stretched like as not. It was low business, though, takin' it in the crust, an' if I see him I'll speak me mind to him."

He reached over to pat Violet's shoulder. "But dinna greet, lassie, the woods is full of deer. Come, come, now. I'm ready for me supper the night, an' no mistake."

"The mush is lifted. Sit you down at the table and begin then," said Martha. "You can have your choice of milk or bear's oil to eat on it. You'd better stick to the milk though, Violet, if you're feeling any ways donsie, for the oil's pretty rich."

Violet felt better as she ate. She carried her gourd back to the pot for a second helping of mush and wondered then why she had wept. Later she cleared the few supper things away while Martha did the milking, then at last sat down beside her mother on the settle, ready for the evening's knitting. There were two candles lighted, and the great fire gave out a ruddy glow along with the heavy smoke, as it roared up the chimney. Her father sat across from them, his feet in their wool socks extended to the warmth as he made a new split broom from one of the hickory saplings piled in the corner. Watch lay asleep at his feet. Outside, the wind had died down, and the village was still.

When Sam began to yawn, Martha put up her knitting.

"You'd better take the Book now, and then we'll get on to bed," she said to him. "Violet's going to have a little wash-off here when we're out of the way."

Sam shook his head darkly. "It's temptin' Providence, that's what it is. Washin' yourself in winter. You mind, you'll rue it yet! But I s'pose there's no stoppin' ye."

"Tut, tut!" Martha said with spirit. "I've thrived on it, haven't I, and so has Violet. A little clean hot water and a chunk of soap never hurt anybody. And as for *you*, Sam, all your rheumatism and your aches and pains didn't come from too much washing, I'll bear you witness to *that*!"

He grinned as he reached for the Bible on the shelf. "I'm fornenst it, anyhow," he said. "Me an' Watch, here, will take our water on the inside. An' mighty little of it there," he added.

Then, suddenly his whole countenance changed. His thick wiry brows drew together; his weather-beaten face settled into a hard gravity. He was doing his best to become the High Priest of his family as became a Scotch Irishman and a Presbyterian!

His long, bony, none too clean fingers leafed the pages. He coughed heavily.

No one knew what this rite of family worship cost Sam Murray. Even after twenty years he still suffered acute embarrassment each time he raised his voice in evening devotions. But there was no way out of it. Added to his own sense of responsibility in the matter was Martha's adamantine will.

"Where God gives me home, there will I give Him homage," she had said at the beginning. And though through the years the homes had been rude enough, the homage had not been lacking.

Sam began now, as always, with difficulty. A curious paralysis of the vocal chords seemed to attack him as soon as he started to read aloud. When he had gone but a few paragraphs he coughed again and looked across apologetically at Martha.

"Me throat's as dry as a corn cob," he said.

He rose, laid the Bible carefully open on the chair, and walked over to the shelves above the bench, took down the whiskey bottle which always stood there, and drank a good, long draught.

"There," he said, wiping his mouth on the back of his hand. "Mebbe I can do a little better now that I've wet me thrapple."

He picked up the book, allowed his face to settle once more into its somber lines, and continued the chapter, which happened to be a long one.

The prayer that followed was in a sense easier for all of them. Sam, acting upon the not illogical assumption that he was speaking then not to his family but to the Almighty, dropped his voice to a low inaudible mutter and proceeded slowly with a series of completely unintelligible petitions. This method relieved him of embarrassment and left his family undisturbed to pursue their own trains of thought.

Now on this night, as usual, Martha knelt with her hands tightly clasped before her on the settle, her lips moving in her constant straining cry to the throne of grace:

... *She's so pretty and so delicate made! O God, have mercy on me if I've thought too much of the beauty of her, but Thou knowest she's too tender for this wilderness life.... Open the way if it be Thy will that she may get back to the east far from all this. Even if I have to give her up.... O God, spare her what I've gone through! Spare her.... Spare her!*

Violet's head drooped upon her hands. She sensed the warmth of the fire meeting and turning back the cold draught from the door. She was relaxed and comfortable now as though a gentle balm had been infused through all her veins. No longer did she feel like weeping. This was well; and yet, somehow, she did not wish to lose completely the sweet hurt that had been in her heart. She clung to that tender grief that had filled her body. By tomorrow, would all the strange sorrow for the fawn be gone, she wondered.

It would feel good to have the wash-off. Mother was right about that. It helped the body to bathe it sometimes, and it made you think nice thoughts, too. She could take her time tonight, close to the fire, since Brother was not here. Even with him safe up in the cockloft in his bed, she always hurried a little if she was taking a wash-off. For what if he thought she was done and in her own bed against the kitchen wall, and would come back down the ladder for something? Tonight she would not hurry. . . . But she hoped he was safe. In the dark depths of the forest now he and David would be asleep in their camp, with danger a plenty around them: *O God, wilt Thou watch over Hugh and keep him from all harm and bring him safe back—soon, if it be Thy will. . . . O God, grant that nothing ever happens to my brother Hugh.*

The sudden break in Sam's low, inarticulate murmurings was the signal that worship was over. He himself rose with difficulty and, having replaced the Bible on the shelf and arranged the huge backlog in the fireplace, approached the wider of the two beds built across the end wall. In a moment, by the simple expedient of removing his breeches, he was ready for the night.

Martha was busy now, putting some water in the big black pot on the crane, laying another log to the front of the fire, and then searching for some clean cloths in a bag that hung from one of the shelves.

"Here," she said to Violet. "Here's an old hunting shirt I washed up. You can use it to dry yourself. It's well-nigh in tatters, but you can bunch it up in your hand and it'll serve fine. Use plenty of soap, and see that the water's good and warm. Just put in a little snow at a time, for it's like to cool it off too quick, and I don't want you to get chilled. Be careful, now. Well, I'll be getting to bed."

In a few minutes she had let down the brown curtain that represented her inexorable stand for those decent privacies which every phase of wilderness living constantly encroached upon.

Violet was now alone—or as nearly alone as one could

ever be in the cabin. She began to move about with a small inner excitement. She fetched the wide firkin from the corner and the pan of snow from the drift beside the door. She laid the old hunting shirt and the piece of homemade soap on the settle near the fire; then, having snuffed out the candles, she began slowly to undress. To-night she would undress completely. This in itself was a strange thing, a moving thing, a mystery. For she was unacquainted with her own body. There was never time nor reason to look upon it, except on these rather rare occasions when she bathed.

The water was hot now. She dipped it carefully into the firkin with the long-stemmed gourd, added enough snow to cool it, then, putting aside her last garment, stood naked in the fire glow.

She looked shyly at her own flesh. It was fair and white and beautiful. She touched her breasts with slow, gentle hands, wondering as she did so if this might be a sin. She smoothed the softness of her thighs. Then, feeling each sensation with acute joy, she set one foot cautiously in the firkin, then the other, and began with a bit torn from the old hunting shirt to carry the clean warmth of the water up to her face, her neck, her arms. As she stooped and straightened again, her hair loosened and hung curling on her shoulders. She smiled. It felt good that way. Now she was altogether light and unburdened.

From behind the brown curtain came Sam's heavy, uneven breathing, and soon that of Martha, lighter and more steady. Her mother had evidently fallen asleep at once—as she did sometimes now in the surcease of win ter, Violet thought. Then, knowing herself now shut off even from a shared consciousness, she paused to marvel again at the personal solitude in which she was enshrouded. As to her body itself, not even her mother had ever looked upon it, in so far as she knew, since she had been a child. Her heart, too, was now most curiously alone, and so she was free to think of many things, partly acknowledged, partly surmised, but wholly mysterious. She thought of love, of marriage, and of when and how they would come to her. Hen Wilson was beginning to make up to Peggy Shaw. Peggy pretended not to notice, for she was so young, but everyone else knew. And Dave Shaw was in love with Betsy Kinkaid! Every girl was married by nineteen, and some much earlier. For herself she didn't want marriage, not while they could all be together as they were. She wished there could be years and years without any change. Just her father and mother and Hugh and herself, with the war ended and all the men of the Eighth Pennsylvania home again and old Guyasooter and the Injuns quieted forever. If there were no rattlesnakes and no Injuns, what a nice place Hannastown would be! Crops would get better each year if there were no more raids, and then there would be money to buy things from the traders: she would have a ribbon for her hair maybe some day, and a bit of lace ruffle like a fine lady, and Hugh would take her to Fort Pitt and walk with her in the Artillery Gardens, and Mother would have some boughten dress goods and the pewter candle molds; *and flowered plates* . . .

Violet drew a long sigh. That was the way she would like things to be for always and always.

She stepped out of the firkin at last and turned toward the fire; then she began to dry herself with the cloth, sensing the warm glow as she rubbed, and relishing the fresh soapy scent of the clean skin.

Suddenly Watch raised his head and got up. Trained to that silence which might mean the difference between life and death, he made no sound, only moved toward the door. Violet, lost in her musings, paid no heed, thinking vaguely that he was feeling the heat of the backlog as he often did, and was seeking the cold draught.

Then in a sharp second of time she heard the door behind her open and close softly. She herself made no sound or movement. She could not. Her throat was numb, her limbs stiff, her heart like ice in her breast. Someone had entered through the door she had forgotten to bar when she brought in the basin of snow! Someone stood there now, sharing her white solitude.

She clutched to her the damp, tattered garment. Slowly, as she was able, she turned her head. It was Hugh who stood there. Hugh in his fringed hunting shirt and leggings and coonskin cap, with a load of fur across his shoulders and the wild smell of the forest and fresh peltry upon him. But he stood rooted also, as though bereft of all power either to leave the cabin or to hurry on up the ladder to his own bed in the loft. He stood motionless, without breath, his dark eyes filled with a strange fire, pinioning her.

She felt them scorch her with shame and terror. Sud

denly she was herself the young fawn caught in the crust, waiting for death—or was it life?

She sank down behind the end of the settle, and crouched there, for full well she knew that however close she had gathered the old shirt to her, it had poorly concealed the fairness.

It was all but a moment, though it had been long enough for the voice of the whirlwind and the seven thunders; then she heard a quick movement by the door. It opened and closed again. Hugh had gone out, back into the night somewhere. It did not matter where. It mattered only that he was gone; that she was free again, if ever she could be free.

She snatched up her clothes while tears of bitterness ran down her cheeks. She put on the garments in which she must sleep; then, stumbling along over the floor, she put away the firkin, the basin, and the soap until everything outwardly was as it had been before. Beside the door she paused, trembling. Should she bar it with Hugh waiting outside somewhere in the cold? A fierce anger shot through her. He was a stranger now to her. Not her brother, the brother she had so loved. Never that again. He was a stranger whose burning eyes had wounded her beyond healing.

She pulled in the latchstring, slid the great wooden bars into their places, and crept to bed. There she lay, shivering, weeping, waiting.

The fire crackled and threw shadows on the wall like Indians dancing; the wind rose again outside and swept across the cabin roof; the sounds of her parents' sleeping came from behind the brown curtain; and the clock struck twice.

Then she heard another sound as of someone feeling for the latchstring. This was followed by the family knock—a loud blow and three quick taps. At once her father woke with a start and jumped up.

"Why, that must be Hugh," she heard her mother speak anxiously. "Back at this hour! Hurry, Sam, and see if he's all right."

There were steps on the floor, the sliding bars of the door, and then Hugh's slow, deep voice.

"Dave got sick and I thought I'd better get him home soon as I could. It begun to look to me today like lung fever."

"Why, my!" Martha said. "I'll get over the first thing in the morning. Poor lad! I doubt the trip was too hard on him. Are you all right, Hugh? You look bleached yourself."

"I'm all right."

"Will you have a bite to eat before you get away to bed?"

"No, I'm not hungry."

"You got a good few pelts here," Sam put in.

"We didn't do so bad. Well, I'll get on up."

Violet heard the creak of the ladder as he climbed it; she heard his few movements on the loose boards of the cockloft, the twang of his bedcords as his body settled upon them. Then silence from above.

Beyond the curtain her father spoke very low.

"Guess Vi'let slept right through. She'll be in fine fe

tle tomorrow when she hears Hugh's got back. She sets an awful store by him. Sometimes I jist wonder . . ."

But Martha's voice made no answer.

Neither did Violet's heart.

From the Journal of Martha Murray, Hannastown, Penna.

Jan. 16, 1778 Will set a line while alone. Violet gone with the girls to race on the crust. Glad they're having a bit pleasure. Hugh and Dave still away on the hunt. Hope and pray no panthers drop on them. Sam hauling logs this afternoon with the Brisons' horse. Dipped candles this morning, 90. A messy business. It's maybe wrong of me to hold out for the pewter molds but these cheap tin ones like the traders carry get so dinged and out of shape I'd as leave dip and be done with it. If we can once get a good crop some year I'll set myself for the pewter ones. But I won't borrow. Bad news come that the Senecas are on the warpath. Oh dear if it isn't one tribe it's another! Sam greatly upset I could tell. Mrs. Huffnagle had letter from Mike yesterday from camp. They're at a place called Valley Forge nigh Philadelphia. Says it's cruel cold and clothing scarce. They've built their own cabins and put a wide shelf sort of again the wall where they sleep together with their bodies and feet touching for warmth. Glad Sam isn't among them with his rheumatism. Poor lads. I sometimes wonder to myself if the war is worth while. If they'd all just been patient a little, the trouble might have blown over. No one king lives forever. I daresen't say this to Sam though for he's so hot to fight. And it's maybe wrong even to think it. The next king might have been as bad and

42

my father used to say liberty was the only commodity that could never go so high in price it wasn't worth paying for. Hugh's the same as Sam about the war. He's as like him in some ways as if he was a born son. He's not contrary though. Leastways not yet. I get so *fashed* with Sam sometimes and then my conscience pricks me. He never seems to take thought of all I've borne. Never once since I married him has he said Are you aweary? Never once. Maybe it's me that's contrary at that though for if he ever did ask me if I'm aweary then it would be easy to say bright-like, No Sam not a bit. I'm fine. It's just to know he cares, that's all. And back of everything is the worry for Violet. Today, looking at the girls so innocent and happy-like, it came over me stronger than ever. Another thing Mike Huffnagle wrote was that they hear there are 20,000 British troops in and about Philadelphia and General Howe has seized Mary Pemberton's coach and horses and rides round the town with them. I mind her father's coach right enough. This is maybe the same one. The town will be different now, though, from when I knew it even without the British. It seems like another world from this. Today is little Sam's birthday. He'd be twenty-one if he'd been spared. There's some things you have to put behind you to save your reason. I doubt if Sam remembers the date so I won't say anything. Well, I must stop now and put on the mush. Weather clear and cold.

II

The Panther

Hugh was dreaming as the first gray hint of dawning stole into the cockloft. He thought he was back in the forest, working with Dave to fashion their rough camp. Once again he was choosing the site in the lee of a great fallen tree. The snow was lighter there, and it was easy to dig down to the thick bed of leaves lying beneath it. He was driving stakes eight or ten feet from the log and making a back-slanting frame of limbs and branches over which skins could be spread. He was laying the buffalo robe underneath, starting a fire in front of the rough lean-to, hobbling and blanketing Ranger, when all at once he started up at the sound of Dave's sharp, dry cough . . .

But it was not Dave he heard, and he himself was no longer in the wilderness. The sound came from below, and then all was quiet, for the thin cold twilight of the morning showed that the time of rest was not yet quite ended.

Still dazed and uncertain from sleep, he blinked and peered from underneath the edge of the woven blanket. He saw the dim outlines of the chinked-in logs, the rafters of the low roof overhead from which hung flitches and hams and bunches of herbs; he saw the keg of fat in the corner waiting for soap-making day, the nuts spread upon the floor boards, and the pile of corn beside his bed.

Yes, he was back at home in the cockloft, and with the knowledge he was suddenly and completely awake. Even with the strange emotions which had rent him the night before, his overtaxed body had betrayed him at once into sleep. Now, with his mind alert, he could think about this which had befallen him. For he was not the person who had set out five days ago for the hunting trip with Dave. As though he were meeting a stranger he saw himself as he had been then. Six feet two in his moccasins, broad of shoulder for his eighteen years, quick-footed as an Indian, the best shot left in the town, next to Sam Murray himself, he had been content enough for these months at least, since he couldn't leave the family to go with the regiment, to hunt and trap and do some scouting and then sit by the fire in the evenings watching Violet knit! Even when he had found his eyes constantly upon her, even when he had heard himself asking, "Where's Sister?" the moment she was out of his sight, he had never realized what was going on behind the doors of his heart.

For she had truly seemed a sister to him. From that first day back in the Cumberland Valley ten years ago when the Indian raid had left him homeless and alone, and bereft the Murrays of their sons, he had felt himself a part of their household even as though blood bound him. The constantly recurring frontier tragedies cemented many oldments of families into fast units. Danger and death brought forth new sons and daughters even as birth.

Except for the dull revengeful hatred of the redskins which never left him, his mind had been at rest as the years passed, and his maturing body, tempered each day by the hardest physical exercise, had known quiet and appeasement. In spite of its strength and prowess it had been the body of a boy. He knew that now, because he had suddenly become a man with the weight of man's desire full upon him.

He thought of last night. He had gotten Dave safely home, had quietly put Ranger into the stable, all the while hoping the family might still be sitting around the hearth—as the Shaws had been—when he came in. He wanted to surprise them, so he came up the snowy path on noiseless moccasined feet. The latch string was out. He opened the door softly and stepped in, closing it after him. Then and not till then did he see the white gleaming shape against the ruddy glow.

He could not move. Fire and darkness, ecstasy and terror all swept over him. A new and burning mystery overpowered him. He had slain the panther in the wilderness but he was weak before this tender miracle.

It was not until she had sunk down behind the settle that he realized what his eyes must have revealed. He had left swiftly enough then. Was it a sound of weeping he had heard as he was going out the door? He had walked back and forth endlessly along the beaten cart way. There were plenty of lights at the tavern. There would be a great fire going in the fireplace there and enough noise and confusion to be welcome after the solitude of the fo est. There would be the clatter of drinking mugs and the click of metal as travelers' coins were slapped upon the thick table, or a hunting knife clipped against a rifle.

There would be the sound of hearty voices and stories to be listened to avidly from a warm corner. He might go in and lose his new thoughts there.

There was light also at the Shaws', where they would still be caring for Dave, and at the Brisons', where James, the scribe of the town, would be sitting at the table, his thin, scholarly face bent into the candlelight as he wrote letters or copied the court records. He could go to either house and be welcome, slipping back quickly into his old self.

But the still night and the cold and the darkness were better. The hot blood could rise in his face here and none could see it; his eyes could tell their strange and sudden tale, and none would be the wiser.

So he had trudged back and forth in the narrow track, shifting the pelts on his shoulders, holding the burden as though its weight would minimize the trouble in his heart; using all the strength left in his already weary body to hold out until he was sure Violet would be long in bed and asleep.

His thoughts then had been sadly confused. He had been to weddings where the bridegroom was little older than himself; he had seen some of his own friends turn suddenly shy and soft about a girl; but he had been conscious of the whole pattern of family life only as a background, even as the great wilderness stretched about him, near and yet remote. That he, himself, should ever alter that background by breaking into it with a new pattern of his own had, curiously, never once occurred to him.

Now, as he lay in the cockloft, his thoughts were all too clear. This new tumult of his heart, this mortal longing of his flesh was love; and it was directed toward Violet. Could there be shame in this, since no blood linked them? Surely there could be no shame. And yet there was an unseemliness about it; an ugly shock of strangeness which destroyed the joy his heart would otherwise have felt. For in the eyes of all the village he was brother to her.

When they had come to settle in Hannastown he had already left his own name behind him. It was as though the waters of the Juniata and the Loyalhanna had washed it out, and the towering Laurel and Chestnut ridges had shut it away forever. He had ceased to be Hugh McConnell; he had become entirely Hugh Murray. And this had seemed natural to him. Every tie but that of birth bound him to Sam and Martha. They had long been father and mother to him in thought as in name, and *Violet was his sister*. All roads of his thinking led back to this fact.

He groaned within him, as the everyday speech of the village rushed bitterly into remembrance. For the relationship was not merely tacit. His own voice had declared it a thousand times. And how did Violet herself feel? This was the question he had put off asking his heart until the last, for from the answer there could be neither argument nor appeal. And bitterly he knew what it was. A thousand thousand trifles of which the texture of their daily living was made gave evidence of the way in which Violet regarded him. The word "Brother" fell so gently, so tenderly from her lips. Her eyes, the color of her name, were so deep with innocence when they smiled into his.

Yes, it had indeed been the sound of a sob he had heard from behind the settle last night. And what wonder? If his own heart had been free and clear, he would have gone quickly toward the ladder, never turning his head again. He would have said over his shoulder, carelessly, even laughing-like, "Hello, Sister. Havin' a wash-off this nice warm night?"

That would have been all, and Violet would have laughed too, even through her maiden flurry, her voice with a dozen questions following him to the cockloft.

But this was not what had happened. He had stood there watching her with eyes of desire while the fires of hell gat hold of him.

He jumped up suddenly now, put on his breeches, tightened the belt of his hunting shirt, caught up his moccasins and crept down the pegs in the wall which served as a ladder. Sam was already building up the fire. He looked with affection upon the youth who could meet him now eye to eye. He and Hugh were of the same breed, though Hugh's own Scotch ancestors had spent less time in Ulster than Sam's. They were congenial in a deep, unspoken fashion: both hard-boned, and strong-muscled from that relentless selective process which had left countless small graves scattered on both sides of the Atlantic; both strong-willed from generations of danger-driven men; both capable of Celtic heat in either love or hate.

In short they were Scotch-Irishmen: honest, fearless,

proud, profane, intolerant of restraint in any form, furious at the least show of injustice, loathing the Pope, venerating Calvin, hating the Indians, cleaving to their friends, always passionate, always prejudiced, usually invincible!

Sam kicked a log now viciously.

"This here damned hickory takes so long to ketch, you can't even spit on it without settin' it back. So Dave got sick, eh?"

"Yes. I don't think he was feelin' so chirk when we left, but he wouldn't give up till he was clean laid out. I made him ride Ranger all the way back. It was heavy goin', I'll tell you."

"Must ha' been. I was surprised for sartin last night when you come bustin' in at that hour. Wait till Vi'let knows it! She slept right through, I guess, but she'll stir fast enough now. Hey, *Vi'let!* Here's Hugh home!"

There was no sound from behind the farthest end of the brown curtain, though Martha's moccasined feet could be seen moving beneath the section that screened her own bed.

Sam looked puzzled.

"It ain't hard for usual to get Vi'let up," he remarked. "She's goin' to be surprised this mornin'. *Vi'let!* Jump up, lass. Here's somebody back again!"

Hugh bolted suddenly for the door. "I'll be gettin' out to the stable," he said. "I've—I've got something to tend to out there."

Sam's sharp gray eyes looked at the young man's flushed face.

"Now what the devil's up!" he exclaimed half under his breath.

But Hugh waited to give no reply. He went out quickly and followed the path to the rough shed which housed the beasts.

He had built this stable himself when they had reached Hannastown six years ago. He was only twelve then, but strong and eager. He had begged to be allowed to start the shed while the other men worked in rearing the cabin.

So it was his hands, growing harder by the day, that had cut and set the chestnut saplings and filled in the cracks between with straw and leaves and mud. The roof he had thatched with buckwheat straw from the Brisons' field, and wilding weeds from the deep, primeval growth of their own new land. Over this he had strained and bent more young saplings to hold down the crude thatch and weighted it all over with heavy stones.

When it was finished he had felt for the first time the stir of his man's strength to meet and conquer that force of nature which rose from cosmic deeps, too implacable ever to give quarter. He had felt this still power pitted against him then, not as an enemy like the Indians, even though it might be the means of slaying them all at the last, rather than the tomahawk. In a vague way he knew—as every frontiersman knew—that Nature willed neither his life nor his death; that it was against her vast and remorseless indifference that man must strain and struggle and conquer if he could.

So Hugh, when he had finished the shed, boy though he was, had felt with pride his first sense of individual mastery. With his own bone and muscle he had fought and won one small battle against sun and wind and driving tempest. He had saved the cattle from all this and from hungry wolves and bears besides.

But now as he stood here, with the sun rising above the Chestnut Ridge and the pale, cold breath of the new day blowing over the valleys and the spreading wilderness, he knew that Nature was not done with him when she threw up the great forest and the heavy rank weeds; when she spewed forth rocks and sent the raging storms; when she nurtured the rattlesnake and suckled the wolf. He had already learned to do battle against these.

Now, she had caught him, all unawares, in the coil of another of her laws as inexorable as growth and decay, or heat and cold. Hugh gave it no name. How could he know that it was the *law of continuance,* the only one indeed in which Nature was greatly interested? He only knew that she had decreed, "Let this young man feel the burning fire of love," as calmly, as mercilessly as she had willed the north wind to blow and the snow to cover the earth.

And once again against her might he must struggle— for Violet's sake.

With a quick movement he opened the low door and entered the stable. It lay just inside, the thing he had come out to find before anyone should stumble upon it. He had placed it there in joy last night, his heart leaping at thought of Violet's coming pleasure. He had not stopped to think then that young men hunted and slew panther not for their sisters but for their sweethearts. He rea ized it now. It was for love that he had risked his life yesterday when he saw the sunlight fall on the rich orange and lemon tints of the tawny coat.

The big painter had been sunning itself on the breast of a splash dam, when he spied it. For a moment he had stood watching his prey, for the wind was in his favor. It was by far the largest and most beautiful of the creatures that he had ever seen. His heart jumped in his breast. He would have a skin for Violet that would surpass any in the town, and he would not mar that skin by the slightest error in marksmanship.

He crept closer. The great cat had begun to roll playfully in the snow, every muscle moving, its head jerking quickly, its jaws open. Hugh crept on. A painter would not start a fight, but when once frightened or aroused it was the most murderous of enemies. It would have been safe enough and easy enough, Hugh knew, to fire from where he stood; but he was mad with his desire to get a perfect skin. So he had stealthily pressed forward.

And at the last there had been one terrifying moment when the panther sprang in fury. Death had been in the air, closer than it had ever been to Hugh. But his nerves had been like steel; his muscles as steady. The aim had been true and the shot had gone home—*through the eye*.

Now the panther lay at his feet, the tawny pelage unblemished. It was a huge beast, eight or nine feet long, Hugh surmised, from nose to tail tip. He had brought it home across Ranger's neck, in front of Dave, for it weighed as much as a man. He stooped now to study it more closely. He had seen many painter skins, but this one was

surely the most beautiful. He touched the soft yellow-
tinted hair within the ears and stroked the gray throat
and the pale yellow below the neck. Then he shivered in
spite of himself, drawing his hand abruptly back. There
was a dark spirit in the panther, so the Indians thought:
some connection with Machtando, the Evil One. Sam always said a painter cry was the only thing that ever scared
his liver, and while Martha would praise a fine skin
quickly enough she would never taste mouthful of the
meat (if she could help it) even though it was white as
chicken and tastier than pork. And Violet had begged
him to remove the cruel jaws before he made her the rug.
. . . Maybe there was evil in the great cat, something bod-
ing and sinister. Perhaps it had lured him on, as it lay
sunning itself in the snow. Perhaps by the margin of that
time which he had taken to kill it, he might have been
saved from those moments last night which had brought
this new misery to him.

But here it lay now, dead, at his feet. What should he
do with it? Should he give it in triumph to Violet as he
had long promised her? Should he tell her the story of the
fight, carelessly of course, but watching her face whiten
with fear and then glow again with pride and pleasure?

He shook his head even as his heart sank within him.
He must not do that. Never did brother give sister a gift
such as this; not a gift bought with near death. He must
part with the panther; take it up to the store and trade it
for what he could get, as he would do with the other pelts.
For by so doing he would be fighting the new enemy, and

surely wiping out from Violet's memory something of the unguarded secret of his eyes last night.

He fed Ranger and Reddy, the cow, counted all too easily the few sheep in the stockaded lean-to, back of the shed. No wolf depredations last night.

Then outside again, he stood for a moment in the cold new daylight, a young man, born of the wilderness, inured to danger, but confused and stricken now by a struggle in which no man's hand could lend him aid.

When he reentered the kitchen, everything looked as usual. Martha and Violet were busy at the fireplace with Sam warming his back comfortably in their way.

"Well, Hugh," Martha said, her thin face alight with its quick feeling, "how are you, lad?"

"I'm all right, Mother."

Violet spoke without turning. Her voice was strained. "Did you have a fair trip?"

"Fair—Sister."

The word stuck in his throat, but he got it out. He saw Violet's quick glance with something, he imagined of relief, in it. Martha was speaking of Dave as they all sat down to their breakfast.

"I'll hurry over as soon as I can and take a bit of elecampane. They mebbe won't have any, and if it turns to lung fever there's naught as good. But I hope it's just a little brash. Did he have any luck before he got donsie?"

"He got a few pelts."

"I s'pose you didn't run into any painters," Sam put in.

"Just one."

Martha and Violet both looked up.

"Oh, dear, I was afeard of it, and so was Mrs. Shaw! Was it overhead on a tree when you saw it?"

"No. It was rollin' in the snow. I got it. It's out in the stable."

Sam struck the heavy board before him in delight. His pride in his foster son's prowess was immense.

"A good job, lad. A damned good job! It's goin' to be hard soon to tell whether tane or tither of us is the best shot. How many feet off?"

"Six, mebbe."

"God a'mighty, that was hot work! Kitten, was it?"

"Pretty fair size." He could feel Violet's eyes upon him. The thing must be done quickly. "Fact is, it's about the biggest I ever seen. I thought I'd trade it."

Sam didn't wait for Martha to finish her excited comment. He got up from the table.

"Damme, to hear you talk you'd think killin' a painter was as easy as kissin'. I'm goin' out an' size up the critter!"

Hugh rose too without looking at Violet and followed Sam to the stable.

His heart was heavy. Not all the older man's rich stream of profane praise could lighten it. When he went back to the cabin later for a measuring stick he found Violet alone as Martha had already left for the Shaws'. She turned from her work.

"Was it—was it close danger, killing the painter?"

"Well—pretty close. Titch an' go for a minute, mebbe."

"But if it was playing in the snow, what call had you to go so nigh-hand it?"

"I was set on a perfect skin, I guess. Just an idee."

"So's you could trade it?"

Her voice was very low. Hugh could see the tender rise and fall of her young breasts under the kerchief. He could see the long lashes shadowing the deep blue of her eyes; like a hot sword in his flesh he felt the beauty of the half-parted lips.

He thought the words would strangle him, but he spoke them harshly.

"Why else?"

She turned from him and bent over the fire.

"It's best to trade it. If you'd kept it, I could never have borne sight of it."

She said no more, and Hugh, wondering wretchedly just what she meant, got his measuring stick and went back to the stable.

With quick deft strokes he skinned the panther, cutting from the throat to the tail, then carefully down the inside of each leg to the foot. The knife slipped keenly underneath the thick soft fur while Sam stood by, watching. He knew the boy was not as elated as he should be. He saw the hard set of the jaw and the forbidding look in the dark eyes, and wondered. Well, he was man grown now and must bear man's troubles as they came. He began to talk a bit at random to ease the lad's mind, whatever was heavy on it. He told the tavern news of the east and the west and what had befallen Violet yesterday on the crust. Hugh glanced up once at this latter information but still had nothing to say; he only went on stripping off the tawny fur.

"Curin' it?" Sam asked after a silence.

"Thought I'd trade it green," Hugh replied.

"Right nice to keep it. First one you ever shot, an' all."

Hugh only bent to his task. "I always hate to take the salt," he said, "but I'll get it back an' more when I do my full barterin'."

"That's right. We're runnin' a bit low, an' we don't want to get to the point of usin' hickory ashes like the Duncans."

He went over to the corner of the stable and lifted a large gourd shell from the floor. In it was a commodity infinitely precious. The essence of all flavor, the very life of taste and appetite for both man and beast, it admitted of no real substitute and was as valuable in the Back Country as gold itself. The brackish swamps with their rich deposits along the Conemaugh and the Sewickley rivers had not then been discovered, and the town of Saltsburg was not yet born. So the white grains that lent zest to the palate and savor to all living were brought from the east on laden pack horses; were bought by the frontiersman with careful bargaining and then guarded by the housewives as though they were rubies.

The contents of the big gourd was a mass of dark coarse "rough" crystals of the kind doled out to the beasts. Even so, Hugh, who now had the full hide severed, took a gingerly handful and rubbed it carefully into the skin, wasting no grain.

When he had salted it all he stretched it from peg to peg on the outside of the stable.

"I'll give it twenty-four hours, no more," he said. "Then

I'll take it over to the tavern an' hope for good tradin'."

"You're in a hell of a hurry to part with it, ain't you?" Sam said, eyeing him. "It's worth showin' round a little first, anyway."

From where they stood Hugh could see Violet leaving the cabin and starting for the spring. Her light brown curls were blowing below her knitted scarf.

"What signifies killin' a painter?" he said, trying to keep his voice careless. "There's other things would make me feel prouder-like."

Jan. 17, 1778 Will set a line while the folks are all out. The boys got home late last night from the hunt. Dave took sick in the woods so Hugh got him back as fast as he could. I was afeard of this. Sleeping with their feet soaked and all. I went over first thing this morning and took some of my elecampane. Knew Sarah Shaw wouldn't have any. Was back just now. He seems easier. Cough looser and he's sweat some. I think Dave's in dead earnest about Betsy Kinkaid. You can see it plain on his face when they chaff him. I wish Hugh would take up with Peggy or some nice girl. But love goes its own gait. You can't force it. Met Mrs. Brison at the spring. Says James is back from Pittsburgh but she can't get a word out of him about his trip. She doesn't know how to take him I doubt. James is so fine in the grain. Says she had a letter yesterday from her sister in England and over there they don't hardly know there's a war going on here! It's strange about war. It's death to them that are in it and only a word to them that aren't. Violet upset last night. An Irishman shot a fawn in the crust right under the girls' eyes. I don't know why Violet took on so. It didn't faze Peggy. Haven't seen Betsy since. I let Violet take a wash-off last night to calm her nerves down. I must go over her hair again soon. You have to be on the lookout so cruel often. Am worried over the big bearskin. Watch always lies on it and now it's full of fleas and you can't wash fur. Will get Hugh to shake it good tomorrow out in the snow. It's the crawling, creeping things I can't thole. Hugh shot a panther and Sam more set-up than he is. I'm glad we don't need the meat for the pot for it gives me a grue to think of painter flesh some way. Weather moderating a little. Gray sky. Wind down.

III

The next morning there was more snow, and the flame in the fire was blue. With invincible gentleness the flakes had fallen all night long until now at full daybreak all the hard crystal surfaces were soft as down again. The great trees bowed under their new fardels of white, and the narrow road through the town was covered up as though part again of the trackless wilderness.

"It's going to make hard traveling for Court week," Martha said as she baked an extra johnnycake while the fire was right. "But oh, I'm ever glad to see the snow."

"It's good you got your racin' in yesterday," Sam observed to Violet. "You may not get a crust again like you for a year to come."

"What was the Irisher like?" Hugh asked abruptly.

"He was fat," Violet said slowly, "and he had a red face. And when I went up to him to—to ask him not to shoot, he had a smile that was ugly-like."

"Well, well," Martha said. "It's all past now, and he's on his way to Pittsburgh belike. The next batch of stragglers will be along soon enough for Quarter Sessions. It'll mean busy times for James again. I doubt he'll be in early

62

this morning for his pens. We haven't seen hair of him since he got back from Pittsburgh."

"It's fine to be able to write the way James does," Violet said. "If he lived in the east instead of the frontier he'd be a famous scholar. Mrs. Brison says he reads till the dawn, and it's five times now he's gone through our book of Shakespeare."

Sam's tone was dry.

"An' he don't know which end of a cow the tail's on. Mebbe if he'd go to bed like a Christian instead of sittin' up all night he wouldn't be so slack in the twist."

"Whisht," said Martha, raising her finger, for there was the sound of stamping feet at the doorstone, and then a knock. "That's likely him now. Run, Violet."

Martha was right. It was James Brison who entered the cabin trying to bring as little snow as possible with him. He was a slender young man in his late twenties, with a finely cut, ascetic face which in London or even in Philadelphia would have been reckoned handsome. Here in Hannastown, men thought it weak. For, though his dress was the same as that of Sam or Hugh, the look of the frontier was not upon him. His gray eyes were not made to sight along a gun barrel, and the curious, indefinable air of physical sufficiency which enveloped the native woodsmen did not rest upon him. Another setting of another face held him in thrall. It was an accident of nature that he was living in the Back Country of the new world, copying the court records in a rude log building, the first seat of justice west of the Alleghenies, instead of sitting in the ancient House of Lords or wearing a white wig in the Law Courts over against Temple Bar.

His voice was not so heavy as Hugh's, and his words came more quickly as he greeted the family now and sat down on the settle.

He always felt pleasantly at home in Martha's cabin. Though Tom Brison had begotten him and Jane Brison had borne him, he was no son of theirs. They took what comfort they might in his skill with speech and pen, and yet he was a stranger to them as he was to most of the dwellers in Hannastown. But Martha understood him even as she knew the deep desires of her own heart. And in this understanding he basked and became in her presence the person he was meant to be: a man of strength, if only the challenging forces had been the law and diplomacy instead of Indians and the wilderness.

"I was just saying you'd be in soon, and I've got them all ready for you," Martha spoke as she reached for a wooden noggin on the end of the mantelpiece. In it were a half-dozen pens made from the quills of a wild turkey wing.

James took them smilingly and touched each one in turn with his long, sensitive fingers.

"They're as nigh perfection as anything can be in this world. I'd never have the pen of a ready writer if it weren't for you, Mrs. Murray."

Martha beamed. "It was my father long ago taught me the trick. His pens were always a wee bit sharper and smoother than anybody else's, so it pleasures me now to make them the same way. Will it be a busy court week, think you?"

"There's no telling. The January sessions are usually dull enough. Felonies are apter to flourish better in fall or spring, it seems. There might be a case or two of treason."

"I hope they put the screws on them," Sam sputtered. "We've got enough troubles round here without any damned Tories stickin' knives in our backs. Have you got wind of any new ones?"

"Not just around here," James said. "In Pittsburgh now—"

"Oh, tell us what you saw in Pittsburgh, James," Violet cried eagerly. "We've never questioned you since you got back."

He smiled at the girl.

"Why always Pittsburgh! Pittsburgh!" he asked teasingly. "It's scarce bigger than Hannastown, and yet to hear the women talk you'd think it was Philadelphia or Boston. There are a few more taverns there and a scattering of velvet stocks and knee buckles, but never a preacher more than here!"

"Oh, but there's a deal of difference for all that. There are ladies there, and happenings, and—and excitement. If I could, I'd go to Pittsburgh once a month and walk in the King's Artillery Gardens—"

"It would be poor walking there today," James said, laughing.

"You know I don't mean the winter! And it *is* a passing fair sight, they say, with the Allegheny flowing to the one side and the apple trees to the other, row on row, all covered with flowers or fruit in its season!"

James' cynical gray eyes softened. "What have we here, Mrs. Murray? A budding poet? A young disciple of beauty?"

Sam cleared his throat raucously. He had small patience with any flights of fancy.

"Hugh shot a painter through the eye! Biggest one I ever seen. You'd better take a look at the hide afore he trades it."

A change passed over James' face. He was no shot. His fingers always trembled on the trigger. It was a bitter shame to him, and Martha was quick to speak up now to save his embarrassment.

"You were telling something about Tories in Pittsburgh, when Violet would have her say."

"Yes," said James. "I was at the Fort giving General Hand some letters. One of the soldiers told me there's strong feeling still against Captain Alexander McKee. Last month the Board of War sent orders to Hand to send him to York so Congress could deal with him; but he took sick, and Hand let him stay on at home. He's got a farm out at McKees Rocks. But the soldiers all think he's playing possum and will be up to something yet."

"They ought to stretch hemp, every Tory son of 'em. Here we got a country. A new, big country. We're goin' to be a nation some day under no dratted old King's bid or beck. I tell ye, it's worth sacrificin' for! There's some would just jouk an' let the wave go by. But you never get your liberty thataway. You got to fight for it. Iffen i wasn't for this blasted knee I'd be doin' it now. In the thick of it, I'd be. I'd even rot willin' at this damned Valley Forge place with the rest of 'em if it was keepin' a tyrant's hand from ever touchin' me an' mine!"

"Yes, yes, Sam," Martha said soothingly. "Don't fash yourself now. You've got to take what comes from the Lord in the way of sickness as in all else. Mebbe you *would* fancy a sight of the painter, James. It's a fine one."

She had to choose the lesser of two evils quickly. In another moment Sam would be completely out of hand, and she knew it was even harder for James to be reminded of the fact that he was useless as a soldier than that he couldn't hit a panther.

"Come on," Hugh said, speaking for the first time. "I'm just startin' off with it."

James stood up and put the pens carefully within the folds of his shirt, thanking Martha again with a slight inclination of the head that made her think of callers in the old parlor of her girlhood. At the door he turned.

"Oh, Violet," he said. The name always sounded different on his tongue, for he was the only one who gave full length to all three syllables. "I'll tell you a secret. Some fine day if you want to go a-journeying, set out for the big oak tree on top of the hill here and give a slow turn around—north, east, south, and west. You'll see a fairer sight than any in a dozen far towns and cities put together, I'll wager."

He hesitated, then added in a lower voice:

"Beauty itself doth of itself persuade
The eyes of men without an orator."

"James is so queer-like," Violet said when the young men had left. "I never can make out whether he's making sport of me or not."

"He's half cracked with too much book readin'," Sam said disgustedly. "He needs to scalp a few Injuns to tone up his liver, that's what."

Outside, by the stable, Hugh carefully took down the hide and shook the snow from it while James watched him.

They had met at the Shaws' the night before. Dave, who was better of his fever, had sat propped up in bed and talked to them between spells of coughing. He had asked how Violet liked her present, and Peggy had pouted that never was there brother like Hugh to shoot a painter for his sister. James had watched his friend then curiously as he stated with unusual roughness that he was disposing of the skin. He watched him now as with set face and no words Hugh rolled it up and put it under his arm. Without guessing the secret James knew that he was in trouble.

"Hugh," he said slowly, feeling unaccountably close, "everybody round here thinks that all I like is to bury my nose in a book or a sheet of paper. I'll tell you something. Just now I feel as if I'd rather have shot that painter than written all Shakespeare."

"It's nought," Hugh said, but he smiled a little as they started off.

They plodded through the snow of the narrow track which, early though the hour was, was broken now by other feet. The town always stirred betimes even in winter, for there was no respite, no let-up from the hard business of living. Trees must be felled, logs hauled and chopped, water must be carried, soap made, candles dipped, grain ground, yarn spun and knitted, aside from the caring for the stock at home and the hunting and trapping of the wild things of the forest.

But while men and women worked hard with seldom an idle hand from daybreak till long after early candle lighting, there was here, in this settlement, none of the monotony of physical toil unrelieved by mental stimulus. The very dangers themselves engendered alertness; the fact that Hannastown lay upon the great Forbes Road over which soldiers and traders, messengers and travelers passed, brought the news of the whole country into it eventually; moreover the character and the temper of the settlers themselves gave to the rough collection of log cabins a dignity transcending the material; for there was then "a spirit working in the world, like to a silent subterranean fire." It was the spirit of liberty, and it was working deeply in the souls of the Scotch Irishmen who settled Hannastown, and the county of Westmoreland.

Because of this on a bright May day in 1775, nearly three years before, a great meeting had been held at the big log house of Robert Hanna. Most of the men present were clad in hunting shirts and buckskins, but there were few powdered queues and a lace ruffle or two from beyond the hills. All, whether in linsey-woolsey or lace, were of one mind. For the news of Lexington and Concord had arrived, along with the knowledge that the colony of Massachusetts had been subjected to a tyrannous system, in which its constitutional and chartered privileges

were denied it. There was hot discussion that day under
the spreading old trees of the primeval forest. How could
a man be sure the same oppression might not spread to
the other colonies? even out here to the Back Country?
Durst a man stand idly by while his fellow Americans
were made *slaves?* Never! Hard hands itched toward their
rifles. Strong, husky, woods voices declaimed their remon
strance.

It was General Arthur St. Clair from Fort Ligonier
over on Laurel Hill just sixteen miles away, who wrote
down the resolutions at last, with James Brison close be
side him to make a copy.

One by one, in clear-cut and noble language, the sen
tences had shaped themselves until the end:

"It has therefore become the indispensable duty of
every American, of any man who has any public virtue or
love for his country or any compassion for posterity, to
resist and oppose by every means which God has put in
his power the execution of this system; and that as for us
we will be ready to oppose it with our lives and fortunes."

At the end of the meeting the men from Hannastown
had gone back to girdling trees and planting corn, while
those from farther in the county bestrode their horses and
rode off. None of them, except perhaps General St. Clair
had given a thought to the fact that they had just com
pleted a document like to the one signed in an English
meadow called Runnymede nearly six hundred years be
fore. And certainly none of them knew that they had con
ceived and brought forth a state paper which, in clarity
dignity, and determination, was to be surpassed only by

the greater Declaration of Independence a year later!

They would indeed merely have smiled grimly if they could have seen the entry made a month after their discussion in the Diary of a visiting Englishman, Nicholas Cresswell. "The people here are Liberty mad, nothing but war is thought of," he penned in disgust.

But the resolutions of the meeting were carried out. The "Liberty mad" men raised a battalion under Colonel John Proctor—whose farm was on the Nine Mile Run— secured a standard for it, and flung it to the breeze before the Declaration of Independence was penned or the Stars and Stripes had been fashioned. The women may have paled a little as they looked at it, for wrought upon the red silk field was the design of their own peculiar enemy. It was a coiled snake, its thirteen rattles raised, its head poised ready to strike. Below, were the significant words, 'Don't Tread on Me"; in the corner, the emblem of the Union Jack.

"If they don't get the point of that, they'll be mighty low in the uptake," Colonel Proctor had remarked dryly.

The rattlesnake flag and its faithful bearer, Lieutenant Samuel Craig, along with most of the battalion were at that very moment hemmed in by the bitter snows of Valley Forge, even as Hannastown was shut in by its deep drifts this January morning.

Hugh and James had now come to Robert Hanna's two-story log house, where signs of activity were already in evidence. A path to the heavy door at the side had been carefully shoveled; the rough stumps which served as hitching posts had been brushed off sufficiently to reveal

the crude iron ring in each; clouds of smoke rising from
the chimneys betokened great fires within; and several
strangers could be seen approaching down the hill.

"No red petticoats today, eh?" Hugh asked.

James laughed. "You're an impertinent rogue. Is that
any way to refer to the garments of the Chief Justice? No,
we've only small fry on the bench today and, for the comfort of my sleep tonight, I hope we'll have only small-fry
cases too. Well, give you good luck, Hugh."

Hugh went on toward the front, or tavern, end of the
big cabin, glancing as he passed at the whipping post, a
softened white cross against the gray sky. There had been
no public whippings now for a session or so, and he was
glad, for Violet's sake. Not that he had any stomach himself to relish the sight of a man's bloody back, but Violet
always took it so to heart even when the victim was some
man from the other end of the county. It was worst in
summer when the sound of the lash and the oaths of pain
could be heard all through the town. Violet would always
run then from the truck patch or the flax field to cover
her ears in the cabin's farthest corner. If the strokes were
falling upon a woman she would be sad all the rest of the
day. Violet! Violet!

He set his teeth grimly and turned toward the low, narrow porch at the front where the tavern sign hung. Two
men were standing there now, leaning negligently against
one of the heavy oaken props. One of them was short, red-
haired, and rubicund; the other was tall, strongly built,
black-eyed, and handsome. Hugh recognized the latter at
once. It was Simon Girty, the interpreter. The other man

he hated on sight. It was he who was speaking as Hugh approached.

"An' so, as I was sayin', I brought it down with one shot as nate as if I'd been gunnin' fur deer all me life! An' that wasn't all the wild game runnin' loose either, bless me good right eye! There was another bit come right to me hand so to spake! I've had a little luck, so I'm stayin' on to do a little more huntin'. For if iver I see a tasty leg beneath a petticoat to make a man's mouth water—"

Hugh had tossed the panther skin behind him and leaped to the low porch platform.

"You skunk! I'll shut your dirty mouth for you!"

The Irishman was quick enough with his fists, but Hugh was quicker. By feinting with his right hand he brought a hard surprise blow with his left to the Irishman's face. Behind them, he heard Girty laugh. It was a trick he and Dave had perfected as they wrestled with each other, for fun, and it had never worked so well as now. The Irishman reeled, and Hugh backed up his first success with a heavy bleach upon the jaw. He knew then that the Irishman was through. He had been drinking, apparently, and his weight was against him. There would be no fight in the usual sense; no crowd from inside would come rushing out to watch, and yell advice and warnings.

Hugh stepped back, his watchful eyes despising his antagonist.

"Get on your way to Pittsburgh, if that's where you're goin'! You've been here long enough. An' mind your big mouth! Mebbe you talk about women that way in the old country. Out here in the backwoods we've got more manners."

The Irishman rubbed his jaw. His face was purple.

"Ye blisterin' young rebel, ye!"

Hugh's countenance darkened still more.

"And none of your *rebel* talk, either! We take no sass here from your old king or any pertainin' to him. You'd best get on your way, I'm thinkin', afore the court yonder gets after ye. They'd rather catch treasoners than felons just now, mind."

The Irishman backed sullenly away, still muttering, and entered the tavern. Hugh picked up the panther skin and turned toward Girty. The man drew him, somehow, though he had said not a word. There was a dark magnetism in the eyes and a power, half friendly, half malevolent, about the large, striking head. He grinned now at Hugh.

"Did you make as quick shift of the painter, there?" he asked, eyeing the skin.

"Just about," Hugh said, embarrassed yet proud.

"Good-sized cat," the other said slowly. "Tradin' it?"

"I thought I might."

Girty reached for the skin and together they spread it out. The man looked it over several moments, then "Come in an' have a drink," he said peremptorily.

Hugh was surprised and flattered. While for several years now he had supped at will from the family whiskey bottle, he had rarely drunk in the tavern with strangers. He followed his companion in to a seat in the corner

Girty ordered two bowls of Continent, all the while watching Hugh with his large black eyes.

"Where d'you hail from, lad?"

"Back in the Cumberland Valley."

The other started. "That's where I was born myself. Chambers Mill in Paxtang on the Susquehanna. What's your name?"

"Hugh—Murray."

"Injuns run you out?"

Hugh nodded. "From the look of things now we didn't make much of a better of it, I'm thinkin'. But we'll get the best of them yet, the red sons of bitches."

Girty drained his bowl and ordered another. He drank quickly again with the air of a man accustomed to large quantities of liquor. His eyes had grown fiery and looked now like burning black furnaces between his lowering lids. He leaned toward Hugh.

"I like you, lad, and the way you fettled that Irishman, or I wouldn't waste words on ye! I'm no talker, but I'm goin' to tell you how I feel about the Injuns."

Hugh was taken aback by the suppressed vehemence of the tone. He watched his companion, fascinated.

"I know the Injuns as well as any man livin', an' what I tell you's the truth. They're as good as the whites."

Hugh drew back as though he had been struck.

"Nobody'll put that down my throat after what me an' mine has suffered from them," he said angrily.

Girty went on.

"I know. That's what all these here pious prayin' Presbyterians say. Now listen. My father was killed by an Injun.

My stepfather was tortured to death by them under our eyes. They took me captive when I was a boy an' I lived with them ten year. I still say there's good in them."

"You're a fool!" Hugh burst out hotly.

Girty's countenance did not change.

"Look ye," he said. "My father was an Irishman an' a trader, an' a devil for drink. There was an Injun back there in Paxtang called the Fish, a good friend of his. They'd get drunk every week an' frolic together like a pair of pups. One night when they was both crazy with rum, they drew knives an' my pap got killed. Might just as easy have been the other way round. No more murder than nothin'. But there was a man—"

He paused as though coolly calculating.

"A decent enough fellow too, named Turner. Friend o' my father's an' afterwards married my mother. He took i[t] for murder an' swore he'd avenge it. So he killed the Fish cold-blooded when the Fish hadn't meant no harm. Well, Injuns don't ever let a thing like that pass. When w[e] moved west to Kittanning, they got Turner; an' I can'[t] say they was wrong."

Hugh's horror was on his face.

"But they *tortured* him!"

Girty shrugged.

" 'Tain't nice to see, but body torture don't last long. It comes to an end. There's other kinds lasts longe[r]. White men don't shoot hot powder in your skin, b[ut] they've got other ways. Nice, refined ways." His voice w[as] bitter.

"You're a strange man," Hugh muttered.

"I'm just showin' you the other side for because I know
t. Now take in Dunmore's War, three years ago. I scouted
ll through that, me an' Simon Kenton. When Old Lo-
an, the Mingo, went on the warpath he had a reason all
ight. Know what it was?"

"Don't think I do."

"Well, I'll tell you. Logan was as good a friend as the
whites ever had. All his family quiet an' peaceful campin'
here on Yellow Creek. An' what happened? A dirty little
assle of soldiers killed them all while Logan was off
untin'. Every last one of 'em."

Hugh saw a change in the black eyes bent upon him.
t seemed as though feeling for a moment quenched their
re.

"My God, I'd sooner watch a man roast at the stake
an see that old feller sittin' on a log, the tears rollin'
own his cheeks, sayin', 'I appeal to any white man to say
he ever entered Logan's cabin hungry and I gave him
ot meat; if ever he came cold or naked and I gave him
ot clothing. . . . And now there runs not a drop of my
lood in the veins of any human creature.' "

Girty took a long drink.

"I interpreted his speech, that's how I come to know.
urdered, they was, all his folks down on Yellow Creek,
' him friendly to the whites all his life an' his father
efore him!"

Hugh said nothing, for he knew by a sudden silence in
e room that others were listening too. The door behind
em had opened, and from the tail of his eye Hugh could
e a man standing there, waiting.

Girty's face was deeply flushed now, his eyes like fire
He half rose from his chair, striking the table before hir
with his fist.

"An' what about Cornstalk! Cornstalk the Shawnee
Wasn't he murdered at Point Pleasant this last Augus
him an' his son when they'd come on a peaceful errand
Answer me that. An' wasn't Cornstalk the greatest ma
on the frontier, white or red? Answer me!"

Hugh, now scarlet with embarrassment, was spared th
discomfort of replying. The man at the door strode fo
ward. It was Archibald Lochry, lieutenant of Westmor
land County.

"Hello, Girty," he said quietly. "What's all this ta
about?"

Girty rose to his full height.

"How are ye, Lochry?" he said. "I was telling this la
here that Cornstalk was the best man I ever knew, an
that he was foully murdered. I'll tell you something els
Lieutenant. You an' your county haven't heard the la
of that murder yet, not by a long shot."

Lochry's face was grave.

"Happen not," he said, "but this end of the count
isn't a very safe one to pick if you want to praise India
There *may* be such a thing as a good live Indian, b
you'll have the devil of a time convincing anyone rou
here of it. Eh, gentlemen?"

There was a deep growl of approval from those sitti
about the room.

"So," Lochry went on, "if I were you, Girty, I'd

asy on the subject of virtues when you're talking of the opper gentry."

A look of cunning came into Girty's eyes, as he swept he group before him.

"Do you call oratory a virtue, Lieutenant?" he asked a a suspiciously soft voice.

Lochry smiled. "I never heard it listed that way."

"All right," said Girty, speaking now to the room, "I'll ust tell you then a little bit about Cornstalk's oratory hat you mebbe don't know. I was out there, out in the hio country when he made the treaty of peace with unmore. We was in a big Shawnee camp that covered out twelve acres. When Cornstalk got up to speak you ould hear him over the whole place. An' what did he y?"

Girty paused and looked about him with his fierce ack eyes.

"He said it was *the whites* caused Dunmore's War! An' e charged them flat with the murder of Logan's family. olonel Ben Wilson was there—you've heard tell of him, guess—and when Cornstalk was done he turned to me d he says, 'I've heard the best orators in Virginny,' he vs, 'Patrick Henry an' Richard Henry Lee; but I've ver heard a speech could touch yon one. My God, man,' says, 'I've got to get away and think this over.' Well, as ook at it, gentlemen, we'll all get a chance yet to think ver. Sittin' down, Lieutenant?"

Lochry sat down at once. Hugh, still flushed and un- y, acknowledged the Lieutenant's brief greeting, then ted to rise. But Girty pushed him back in his chair.

"Sit still, lad. He's the makin' of a good soldier, Lochry He finished up a rantin' Irishman out here this mornin as neat as I've seen lately. An' he's just shot a painter a big as a cow. He'd mebbe like to go in the next cam paign?"

"Again the Indians?" Hugh asked eagerly.

Girty nodded.

"But I thought from the way you talked you was sidin' with them."

"Me? Hell, no! My business right now is fightin' ther same as the Lieutenant here. I'm only sayin' they ain't a devils any more'n the whites are all angels."

"All right," Lochry said sharply. "Let it stand at tha What's the news from Fort Pitt? I heard you were her and I came in today special to see you."

Girty drank again heavily.

"Give it to you in a nutshell. General Hand is sti rarin' to do something to show them back east that he the fellow sent by God a'mighty to save the frontier. He got wind the British have built a magazine out in t Ohio country on the lake and stored ammunition. T idee is for Colonel Hamilton out in Detroit to use it ne spring for his Indian raids. Hand wants to lead an expe tion to bust it up first."

"When?"

"Next month, if he can raise the wind."

Lochry leaned forward.

"Just what do you think of the present state of thin Girty? I know you're fresh back from the Senecas."

"Bad enough," Girty replied, "as near as I can see. C

Guyasoota's one of our warmest enemies now. He's prancin' round like a bull moose in ruttin' season, talkin' about his allegiance to the King of England. He'll be on the warpath next spring sure as shootin'!"

"Had they heard there about Burgoyne's defeat?"

"No. And they wouldn't believe me when I told them. Oh, they're set now to raise hell, that's sartin. Guyasoota says the whites deceived him. Mebbe so. Wouldn't be the first time. How's county affairs, Lieutenant?"

"Quiet for the most part while the snow lies. Are you staying here long, Girty?"

"Just a day or so. I'm tryin' to pick up a few skins to settle a little account back in Pittsburgh."

He stood up suddenly and motioned to Hugh. "I've some barterin' business now with this lad, here. Well, good day, Lieutenant."

Hugh caught the startled look on Lochry's face. It was evident he had more to say and had expected to terminate the interview himself. But Girty had headed for the door that led to the store end of the tavern, and Hugh could only follow, carrying the panther skin with him.

The store was a rough log lean-to which had been added to the original cabin. The heavy puncheon floor, rarely swept, was covered now with dirty melting snow; and a strange reek of green cured skins, ginseng, gunpowder, camphor, spice, dyestuffs, and smoked bacon filled the room.

Girty leaned on the rough counter-table and reached for the panther skin.

"Now, let's us get down to business. I've taken a fancy

to this hide, and I'd like to strike a trade with you. Wha
do you think it's worth?"

"What have you to offer?" Hugh asked cannily.

Girty laughed shortly as though the reply pleased him
Then he left the room, returning in a few moments wit
a rolled blue and red stroud.

He fingered it for a moment without unrolling it.

"You see," he began, "I'm no trader. I scout, I inte
pret, I soldier. But I have some good chances to do a littl
barterin' on the side. I don't bother the usual run o
stuff. I go in for *specialties*. If you want salt an' lead bar
I'm not your man. But if you've got a mother and a ni
sister mebbe—"

He paused, shrewdly watching the color rise in Hugh
cheek.

"—who like a touch of civilized life—well, I've g
something for you."

He opened the stroud, and drew forth a flat obje
about six inches square.

"Now this here ain't one of those lookin' glasses li
George Groghan used to carry to sell the Injuns. In the
you couldn't tell whether your eyes was meant to
above your nose or under it. This is a genuine mirr
like the quality uses back east."

He handed it to Hugh. It was indeed as much a fra
ment from another world as a dropped feather from
angel's wing. Hugh felt an involuntary shiver of antici
tion and fear pass over him, as though, even in handli
it, he were somehow dealing in necromancy. For a m
ror was a rare and strange article in the Back Count

t was thought that Mrs. Hanna had one, but she never
aunted it in the eyes of her neighbors. He had heard
Martha say she suspected Mrs. Brownlee over the hill of
aving perhaps a small bit of one, because of the straight
art in her hair. But no one else in the village had such a
ommodity. Life was too filled with desperate urgencies
or physical vanity to rise and cry for satisfaction. When
woman had to use a thorn for a brooch she was not
kely to miss a looking glass.

Hugh looked around the object now, over it, and
oove it. There was a wooden rim and a handle which he
ngered carefully as though considering the workman-
ip. As a matter of fact he was waiting for courage to
ok at his own image.

"That wasn't brought over the mountains by any ordi-
ary traders," Girty went on. "They can't take a chance
a fancy breakin' things. Besides, it's bad luck to smash a
okin' glass. I got this from someone in Pittsburgh for
ing a favor. What do you think about it? I'll throw
u in a good heavy stroud like this one to boot."

Hugh set his teeth together firmly, raised the mirror in
s hand, and looked full into its shining surface. He saw
air of dark eyes, and a lean, handsome face under the
onskin cap. If he had met that face in a stranger he
uld have inwardly saluted it as belonging to a man of
ength.

"I'll take you up," he said suddenly. "The mirror and
e stroud."

He looked again lingeringly at the panther skin. Per-
os this was best after all. They could use a new blanket,

for sure, and the mirror would please Violet. He would
make it a present to Martha, though, not to her, so his
resolution would still be unbroken.

Girty saw his eyes on the skin. With a quick movement
he drew his knife and cut off a claw which he held out
to Hugh.

"Injun charm," he said. "Means you got the best of
the devil once anyway. Chances better the next time,
guess they reckon. Carry it on you for luck, lad."

Hugh slipped it along with the mirror into the wide
overlapping folds of his hunting shirt, and stuck the neat
rolled stroud under his arm.

"Well, good-bye, Mr. Girty," he said.

The older man looked at him steadily as though calculating his resources.

"About this campaign Hand is gettin' up. If it goes
through, do you want word of it?"

"I'd like it fine."

"I'll mind that."

He turned to the tavern room with the skin, and Hugh
went out the store door into the snow, the mirror hard
and cold against his breast.

As he walked along the narrow track, he was wondering what the womenfolk would say or do when they saw
it; or rather when in it they saw themselves. Sam, he
feared, would be put out that he had made such a poor
barter. But there were still left the other pelts to trade
for salt and household necessities; besides, if he had given
Violet the panther in the first place there would not even
have been the blanket extra to show for it.

He went into the cabin and over to the fireplace.
Martha was churning, and Violet busy at the endless
spinning. The hum of the wheel and the splash of the
dasher stopped as he began to speak.

"I got a couple of things for you, Mother," he said
huskily, "from barterin' the painter."

He flung down the blanket, and Martha exclaimed in
quick pleasure over the color and the texture.

"It's a fine one, Hugh," she said, "and we can use it
mucl well this weather. We'll maybe let Violet have it,
fer she needs an extra ply."

Violet said nothing. He saw that her eyes looked puzzled and hurt. He held grimly to his plan as he felt
within his hunting shirt. He was trembling a little, he
scarcely knew why, as he slowly drew forth the mirror
and held it out—to *Martha*.

"Here's something else," he said. "It's a good one, like
the quality use back east."

Martha gave a cry. Then she stood, making no move to
take it, while her eyes filled up with tears. Hugh and Violet watched her in amazement.

"A mirror!" she said in a strange voice. "An' I'd seen a
ghost it couldn't have startled me more back into the
years. It's as like the one I used to have in my room at
home as one grain of corn to another! Hugh, lad, how
did you ever come by it?"

"From Simon Girty at the tavern. He traded me it an'
the stroud. Take it and have a look at yourself."

Martha slowly reached forth her hand, the tears of
deep nostalgia still blinding her. It was as though she

were reaching for the substance and texture of vanishe
time. She took the mirror and turned it this way and tha
feeling it, fondling it with her rough, hardened finger
but she did not look in it. Instead she held it out to Vio
let, in whose face the hurt was gradually giving way t
excitement.

"Here," she said, striving to keep her voice calm
"This'll soon show you whether you've got a tousy pat
or not. There'll be small excuse for you now if you
curls get strughly."

Violet approached it with a nervous laugh.

"I'm half afeard," she was saying. "I'm afeard I'll ne
know my image, an' then I'll feel strange to myself. Yo
look first, Mother."

But Martha shook her head. "My eyes are bleary. Ju
mind as you see yourself that we're all made in the imag
of God, comely or homely, and it's only the heart th
matters."

Violet raised the mirror cautiously and stared into i
shining surface while Hugh and Martha watched he
They saw her eyes widen, her lips part in a start of su
prise. She bent her head nearer. At last, as though wi
reluctance, she handed it back to her mother, her chee
scarlet.

"I never knew," she faltered. "I never was sure-lik
before, just what I favored . . ."

She stopped, embarrassed, but the waiting two w
loved her saw that she had eaten of the tree of knowled
and knew now that she was fair.

Martha set the mirror carefully on the mantel.

"Well, we must get on with the work. My milk will be old with all our dillying and I'll have a time with the utter. You made a strange-like trade, it seems to me, Hugh. But, as for me, I'm content with it. What your father may think is another matter. He's gone on for more logs, and he said you were to follow him."

All through the day the mirror made, as it were, a light in the dark cabin. The churning and the spinning went on; from without came the heavy sound of the ax blows as the men chopped the newly hauled logs. The wind went howling through the naked trees, and the snow anked and resettled on the roof; the smoke from the re smarted the eyes as the women cooked the meals, and the cold draughts from the cracks brought their usual insidious discomfort. All the same and yet not the same. Something from another life had come to dwell in the cabin. In the fluidly shining surface of the mirror there were memories, there were dreams.

A tinge of excitement colored Martha's manner as she worked. As for Violet, she invented excuses to go often to the fireplace and glance at the magic reflection which repeated again and again the truth she had never fully known before.

Even Sam, to everyone's surprise, accepted the new possession with amused tolerance.

"So," he said that night as he warmed his feet at the re after family worship, "we're gettin' to be gentry an' l, it seems. Damme, if that there painter wouldn't feel nny if he knowed you traded his hide for a mere lookin' ass! Make him feel sort o' cheap, I guess. No cheaper,

mebbe, than I did when I looked in the thing, though
What did you think of this Girty, lad?"

"He's a queer one," Hugh said slowly. "He kept talkin
about the Injuns as if he liked them. But he says he
fightin' them just the same."

"Aye, he's quare an' no mistake. There's a look in h
eye . . . I'd go aisy on the talk with him if I was you
When a man says he likes the Injuns I'm fornenst him a
far as hell an' back."

He turned toward Violet.

"Your brother, here, put a crimp in that Irisher tha
shot the fawn. Was he tellin' ye?"

Violet, startled, looked up, and for the first time sine
the wash-off met Hugh's eyes. He held her to his by th
new force that filled him.

"It was naught," he said. "He's got a dirty mouth, a
I shut it for him, that's all. He's gone on to Pittsburg
I'm thinkin'."

"I'm glad," Violet said. Then, as though feeling som
thing more should be added: "You're—you're awf
strong, Hugh."

"It was naught," he repeated. Then he got up. "I'll
gettin' to bed now, I guess."

He climbed the ladder pegs quickly, and in the col
unlighted cockloft took off his breeches and got betwe
the coarse, woven blankets. Before he lay down he dre
from his shirt the painter's claw which Girty had giv
him, and a bit of linen string. Carefully, using his finge
for eyes, he fastened the claw securely and then tied t
string around his neck. As he lay down he repeat

irty's words: *"Means you got the best of the devil once
nyway. Chances better the next time."*

He closed his eyes. All the more plainly he saw Violet's
s she had raised them to his a few moments ago.

"I'll wear the charm, no fears," he whispered to him-
:lf. "For God knows, I'm goin' to need it."

Below, Martha, her sallow face pale and flushed by
urns, sat knitting on the settle.

"Get on to bed," she was saying to the other two. "I'm
iinkin' I'll finish the heel of this sock while I'm about
."

When the sound of their sleeping came at last to her
urs, she laid by her knitting and sat for a minute, her
eart beating quickly. She smoothed her hair and re-
istened the kerchief at her neck. Then she reached for
ie candle and rose. It was strange none of them had
oticed that she of them all had not yet looked in the
iirror. The hand that held the candle shook, but she
eadied it with the other. She walked to the mantel,
ioistened her lips nervously, and slowly raised her eyes.

For a long time she stood so, reading as though from
me bitter book of remembrance; then she set down the
ndle and sank back on the settle, her head bowed low
 her hands.

When she forced herself to look up at last she stared
rough the dim firelight glow toward the silver sheen
 the mirror. It was like the years of God, she thought,
ross which moved the race of men, breathing their
ief breath and vanishing as though they had never
en. The mirror now was empty, vacant, void, yet only

a short time ago it had held the loveliness of Violet; and
then, so quickly after, the reflection of her own ravaged
face.

For she too had once been beautiful. As she watched
Violet day by day, each feature of her own girlhood
stood out in sweet familiarity. She recalled her father's
voice as he used to say, " 'Thou art thy mother's glass,
my dear."

Even so had Violet been to her. But now this would be
changed. Tonight's truth was an omen, a portent. The
mirror as well as the moving days had warned her that
even as her own beauty had been raped and her heart
torn by the wilderness, so would Violet's be.

Jan. 18, 1778 The rest are all in bed. I told them I would sit up to finish a sock but that was a lie and I'm cruel well paid for it. Hugh traded the panther hide today at the store to Simon Girty the interpreter. He came home with a new blanket *and a looking glass*. Why? Why? Did the hand of Providence send it here? That's what I'm wondering now as I sit all my lone with the wind howling. I feel so sad, so crushed down like, and it's a shame to me. For it shows the vanity and the pride that's still in me. O God help me to purge myself of it. But there's no use covering up the heart from the eyes of God. I know I could bear everything better, even death itself, if I still had my looks. And that's wicked. I must forget myself and the face the years have made for me. It's Violet only I must think of now. Yet I'm a woman and only in my forties and oh it can't be a sin to set down that I was fair once. I mind the first time I met Sam. I had on a sprigged cambric and a pink bonnet. I'd been carrying some custards to old Mrs. Pardee who was sick and the little basket was still on my arm. Sam was coming along the street and he just stopped dead and stared at me. He was so tall and handsome then, and he looked stronger and different some way from the town young men. He lifted his cap and we both knew something had struck us right there. I mind those next weeks. There was no stopping Sam. My father liked him and

said true love must have its way and if he was young again
himself he'd be out on the frontier. But it broke my mother's
heart when I left. She died that next year. She gave me a nice
wedding though and kept up till the very end for my sake.
We had the tea in the garden and my dress was white and
they all said I looked like an angel and Sam's eyes were wet
I mind, when he kissed me. I was so happy and excited-like
I had no idea what I was coming to. Sam got a second horse
and we set out with all my wedding things in the pack sad-
dles. I was too young, never knowing what I'd have to face.
And Sam never told me. Well it's long past now. *But I won't
let Violet go through what I've borne!* I'll save her if it takes
my life! God help me find a way.

IV

The Kissing Party

Martha lay close to Sam's angular body for warmth, his heavy breathing in her ear, while her eyes kept following the shadowy patterns on the log walls about her. The uneven light from the burning hearth was enough to reveal even now the pathetic crudities of the cabin. The curtain, pushed back to let the fire's warmth through, had been spun and dyed by her own hands, and hung by loops of yarn from a wild grapevine strand secured at the ends to wooden pegs in the wall! As she looked, this now seemed to symbolize the harsh discomforts, the bitter makeshifts, the merciless, unending toil of a frontier woman's life. It was not enough tonight to dream she was back again in a room with polished tables, pictured walls, and china dishes row by row on a dresser. She could not lose herself in this girlhood scene as she often did when she was wakeful. The fire in her mind now was beyond putting out with thoughts of the past. Only some assurance for the future could quell it; and the future held only fear unless she could bend it in some way to her will.

So near to her now lay Violet, her eyes closed, her

curls light upon the pillow, her young limbs relaxed in sleep. The very anguish of maternal yearning swept through Martha's heart as she reached out in spirit to her child. Nature had formed her in loveliness; had made a lady of her in blood and bone and flesh. Was not purpose there beneath the fair design? Was Violet not meant by Providence to walk in gentle ways, to be clad in silks and laces, to hear the midday hum of bees in a peaceful garden and the sweet twilight note of a robin from the rooftree?

There were no bees in Hannastown and no songbirds this side the mountains. People said they would come soon, following the path of the settlers. Perhaps this was true, but now there was only the harsh hoot of the owl, the cawing of the corbies and the sad death call of the whippoorwill at dusk! The happy-singing birds were still far away.

Once again she considered all the facts. If only her mother were alive, or her father, that she might send the girl back east to them! But they were both gone now and the old home of her memories was in other hands. She had no near relatives. So if Violet was to go back to safety and comfort it would have to be as a wife. But whose?

The snow started falling again after the turn of the night. Martha felt it even though it was soundless. Long years of watching, listening for the blessed flakes had given her an Indian-like perception. The wind had fallen; the draft through the chinks was suddenly less cold; there was an enfolding hush, and a sensation like

gentle fingers laid upon the brow. It was the snow once
more. She crept out of bed quietly and laid another log
on the fire, being careful not to look in the mirror. They
were all safe tonight, close and safe together, free from
danger and the fear of it; but still she could not sleep.
Her mind, following tortuous paths, wondered and questioned and planned. Thoughts of daring, almost of unseemliness came and passed and left their mark. There
had been a woman back in Cumberland County who had
grabbed an ax and disemboweled an Indian when he was
about to catch up her child. Women could do what had
to be done the same as men, when the time fell upon
them. And if the necessary thing seemed strange or dangerous it made no difference. You had to fight for your
own. That was the first law of the wilderness. And you
had to use the weapons ready to your hand. . . .

All at once the hot procession of her thoughts stopped.
She lay tense and all but breathless, overcome by a new
idea which, the moment it was born, seemed old, so well
did it fit into the accustomed grooves of her mind. The
wonder was that she had never thought of it before!

There was one other person in the town who longed
for the east as she did, though his eyes had never seen it;
whose spirit constantly chafed under the exigencies of
the frontier, because he had been made for a different
way of life. This was James. *James!* In all the times he
had come and gone, borrowing and reborrowing the
Shakespeare, sitting by the fire with his eyes of understanding fixed on her while they talked of things within
their own ken, she had never once thought of him as a

possible husband for Violet! Now, suddenly it seemed
natural and inevitable.

He was not too much older, and he was handsome in
his own way, and clever! Even if he was not strong and
rugged as Hugh was, for instance, he was not *ailing*. Just
studentlike, that was all. And yesterday, as he had turned
at the door to tell Violet about the view from the hilltop,
there had been a soft look in his eyes. She remembered i
now. Maybe already on his side there was a bit of feeling. Men always showed it first in their eyes. She would
watch carefully from now on. As to Violet? Oh, she
couldn't help getting fond-like over James if he would
begin to fancy her! The thing that must be done now, at
once, while peace lay on them with the snow, was to give
them a special chance; to bring them together some way
different from the plain everyday meetings, so that all of
a sudden they would see something in each other the
had never seen before.

Martha lay thinking. It was part of a mother's business
to plan and contrive for her girl's happiness. Sometime
it might be almost as hard a job as fighting Injuns, but
she had to go on, doing the best she could to follow her
promptings. As for herself, she had turned her hand before to many a thing that looked impossible: the brow
curtain, for instance, and the stained chairs and, most of
all, those little times of joy or easement which she ha
made for the children even in the darkest days. Ther
must be some way now to manage this, which here in th
one short span of a night had become to her the mo
important thing in life.

A shiver of fear and hope, mingled, ran through her thin body. This would be different from the time she went to mill and loaded the heavy bags of grain herself when Sam and Hugh had both been down with the shakes; far different from the time she found the rattlesnake den on the far edge of their land and set fire to it herself.

She remembered those days just after the massacre in the Cumberland Valley when Hugh and Violet had sat dazed and white-faced in the cabin, having seen sights no young spirits could bear, and Sam with his eyes like coals and his face set hard in the "killing look" had gone off with the other settlers in pursuit of the Indians. It was then, with her own heart weeping blood, that she had taught Hugh and Violet to play Fox and Geese with corn kernels, and laughed herself to lift the dark spell from them. That laughter had been more the measure of her courage than all else she had ever done. And the sheer triumph of it had given her strength to go on; that was the strange part.

This now that she had set herself to do would be more like that. She would plan and contrive and at last succeed in sending Violet back east—away from her forever. But she would sup from all of that her own strange cup of joy! Violet would be safe. And because of that her own heart would have easement from its worst fear. If only it were as simple now as the old game of Fox and Geese with the corn kernels. Suddenly she caught her breath and lay very still. With the blood pounding in her temples and her eyes hot and opened wide, the plan began swiftly to evolve. As though felling enemies, she dashed down every thought of hindrance.

She had barely fallen into her first sleep at last when Sam began to stretch and turn his head upon the pillow preparatory to getting up.

Sam was a born early riser. He had the native woodsman's ability to sleep at any time upon the command of his senses, to rouse instantly if there was danger in the air, and to wake with finality when the sun rose; and he had no patience with those who could not do likewise. He began to talk now as he always did the moment his eyes were open.

"Martha, *Martha!* Time to get up. Come on now, it' gettin' late. Hugh an' me's got a heavy day in the wood comin'. *Martha!* Ain't a whole night time enough for you to be snorin' it off? You're as bad as Vi'let, gettin' to be Come on now. Snookin' in your bed won't fill the pot."

Martha's head was intolerably heavy, and her eyelid were sore weights; but by force of will she held them open. She had managed this far in her life to keep up with Sam's unremitting energy, and on this particula morning she had her own reasons for wanting to be astir The resolve that had taken her by force in the nighttim was even stronger now by day.

She hung her bedgown on the peg in the wall and dressed hastily. As she was smoothing her hair she stoppe dead-still, considering. There was a personal decision sh must make some time. It might as well be done now Should she shun the mirror from now on, evade it, dodg

t, cringe away from the hurt of it? Or should she accept
ts bitter truth and make a daily companion of it, as she
had been forced to do with many another?

"It's just the *woman* in me that hates the thought of it
o," she whispered to herself. "But it's coward-like to let
t best me. Besides, if I'm stirred up now to do something
about Violet, what signifies having my own pride brought
ow in the dust."

She walked straight to the mantel and looked full into
he shining glass, carefully parting her hair by its reflec-
ion. The image she saw was even more unfamiliar now
han that of last night, but she looked at it steadily. The
hin cheeks looked thinner this morning; the eyes blood-
hot from sleeplessness; and the multiple lines deeper.
But she did not flinch nor let herself think of the past
now as she looked. Here was the present tenement of her
pirit. She must accept it and school herself day by day to
ive with it. Just this matter of living on patiently with a
hurt took most of the bitterness out of it. She had found
hat out long ago. There might come a day when she
ould even smile at the mirror, though now that seemed
unlikely. At least, she had won the fight with herself this
morning.

She hurried about the business of getting breakfast
while Sam roused Violet and Hugh, planning in her
mind how best to make her announcement to the family.
The opportunity, however, like a miracle, came of itself.

Sam was chaffing Violet about the mirror, throwing in
warning to Hugh that there mustn't be too much time

wasted now in seeing how handsome he was. The young
people laughed a little, glancing at each other with con-
straint across the table.

"It's a fine thing you folks ain't goin' to the dance.
Vi'let here'd take so long to prink up her curls she'd
never get there."

"A dance!" Violet cried. "Oh, Father, where is it to
be?"

"Over at Coventry place, at the Pershings'. Least so I
heared them sayin' last night. The Conrads an' the
Heuguses an' the Ackermans an' all them from round the
Nine Mile Run are gettin' it up."

Violet's eyes were misty with longing, and even Hugh
had raised his head to listen. For purely social gatherings
were rare on the frontier, especially among the Scotch
Irish. There was always a joyful celebration over a
wedding, and even a strange season of hospitality and fel-
lowship at a funeral. In between these extremes of experience there were the gatherings in which the need of help
from neighbor hands was made the occasion of a frolic,
the corn shuckings, the maple sugar bilin's, the flax
scutchings, the fulling bees, the cabin raisings! But these
did not occur with regularity, and for the last year, while
the Indian raids had been more and more threatening,
the summer and autumn frolics had been curtailed for
reasons of safety.

Amongst the German element there was always more
spontaneous merrymaking than amongst the Scotch-Irish.
The racial traditions of the former included good living
and a natural acceptance of happiness as one of the gifts

of God. But the latter still bore upon their spirits the stamp of the bleak highlands and the martyr-haunted moors. By nature and inheritance they were better fitted for struggle than for enjoyment; so they sought as a rule a practical excuse for pleasure. It was this realization with which Martha had contended the night before; and with which Violet was now struggling.

"It's strange-like why the Lutherans think no harm in dancing and the Presbyterians call it a sin," she said.

"Whisht!" said her mother. "It's not for us to sit in judgment on others if their consciences tell them different from ours. But it's for us to see to it we follow our own light. As for me and my house, there will be no dancing. But I see no reason why we mightn't have another kind of party ourselves."

The others stared at her in surprise.

"What's that?" said Sam sharply.

"Why, Mother!" Violet's eyes were large with un-dreamed-of delight. "You mean *us* have a party?"

Hugh said nothing, but he had stopped eating.

Martha tried to speak calmly though her heart stormed against her chest.

"It's queer-like the way things just come to you. Last night I lay in bed thinking now with the deep snow and everything quiet it would be nice for us to have the young folks in of an evening, and play some games."

"Oho!" Sam observed. "A kissin' party! Why, what's struck you?"

"Mother," Violet broke in, "we never had just a— *party* before. Will folks think it odd-like to come when it's not for a husking or a fulling or—or even a spinning?"

Martha was ready. "We'll just tell them it's because we had all work and no frolic last fall on account of the Injuns. What do you say, Hugh?"

He raised his eyes swiftly toward Violet and then dropped them.

"Why, I'd like it fine," he said slowly.

"Is it all right with you, Sam?" Martha went on.

Sam, too, was watching Violet. He had started to grumble but changed his mind.

"I guess the younkers can stand a bit play an' no harm done—though I still don't know what set you on this."

Martha hoped the uncomfortable flush on her cheeks would pass for overheat from the fire. Her voice was still calm though, almost casual.

"Just a thought come to me in the nighttime, that's all. We could ask the young folks here in the village and the near-by places."

"When would we have it?" Hugh asked. "It ud be a pity for Dave to miss it."

"Of course we'll wait for Dave; but his mother thinks he'll be feeling chirk again come next week. It doesn't act like lung fever. You got him home in time to save him that, I doubt."

"Friday night, we might say," Violet suggested eagerly. "Friday night week, or even two weeks off. That would give us a chance to get the word around and—and . . ."

She hesitated, as though ashamed.

"And what?" Sam put in. "Let's have it, lass."

"I just meant we would have a little while to *think*

about it before the time and be happy-like expecting it. It would sort of stretch it out longer."

Martha looked tenderly at her daughter. She herself had always been an adept at spreading the smallest bits of pleasure over the longest possible period.

"That's right, Violet. Besides, we'll want to give the cabin the going over of its life and plan a little about what we could have for a bit supper for them. That will be the biggest worry, I doubt. But we'll put our brains in steep and see what comes of it."

"Will we be sayin' a week come Friday then?" Hugh asked.

They all looked at one another over the rude split-log table, considering. The amazed eagerness in Violet's eyes —and in Hugh's—went to Martha's heart. She had a feeling of guilt because she had not planned this purely for their pleasure; but the true reason was so infinitely more important! She trembled inwardly at thought of the far consequences she might be bringing upon them all by this action, yet the iron resolve in her soul supported her. Another element in the morning's discussion gave her comfort. She had the deeply inbred Scottish feeling for *omens;* and there had been a favorable one here. The whole matter of the party had been led up to by Sam's unexpected reference to the Pershing dance. She herself had not had to broach it with sudden irrelevance. This was a good sign.

"'We might say Friday a week," she replied.

"And can we tell the folks right away?" Violet asked.

"You might as well. I'm glad we've a braw good supply

of candles anyhow. When it's near the time you might fetch a bit of pine in, Hugh, and we'll stick it up here and there to dress the walls. The only thing we've got plenty of here is woods, the dear knows, so we might as well make them serve us all we can."

"I can't *believe* it, some way," Violet kept saying. "Can you, Hugh?" For the first time since the night of their dark pain she looked up at him with eyes bright with innocence.

"It's a wonder now, for certain, but they'll all take to it right enough. Would—would you think of havin' a fiddle? I'll venture we could scare one up somewhere, an' Father here could saw us a tune."

Violet clapped her hands, and Sam's eyes looked pleased; Martha, however, was doubtful.

"A fiddle? Oh, I don't know, Sam. What think you? To fiddle for the games would make it a bit like . . . Well, we wouldn't want word to get out we were having a *dance*. That's the only thing."

"The Kinkaids have an old fiddle under the bed. I saw it once, when Missus pulled a box out. I'm a'most sure it had two strings on anyway."

"Ach," Sam said, "what signifies findin' a fiddle when me fingers are as stiff as cornstalks. I couldn't get any more tune out of one now than I'd get milk from a polecat."

But Martha saw there was an old eager look in his eyes.

"After all," she considered, "it would just be the tunes you always used to be playing before we came here. 'It's raining, it's hailing,' and suchlike."

"And 'Oh, Sister Phoebe,' and 'King William Was,'" cried Violet. "Oh, let's try to get a fiddle!"

"I never knowed Kinkaids had a one," Sam said slowly. And then Martha realized from his tone what he had never admitted these last years. He had felt bereft of something precious when his old fiddle had been lost coming over the mountains. No one ever knew where or how the one bundle had loosened and fallen from the pack horse. Sam had gone back patiently over the narrow track for miles when he discovered the loss, but there was no trace to be found of the articles. He decided they must have rolled down the mountainside, or even been picked up by a stealthy straying Indian. In any case they were gone. Martha had made her own moan over the loss, for a piece or two of her mother's china, long treasured, had been in that particular bundle and a few choice pewter spoons. Sam had said nothing then or later about the fiddle. This should have told her the truth. With swift intuitive insight she saw it all now clearly. This was the reason Sam would suddenly turn irritable as he sat by the fire of an evening. He missed the feel of the fiddle under his chin; he had no reason now for the old relaxing rhythm of his foot as it kept time; a familiar thread of his life had been snapped, and he could not mend it. So he hacked and hewed away at split brooms, cursing fitfully under his breath. Martha understood it now, and her heart ached for him. She carried so many pains for all of them that it seemed strange she should have missed this. But it, too, would be with her from now on.

"The thing to do is to stop by at the Kinkaids'," she

said quickly, "and see if they really have the fiddle and will lend it. It wouldn't take you long to get the hang of it again, Sam. Rub your fingers good with bear grease tonight and they'll limber up."

Sam yawned ostentatiously. It was the infallible sign that he was peculiarly and deeply interested in the matter in hand.

"Well, I'll mebbe give the Kinkaids a cry when I get round to it. Come on now, Hugh, we've got heavy work afore us."

"Will you bid the boys then, Hugh, if I bid the girls?" Violet asked eagerly.

Her eyes were, at the moment, clear, unembarrassed, bright.

"Aye, Sister. I'll help you with the biddin'."

A fragile, beautiful mood suddenly fell upon them and filled the smoky cabin as though a breath of June had blown through it. The air trembled and would not be held, but the delicate pulse of it was there; for each heart at the same moment was knowing some sort of happiness.

When the men had gone, Martha and Violet fell to talking quickly and joyously. Something of their woman's heritage denied them by the hard repressions of the frontier was now to be theirs.

"I've a bit more cloth left from the hunting shirts and there's more deer hair in the bag up in the cockloft. What think you about making an extra cushion or so for the settle? If we could borrow a bit of madder from somebody we could dye them yellow. That would make a nice change. Mrs. Shaw might have some."

"And, Mother, the night of the party, the folks can all lay their wraps on my bed, and then we can spread the new stroud over yours for some to sit on between the games—"

"And I've just thought of a thing Mrs. Hanna told me of! We'll get Hugh to cut a smooth short log of a white birch and hollow three sockets for candles, or even *four,* mebbe! We'll set it fair in the middle of the mantel—"

"And with the *mirror* there on the one end and the pine on the walls— Oh, Mother, it's going to be past believin' beautiful!"

Martha's face fell suddenly.

"I hope and pray there'll be none to say it's to show off the mirror we're having the party! That would be a fell blow to me! Never would I want to vaunt myself before my neighbors."

"They'll never think it. They all know we aren't proud folks. But, oh, Mother, *what* can we have for the supper, like?"

At once both women stopped their work and considered their resources. There was in the house a very, very little white wheat flour saved especially for time of sickness, a plentiful amount of corn meal always; some deer bladders filled with maple sugar; an abundance of bear and hog fat; a scanty, priceless gourdful of salt; another gourdful of mountain tea leaves and one of dried roots; some smoked ham and flitch that must last till the following fall; the milk and butter from Reddy, the cow; walnuts in the cockloft; all too few potatoes and turnips in the hole behind the shed; and the potential food of the forest.

Martha sighed a little. "My mother used to have tea parties, I mind, with hot gingerbread and big plates of thin bread as white as the driven snow. There would be damson conserve too, and cheese on a little pink-flowered plate. It's queer-like, how I can see that plate yet after all the years."

"I'd *never* forget a flowered plate, once I saw a one," Violet said wistfully.

Martha straightened suddenly. A strange light came into her reddened eyes.

"You'll see flowered plates a-plenty yet, mind you! You'll have a house some day with papered walls and stairs and a dresser polished fit to see yourself in!"

"Why, Mother!" Violet's voice was both startled and pleased. "Do you honest think so? But I doubt it'll not be till I'm old, the way things are here in the Back Country."

"We'll not fash ourselves about *when*," Martha said. "Let's get back to the supper."

All through the day the planning went on. At every point there were the pressing limitations to confront them; but at last they came to a decision. Game was always plentiful and nary a thing on wings was swift enough to evade the aim of Sam or of Hugh. They would have wild turkey, with corn pone and maple sugar for a sweet finish.

"And if I can beg, borrow, or barter a pinch of saleratus, I can make the pone extra good. I can maybe fix a mulled drink, too, if there's enough value in the rest of the skins Hugh's trading to warrant a bit of spice after the necessities. We'll see."

Never had days flown so fast as the ones which followed, or been filled with such tremulous excitement. On each trip to the spring or the tavern, to the Hannas' or the Shaws' or the Kinkaids', there was long discussion of the coming event. The word had gone over the hill to the Brownlees and over the other hills to the Wilsons. Travelers at the tavern, hearing the conversation, made comment over their bowls of Continent or rum.

"Hannastown's as fancy as Pittsburgh, gettin' to be, what with parties an' such!"

Sam, half embarrassed and half proud at his sudden prominence, brought the remarks home to the family.

Even in the evenings they were all busy in the Murray cabin. Martha and Violet worked on the new cushions, Hugh finished the birch candle holder with infinite care, making delicate carvings with his barlow knife and then turned to the task of making extra wooden trenchers for the guests, to eke out the supply of eating utensils.

But perhaps, of them all, Sam was the happiest in these evenings. He had dropped in at the Kinkaids' one day and after a casual chat had inquired about the fiddle.

"Dear me, yes!" Mrs. Kinkaid had said. "We've got the bones of one here somewhere. I never let them throw it out, for it was my old grandpappy's an' he set awful store by it. Get down under the bed, now, some of you young ones that's soople, an' see if you can fetch it out. It'll be no good to you, Mr. Murray, I can tell you, but you're right welcome to see what you can do with it."

Sam had brought it home tucked under his arm like a child. There was but one string on the fiddle, and the bow was warped and bare. He had applied himself first to the latter. Very gently, making a kind of running commentary on the situation as he did so, he had abstracted from Ranger's tail enough hairs to string the bow. He wet the wood and straightened it tenderly at the heat of the fire. When all was ready he threaded it with a touch incredible in his rheumatic fingers. He whistled as he worked, keeping time once more with his foot.

For the fiddlestrings themselves there were sacrificed two soft brown rabbits that sat quivering with quick terror one sunset in the snow. He had skinned and cleaned them quickly, turning over the small infantlike carcasses to Martha for the pot, but keeping with care the entrails for himself. He soaked the guts overnight, and then, getting Hugh to help him, he cut with the grain, long, tiny threads. Once again with a delicacy past believing, he twisted the slender slivers together and fastened them taut to dry. He spent all of three evenings whittling small wooden pegs and adjusting the new-made strings. Then at last one night—

At the sudden sound they all started and cried out with surprise and delight.

> It's raining, it's hailing,
> It's cold stormy weather,
> In comes the farmer
> Selling out his cider. . . .

The old tune here in the Hannastown cabin, harsh
and thick and uncertain but recognizable! And here sat
Sam, a great contentment on his brown, wrinkled face,
his head bent against the fiddle as a man leans toward his
dearie.

> I'll go the reaper,
> Who'll go the binder?
> I've lost my true love,
> And where shall I find her?

Martha felt her throat tighten as she watched him, and
then sat clapping softly to the time; Violet jumped up
and pirouetted about for the sheer joy of it and Hugh, the
dark look all gone from his eyes, kept calling out:

"Give us another, man! Give us another!"

The Murray candles were the last in the village to be
snuffed that night!

On one point Martha spent anxious thought as the
time approached. She had one possession from her own
wedding that she had kept as with her very life. It was a
silk dress. It lay now wrapped in old linen cloths in the
bottom of a homemade wooden chest under her bed. It
was, of course, for Violet's wedding. But the deep question in Martha's mind was whether the great end would
be served better by bringing it out now and letting Violet
wear it at the party. It would set her off from all the rest;
it would bring her before James' eyes as a creature from
a different world—the world he longed to enter.

For James was coming to the party. She had had un-
told fears before that was finally assured. It was mentioned first in a way casual enough.

"Have you all the boys bid, Hugh?" she asked him one day.

"I think so, Mother."

"Did you speak to James?"

Hugh and Violet had both looked up in surprise.

"*James?* Why, you know he never pays heed nor hap to a frolic. He says he doesn't like to be with a whole boon of folks."

"He told me once," Violet put in, "that time we had the fulling bee at the Shaws' that he'd had a much better night of it with 'Hamlet.' "

"But we must ask him," Martha said eagerly. "It wouldn't be neighborlike not to."

"He's too old," Violet said, "and he'll mebbe spoil the fun. You know, the young folks don't take to James rightly."

"I can *bid* him," Hugh said as though the thing were settled already, "but he won't come."

Martha had been terrified. "Never mind," she said, "I'll see to it."

She had found James writing as usual when she stopped in at the Brisons'; for with infinite pains he always re-copied his court records into the large book kept for the purpose. She told him briefly of their plan.

"And I want you to come, James. Don't say me nay, now. We're scarce of young men, and besides it will do you good to play a bit. You're too stuck to your pen as it is. Isn't that right, Mrs. Brison?"

"Don't I tell him so daily an' duly? To be sure you'll go, James, when a good friend like Mrs. Murray bids you." Mrs. Brison was short and fat and practical. "It'll be a kissin' party, I reckon? Well, as I tell James here, a thriving land is aye a wiving land, an' if all the young blades paid as little heed to the girls as James does there'd be a poor lookout for the Back Country. You don't get bairns out of books, I keep tellin' him."

James' thin face colored at his mother's bluntness. There was not much understanding between them; Jane Brison could never make out why a son of hers should turn tail at a gun, and the shame of it never left her. It was almost as unvirile a thing on the frontier to reach the age of twenty-eight unwed.

"I'll go, and my kind thanks to you, Mrs. Murray," James said quietly. "If I'm not much good at the sterner sports I surely should not refuse to lend my presence to the milder ones. It remains to be seen whether I'll be a failure there too."

Martha sensed the thin irony, and her heart was not at peace. All the way home she had felt James' eyes uncomfortably following her.

She was feeling them upon her now as she tried to decide what was best to do about the silk dress. Should she take it from its wrapping and let Violet array herself in it, making the occasion thus marked past all forgetting? Or should she keep it for the wedding gown as she had always planned? She had redyed Violet's linsey-woolsey at any rate, and her linen kerchief was clean and ready. . . .

She decided at last to let the precious silk await the ultimate consummation of her planning. Yes, it would bide where it was until the wedding. She must rely now on the unusual quality of the party itself and upon Violet's own fresh beauty to quicken James' senses.

When the great day came at last, all was in readiness. The biggest logs the fireplace would hold had been lugged in by Hugh's strong arms and stacked at the side of it; the wild turkeys had been shot and plucked and drawn and were even now in the great iron pot on the crane; the cabin was as clean as relentless woman hands could make it; the mantel, wonderful with the row of candles set in the birch log in the middle, the mirror at one end and the fiddle at the other!

"Now, before we get too throng," Martha said as they finished breakfast, "I wish you'd get out to the woods, Hugh, and bring in a good bunch of pine. It'll look green and fresh-like and make a decoration. You might ask Dave to go with you, but it's maybe better for him not to overdo when he's saving up his strength."

Sam chuckled. "He told me yesterday he'd be ready to do as much swingin' an' kissin' as the next one tonight."

Hugh tightened his hunting shirt, sharpened his knife, stuck it in his belt, and picked up his coonskin cap.

"Ain't you comin' along then, Sister, to help fetch the pine?"—looking the other way.

"Why, yes," Martha said quickly. "Go along, Violet. You can carry a load after Hugh cuts it. We might as well have a plenty."

Violet's cheeks flushed. She caught up her shawl and her long knitted scarf, and in a second the two were outside. It was a bright morning, and the new world sparkled.

The sun was still in the east above the far ridges, the great stretches of snow over the cleared spaces sloped away like fields of asphodel; while beyond on every side, high to the north and west, low to the east and south, was the deep wilderness. Hugh struck off along the track he and his father and Ranger had made the day before when they hauled logs. Violet's moccasins were well stuffed with deer hair, and her woolen stockings, heavy and warm. She plodded happily beside him, and neither spoke.

At last they entered the woods. Even though the trees bore crests of snow instead of leaves there was heavy shadow here, lightened only by occasional pale streaks of sunrise amber. There was a silence too, of more substance than that of the open. This silence had a texture woven of the hushed heartbeats of hidden, living things. Hugh and Violet felt it and adjusted themselves instantly to it, for they were both children of the forest. They moved, light as Indians, over the rough broken trail between the trees, their eyes instinctively alert, their ears open for the least break in the strange live stillness.

They reached the clump of balsam and hemlock which Hugh had marked the day before, and began upon their work. Violet piled the branches on the snow as they fell under Hugh's knife. There was white spruce near by too, and the sharp sweet resinous scent filled their nostrils.

At last Hugh paused and looked around.

"Is it enough, think you?"

"There's a good lock of it here."

"This one more with the cones, then, an' we'll be gettin' back."

But when he had the branch, he laid it down with the rest, shut up his knife, and came over beside Violet. A little shaft of light fell through the thick trees upon her face. Hugh straightened his hunting shirt and stood there, looking down at her, his hands in his belt. Would the furious beating of his heart break the quiet and call the wild things from their holes, he wondered.

"There's something on my mind to say to you, Sister," he began. "An' I hope you won't take it ill. It's about"— his voice dropped—"the night I got home from huntin'."

Violet's dark blue eyes fell now before his, but she said not a word, only moved the snow with the toe of her moccasin.

"It's been like pain to me ever since, the way it was that night. An' I've wanted to tell you it was the startle you give me that made me wait, standin' there like a gawk—"

He swallowed hard.

"It was just the startle, mind. I wanted you to know, an' think naught of it."

And then Violet made a sudden quick step forward. She came close, catching his arms, her eyes cleared of all shame, and bright.

"Oh, Hugh, I've got easement now with you telling me this. I set such store by you, Brother, and it's seemed these last weeks as if you were farther away than when you were in the forest even. And that was a worry to me. And now we can be the same as if it never happened, can't we?"

"Just the same," Hugh whispered thickly.

There was no effort, no volition, no conscious movement, but all at once they were in each other's arms. Was
it sister, was it brother? Was it sweetheart, was it lover?
Why should they ask? Why should they care, when their
lips, young, warm and virgin, met and held and met
again? The passing sweetness of it! The piny air, the
deep, white solitude, the forest enfolding!

At last they stooped to gather up the boughs, and then
made their way back, laughing nervously, talking in
broken sentences, trying to deceive each other, trying to
pretend they did not know what had happened to them
in the forest stillness.

The pine, as Sam himself acknowledged by evening,
"just fettled things right." They tucked it in the shelves,
behind the wooden pegs; they covered all the unsightli-
ness with its fair fresh green. The great fire roared up the
chimney, the bright stroud adorned the double bed, the
new cushions graced the settle, the candles were lighted
in their wooden holders, pleasant odors of the turkey and
pone and the spicy drink mingled with the fragrance of
the pine. Even Martha smiled with pleasure and satisfaction as she saw the room ready at last for the guests; but
more than the room was the brightness in Violet's eyes
and the red flush of happiness on her cheek!

There were sounds of chatter then from the girls outside and of loud calls and whistles from the boys. They
were coming! There was a pull of the latchstring, Hugh
sprang forward to hold open the door, they were inside,
laughing, exclaiming, calling one another to witness the

marvel of the festive cabin. It touched Martha to hear them, in their artless ignorance of better things.

James was the last to come. He entered quietly while the first circle was forming, and Martha pushed him toward it even while he demurred. Violet turned around and, seeing him, flashed him a smile and caught his hand.

"Oh, James, you're just in time for 'King William Was'! Come on here, beside me!"

Sam struck up the fiddle, and the circle began to move, the girls in their blue and green linseys and white kerchiefs, the boys in their buckskin breeches and fringed shirts with an occasional red plaid to set off a pair of wide shoulders. Dave Shaw was dragged into the center of the ring, his round face a bit pale from his illness, but his eyes bright and his laugh sounding out above all the rest. He gave a quick smoothing to his bear-greased hair, executed a few fancy steps to show he was in fine fettle, then settled to keep watch on the girls as they moved past, dimpling and giggling even while they sang:

> "King William was King James' son,
>   And of a royal race he sprung;
>   He wore a star upon his breast
>   To show that he was royal best."

Dave shifted from the center a trifle, for it would soon be time to choose. And they all knew who it would be!

> "Go choose your east, go choose your west,
>   Go choose the one that you like best;
>   If she's not here to take your part,
>   Go choose another with all your heart."

Dave made a sudden snatch at Betsy Kinkaid, and pulled her, prettily protesting, with him back into the center of the circle. The voices rose louder with a high obbligato of girlish laughter.

> "Down on the carpet you must kneel,
>   Just as the grass grows in the field;
>   Salute your bride with kisses sweet,
>   And then rise up upon your feet."

The two knelt down, not on a carpet but on the hard plank floor. But it could as well have been a velvet cushion. The mood was as gay, the young hearts, for these precious moments, as light, the kiss as hearty.

Round and around went the circle again with a new lad each time in the ring. The wind rose and howled over the cabin roof, once a death-chilling sound came from the wilderness, but the singing voices drowned it out. The great logs crackled and flamed in the fireplace especially when a draught of icy air came from the door as a neighbor slipped in to sit in the corner and watch the fun. The plank floor creaked with the weight upon it; the color rose higher in the girls' cheeks, the boys flung their broad shoulders and shouted the words louder. And the kissing went on—sometimes to the accompaniment of scuffling and coy resistance, sometimes accomplished quickly and simply as though hand were merely meeting hand.

Martha watched from the kitchen end of the cabin while she set out the trenchers and noggins and tested the turkey. A few of the girls were called into the ring center over and over again. Violet was one of these, her curls flying free, her lips and cheeks red from the quick exercise. There was a grace about everything she did which drove the knife into her mother's heart more than beauty alone would have done. It was the grace of a lady born.

Back east, in Philadelphia, even with the war going on, there would be great parties this winter. Men in shining braid, fine wrist ruffles, and carefully queued hair would be gallantly leading beautiful women through the minuet. Candle shine would fall like pools of living light on polished mahogany; and old wine and dainty delicacies would be dispensed from stately dining rooms. But among all those women back east whose lives were pleasant and easy not one would be as beautiful as Violet. Not one!

She stopped suddenly, her hand tight upon a noggin. James was the last one to be pushed into the circle. It was his turn now in a moment to choose a girl, and the others were shouting at him, half derisively.

"Get your spunk up now, James!"

"Kissin' ain't as hard as it looks."

"You wasn't born in the woods to be scairt of an owl, was you?"

"Time you got down to business, James. You'll never learn younger!"

So the boys' shouts ran to the high descant of the girls singing. Martha could see that James was embarrassed and annoyed. He stood there listening, watching, his face pale, clean-cut like a cameo.

He's got the high-born look, too, Martha thought.
They'll make a fine couple.

Violet was not singing or calling. She moved past, understanding his deep shyness, and smiled at him reassuringly.
He caught her hand suddenly and drew her in.

> "Down on the carpet you must kneel
> Just as the grass grows in the field . . ."

They knelt together, and because James was older and
his face grave instead of laughing the loud guffaws of the
boys were hushed a little. Martha's own heart stopped
beating as she watched him. For once she had no eyes for
Violet. It was James she saw as he bent his head and kissed
the girl slowly and quietly upon the lips.

Then the noise grew louder than ever. The couple in
the ring rose, the circle broke and scattered, and the cabin
walls shook to the noise and the laughter, for this was the
end of one game and the next must now be chosen.

"Come on, come on," Dave shouted. "Join up hands
now for 'Lily in the Garden.' "

"No. 'Sister Phoebe!' We want 'Sister Phoebe'!" Peggy
Shaw called.

Violet added her plea.

"Oh, yes, 'Sister Phoebe!' It's the best."

Hugh caught her words and at once raised his hand.

"Get your partners for 'Sister Phoebe,' and get in the
ring."

His heart felt a quick tender pang, for the words might
have been written for him and Violet.

Sam played the tune through, and Martha listened to the plaintive cadences, feeling bound by it to all that had gone before her. For these old words and melodies were the folk songs of England and Scotland, borne without loss in brave hearts across a stormy Atlantic; carried, indestructible, over the mountains to be heard now in the western wilderness and still to be borne on, along the Monongahela, the Allegheny, the Ohio, south and north, and then on, on into the deeper unknown west. Strange that of all man's possessions it should be the frail echo of a song's lilt, the fragile memory of a rhyme that should be imperishable! So Martha thought, as she stirred the turkey stew.

The circle formed with new partners, and the young voices rang out again:

"Oh, Sister Phoebe, how merry were we
   The night we sat under the juniper tree,
      The juniper tree, I, oh.

"Take this hat on your head, and keep your head warm,
   And take a sweet kiss, it will do you no harm,
      But a great deal of good, I know."

It was Hugh in the center, but he did not look at Violet. She knew he would not call her in the game, and something within her gloried in the fact. He called Jenny Hanna and kissed her with quick heartiness. Now it was Jenny's turn to remain in the center and choose. Round and round flew the linsey-woolsey skirts and the buckskin breeches as the rhythm changed and quickened.

"If I had as many lives
  As Solomon had wives
    I'd be as old as Adam;
  So rise to your feet
  And kiss the first you meet,
    Your humble servant, madam."

Then again the slower, plaintive melody:

"Oh, Sister Phoebe, how merry were we
The night we sat under the juniper tree."

When they stopped at last, the girls sat down on bed and settle and the boys dropped to the floor. The warm blood still raced in their veins, and all the fires of youth flared high. The hot young eyes of the lads sought the bright provocative gaze of the maidens, and the pulse of stirring life was in all the air. Martha, watching, praying unworded prayers, saw the still severity of James' face relax and a faint color rise in his thin cheeks. He was laughing with Dave Shaw, but his eyes were somewhere else. . . .

Violet skipped through the group of lads and over to her mother.

"Would we play a game of Hurly-Burly now, think you, before the supper?" she asked eagerly.

"I think you might. I'll have things ready by then. Mind none of you get too close to the fire in the scrimmage."

"I'll get Hugh to help me with the telling," she said. "Oh, Hugh!"

He was beside her in a second, standing so close that their hands met in the folds of her dress. No one saw, or paid heed. Was he not her brother? But the very essence of their own souls seemed to meet and join at the touch.

"It'll be Hurly-Burly now, Hugh. Will you tell the girls what to do, and I'll tell the boys."

"As you say, Sister. Will we keep it inside?"

"It's such a night, I guess we'd better. Make it funny now."

Hugh clapped his hands.

"The next game's to be Hurly-Burly!"

Shouts of acclaim greeted the announcement.

"I'll give the girls their orders, an' Sister here will tell off you boys. Quiet now, all. We're startin'." Around the seated group on the floor went Violet, stooping to whisper through her cupped hands in each lad's ear. Pete McHarge was to pull Peggy Shaw's hair; Dave was to bring Jenny Hanna a gourd full of water; Hen Wilson was to kneel before Betsy and loose her moccasins. On she went, growing more inventive as she progressed until she had completed her task. Hugh was only a few moments behind her. When he had finished there was a moment of suppressed giggles and half-hysterical silence, while all waited for the word which would bring pandemonium. Suddenly it came.

"Hurly-Burly!" shouted Hugh.

As he spoke, all dashed to obey their orders at once. Then the noise, the shouting, the confusion, the hilarity!

"By God," Sam said happily to Mrs. Shaw in the corner, "I'll bet there won't be a damned panther left in the woods by tomorrer. This here noise ought to skeer them to hell an' gone."

It was a long time before the din ceased and the young people flung themselves down again to rest exhausted. The lads then straightened their shirts and settled their belts while the girls aided one another in tidying ruffled hair braids and refolding twisted kerchiefs.

Violet had gone to help her mother and Mrs. Brison get the supper lifted, and Sam was deep in a hunting story with old Peter Hill who was always to be found where free victuals were, so it was Hugh whose keen senses heard and felt the presence of a stranger without. The sound was of a slow, inquiring foot along the frozen cart track and up to the cabin. He stepped out swiftly and shut the door behind him. A man stood there whom Hugh had never seen before.

"Well, stranger," Hugh said.

"This here the Murray cabin?"

"This here's it."

"I'm lookin' for a young fellah by name of Hugh Murray."

"I'm him."

A burst of shouting and laughter came through the chinked logs.

"What's goin' on? A weddin'?"

"No. Just a kissin' party. Want to come in?"

"No, thank ye. I'm too hell tired even to *kiss* a girl to-night. I just come from Pittsburgh, an' I got a message for you from Simon Girty. Know him, don't you?"

"Seen him a coupla times."

"Well, he says this new campaign again the Injuns is startin' off on the 15th, an' if you're itchin' to go you're to be at the Fort by then. You have to have a horse an' food enough to run you for a while. General Hand's givin' out the ammunition. Thinkin' of goin'?"

"I might. An' I'm obliged to you for the message. Sure you won't come in an' have a drink?"

"No, thank ye. I'll be gettin' back to the tavern. Well, luck to you an' plenty of scalps!"

"Thank ye kindly, an' a good journey."

Hugh reentered the cabin, his heart beating fast. He had wanted sorely to go east and fight the British, but with Sam flat on his back that had been out of the question. Besides, they hadn't been eager for young lads in the Eighth; it was the men in their twenties and over who had marched away. Now, with the new weight of love upon him, he was eager to prove his manhood. He suddenly saw ahead of him, dim but beckoning, a time when by the might of his own exploits he could stand up firm and strong, able to throw off the yoke that bound him; able to speak his own name and, as *Hugh McConnell* instead of Hugh Murray, admit openly his love for Violet. The very daring of the thought sent through him a warmth that reddened his cheeks and made the blood tingle to his finger tips.

He gave a spring, a yell, and landed in the middle of the group.

"One more game before supper," he shouted. "Up with the fiddle there! Everybody on their feet. Come on, Sister, you start it off! 'Lily in the Garden'!"

Martha and Violet both looked up with surprise.

"He's fair beside himself with excitement," Martha said. "Well, it'll do him good. Get away then, Violet, and go on with the game. We can hold back here a little." She lowered her voice. "Pick James, why don't you, just to put him at ease."

It was sweet excitement, the girl thought, as she ran to take her place in the center of the new ring. To see Hugh like this, his head thrown back, his dark eyes burning-like, his firm white teeth in full view because of his laughter. He was the handsomest one of all and the strongest.

"All right, Brother, I'll be *it!*"

Sam was already sawing out the old tune, his ear pressed close to the fiddle, his bow swinging joyously. Violet stood in the center shaking back her curls, her cheeks bright with blushes, her hands nervously working with her dress.

In a sudden burst the voices came:

> "There's a lily in the garden
> For you, young man;
> There's a lily in the garden,
> Go pluck it if you can."

In a moment she must choose. Her own eyes were full of light though she did not know it; and her heart conceived a thought which went through all her body, like a shuddering rapture.

It was time—now. . . . "Pick James," her mother had whispered. Anyone—it didn't matter who. . . . Hugh would understand why she didn't call him into the ring just as she had understood . . . Anyone—James as soon as any. . . .

With her face all lovely and the candlelight soft on her hair, Violet smiled at James and touched his arm as he passed by in the circle. She had not noticed before that James' pale face, too, was flushed; that he had been singing and shouting and executing fancy steps along with the others. But there had been sly remarks going round the circle. James, the old bachelor! James, who wouldn't never look at a girl even! Well, watch him now, would you! Not as slow as we thought him, old James!

Dave Shaw had just poked Hugh in the ribs, and given him a comment behind Jenny Hanna's back, so from looking only at Violet he now saw James; the whole circle, keyed to quick sensitivity, saw; and Martha from the table saw as through a mist.

For James was suddenly no longer the coward, the hermit, the weakling, the Scribe. His arms seemed strong enough, in all conscience, as they crushed Violet to him, and swung her in breathless whirls before the kiss. The burning in Hugh's body grew hotter, and a fear like lightning struck him. Then he flung up his head and laughed it off. Not James. He'd never be fool enough to think fear of *James*.

> "There's a lily in the garden . . .
> Go pluck it—if you can."

It turned out to be the gayest game of all. High rose the fiddle, bright roared the flames, fast flew the merry feet.

Then came supper, with healthy appetites to add grace to the plain food. The wild turkey was tasty and tender, and the corn pone, baked on its clean ash board in front of the fire, had the peculiar lightened flavor of the borrowed saleratus. With maple sugar to sprinkle upon it and a noggin of the mulled drink to top it off, the young folks ate and drank lustily, praising the victuals until Martha's face was bright with pleasure.

It was not until the meal was nearly finished that Jenny Hanna gave a cry.

"A *mirror!* Violet, you never told us. Wherever did you get it?"

There was a quick chorus of excited questions from the girls. It had been Martha's idea at the last to place a pine sprig half covering the looking glass, so fearful was she that her neighbors might accuse her of pride.

"If they see it in spite of me, then well and good," she had said.

And now it was seen. The girls gathered about the mantel, while the boys chaffed loudly. With hands gripping the mysterious rarity they passed it carefully round the circle. There was a constant confusion of sound, but Martha, looking on, paid no heed to that. It was the faces she watched, the innocent, eager faces that must now watch flesh and spirit meeting distinctly, perhaps in the case of some for the first time. The fair-favored ones dimpled and smiled and spoke foolish disclaimers. But Sarah Waters, the homeliest girl, and poor Enoch Henderson who had had the pox, looked, and then with eyes stricken, passed the mirror hastily on. And a moment before,

Martha thought with pain, they had been happy and lighthearted as the rest! Oh, there was grief in a mirror! She was not sure she was glad to have it. Maybe the panther skin would have been better. Ah, well!

"I know a game," Dave Shaw was shouting. "It takes a lookin' glass to play it with, so that's why we've never done it. I seen them at it once over at Nine Mile Run."

"What is it?" Hugh asked.

"It's like this. The room's got to be as dark as you can make it. Then the boys form a circle an' the girls all keep back except the one in the middle. She holds a lit candle an' the mirror, but she's blindfolded. The circle keeps movin' till she says 'Stop.' Then someone unblinds her an' when he's in his place again she holds out the mirror an' the face she sees back of her in the glass will be her fate."

Martha intervened, "But be careful of the mirror, mind."

"We'll be careful. Come on, now, let's get started. There's magic in it, the Dutch say. Sometimes you see a face that ain't in the room at all. Put out the candles, Hugh—all but one."

"What of the firelight? Here, Father, you an' them that ain't playin' stand in front of it, like." Hugh was excited now too. "Get to the one side, girls, all of ye. Now, boys, fetch up the circle. Who's to be first?"

"Not me," Betsy Kinkaid said shortly. "I think it's a fool's game."

There was a peal of girlish laughter from the others. "She's afraid she won't see Dave in the glass, that's why."

Betsy's face did not flush. Instead it looked white. "I'm not playin'." And she sat down on the bed.

"Come on, Jenny, start 'er off," someone called.

Jenny Hanna threw her head in the air. "I'm not afraid. Fetch me the mirror and the candle. Here, you can use my kerchief for the blindfold."

"Jenny's the one! Jenny's no coward!"

Dave fastened the kerchief and led her to the center of the ring. The room now was in darkness except for the one burning candle in the girl's hand and the faint russet shadows on the wall. The sudden quiet was eerie, for the moccasined feet of the boys made no sound as they moved slowly around. There was only the chill sigh of the wind as it swept across the cabin roof.

"When you feel there's something in the mirror, then you call 'Stop,' " Dave whispered.

"*Stop!*" Jenny said quickly.

Dave untied the kerchief. "Don't look till I'm back in my place! . . . *Now.*"

Jenny opened her eyes.

"It's a Britisher!" she cried, startled.

James Brison laughed. "Oh, you've just caught sight of Ben's red shirt here behind you!"

Jenny slowly lowered the mirror. "Maybe so. It was a bit blurred-like." But she did not joke as she had done at the beginning, and she whispered to the other girls as she took her place among them.

Dave was elated.

"I telt you there was magic about it! Come on now. Nancy Wilson next."

Nancy came forward slowly, her lips smiling. Everyone knew her lover was Matthew Jack off now with the Eighth.

"I hope it tells true," she said, and allowed herself to be blindfolded.

But when she looked at last, she gave a small sniff of disgust.

"Why, all I see's James Brison behind me as plain as day!"

"Well, he looks a thought like Matthew at that," someone suggested.

The weird spell seemed for the moment broken, and there were outbursts of laughter as the game went on. One lad after another was reflected in the mirror, and by a little adroit shifting of the circle or a bit of leaning this way or that it was as often as not the right one.

When Violet in her turn stood for a long moment silent and then said very low, "I just see Brother," there was amusement and demurring.

"Oh, try again. Brothers don't count. Come on, Violet."

But Violet would not do it again, and Hugh hurriedly called up the next girl.

At last all had taken their turn but Betsy, who still sat, silent, on the bed. Several of the boys made a sudden rush toward her and dragged her, protesting, into the ring. Dave blindfolded her as he had done the others while teasing comments filled the air. His hands were a bit unsteady as he touched her smooth braids.

Perhaps it was the look of fright on Betsy's face, but the strange quiet fell again upon the room as the circle moved about. Once again could be heard the moan of the wind and a faint wild cry from the forest. The candle shook in the girl's hand and sent a trembling reflection in the mirror.

The noiseless feet passed and repassed again and again before Betsy said, "Stop." Then when her eyes were freed she looked, and a scream cut the air. There was a quick intake of startled breaths, while for a moment she stood rigid, her dark gaze fixed; then with a sob to tear the heart, she threw the mirror from her to the floor.

"It's not *so!*" she cried. "It's a lie, I tell you. It's not him. How could it be? It's a bitter, bitter *lie!*"

She was shaking now, the tears wet on her face.

Martha took charge swiftly.

"Light all the candles quick, Hugh. Stir up a good blaze, Sam, in the fire. Come, come, Betsy child. It was a silly game. What fright could you take at shadows? Sit here, now, a minute and dry up your tears. What about a nice tune, Sam, to liven us all up?"

She went about quickly, bringing back the ordinary atmosphere.

Hugh had rescued the mirror, his own face startled and grave.

"It ain't broke, Mother," he said softly as he handed it to her.

"It's a good thing," she replied, also in a low voice.

The cabin was alight now, and the young folks, with the quick resilience of youth, were laughing at what had chilled their hearts a moment before. Even Betsy succeeded in smiling wanly and agreeing that she had given them all a foolish scare. But no amount of coaxing would

make her open her lips as to whom she saw in the mirror
To everyone's surprise it was James who now took charge

"What about some songs?" he called above the hub-
bub. "What about 'Yankee-Doodle'? Come on, let's try it
Everybody's singing it back east."

Sam fumbled a bit while James hummed the air. Ther
he caught the tune. He smiled over it, his foot smartly
keeping time.

"Ready now, everybody! The words are easy!" Jame
urged them.

> "Father an' I went down to camp
>   Along with Captain Good'in
>   An' there we saw the men and boys
>   As thick as hasty puddin'.

Come on now."

They started a bit hesitantly, but soon they were all i
the thrall of the rollicking rhythm. Most of them ha
heard it sung or whistled by passing travelers, and Jame
proved a good leader. His face was all aglow as he let hi
full voice out now, waving his arms to the beat.

> "Yankee Doodle-dandy,
>   Mind the music and the step
>   And with the girls be handy!"

They sang it over and over again. They kept on sing
ing it until the girls declared finally they must go, an
there was the confusion of putting on shawls and sayin

heir thanks and good-byes. And then they sang it along
he narrow snowy street, delighting in their own uproar
n the still hours of the night.

James was the last to leave. He bent above Martha's
and like a fine gentleman.

"I feel as though I've been dead for years and just come
live tonight," he said, his eyes shining.

Then he took Violet's hand and kept it in his own
while he called a laughing thanks to Sam and Hugh. He
vent out quickly then just like the other young blades,
nd they could hear his voice shouting "Yankee Doodle"
vith the rest.

"Damn my gizzard if James don't act half human to-
ight," Sam observed.

"Oh, Mother, it was *wonderful!*" Violet said. "Wasn't
just wonderful past believin', Hugh?"

"It was that," Hugh returned. "It was the best I ever
as to, even countin' corn huskin's."

They put the few pieces of furniture back in place, and
elped Martha carry the soiled trenchers to the fireplace
 be burnt as needed.

"It's late now, and we can finish in the morning. I
oubt you'd better give us a short chapter the night,
am."

Sam had set his fiddle carefully on the mantel, finished
e mulled whiskey at a long draught, and taken down
e Bible. He swore quietly at his rheumatic fingers as
ey fumbled the pages. Finally he found his place and,
 his usual low unintelligible mutter, proceeded with

the devotions. He was in the habit of pausing occasionally
for a comment between chapter and prayer. Martha always considered this unbecoming but knew nothing could
check Sam when he wanted to speak.

Tonight as he closed the Bible he looked up.

"What in hell was wrong with Betsy tonight? Screamin'
out like a wildcat?"

"A bit of girlish vapors, I doubt," Martha said shortly.
"Pay no heed to it."

At last in the cabin all was quiet; Hugh in his loft, Violet asleep in her bed, Sam beginning to breathe heavily.
Martha lay awake, strangely shaken with happiness. Sam
had held her close to him as he had not done for many a
long, long night. The tenderness of passion was so soon
lost in the hard wilderness, leaving behind only physical
necessity.

Now Martha lay trembling a little but warm and most
curiously glad. The party had been all she had dreamed
it could be and more. The look of James as he left! The
light in his eyes as he held Violet's hand. There was no
doubt he'd come alive this night. In a half-trance of relief
she lay planning the consummation of her hopes.

There were others awake also in Hannastown at this
hour when the wind dropped and the stars were high and
clear above Gallows Hill. Betsy Kinkaid lay in bed between her two sisters, face down, so that her weeping
might not wake them; James Brison was staring wide
eyed into the blackness of the roof above him with a tune
running through his head. His lips moved, smiling, as
they formed the words:

And take a sweet kiss, it will do you no harm,
But a great deal of good, I know.

In the cockloft at the Murrays', Hugh tossed on his rough tick planning how to break the news of the campaign in the morning and how to arrange the details of his leaving.

But Martha, of course, knew naught of all this as she turned at last toward Sam's hard back, and fell asleep.

Least of all did she know that Violet's last waking thought had been of the kiss in the forest!

Feb. 3, 1778. Well, it's over and pretty nice over at that.
Never did I think we could make this cabin look as wel
Of course the firelight and candles soften things down consid
erable, and the pine hid many an unsightly spot. It touche
me some way to hear them all exclaim. They've never see
a proper house, some of them. The pone was the best I eve
put in my mouth if I do say it. Hugh got a nice bag of sa
and a little *saleratus* at his last trade. And what a difference
pinch of that does make in the pone! I used fresh buttermil
He got a few spices too, though I questioned whether w
ought. The mulled drink was as tasty as you please. I mu
say I wasn't ashamed of the vittles even though they wer
plain. There was a plenty too, which gave me a good fac
Sam was like a boy himself over everything, especially th
fiddle. I doubt he'll be better tempered now he has it. Neve
have I seen the young ones as frolicsome. Hugh said it wa
better than any husking he ever was at, and Hugh never sa
much. There was just one thing to mar. They started a fo
game looking in the mirror to see their fates. Betsy Kir
kaid got a scare some way and cut up a regular dido. W
clean in hysterics. She looks pale to me. I hope she'll n
go consumptive like their Belle. Oh but I dread that diseas
I believe I'll drop a hint to Mary Kinkaid to watch out a litt
for Betsy. Mary wouldn't see anybody was ailing till th

138

were dead and laid out under her eyes. She's so husky herself.
But we got everything righted after Betsy's spell last night.
They had plenty kissing and a right good time! The fiddle
sounded fine. You could tell what every tune was before they
started to sing even. Sam says cat gut would be better than
the rabbit, but he did wonders with that. I don't know how
to write about the way Violet was last night. Sometimes I'm
fearful I set too much store by her looks. But dear God how
can I help it? She's my child spared to me out of all our
desolation. And she's so lovely made and all! I'd be acting a
lie to my own heart if I didn't ever think to myself how
comely she is. I never say word of it to the neighbors, never
even to Sam. But here dear God what sin can it be? Thou
dost see all with the eyes of Truth. Last night her cheeks
were like a flame and her eyes like stars. Her curls were like
shiny silk. Her smile just lighted up the place. Oh I pray her
teeth may stay long with her. They're so white and even. I
fear sometimes for them being too white. Mine were that
way and they didn't last. My mother always said yellow teeth
stayed longer with you. Look at Sam. His are like saffron
and he's got nigh all of them even the stumps don't ache him
like mine do. Well maybe Violet's have some of his substance
as well as mine. She seemed nigh bewitched last night, she was
so gay-like. Every move of her light and easy like a lady ought to
be. James Brison came and *was a surprise to all!* He took part
in the games and could kiss with the best of them. He and
Violet were partners more than once. He seemed changed-
like and youngish. He set them all going on the new army
song at the end and led them off as well as if he was precent-
ing the psalm. Even Sam and Hugh said James acted lively.
It wasn't just me thinking it. There are some things I can't
write here for fear this might some day fall into stranger
hands. I'll set down though that I've seldom felt as cheered
so over *some things* as I do right now. Hugh is set to go on

an Injun campaign. That keeps me stirred up of course when I let myself dwell on it. That Girty man sent him word and he's height to go. Sam eggs him on, for he thinks one of them ought to be fighting. And Hugh's a man now. I've got to face that. I'll taste my bit of happiness now though while I can. If you never stop the littles, the muckles are like to pass you by! I feel lifted tonight some way. In spite of all I do feel lifted.

V

The Squaw Campaign

The news that Hugh was going on the campaign spread quickly through the town. General Hand's latest call for men had been mentioned around the tavern by Lieutenant Lochry, but small note had been taken of it. Lochry himself was decidedly half-hearted in the matter, for last October's episode was still fresh in his mind. Hand had called then for five hundred men from Westmoreland and Bedford counties to be joined by fifteen hundred Virginians. They were to descend the Ohio River to the mouth of the Big Kanawha and then to march overland against the Shawnee towns on the Scioto.

Lochry had expostulated with Hand upon his unreasonable demands. The whole border, he told him, was drained and distressed. Practically all the strong, adventurous young men had gone east to fight the British. Those who remained were either lads or men needed to defend their families. But the general was obdurate.

The upshot of it was that Bedford County had sent no men at all; with the greatest difficulty Lochry had raised a hundred; the Virginians, in their turn, failed to appear except for a few poorly equipped squads, and Hand, after a brief excursion down the Ohio, had given the project up in disgust. So had the men. Hannastown therefore was dubious about this new venture.

But no one tried to dissuade Hugh. In these years of tension and danger no man dared ever say to another "Stay thy hand." In addition to this there was a feeling that Hugh, by his message from Girty, had been especially called. This was the view the young people took. Dave Shaw in particular. He and Hugh stood out by the stable talking it over the night before Hugh left.

"God, I'd like to be goin'," Dave said wistfully. "But can't raise the horse. You're lucky to get Ranger."

"That's all I'm worried about. I hope nothing happens to him. Before spring plowin'. Father says to go on though. He feels one of us ought to be fightin'."

"You know what they're sayin' now round the tavern?" Dave went on. "They say Hand's offered to sell all the plunder an' divide the cash among the force. Mebbe you'll come back rich, Hugh."

Hugh laughed a disclaimer, but his shoulders squared a trifle.

"Oh, that's just talk to get the men. If I can kill a few Injuns I'll be satisfied."

"Havin' the word direct an' all, you'd ought to go. Where will you be meetin' Girty?"

"Semple's tavern tomorrow night."

"Good deal of stir round Pittsburgh one way 'nother," Dave said, still wistfully.

"Will be a change, sort of," Hugh admitted, not wanting to seem too eager.

The boys stood silent in the darkness. Hugh felt that Dave had more on his mind.

"Great party tother night," he said at last.

"It was, that."

Pause.

"Don't know what struck Betsy."

"Oh, girls are queer. They get notions."

"Fancies, kind of."

"Vapors. Don't mean anything."

"I wisht afterwards I'd never started the game."

"It was all right. She soon got over it."

"Just a notion, I s'pose."

"That's all. Just a fancy-like."

They walked back to the house.

Hugh left before break of day the next morning. The air seemed like a continuous draught of cold water to him after the smoke and hot fried grease smells of the cabin. He rode along, in the pale dusk, letting Ranger pick up the track. The adventure upon which he was setting out had taken on for him the dimensions of a colossal gamble with the greatest of stakes at the end. If in this campaign he proved himself indeed a man, if he came back home with distinguished success behind him and, as Dave had intimated, a supply of cash in his pocket, he would stand forth then in a new personality, assert his own name and ask for Violet in marriage. The daring of the thought made his head swim. He pondered on the kiss in the fort, realizing that all the while he had been saying, "Just the same, Sister," he was feeling the new fire that all but

overcame him. Did she, too, feel it, even without knowledge?

The sun rose above the eastern ridges and a brightness
fell upon the snow. The day, at least, he reassured himself, would be fine, which made the going easier; and with
steady travel he should reach Pittsburgh by night. The
temperature had risen slightly, also, and there was now
no wind; so, aside from the fresh chill of the air against
his cheeks, he rode on warmly and in comfort. The thrill
and novelty of his errand quickened his pulse; and the
fact that he was not far from Bushy Run sent his thoughts
flying in new altitudes of ambition. For this spot was
sacred ground. Though the great battle had taken place
fifteen years before, Hugh knew every detail of the story.
It was more vivid to him now, as he felt himself for the
first time a fighter, than it had ever been before.

He was riding through the snow, but Colonel Bouquet
and his heroic little army of Highlanders had toiled over
the mountains in the new world's summer heat—unknown
and intolerable to the Britishers—to raise the siege of For
Pitt. They had met the Indians at Bushy Run and by in
credible sagacity and courage had defeated them in ac
tual battle. Hugh thought of those hot August days when
the Indians held the springs and the torment of thirst ha
been harder for the soldiers to bear than bullets; but th
courage of the famous Black Watch had not failed.

It had been a signal victory, for Guyasoota himself ha
been the red men's leader, while Pontiac, the maste
mind, waited watchful in Detroit to learn the outcome

Now, Hugh thought as he rode along, the times wer

darker than they had ever been. For the Americans were ranged not alongside the British as then, but against them; while their old and constant enemy, the Indians, still harassed them with deadly success.

If the tale Girty had brought back from the Senecas was true and Guyasoota had gone over to the English side, then, look out!

Hugh had seen Guyasoota once some six years ago, the first time he had also seen Girty. Sam Murray had had an errand over to Nine Mile Run and had taken Hugh with him. They stopped, as most people did who passed that way, at Colonel Proctor's. There, in the corner by the great fireplace, sat a very tall, dignified, and handsome Indian dressed in scarlet cloth turned up with lace and a high gold-laced hat. His martial manner had been unbroken by speech though he acknowledged the introductions with solemn bows. The man with him was Simon Girty, his interpreter, who had explained to them that the Seneca chief was on his way to Philadelphia and from there to Sir William Johnson's to see about some treaty or other. Hugh recalled only his surprise at the chief's appearance. It was the first time he had ever thought of an Indian as a person one might meet with on terms of equality.

Sam Murray, sensing the boy's reaction, had set about dispelling the illusion as soon as they left and were on their way home.

"Son," he had said, "if you dressed up the devil in gold lace his horns would still show, mind ye."

Later on he remarked, "Never forget, Hugh, there's

jist one time an Injun looks handsome. That's when he's
damned good an' dead."

Hugh's mouth twitched to a smile now as he recalled
this conversation. His father need not have worried. His
own longing for revenge was deep enough. But the fact
remained that Guyasoota was probably their most powerful enemy and to that extent must be thought of with
respect.

With young dreams of prowess in battle, delight of
love, and far vistas of newer and still richer country beyond the Ohio filling his mind, Hugh rode steadily, with
only a brief rest once while he fed Ranger from the bag
of grain behind him, and ate himself some of the pone
and jerk which Martha had packed as his campaign provision. His woodsman's eyes were sharply alert as he stood
quietly for these moments beside the horse. Now in winter the famed Forbes Road was only a narrow, blurred
track, and the wild forest pressed closely upon it. Once
there was the skeleton of a buffalo veiled by snow, a victim no doubt of wolves, those dark, hidden creatures of
the night. A moose had lumbered past within the last few
days, Hugh decided from the half-filled tracks near by, on
his way to the clump of evergreens on the southern hill
where he would feast on the moss and the bark.

Closer beside him now was an odd trail which the
young man recognized instantly: the two small foot marks
almost side by side and close together with a long stretch
between the tracks. Hugh's eyes narrowed, measuring the
distance.

Must be fifty inches between jumps! he conjectured.
He was set for hell an' gone, that fellah!

Then to his own surprise he heard himself speaking
loud.

"I don't like a weasel, the dirty bloodsucker."

Ranger had finished his meal now, so Hugh mounted
astily and went on, his eyes ever keen, his heart beating
igh.

He reached the outskirts of Pittsburgh in the early
usk. As on the other occasions when he had been here he
ad a quick feeling of disappointment that the town was
ot larger; only some forty-odd houses—not many more
an made up Hannastown. But as he rode along the
tty street, also as at other times, this first disappoint-
ent vanished. There were lights here, many of them
ining through real glass windows, and there was excite-
ent beginning even at this moment as a half-dozen
unken Indians came out of a tavern and went lurching
d yelling along the path. Traders, probably, in to
change their furs for rum and blankets. Hugh sat
raighter, more watchful than ever but liking the noise
d hoping for more, while the rough fort town began
ain to work its spell upon him.

The whole setting of the place was unusual and pic-
resque. It lay in a stormy triangle formed by the inter-
ction of two great rivers. From the south rolled the
w, yellow waters of the Monongahela; from the north,
e wider, swifter flood of the Allegheny. At the point
here the two streams united to form the Ohio (the Beau-
ul River, as the Indians called it) there rose now on the
ins of the old French Fort Duquesne, the battlements
d pentagonal bastions of the fortress named for the
ime Minister across the sea. This was young Pitts-

burgh's crown and reason for being; and, paradoxically enough, it was because of the heavy bristling cannon and the stone magazines overlooking the rolling rivers, that certain gentler aspects of life were present in the rude frontier town.

For there *were* a few satin petticoats lifted above the mud or snow of the streets, just as there were occasional bright waistcoats and well queued wigs in the taverns or stores. Here and there in the larger cabins might be found a woman with eyes still wet from a reading of "Clarissa Harlowe," or a man who argued with his companion over a bowl of rum as to the merits of Johnson or Hume, or— more pertinent still—the authorship of the Junius letters.

In Samuel Semple's big two-story tavern there was actually a billiard table and the latest Philadelphia paper (none too late, of course) to be read by the fire.

In the summer still more noticeable elements of gentle living were present; for then the King's Artillery Gardens on the bank of the Allegheny burst into bloom and leaf and, in the shade, along the pleasant paths strolled the officers of the garrison and such gentry as the town afforded. There was handball, too, played in the dry moat around the fort, and occasional ferry excursions, carrying a party of ladies and gentlemen across the Monongahela to view at close range "Coal Hill," the tall green mountain which the depths of coal had become ignited and now poured forth volcanic smoke and flames.

For the most part, however, winter or summer, this Pittsburgh, this edge of the western frontier, this outpost of the Back Country, was a dirty, dangerous, exciting ixture of muddy bordering waters and muddier streets; f ill clad soldiers, rough traders, Indians and tavern eepers; of boats setting out by way of the Allegheny .iver, French Creek, and Lake Erie to Detroit; of boats oming in from LeBœuf or the Illinois; of express riders inging wearily off their horses with dispatches from the ist; of fighting packers and wagoners; of travelers fraught ith evil report and good; and—most important of all— : a few steady, stalwart pioneer citizens who put their oots down firmly as they built their log cabins and, in so oing, simply and unconsciously planted a city.

Hugh now rode on toward the Fort in the gathering arkness, then turned sharply left along the Monongahela ank. For it was here in this row of houses that Semple's avern stood. It would have been easy to locate even if : had not seen it before, for there were more lights vis- ole here than in the other cabins, and a busy confusion · men going in and out its heavy door. Hugh tied Ran- ·r to one of the rough posts and started up the steps. On e platform he stopped short. A man with a stocky figure id a florid face passed him unsteadily and all but fell. It as the Irishman!

Hugh's foot itched to send him sprawling with one easy ck, but he refrained. The man was beyond recognizing m, and even with a skunk like that there were certain cencies to remember. His own face was glowering, how- er, as he opened the door and entered the tavern.

A warm wave of burning wood and cooking food eeted him, mingled with the pungent reek of soaking ilt liquor from the heavy oak tables and the kegs along

the wall. There was the smoke from real tobacco, too, n[...]
the dried sassafras leaves with which Sam all too often ha[...]
to fill his pipe. The smells to Hugh's nose were all sedu[...]
tive and good. He drew a full breath and advanced t[...]
ward the fire where several men were standing. One [...]
them turned quickly. It was Girty.

Hugh was struck anew with the man's powerful shou[...]
ders, large head, and piercing black eyes. "A bad enemy[...]
he thought to himself. "I hope I'll keep him a friend."

Girty half smiled at the lad but made no other motio[...]
of greeting.

"You got here, I see," he said finally. "What abo[...]
some victuals?"

"I'm thinkin' they would go fine," Hugh answere[...]
"I've got no cash, but I've some pelts I reckon will see [...]
through till we get started. I've got provisions for t[...]
campaign all right," he added.

Girty made an abrupt gesture.

"I've a few shillings burning my pouch. We'll eat he[...]
Keep your pelts till you need them."

He made a sign to one of the serving men and led t[...]
way to a table. Hugh's cheeks flushed with exciteme[...]
To eat at Semple's Tavern like a regular traveler w[...]
overwhelming to a degree. It seemed the perfect and a[...]
picious beginning for his great adventure.

Girty ordered supper and two half-pints of whiskey[...]

"Know anybody else in here?" he asked Hugh su[...]
denly.

"Nobody."

"Well, you might as well see all the sights you c[...]

That's Semple, himself, over by the fire. The one with the gray hair and the fat belly. Likes to hear himself talk, but honest as daylight. That's Mistress Semple coming this way now. She's got a tongue, yon one. And if you don't believe she's loyal to the King, just ask her! *You'll* see!"

Girty chuckled as Hugh's eyes grew wider, watching the ample figure of Mrs. Semple as it moved with a swish of flowered petticoat between the tables.

Girty leaned nearer. "I'll tell you a story about *that* lady," he said, speaking from the corner of his mouth. Two year ago last August, time they had the Liberty Pole set up here an' a lot of fussin' over the *tea* business, the wind got out that Simon & Campbell were still sellin' tea. So Colonel Arch Lochry an' about twenty Westmorelanders rode into town one night to teach them a little patriotism."

"I mind about that," Hugh said. "I heard tell of it then."

"Well, they cleaned the store out of tea an' carried it up next day to the Liberty Pole an' burnt it. It made a stink all right—two ten-gallon kegs, an' boxes and bags. But the best fun come when they got done an' dropped in here to wet their whistles."

Mistress Semple had approached them with her brass-bound tankard, so Girty waited till she passed on.

"Nobody knows how she fixed it up, but old Semple an' the help was nowhere to be seen. Just the lady herself, sittin' in her chair in the corner there on a big fat bag of tea just the mate of the ones they'd burnt up! They was struck dumb, for they was sure there wasn't a leaf of it left in Pittsburgh. How she got it away from the store God knows. But there she sat with it!

" 'I'm sorry I can't rise to serve you, gentlemen. I'm somewhat indisposed the day, an' my disease ain't *treason* neither,' she says as cool as a snake.

"Well, none of them dast lay hand on her—you can see for yourself what a look she can give you—so they drew themselves some rum, threw their money on the tables an' left, sheepish-like, an' she kept her tea. *There's* a woman for you!"

Hugh joined in Girty's heavy laugh; then he saw his companion's black eyes grow suddenly blacker under the heavy brows. Two more men had just entered the tavern and made their way toward the roaring fire near by. One was a tall blond man whom Hugh recognized. It was Colonel William Crawford who had been one of the justices in the Hannastown court until he had taken Virginia's side in the boundary dispute. The other man looked vaguely familiar, but Hugh could not place him.

"Who's the man just come in with Colonel Crawford?" he asked.

Instead of replying directly, Girty turned to look at Hugh.

"You know Crawford?" he asked.

"He used to be Judge out there a few years back."

Girty's voice was bitter.

"He's been damned near everything an' never got his skin scratched yet, that fellah. Luck, that's what he's got!"

"An' the other man?" Hugh persisted. "I've seen him somewheres."

Girty's voice was not much less bitter. "*Him*. Don't you now him? That's Morgan. Indian Agent here."

As though he had heard his name, the man in question urned and looked full at them. He was shorter than rawford, with a round, genial face under his wig. He odded curtly to Girty and spoke his name, at which rawford also turned toward their table. There was in is bearing, as Hugh had remembered, a certain dashing irit and courage.

"Well, Girty," he said with attempted joviality, "I hear om General Hand you are to be one of our company on e new campaign. He has close to five hundred men now, e says. With that force we ought to do something this me with the Injuns, don't you think?"

Girty's great head seemed to sink deeper into his thick eck. Hugh had the sensation of tremendous power and atred combined, emanating from the man.

"We might," he said slowly. "Leastways we all got *orses* if nobody takes 'em from us, eh, Colonel?" he lded, looking insolently up at Morgan.

Colonel Morgan seemed annoyed.

"Still harping on that horse business, are you, Girty?" e said shortly. "I thought that was closed and finished."

Girty's black eyes were very bright.

"There's a number of things, gentlemen, that ain't osed and finished yet. An' as to my horse that was took om me by you, an' the rest of the money owed me by the nited States of America—well, I've still got a copy of the ll. But I'm not goin' to wait much longer on gettin' id."

Morgan laughed, and with it his face resumed its naturally kindly expression.

"Good idea, Girty. Never expect pay from the government. The wheels turn too slow. Besides, you know well enough that horse wasn't legally yours. Well, Crawford shall we see what Mistress Semple has to offer in the way of refreshment?"

"It was as legal as most things are in the Back Coun try," Girty said, raising his voice. "An' don't forget there's some governments that *do* pay their bills."

The others went on without answering, to sit at a table near by where they were at once joined by companions Hugh caught the introductions.

"Seems like everybody's either a major or a colone round here," he observed innocently.

Suddenly he felt Girty's heavy body tremble with anger

"All but me," he gritted through his teeth. "I'm still second lieutenant. That's all. That's good enough fo Girty! Let him risk his skin. Send him to the Mingoes send him to the Senecas. Send him to the Shawnees. Send Girty. But never raise his title *or* his pay."

He leaned close, his dark face heated by the drink.

"All last year I worked recruiting men for the army. raised a company. *I* did. Me, myself. Thought at the leas they'd make me captain of it. Well, that damned Craw ford over there fixed that. Got John Stephenson, h brother-in-law, put in command. Of *my* company, min you. They've sent them down to Charleston now, ar they can rot in hell for all I care. An' so can those tw *colonels*."

He pulled a skin pouch out of his shirt, and from it
drew a dirty paper.

"Read that," he said. "That's what they owe me in
money. Morgan hired me as interpreter two year ago
come May. I did more work for him than any other interpreter he had. Then in three months he discharged me.
'For *ill behavior*,' says he. The damned old pretty-face!
If I got drunk it was none of his business. Look at what
they owe me, an' never a penny of it come!"

Hugh spread out the greasy paper, on which a thin let-
tering still showed clearly:

THE UNITED STATES OF AMERICA
To Simon Girty, Dr.

	£	s.	d.
To a horse taken by George Morgan and given out in service of the public	20		
To cash expended on journey to Indian Country	3		
To hire of horse	0	15	0
To finding horse when lost	0	15	0
To rum to chiefs of Indians at their request	0	15	0
To horse shoeing	0	3	9
For meat	0	3	9
To an Indian who accompanied me to buy leggings with	0	7	6

My constant wages in the service and extra pay
when in Indian country Mr. Morgan knows. It
is therefore not inserted here.

Errors excepted.

His
SIMON X GIRTY
mark

Hugh read it slowly and then handed it back, his main surprise being the fact that Girty could not write.

"It's fair enough, ain't it?" Girty urged. "An' it was none of Morgan's damn business how I come by that horse. It was mine then as much as anybody's, an' I ought to have been paid for it."

"Now, what's the rumpus?" said a voice behind them. "Divil a time I come on you, Girty, that you ain't raisin' hell over something. Move over an' give a man a bit o' sittin' space, will you?"

To Hugh's surprise, Girty grinned at the newcomer and made room for him.

He was a young man, short, snub-nosed, and apparently Irish.

"Hello, Matt," said Girty. "I didn't know you was in town tonight. This here's Hugh Murray from Hannastown. Goin' on the campaign with us. Matt Elliott," he added, nodding from the one to the other.

The new young man eyed Hugh earnestly.

"Pretty red-hot Americans out round Hannastown ain't you?" he asked.

"Yes, sir, we are," Hugh said strongly. "We've no use for Tories, that's a fact."

Young Elliott looked off over the room.

"Such fine Americans we got. Such good Yankee Doodlers. An' yet, if you scratch one of 'em, he'll bleed British blood same as the Tories. That's what makes it a little confusin'. Course, now if you scratch an Injun . . ."

He glanced at Girty meaningly and began to speak in a low tone in a dialect which Girty answered. Hugh guessed it was Shawnee but was not sure. They seemed to have forgotten him, so for the moment he turned his attention back to the room at large. It was filled now, and there was loud talking and heated laughter from every corner.

Although Hugh was by birth and nature a child of the forest, he had quick perception for the swift-running emotions and powerful crosscurrents of human life. He knew now that in this room were meeting in the persons of men some of the great issues of the new world. There was in the heavy, liquor-scented air, the pulse beat of nations at arms. It was not only the uniforms that showed it. It was the sudden wheel, the wary glance, the sharpness of the eye, the hot blood rising in the cheeks.

He looked again at Morgan, the Indian Agent. Hugh had heard much of him. For years he had been an important trader in the far Illinois country representing the Philadelphia firm of Baynton, Wharton & Morgan. His reputation for honest dealing with the Indians had won him his present appointment. Now his mission was the tremendous task of keeping the red tribes at peace during the present war; for if the British should attack in full strength from the west, and the Indians join with them, it would be bad indeed. Perhaps fatal.

There had been a good deal of talk about Morgan in the tavern back at Hannastown. Sam Murray for one, and Archibald Lochry for another, had declared he was too easy on the Indians—too friendly with them, too anxious to make peace at any price; that perhaps, indeed, he even had Tory leanings. When a man was so close to an

Injun that the chief named his son for him, it wasn'
wholesome, Sam Murray said. That was the way it wa
with Morgan and White Eyes of the Delawares. Th
young buck was called George Morgan White Eyes and
it was said that Morgan was going to take him back eas
to educate him at Princeton College when he was ol
enough. Sam had snorted over this report and said tha
would be trying to make a silk purse out of a sow's ea
and no mistake. Hugh, watching the ruddy kindliness of
the Indian Agent's face now, felt that he could be trusted
Whether he would succeed in his great task was anothe
matter.

Colonel Crawford also was close to the stream of n
tional events. A Virginian by birth and a valued frier
of General Washington's, he could be heard now givir
his predictions on the war in general and the comir
campaign in particular.

"Five hundred horsemen—two hundred of which I'
proud to say I've brought myself from the Youghioghe
—gentlemen, I tell you this time we'll accomplish all Ge
eral Hand has laid out for us to do and more. W
knows? We may even go as far as Detroit and have a s
sion with Hair-Buyer Hamilton, himself!"

A groan and a hissing spread over the room as Color
Crawford's remark was repeated from table to table.

"Go after Hamilton!" someone yelled.

"A red-hot bullet for the Hair-Buyer!"

Suddenly the door opened and a traveler entered,
spent from his journey, so dirty and tattered and forde

that the men, eating and drinking and shouting, stopped and looked at him.

He slouched in and all but fell into a chair as Mr. Semple went quickly forward and put a noggin of whiskey to his lips. It was no new thing for express riders and army messengers to fling themselves from their horses and enter the tavern exhausted, for they traveled fast and far. This man bore the stamp of strength and great endurance. He finished his whiskey at one draught and then in a low voice began to talk to Mr. Semple.

In a few minutes the host raised his hand for silence.

"Gentlemen," he said, in his full, pompous voice, "this messenger brings news. Disturbing news. Portentous news for all of us who are at work to build up the frontier of his great new country. Anxious news for all of us who admire the courage, the prowess, the sagacity of those leaders who—"

"Well, damn it! What's happened?" yelled a voice from the back.

"Get to the point. To hell with the oratory!" came from Girty.

Mr. Semple's full cheeks seemed to collapse somewhat. He moistened his lips as though for a peroration, then thought better of it.

"Daniel Boone has been captured by the Indians," he stated briefly.

At once the tavern was in an uproar. Those who did not know Boone personally, knew of him. His name was the frontier symbol for that intrepid and miracle-working power of the white man to overcome the wilderness.

Girty had sprung to his feet. "How'd it happen?" he called out. "I don't believe there's a redskin livin' could catch Boone. He's as quick as they are."

There was a sudden movement toward the traveler, who now, since his whiskey, sat up and looked about him with interest. Hugh pressed forward with the others and stood close to him, as he answered the questions rained upon him. With an odd twang he told his story.

"I just come from Kaintucky, part by boat an' part by trail. First of Janawary, Dan Boone an' twenty-nine others went to the Blue Licks to make salt for the different garrisons. He sent three of them back with a load at the end of the month, an' that's the last was seen of him. An Injun we know, though, told us a band of about eighty Miamis got Boone an' the rest of them an' took them to Chillicothe an' on to Detroit mebbe—if they let 'em live that long."

There was a sound in the room like angry bees swarming. There were curses and sporadic shouts. Suddenly Colonel Crawford leaped to a chair and lifted his arm.

"Gentlemen! *Gentlemen!* This new piece of bad news is only another evidence of what our frontier is facing. Peaceful settlers are massacred in their own fields! Women see their infants slaughtered on their very hearthstones. Youths are carried off into captivity. When these snows melt, not a log cabin this side the Blue Ridge, not a fort even, is going to be safe from attack. And if enough tribes join up with the British—"

A ferocious growl now spread among the men. Hugh, with no conscious volition, found his own voice joining it,

"Are we *Americans?*" Crawford went on. "Are we citizens of a great new country fighting for our lands, our homes, our liberty? Are we going to see this thing *through?*"

"Aye, aye," roared the crowd.

"Let us not fear then. Let us go forth to crush the Redskins and the *Redcoats* together!"

Cheers and laughter.

"Only tomorrow, as most of you know, we start five hundred strong for the mouth of the Cuyahoga River, where a magazine of arms and provisions have been stored by the British for the use of their Indian allies next spring. We intend to destroy it. Let's have a toast, gentlemen, to send us off!"

Someone quickly handed him a noggin. He raised it high.

"To General Hand and the success of the expedition!"

There was the sound of stirring feet, of clinking tankards, and the dull scud of wood against wood as noggins left the table.

When the toast was drunk another voice rose above the crowd.

"To Colonel Crawford, soldier and gentleman!"

Hugh, raising the liquor to his lips, saw that Girty made no move to drink.

"What's maggotin' you?" Elliott was saying in a low voice. "Me now, I'd drink to the divil himself if the rum was good enough."

"I'm a little perticular who I drink to," Girty drawled with dark brows.

Suddenly he threw up his great head and shook the black hair out of his eyes.

"To the safety of a brave man—Dan Boone," he called out.

There were wild cheers then, and after the toast a general movement of departure, for the hour was late. Hugh was anxious about Ranger and his own plans for the night. As though reading his thoughts, Girty voiced them.

"Now about your horse. There's room in my stable, an I can bunk you at my cabin for the night." He turned toward Elliott. "I took a fancy to this lad out at Hannastown when I saw him down that bull-necked Irisher that's been hangin' round here of late. An' he can hit a panther in the eye, this fellah. How's that for a shot?"

Elliott surveyed Hugh's tall, muscular frame. "That's pretty damned good. Too good for just stayin' round Hannastown, I be thinkin'."

"What I was thinkin' myself," said Girty.

Hugh felt oddly mature and warm with power as they all left the tavern. He liked Girty in spite of his father's qualms. He liked the snub-nosed Elliott. And for his own prowess they evidently liked him.

He bestrode Ranger and followed the two as they plouted through the snowy streets. Before a small cabin near the fort, Girty stopped. The rough shed behind had not been built with the care of the Murrays'; but there was an extra stall, and Ranger was soon bedded for the night next to Girty's black mare.

Once in the cabin, which was bare and dirty enough, Hugh had a shock. A squaw was bending over the fir

Girty spoke to her sharply, and she scampered up the ladder to the loft.

"There's a bunk for you, lad," Girty said, indicating one of those against the wall. "Fall in, for we may be off for a good long ride tomorrow."

Without a second invitation Hugh flung himself on the rough bed and pulled the dirty blankets over him. He knew as his body relaxed how completely tired he was. In an instant he was asleep.

He woke suddenly, but from long training made no slightest movement, only felt the complete recurrence of consciousness. Elliott evidently was just leaving. What time it was, Hugh had no idea.

"I tell you, I'm not decided yet. I'm goin' to wait till after this campaign," Girty was saying in a low voice.

"That's your word then, for McKee?"

"That's my word. When my mind's made up, I'll let him know."

"All right, but I thought you had enough stickin' in your craw now to settle you."

Girty's voice was firm.

"That's my own business. When my craw gets full, I'll tell you."

"Hand's got wind of something. He's ordered McKee to go to York an' report himself to Congress, but McKee's playin' possum. Pertendin' to be sick an' keepin' to bed, so he don't have to go. But the fat's goin' to fall in the fire some day."

"All right. I'll tell you my mind when it falls."

"You're the divil of a chap, Girty! Well, good luck on your little ridin' party."

"Get out of here," Girty answered pleasantly, "before I kick your backside!"

The door closed then, and Girty put new logs on the fire, blew out the candle, and hurriedly climbed the ladder to the loft. Hugh was too weary to ponder, and so again he slept.

The clink of iron vessels awoke him. The squaw was bending over the fire, while palest daybreak could be seen through the small glass window. Girty was cleaning his rifle and looked up quickly as Hugh sat up and swung his legs to the floor.

"Well, lad, are you ready for the day?" he asked.

"Fine," said Hugh. "I'll be givin' my rifle an extra look over, too."

The squaw never raised her head, and Girty paid no more attention to her than if she had not been there.

They got their guns in prime order, ate the food set before them on the plank table, then fed the horses, checked over their provisions and finally, as the dawn became day, rode off to the fort. Hugh's excitement quickened as he looked upon it in the light. While the terrible flood of 1763 had undermined three sides of it and sent some of the ramparts tumbling into the moat, it had been largely rebuilt and was now an impressive fortification.

"Thought we'd come up early an' sign you up," Girty said. "You'll mebbe meet the General himself. Ever see him?"

"Never."

"He's only been here now since last June, an' it's my opinion he ought to have stuck to makin' pills instead of fightin' Injuns. He was a doctor in the fust place, you know. Was out here oncet before as surgeon to the Royal Irish when they was garrisoned here. Then when this war started he got into some of the big battles back east an' Washington made him brigadier general. Young feller, too, for that. Younger'n I am."

Hugh detected a bitterness behind the words and recalled the conversation of the night before. Now in full day the brooding look in Girty's black eyes was more apparent.

They had reached the outer work of the fort now—a long embankment reaching from the Monongahela to the Ohio across the triangle of the confluence. They passed through a narrow aperture in this embankment and crossed a drawbridge that, to Hugh's astonishment, led to a regular island in a moat! A second drawbridge led from this curious island, through a gateway in a high brick and earth wall, into the inner fort.

Here Hugh could see about him an irregular pentagon with five elevated bastions. The two landward sides were of brick and earth reenforced by stone, and the other three were of earth topped by stockades. Built into the walls or set against the stockades were shelters for the garrison's guns, while near them were the barracks and storehouses with their roofs rising over the top of the fort.

The whole place now was a scene of activity. Soldiers

in uniforms and frontiersmen in their own dress were moving about. Many of them knew Girty and spoke to him—quite respectfully, Hugh thought.

"I'll name you off the bastions here if you'd like to know," Girty said, seeing the lad's look of absorbed interest. "That one to the southwest is the Monongahela; the southeast one's the Flag—for because that's where they hoist it; the big one north of that is the Grenadier; the next one's *Music!* God knows who ever give it a name like that. Course the bugler stands there, an' they *do* have band concerts once in a while, but still it seems a damned womanish name for a bastion. Last one's the Ohio."

"Thanks," Hugh said. "I'd like to mind them."

They were now before a brick house with the Commandant's insignia above the door. Girty knocked and a soldier answered.

"New recruit for the campaign come to sign up," Girty said.

The soldier nodded and pointed to the room on the right of the narrow hall. In a moment Hugh stood before the General. He was indeed young-looking, except for the baldness that spread well back over his head. His nose was long, his mouth kindly, his chin firm.

"Another recruit, General," Girty said. "A lad that can hit a panther in the eye."

"So?" said the General. "That's a good recommendation, Lieutenant. What's the name?"

"Hugh Murray."

"Provisioned?"

"Yes, sir."

"Very good. Sign here. Just for the duration of the campaign."

Hugh wrote his name at the end of a long list, his firm letters showing the result of Martha's careful teaching.

"Be in front of the fort ready to start at ten o'clock," the General ordered.

"Settin' off today then, sir?" Girty asked.

"Today. The sooner we get on with this business, the better."

"Right, sir," Girty replied, "if you're sure of the weather."

He saluted; Hugh tried to, awkwardly enough, then ashamed of the gesture. Among the fighting men he found around Hannastown there was little saluting. When a man put his hand to his head it was usually to scratch it. The wide ground in front of the fort was fast filling as they reached it. Colonel Crawford could be seen on a handsome bay, getting his two hundred Youghiogheny riders in form. Girty became busy at once and, as Hugh noticed, all soldier. He rode swiftly about, giving the hour for starting and checking up with the men on their provisions. Once he dismounted suddenly, and picked up the forefoot of a horse near him.

"Shoe's loose," he told the rider. "He'll cast it in a day's travel. Better get off to the blacksmith in a hurry and get it fixed up."

As it neared ten o'clock, the men had been divided into companies of fifty, each under a leader; the flag had been hoisted on its bastion; cheers and shouting came from a large group of citizens gathered to watch the start; and

General Hand, proud and determined, flashed out at the head when a signal shot was fired. They were off!

Hugh had a feeling close to ecstasy as he rode along. He was accustomed to solitudes. This close union with five hundred other men, all pressing on with singleness of purpose and the same intent of heart, this fusion of courage and strength and the determination for victory, was new to him; but he felt it as though it were a tangible cloud enfolding him. The sound of the two thousand shod hoofs upon the snow was like martial music to his ears. He had been waiting, then, for this great moment for the triumph of his new manhood.

The plan was to follow an old Indian trail which ascended the Ohio to the Beaver River and then up that stream and the Mahoning toward the Cuyahoga. In a necessarily long procession they moved forward up the snow-covered trail. Girty, who Hugh soon discovered had the eyes and nose of an Indian, was asked by the General to stay at the front as guide, and so Hugh found himself in a position of relative importance at Girty's side.

Girty kept watching the sky and sighting off between the trees if any snow fell from the limbs.

"I don't like the look of the weather," he said at last. "Smells to me like rain. But you can't tell the General anything."

Hugh also had been aware of a heaviness in the atmosphere which increased as the day wore on. By evening, though, there was still no actual fall. They made camp in an open spot in the forest not far from the mouth

Suddenly his fingers encountered a soft, fuzzy object that felt like a kitten. This would be one of a pair of new cubs probably, born in their January month and sleeping now, he devoutly hoped, beside a drowsy mother. Hugh drew his arm out as quickly as possible, replaced the wet leaves and brush at the entrance, and loped off along the track he had come. It was darkening now, but he kept to the landmarks he had noted and finally heard the sounds of camp ahead of him. The others were all back, a few of them with the scanty birch bark; but only Girty, except himself, had secured the coveted leaves. Hugh's heart swelled immeasurably at Girty's look of approval. Between them they had enough dry material to start a blaze in a sheltered spot, and with the wet birch bark and pine added, soon had the first great fire roaring up through the cold of the night. Others soon followed. The men warmed their stiff hands and feet, but to dry clothing was impossible. They lay wretchedly that night in what shelter the forest afforded.

The next day it was still raining. Before the mount, small groups of the men stood together talking in low, querulous voices. A grumbling dissent now seeped through the force even as the wet seeped into their bones. But the General ordered an advance. It was slow, intolerably heavy going that day and the next, with the rains continuing intermittently. As they neared the Mahoning the level valleys were covered with water, and each small fording, which in dry weather would have been easy enough, now became a hazardous undertaking. The Mahoning itself was a dangerous torrent.

By the fourth day the grumbling had become not only audible but violent. General Hand ordered a halt before noon and rode about among the men.

"It's not lookin' too good, General," Girty said shortly. "It'll be the devil to pay if we try to cross the Mahoning. It's my opinion we'd never make it, not with these waters."

The General's face was white and grim. "We started this campaign and, if courage and resolution will finish it, we're going to carry it through."

"You're the master, sir," Girty replied, "but five hundred's a lot of men to send to hell at once. . . . Not countin' him an' the *Colonel*, yonder," he added after Hand had passed on.

Apparently Colonel Crawford and most of his men were of the same opinion as Girty, for when the General rode back he was grimmer than ever. Hugh thought he looked actually sick, and his own heart shared the desperate, sinking disappointment.

"Girty," he said shortly, "do a little reconnoitering, will you? See what the prospects are on that bit of higher ground to the east. It may pay us better to drop the old trail now."

"Good, sir," Girty answered, as he dismounted and started off on foot.

In a surprisingly short time he was back, his eyes bright, his whole body alert.

"I found tracks," he said. "Indians. Goin' north'ard. There must be a settlement of them hereabouts."

The change in the General was electrical. He set off down the line, repeating the news to his leaders and giving orders. At once every man was on his horse and eager for the command. The doubtful future had become the exciting present.

Hugh felt his own sprits rise suddenly to their former pitch. Above all discomfort of body rose the lust for the chase and the lure of physical triumph.

They all headed for the high ground, where they halted until Girty pointed out the footprints and they struck the new trail. There was no sound then except the soft swash of the horses' hoofs, each man riding warily, grasping his rifle.

At the end of an hour, Girty held his rifle high above his head, and General Hand gave the signal to halt. Before them could be seen a small village of huts in a grove. A tremendous excitement passed from man to man as low-voiced orders were given as to the method of attack.

They were to go forward at full gallop, spreading out as they reached the village in order to surround as much of it as possible. Every man sat tensely waiting for the charge. The command came; they sprang forward, all five hundred in formidable array. They galloped through the grove and were almost on the huts themselves before there was a sound. Then piercing the air came the high shrill despair of women's screams. Hugh could see moving forms starting to flee back toward the forest. He fired at one of them and it fell. There were more quick shots, but only one other took effect.

Girty's voice sounded suddenly above the firing.

"Can't you see they're only squaws? An' kids. There's no one else here."

All at once, more quickly than one could have thought possible, there was a complete and awful silence. Before them lay the patch of empty huts, with an old man and a squaw dead where they had fallen. Another squaw coming last from her home was caught by the two men nearest her and now stood with her face on her breast.

"Don't kill her!" General Hand said sharply.

"Why not?" the men clamored angrily.

"She may have information for us. Talk to her, Girty, will you? See what you can find out."

Hugh felt dazed by the sudden turn of events. His blood had been hot for battle, for the curdling cry of warriors, for the clash and noise of a struggle, and for feats of incredible strength and daring.

Instead now was this cold silence, with the two still figures lying in the mud. Girty was talking with the captured squaw. Hugh could not understand the words but was surprised at the low, civil tones of the interpreter's voice.

At last he turned toward the General.

"She says—what you can see for yourself—there's no warriors here. They're all off on a hunt. The rest of the women an' kids got away. They're all Delawares. Wolf clan. She says ten Wolf Injuns are making salt at a lick ten miles up the Mahoning. That's all I can get out of her."

The General's face showed a bitterness as keen as Hugh's own.

"Take a hundred men, Girty, and follow to the Salt

Lick. Don't let an Indian escape. We'll make camp here for the night."

Girty picked his men quickly—passing over Colonel Crawford's group entirely—and started off again along the Mahoning. Hugh rode beside him, hope slowly rising once more in his breast. After all, ten warriors slain and captured would not be a bad day's work. He knew the accuracy of his own marksmanship, and warm and strong beneath his rain-soaked garments he felt the seasoned muscles of his body. Girty rode in silence, leaning forward a little in the saddle, his black brows drawn, his eyes quick and furtive.

The ten miles were long and heavy. The rain had stopped, but wind now lashed the trees and made the roar of the Mahoning louder. A cold sun shone through the dripping branches and still shone when the men suddenly came on the lick, so that the scene stood out as though painted with white on a dark canvas.

There stretched in a round shallow depression the gray-white shaly deposits of salt worn smooth by the rough licking tongues of deer and moose and bear. At one corner plying their spatulate pieces of wood, squatted four squaws and a young boy. They were taken entirely by surprise, for the horses' feet had made no sound against the rattling wind; even so, Girty's oaths sounded above their screams.

"Squaws again, by God! Don't shoot them. There's only squaws here! Hold your fire, men!"

But the men were far past restraint, even if the General himself had been there. They had come a long, hard way; they would not be cheated of their red quarry. The shots rang out. Two squaws fell forward, their heads in the shallow crater, one leaped high, screaming, before she dropped; the boy fell backward from Hugh's bullet, still clutching his bowl of salt; the fourth squaw ran toward Girty, falling on her knees before his horse. He spoke swiftly to her in Delaware, while once again a silence fell. There was only the crying wind and the still figures staining the gray-white of the salt lick. It was not natural.

"I'll take this one prisoner," Girty said. "Well, let's get back as fast as we can."

He slipped a rope around her waist and hitched the end to his saddle. She made no sound, only trudged beside the horse, her head bowed.

Hugh could hear the other men, now talking as they rode along. There was some laughing and chaffing, but for the most part a heaviness held them.

When they reached the village of huts, Girty turned the squaw over to the General.

"Another prisoner of war," he said ironically, and then told him briefly what had happened.

It was a bad night. There was some food, but little enough. The huts were dirty, the blankets full of lice, while outside the rain began again in earnest. The men were utterly discouraged, and Girty at least, openly scornful.

He spoke to Hugh as they lay side by side on the floor of one of the huts. There was in his voice again that intense bitterness which Hugh had noted before.

"I'll fight Injuns as hard as any man if there's a leader

that knows what he's doin'. But to come out under a leechin', pill-makin' jackass to shoot a few squaws! Yes, sir, that's what it's turned out to be, a *squaw campaign*, by God. An' it's settled my mind for good now, damned if it hasn't."

He spoke as though entirely out of Hugh's ken. "My craw's full at last. My mind's made up."

Hugh, with the peculiar misery of his own that seemed to drown his very heart, remembered the low voices of Girty and Elliott that last night in Pittsburgh and wondered.

The next morning, General Hand, his long nose longer and thinner than ever, his cheeks pale and his mouth set, announced that it was useless to go further, on account of the weather. They would have to return to Fort Pitt as speedily as possible.

On the way back, along with the cold and the wet, two phrases, drifting ominously up and down the lines of riding men, seemed to weigh down the spirits of all. One was Girty's ill coined sarcasm; the other was, "This'll be the finish of Hand!"

They reached Fort Pitt on a late gray afternoon, their trophies the two Indian squaws. Their formidable force of five hundred horsemen had slain one old man, four women, and a boy!

The men dismounted stiffly and sought the taverns; the General went slowly into his office and bolted the door behind him. He knew and all the men knew that by that mysterious osmosis of intelligence which obtains in any settlement of human beings, it would be less than an hour before the damning words, "Squaw Campaign," would have penetrated to every part of the town. Nay, more. They would be carried up and down the border by every messenger and traveler until the frontiersman, sitting by his fire cleaning his own rifle, would laugh with derision at this latest major effort against the Indians.

Hugh found himself sticking to Girty, who for some reason did not go to Semple's but contented himself with a smaller tavern near his own cabin.

"Thinkin' of startin' on home tonight?" he asked.

"I thought I would."

"Better stay the night with me an' get the chill out of your bones. You can leave early tomorrow."

Hugh considered. He felt half dead with weariness. "I'll do that, thanks," he said.

The squaw was stirring something over the fire when they entered the cabin as though she had not moved since they left her. Girty spoke sharply to her, and, with a half-glance toward Hugh, she busied herself over her stew and then quickly set it on the table before them. It was hot and, after the days of jerk, actually savory.

Girty turned his wooden bowl slowly round and round when he had finished.

"There's some," he ventured carefully, "that thinks the Americans haven't got a chance to win this war."

"They're liars," Hugh said quickly.

"Mebbe so, but take a look at what's goin' on. The Wyandots an' the Mingoes an' the Senecas an' some of the Delawares has all gone over to the British. And you mark me if the Shawnees now aren't goin' to be the fiercest of the lot. Cornstalk was the one that held them off before. He sided with the Americans. What did he get for it? Seven bullets through his body when he'd come, peaceable, to warn them. An' Ellinipisco, his son, with him! I knowed them both. Now, you can't blame the Shawnees for goin' British. They'll raise hell to pay for Cornstalk's death, all right."

Hugh's strong chin merely hardened.

"We'll raise hell on them, then. We've got to wipe 'em out, that's all."

Girty considered. "They say Washington's about finished there in this Valley Forge. Troops freezin' an' starvin'. Some say he'll have to surrender before summer."

"That's another lie," Hugh said hotly. "*The Eighth* is here, an' they don't write back nothing about surrendering."

Girty shrugged.

"Mebbe. I ain't sayin'. This is just the talk I hear. Wondered how you felt about it."

"Well, I guess Americans ain't likely ever to give up. That's the only way I figure it."

Girty's black eyes rested on the young man across from him.

"Kinda wish you an' me could stick together, son," he drawled. "But we mebbe got to go our own ways. Still got your panther claw?"

Hugh opened his shirt.

"Hang on to it. Injun luck won't do you no harm. Well, I'm goin' to get some sleep."

It was still not dark when they threw themselves into

their bunks along the wall. The squaw had disappeared, though Hugh had not seen her go. As he settled himself Girty spoke again in a low growl.

"This whole damned business we've just been through makes me sick to my gizzard."

"Me too," said Hugh sadly. And then he was asleep.

The trip home next day was physically easy. There was no rain; instead, a light, delicate flutter of fresh snow flakes. But Hugh's heart was oppressed with a heavy weight. He was returning defeated. There had been no victory and no spoils. His great game of chance had been played, and the stakes lost. He was Hugh Murray still, a man yet not a man; too young in all eyes for a soldier, but old enough for the pains and sorrows of love. Through no fault or lack in his own nature he would now be associated not with battle and its hard glory but with a laughingstock tale, a story of derision.

"Come on, Hugh, my lad, tell us about your 'Squaw Campaign.'" He could hear the voices even now at the tavern or about the fireside, and he winced.

One other fact puzzled him sorely. He had killed his first Indians, and the remembrance brought him no joy. The exultation he had dreamed of would not rise within him. If there had been heat of battle, it would have been different, he argued. But the memory of that strange quiet after the screams and the firing, and the prone, unmoving figures would not translate itself into the thrill of revenge. He felt confused and in a curious way stricken, as though he had lost his way. In spite of himself he kept thinking of the scene at the salt lick. The boy was no much younger than he. . . . There again it was the after quiet that had shaken him, and taken away all the conquering glow which should have been a part of it.

A mile from Hannastown, Ranger went suddenly lame. Hugh jumped off and felt the forelegs anxiously. A swelling had set in, in the right upper joint. This, he felt miserably, was the last insufferable stroke.

He walked the remainder of the way, encouraging the horse as best he could.

At the top of the last hill the lights shone out through the lacy veil of snow. There lay the town just as he had left it; but he, returning, was not the same. Did anyone ever go forth and come again without change? What far boundaries the spirit could cross in a short week of days! The hopes with which he had set out had been like the fire of life in him. But how could he say now, *I am not her brother!* All the strong words he had dreamed of speaking in his hour of victory were now as empty echoes on the wind.

He moved slowly up the narrow track toward the Murray cabin with Ranger limping painfully beside him.

February 23. Hugh back last night in safety thanks be to God. The campaign was nothing much when all was done, just put some squaws to rout. The high waters held them back. Hugh seems troubled over it that they didn't do more. I suppose it's natural for men to want to kill their enemies. Just the once I knew how it felt may Heaven forgive me for it. When I saw my boys lying in their own blood I could have killed too. But the feeling tore at me like a burning sore. I could scarce thole it. When it passed I felt eased even in my anguish. But it's different with men. They can hold the feeling longer. Maybe they have to. Maybe women aren' strong enough to bear it or maybe, because they have pain enough without that, they *won't* bear it. I don't know. Men have plenty to bear too. They do the things that have to be done and keep their thoughts to themselves. I often consider that looking across at Sam of an evening. Blessed be the Lord which teacheth my hands to war and my fingers to fight. That's what they have to say whether they like it or not. Yet they have a hard time too men have. And they keep it so to themselves. I'm like to forget that maybe when I get fashed with Sam over little things. Besides the few squaws there was a young boy killed Hugh says. It just come over me maybe his mother is in her anguish now the same as I was once. I've always hated the Injuns so I could think of naught but th

184

savage in them. Maybe it's just the same with them in some things as it is with us. Oh but life's the hard riddle. You could go mad thinking on it if there wasn't a greater Power to stay yourself by. Ranger hurt his leg some way on the trip. If it lames him I don't know what we'll do. It's the joint. Watch got his paw in a bear trap too. It didn't take it clean off just tore it. I've been poulticing it steady. The poor beast is patient as a child and so knowing. My heart goes out to him. The Wilsons had a letter from their Joe from camp. He says General Washington's a fine man. The soldiers don't fault him but they're having a bad time of it. Joe's feet both froze so deep he thought to lose them but they're better. Several men he says have lost limbs from freezing. Poor souls. Says they would all rather be fighting than waiting but no help for it. At that though he says there's been few deserters and *none* from the Eighth. Passed Liz Smith on the way to the spring today. She was pleasant as a basket of chips. Held me no ill will it seems for the talking to I gave her. I'm sorry for the poor creature indentured as she is but I couldn't have her making eyes at Hugh. He may never have paid heed or hap to it but I wanted to make sure with her so much older and all. A young boy can be taken in. Hugh doesn't seem to make up to any of the girls. But he has time yet. Finished another stint of spinning today and will turn the second heel on Sam's socks tonight. Weather still cold with light skift of snow last night.

VI

The Blind Preacher

It was Sam who brought some comfort to Hugh's troubled heart in the next few days. He had told his story with bare and undramatic truthfulness to the family group the night he reached home. Martha and Violet were so relieved to see him safely back that they seemed not too greatly disturbed by the fact that the campaign had ended in humiliation. Sam made no comment until he and Hugh went out to look at Ranger's leg. Then, carefully, he began going over the facts.

"It was the high waters, then, stopped you."

"Yes."

"How many Injuns killed altogether?"

"Six."

"Did you—was you lucky with a shot?"

"I fetched down two."

Sam stopped rubbing Ranger's joint and straightened.

"Two outa six! By God, Hugh, that wasn't bad. Which uns was yours?"

"Woman an'—the boy."

Sam spoke no more until they were leaving the stable The world was whitening again, and all the wide uni verse was silent about them. Sam stopped, and stood holding the lantern, which threw a thin, living light ahead of them.

"They killed my sons," he said in a strange voice, "an' they killed your mother. You done a good job, Hugh."

From then on Hugh felt a change in Sam's attitude toward him. There had always been fondness and a good-humored understanding; now, there was respect.

And slowly, night by night as he lay in the cockloft, he felt his one burden easing a little, even as the other one grew. Because of Sam's reporting of his part in the campaign, there was no finger of derision pointed at him though the townsmen discussed the whole affair with bitter laughter. It was known now that General Hand had sent in his resignation at once to General Washington. It would have to be passed upon by Congress, but everyone around Hannastown thought it would be accepted. A good man, Hand, in a regular war, belike; but no knack at fighting Indians. There would soon be another in the long line of commandants at Fort Pitt.

"Oh, well," as Martha said, sighing heavily, "among them be it!"

For Hugh's other burden there was no rest. All the more because Violet since his return acted like her former self. The cloak of restraint had fallen away, and she seemed at her sisterly ease with him. She was spending much time now with Betsy Kinkaid who, Martha kept saying anxiously, had "a peaked look." The girls went together to the spring for water or walked in the near-by woods, their heads close, their arms sometimes around each other. When Dave or Hugh tried to approach they turned away, Violet with some joking comment, Betsy with her face in her shawl. Hugh knew that Dave was anxious, but he had no comfort for him. It was all he could do to master his own heart.

It was toward the end of March that the dire news came which shook the frontier from Pittsburgh to Boonesborough and brought Hugh to a strange prominence in Hannastown. Sam, because of his new man-to-man treatment of the lad, was wont now to take him along to the tavern, so that they were both there one raw night when the word came. An express threw himself from his horse and entered the big room with ice clinging to his hair and beard. He brushed his face hurriedly and moved toward the fire.

"Well, men," he said excitedly, as the group stopped talking, "there's the devil to pay now, an' no mistake."

The frontiersmen, accustomed to every form of disaster, real or presaged, hardened their faces and waited.

"A bunch of Pittsburgh Tories has gone over to the British!"

"Who are they?" someone shouted.

"Aye, well may you ask," the express continued, glorying a bit in the suspense. "Captain Alex McKee for the head of it. He's been mixed up with the British, you know, for two year or more. Last night General Hand heard somehow he was goin' to light out, so he sent troops down to his farm to head him off. They was too late. McKee an' his cousin an' a couple of nigger servants was gone. An' with them Matt Elliott, the trader—an' *Simon Girty*."

There was a silence like death in the room. Every man's face had paled. In all the Revolutionary struggle, this was the heaviest, the most calamitous blow that had yet fallen upon the border. Captain McKee was a man of wide influence all along the frontier. He had been an Indian trader himself, and for a dozen years before the Revolution had been the King's deputy agent for Indian affairs at Fort Pitt. He had even served here at Hannastown itself for a time as a justice of the peace. He was intimately acquainted with most of the Indian chiefs, and it was even widely whispered that he had an Indian family in the Shawnee nation. Now he had gone over to the British!

But even the thought of McKee as an enemy did not strike as much terror to the hearts of the men sitting in the tavern as that Simon Girty was now against them.

Girty, with all his intimate knowledge of the frontier, Girty who had scouted from one end of it to the other, who knew every stream, every hill, every trail, every settlement, every isolated dwelling, and every pathetically weak fort or stockade in Westmoreland County—Simon Girty who as interpreter had been intrusted with all the secrets of the whites, had turned traitor to the American cause and would now be in league with the redskins!

It was Hugh who, to everyone's surprise, broke the heavy silence. Forgetting his usual reticence, he sprang from his chair.

"I know something about this," he exclaimed. "I heard them talkin', Girty an' Elliott, but I didn't take it in at the time."

The men leaned forward, shouting to him, pressing him to tell all he knew.

"Elliott came into Semple's the night I was there an' started talkin' to Girty—I think it was in Shawnee."

"Aye, it would be that," the express volunteered, "for Elliott was sent on messages to the Shawnees often."

"Then that first night I stayed in Girty's cabin, Elliott was there, too, till late. I woke up once an' heard them Elliott says, 'So that's your word for McKee, that you ain't decided yet?' 'Not till after this campaign,' Girty says. 'When my craw's full, I'll let him know.'"

Hugh's face flushed with the telling of it. Bit by bit certain words and incidents were piecing themselves together. He presented them to the fear-harried group who craved eagerly new details and more and more tal' to stave off the moment when each alone must reckon with this new threat.

"He was grulchy-like when he spoke of the government. He said they owed him money, an' he showed m' the copy of a bill. He couldn't abide Colonel Morgan, for he says he took a horse from him once an' never paid him an' then discharged him. He was interpretin' for Morgan."

Lieutenant Arch Lochry, who was in the room, had risen and come nearer.

"Go on, lad," he said. "These things you're telling ar' all straws in the wind. What else did you find out?"

"He hates Colonel Crawford like pizen. He hates him worse than Morgan a long sight. He says he raised a company himself last summer, an' then, instead of gettin' to be captain, Crawford put in his brother-in-law. He hates him for other things too, I think—I couldn't rightly say what."

Back to Hugh's memory came the sight of Girty's dark face by the campfire when he had inquired insultingly for Crawford's family.

The candles were low in their sockets before the tavern emptied that night. With grim faces the men discussed the bitter facts before them. The British were still in possession of Philadelphia, the American Congress had been driven to York. Washington's army was reduced to a starving, naked remnant at Valley Forge. Here on the frontier, with food and ammunition both scarce enough, with General Hand a failure waiting to withdraw from Fort Pitt, with the lands beyond full of hostile Indians ready to descend upon the whites at the first breaking up of the snows, and with Detroit still in the hands of the infamous Hamilton, the men of Hannastown set their teeth and accepted this last desperate blow: the defection of the Pittsburgh Tories.

At the end, Lieutenant Lochry stood up, a tall, resolute figure, and lifted his noggin of ale. Every man rose and waited.

"We'll still drink—to *Liberty!*" Lochry said simply.

They emptied their cups and went out quietly into the night, on to their cabins where the women would be waiting.

Lochry walked along with Sam and Hugh before returning to the fort, where he and some of his rangers were making repairs. He was still questioning Hugh as to what he had seen and heard.

"Was there anything more, Hugh? Think, lad. I'd like to see the bottom of this."

Hugh hesitated. He had feared to praise himself by recounting in the tavern the strange conversation of that last evening with Girty. But now, slowly, he repeated it as well as he could.

"We'd got back, you see, from the—campaign. He told me to bide the night with him. He said, sort of slow-like, that he'd be pleased if we could travel together, an' then he set out to tell how hard put to it the Americans was and how like they'd be to lose the war."

"The damned bugger," Sam put in viciously.

"And what was your reply?" Lochry questioned.

"I never thought what he was aimin' at, or I guess I'd have given him a clout. So I just said as far as I could see Americans wasn't ever likely to give up."

"Good for you, lad," Lochry said. "You couldn't have said better or truer."

"The dirty varmint," Sam kept repeating under his breath. "To think of him tryin' to seduce you. I'd put a bullet in him myself if I could. Aye, you always need a long spoon when you sup with the devil, like I told you. Well, what do you be makin' of it all, Lochry?"

Even in the darkness they knew that the Lieutenant's Irish face was twitching in a smile.

"I think I'll be makin' my will," he said dryly, "and

then I'll be makin' it as hot for the enemy as I've powder to make it."

"An' good luck to ye," said Sam. "We're with you to the last ditch, Hugh an' me, for what we're worth—eh, lad?"

"We are that," Hugh replied gravely.

Through the next weeks there was talk of little but the flight of the Tories. The men's faces looked harder, and those of the women more drawn as further news filtered in. A friendly Delaware Indian had come to Pittsburgh and reported that the seven renegades had gone straight to Coshocton, the capital of the Delaware nation, and had tried their best to persuade that tribe to start war against the colonists. A long debate had followed then with White Eyes, the chief sachem, stating again his friendship for the "buckskins," as he called the Americans, and his determination to remain at peace. Against him in the argument was pitted Captain Pipe, an influential chief, who urged the tribe to follow the advice of the visiting white men and wage war on the frontier. White Eyes, by his character and his oratory, had at last prevailed in the council, and the Tories had left and gone on to the Shawnee towns along the Scioto River.

This latter was dark news indeed, for McKee would be received warmly by the Shawnees; and according to still another report James Girty, one of Simon's brothers, was already there on a peace mission from the American authorities at Fort Pitt. There was little doubt that he would now join himself with the renegades.

Questioned over and over by the townsfolk and even

by passing travelers, Hugh repeated the conversations he had overheard. He remembered now and mentioned Girty's strong feeling over Cornstalk's death. This would be further reason for the inciting of the Shawnees.

There were other men too who recounted what they knew of Girty, good and bad: that he had saved a fellow scout's life in Dunmore's War; that during the Virginia border troubles he had saved the wife of Colonel Aeneas Mackay of Pittsburgh from the blow of one of the rough soldiers who were attacking the homes of the justices there. He never broke a promise, one traveler said, and would always help a friend, but he was the devil incarnate to an enemy.

"Well, there's no one round here as I know that's any friend of his lessen it might be Hugh," Mr. Brison said once.

Hugh flushed, feeling the panther claw under his shirt.

"He knows how I stand, anyway," he said dryly.

By the last of April they all knew that the Tory troubles were not over in Pittsburgh. Captain McKee had done his work insidiously and well before he left, and of course agents of Hair-Buyer Hamilton were at large all along the frontier. The news came that Colonel Crawford, who was in command of a detachment of the Thirteenth Virginia Regiment stationed then at Fort Pitt, had discovered a plot by some of its members to blow up the fort! At the last moment this had been averted; but a score of the traitors, along with a few Pittsburgh citizens, had got away in a garrison boat and fled down the Ohio.

Each day now the Hannastown men, as they could

spare the time, haunted the tavern to learn what word
the latest express had brought; while the women went
from door to door passing on the news as it came.

Martha, with the new fears pressing constantly upon
her, had gone down one morning to speak to Mrs. Brison,
whose plump, comfortable face and unimaginative mind
always seemed to relieve the tension of her own spirit.
James was writing as usual by the table. He smiled with
pleasure to see Martha. His smile had become readier of
late, and his eyes less reserved. Even Sam had commented
upon it.

"James is actin' sort of chirk these days. The kissin'
party must have fettled him, somehow."

Martha kept each phase of his changing manner in her
heart. It could not be hurried, this thing she was planning. James would move slowly and with conscious care
even in love making. But if only one day the great fulfillment came . . .

They were all talking together now of the recent events
when there was a knock at the door and Colonel Proctor
himself entered the cabin. Mrs. Brison hurried to set him
a chair by the fire, and James bestirred himself quickly
to place a new log on the blaze. Martha was of two minds
whether to go or stay, but when she rose the Colonel
urged her to remain.

"Stay out your call, Mistress Murray. I'm just stopped
in to get James here to back a letter for me, an' then I
must be gettin' on home. I've been to Pittsburgh to find
how things stand, an' they're bad enough. I've wrote a
letter, here, James, to President Wharton. If you back it

now, I'll leave it at the tavern for the next express."

"I'll do it with pleasure, sir," James said, a faint twinkle in his eye; for while the Colonel's spelling and penmanship were both highly individual he always wrote his own letters. The address only, he turned over to James, the village scribe.

Colonel Proctor now gave a long sniff, twisting his mouth sidewise in the process, unfolded a small paper and scanned it.

"I've just set down the facts plain. If he's got eyes he can read them, an' if he's got any bowels of mercies he'd better do something about them. Here's what I wrote:

> Westmoreland County
> April ye 26, 1778
>
> To Pres. Wharton
>
> Honoured Sir,
>   I am able to inform you that Capt. Alexander McKee with sevin other vilons is gon to the Indians and since there is a Ser't and twenty od men gon from Pittsburgh of the Soldiers. What may be the fate of this country God only knowes, but at Prisent it wears a most Dismal aspect.
>   I am, Sir,
>   Your most sincare and very humble servant,
>   John Proctor."

"Is there any more news of the traitors?" Martha asked eagerly.

"They've sent after this last batch and may catch 'em. The first ones though are gone far enough by now. Mebbe to Detroit itself! They'll get a good welcome there, devil take them."

"What's to become of us, Colonel?"

Colonel Proctor's heavy brows met above his strong nose. In many respects he was the most important man of the countryside. He had been with General Forbes' army twenty years ago when it made its way over the new Great Road to take possession of Fort Duquesne. In recognition of his military services then, the Penns, by special grant, had set aside three hundred acres of land on the Twelve Mile Run to be known as "Proctor's Plantation." From that time on, the Colonel's place had been the seat, not only of the first religious services, but also of numberless conferences when important travelers stopped at the big log house to consult about county, state, or even national affairs.

"What's to become of us, Colonel?" Martha asked again, quaveringly.

The Colonel rose and stood for a minute without speaking. Not as young as he once was, but still a soldier, a wise man of affairs, a burning Presbyterian and a patriot to the last drop of blood—this was John Proctor.

"We've got to hold fast," he said slowly. "Say your prayers and be ready to melt your spoons into bullets if we need them. And oh, that minds me of an important piece of news. Spread it around as much as you can. There'll be communion at the Meetinghouse on the second Sabbath of May. The Reverend James Waddell will officiate."

"The Blind Preacher!" both women said in a breath.

"Aye. He's visiting at his brother Robert's just next

my place, and he'll give us a service. We set it on a bit so's to allow time for the word to get round."

"We'll spread it, Colonel, no fear," James said quickly. "It will be a grand privilege to sit under the Blind Preacher again."

"If things just stay quiet—" Martha began.

Mrs. Brison interrupted. "Well, if I'm to be killed I'd as lief it was on the way to the Meetin'house as anywheres else. Preparatory service on the Saturday, I suppose, as usual?"

"That's the only disappointment. He's not fit to preach twice together. He's ailin' bad, so we'll have a brief prayer meetin' before the regular service an' try to do with that. Well, I give you good day, ladies, and thank ye, James, for your kind service."

He held the letter up before him and read slowly:

"His Excellency Thomas Wharton,
        President of the Supreme Executive Council of
                Pennsylvania.

"Fine writin', James. Fine writin'. There's none can beat you at that. But what about this fellow, Mrs. Brison? No sign of a wife yet for him?"

"Ach, it's sickening, right enough. I keep at him, but what's the good? An' all these pretty girls round here, too. You'd think *he* was the blind man."

Martha, watching James, saw him flush a little.

"Oh, I might surprise you all yet," he said, smiling.

"See you do it, then," adjured the Colonel good humoredly, as he bowed again and took his leave.

When he was gone, the three sat on talking with a tremulous eagerness of the coming service. Even if their devout souls had not craved the solace of the church, their secular senses would have been stirred by the thrill of the coming gathering. For many years the only place of worship for the Presbyterian settlers along the Forbes Road had been "Proctor's Tent," so called from the fact that a rude shed sheltered the visiting ministers from the exigencies of the weather and in itself suggested a certain setting apart of that which was holy from that which was presumably less so. In front of this rough altar the congregation had ranged itself along a low hillside, the women seated on logs, most of the men standing, their rifles in their hands.

Four years ago, however, the "Presbyterian Congregation" had formally received a grant of land from the Penns near the original Tent, and had erected a log meetinghouse. Toil and sacrifice had gone into it; prayers and tears had hallowed it. It had been in the eyes of all the Scotch-Irish, far and wide, the sign and symbol of their ultimate conquering of the wilderness. It was long since many of them had sat decently in a dedicated house of God, and partaken of the sacraments under the roof of a sanctuary.

Bare enough the building stood on its lofty hill, square and plain, like their own cabins; but a dignity invested it, for within, created by the fervor of the worshiping souls, as real as though shrouded by the ancient temple veil, rested, in truth, the Ark of the Covenant.

The services were of necessity irregular, for there was

as yet no stated pastor; but when a young theologian freshly graduated from Princeton College came out to the frontier to see the world and try his missionary zeal on the Indians, he always stopped for a Sabbath at Unity, as the new church was called. And other pioneer ministers—Reverend John Finley, Reverend James Power, and the famous Dr. MacMillan—had all officiated here when they were passing through.

This coming service had in it more poignant promise, however, than if any of these were to preach; for James Waddell with his sightless eyes could see the heavens open and bring the vision to the waiting souls before him. He lived in Virginia and came only at intervals to spend some time with his brother at the headwaters of the Fourteen Mile Run. His last visit here was three years ago, and even then he had been frail and trembling with palsy. No one had felt he could ever return.

"It's like an omen, sort of," Martha was saying. "Just now when everything looks so dark and we don't know where to turn or what's to befall us, the Blind Preacher comes back to point us the way. Oh, if only there's no bad uprisings before the time!"

"It will be a sight for sore eyes, too, to see the folks from all around the county that we haven't had a crack with since last fall," Mrs. Brison said complacently. "And we must see to it the word gets passed along in all directions. Well, this will take our minds a bit off our other troubles."

"That it will. I'm glad to have one fair piece of news to take back with me now. Violet's been a little down hearted these days, which isn't like her. She just needs a bit of chirking up. I guess we all do in times like these. Well, I must get on now. Drop in when you can. There's always a welcome ready." She spoke as to Mrs. Brison, but she looked at James.

On the way back Martha stopped in at the Kinkaids' to give them the word. She found Mrs. Kinkaid with a pot of soft soap on the fire, the penetrating stench of it filling the cabin. There was never any pretense at order at the Kinkaids', for there was a big family of them, from Betsy, now sixteen, to Samuel, three. Things were always "through other," as Martha was wont to say. Now, she had barely entered when Betsy, her eyes staring, her hand over her mouth, brushed past her, out of the cabin.

Mrs. Kinkaid went on calmly stirring the soap. She was, in a sense, a typical frontier woman: strong, determined, inured to hardship, her eyes sharp, her features set. Not a woman to evoke dalliance even though she had still a sort of comeliness; but a woman who could shoot a rifle when it was necessary, and who had more than once killed a rattlesnake by stamping on it with her moccasins.

"This soap sets up an awful stink, but I had to make it before my grease spoiled. I never knew Betsy to take such a scunner to it before. She's been pukin' all morning. Draw up a stool, Mrs. Murray, if you can stomach this."

Martha's face, beside her neighbor's, looked sensitively thin.

"I've been noticing Betsy. She seems a little dwiny this spring, doesn't she?"

"Oh, I doubt it's just workin' in her to get married. I wisht she an' Dave would hurry up an' on with it. It's best for young uns to get settled early before the pigs run through it. There's something wrong between them now, but I can't riddle it. Oh, it'll come right. Girls are full of vapors at this age. How are you all, and is there more word of the renegades? I'd shoot them down with my own hands if I could get nigh them," she added, her eyes snapping.

"No new word except that they've sent after the last ones. But I have other news, and good at that. There's to be Communion at the Meetinghouse the second Sabbath in May, and the *Blind Preacher's to officiate!* He's back again at Robert Waddell's."

Mrs. Kinkaid paused in her work, her hardened face moved by rare emotion. She drew a deep breath.

"The Blind Preacher! An' we thought never to hear him again. Well, that's something to fix our minds on now. Is there Saturday preachin' too?"

"No. He isn't able for two services, so I doubt we'll all have to prepare our hearts in our own way. Well, I just gave a look-in to tell you. I was at the Brisons' when Colonel Proctor stopped there and told us. Now I've got to get on home."

Mrs. Kinkaid pushed two small children out of her way with a strong arm. Little Samuel bumped his head on a stool as he fell, but she paid no heed to his tears. Bairns had to learn early to fend for themselves.

"Well now, I take it kindly you brought me the word. I'll pass it on and tell Tom to do the same."

As Martha left she met Betsy face to face. Her heart went out to the girl, all the more since she knew Mrs. Kinkaid would pay scant attention to minor ills.

"Are you sick, child?" she said gently.

At her voice Betsy's eyes swam with sudden tears.

"It's the soap," she said. "I never could abide the smell of it. I don't know why she couldn't 'a' waited an' made it all outside."

"It's just a bit of *soft* soap," Martha said. "It'll soon be done and out of the way. Come on down when you've finished your work, and you and Violet can do your knitting together."

As she went on home her brows knit anxiously.

"She's got a consumptive look about her, but God grant it may be nothing boneset tea won't fettle!"

By the next week everyone, not only in Hannastown but in the lonely country cabins on all sides of it, knew of the coming service at Unity. The various messengers carried other word also: The troops who had gone down the river to overtake and capture the latest renegades had come on them near the mouth of the Muskingum. A few of them had escaped to shore, and some were killed on the spot; the rest were brought back to Fort Pitt, where they were tried by a court-martial. The three leaders had been executed, and the others publicly whipped on the parade ground of the fort with a hundred lashes on the bare back. There was still bitter talk among the men. If McKee and Girty had only been brought back to justice too, they lamented! For this that had happened was not merely the matter of one man's standing by the King's cause and another by that of the Americans. This was no mere difference of honest opinion. This that had been done was *betrayal*, with perhaps death for them all at the merciless hands of the Indians, in consequence.

Like a golden thread, though, through this black weaving of anxiety, ran the plans for the coming communion; while over the countryside moved the unflinching miracle of the spring. No threat of coming disaster could stay the soft winds or hold back the spreading green. The snows which had buried the Great Road and the forests, and lain on the mountains like eternity's own vast weight, had gone at the last as suddenly and as completely as yesterday's cloud. There was an invincible joyousness now among the wild things of the wood. They moved and wrought in a present delight. Already in April the busy beaver people had begun building slack waters and felling quaking asps, though they would not construct their dams until late summer. The bears had wakened and come out of their winter caves and now, with their cubs behind them, were padding through the forest in search of ants' nests, grubs, and roots; or were teaching their young to avoid the stem of the water hemlock, so sweet and yet so deadly, and the "death angel" mushroom which would close small bears' eyes upon the new bright world forever.

The little fawns in their fresh spotted velvet coat sniffed the honey-sweet air and exulted in the shadow of the purple laurel or among the scented beds of May apples, while everywhere in the mottled pattern of the forest hopped soft brown rabbits, warm with new life never knowing that perhaps some day the terror of a weasel might fall upon them.

Each morning now, Sam and Hugh, their rifles close at hand, started work in the fields, trying to get the new crops in; or girdled more trees in the thick woodland to increase their productive acreage. Though Ranger still limped a little the leg was settling to normal size, and Hugh's fear that the campaign had permanently crippled the horse was now abated. He had been faithful in his care of it, rubbing night and morning with bear grease as though the rheumatic joint were one of Sam's own.

The two men worked with a desperate energy, knowing that any day a sudden raid or even the sight of skulking forms among the trees would keep them from their tasks. Early in April it was known that the Senecas had crossed the Kiskiminetas and the Conemaugh, and entered Westmorland County. They had come down on Fort Wallace, about sixteen miles from Ligonier, where ammunition and supplies of salt were stored. They had helped themselves, killing nine rangers and wounding their captain. This meant that the spring outrages had begun; but so far Hannastown was quiet.

In the cabin and in the small truck patch behind it, Martha and Violet toiled as unceasingly as the men, with Hugh running back from the fields at intervals to make sure all was well. It was cruel, Martha thought often, not to be able to enjoy the warm, sweet air and the delights of spring without the tense muscles, the strained eyes, the quick-beating hearts that meant eternal vigilance against the redskins—and the snakes!

"God forgive me!" she said once as she and Violet planted potatoes and hoed the flax. "I believe I dread the rattlers a'most more than the Indians."

But there was no outcry and no alarm in those days that led up to the May Sabbath for which their hearts waited. Martha's thoughts dwelt happily upon the re-union with old friends and far-away neighbors which the day would bring. She would see Mrs. Proctor and Mrs. Lochry, both of whom she admired. There would be the Sloans, the Shieldses, and the Craigs from the Derry settlement. And dearest of all to her would be the meeting with Hannah MacRoberts! Though Hannah was still a young woman she and Martha had been close in spirit since their first acquaintance two years ago. There was a native fineness in each which rose to claim the other a friend. The MacRobertses had a lonely cabin back in the hills, but they never missed a service.

Martha had done all her slender resources permitted in making her family presentable for the occasion. Her kerchief and Violet's were bleached white as the driven snow; the men's hunting shirts were freshly fringed; and there were new moccasins for them once around.

As a rule when they went to church, Martha and Violet both rode Ranger with Sam and Hugh walking near, but now with the horse's stiff leg, it was thought wise not to overload him.

"I'd rather walk anyway," Violet said as they planned. "I'll walk with Brother, and then Father can stay close with you. There'll be a fair company of us. Half the town's going, it seems. Oh, I *hope* it's a good day."

And it was. Bright and fair with just enough warmth to make the light breeze soft to the brow and to bring up from the earth the rich smell of soil and matted leaves as well as the scent of serviceberries and the flowering thorn.

There was, as Violet had predicted, a goodly company setting forth. The Shaws, the Brisons, the Steels, the Kinkaids, the Hannas, the Wilsons, Mrs. Brownlee and her older children from over the hill—in fact, all the Presbyterians except Lieutenant Lochry who, with his rangers, was still at the fort and would keep guard over the town. There was, of course, no laughter or unbecoming levity among the group as they left the village, some on horseback, some afoot, for this was the Sabbath. Besides there was the dark necessity for quiet as they proceeded. Every man and boy held his rifle while his eyes, trained by years of wariness, raked the forest as they passed through, watching with hard set faces for the glimpse of a red face or a feather at the side of a tree.

But though there was no levity, and though fear rested upon them all, there was still manifest a spirit of subdued gladness. For they were all Scotch-Irish, with their intense racial hunger for religious observance; and now this hunger was about to be satisfied. They were to sit today, along with friends and acquaintances whom they had not seen for months, at the table of the Lord.

Violet and Hugh walked close together without speaking. The mirror had imaged them both before they set out. Violet knew that her eyes were a deep, shadowy blue and that the white kerchief became her well; Hugh knew that his face had the strength of a man's and that this spring his shoulders had broadened. They were both conscious, too, of the sweet impact of the spring weather and of the fact that all about them in the waking woods there were wild things mating. They felt, as they moved on together, the tender, throbbing wave of life that surged through the forest as warm bodies passed with liquid hidden grace between the trees, and unseen eyes watched from vantage points with their own curious, bright wisdom.

Between Violet and Hugh, as always, there was a silent understanding of all the meaning of the wilderness. But they spoke little.

"It's a fair day, Sister," he said once.

"Oh, it's bonny. I'm right content to be going to church today."

It was not till the first miles were behind them that James Brison and Dave Shaw came forward casually and joined them. Dave was not inclined to speech; he had hoped Betsy would be along but she had resolutely insisted upon staying behind to watch the younger children even when Mrs. Huffnagle, who was a Lutheran, had offered to keep them. But James was unusually talkative. He spoke in a low tone of the Tories and the weather, of the Blind Preacher and the state of the American army; he started to quote Shakespeare and then, as though remembering the day, ended up with a verse from the Song of Solomon. All in all, his high spirits and general loquacity caused the others to glance at him in surprise.

"I doubt our friend James must be in love," Hugh said once under his breath to Dave.

"God help him then," Dave replied.

The pain in his voice made Hugh wince. Though he had spoken in jest about James he was brought back suddenly to the reality which lay upon both Dave and himself. He glanced at Violet with the sunshine on her hair and throat. For the first time the thought went through him that she was too slightly formed for a frontiersman's wife. Even now at home when she bent over the hoe in the truck patch he was always saying when he could, "Here. Give it me. I'll finish it up sharp for you." But a wife. In the Back Country a wife had to bear and endure and work the same as her man. Only more.

Hugh flushed hotly and looked quickly away into the forest. There were thoughts again in his mind that he had no right to think. And on his way to the Lord's table too. It was strange how peaceful and pure the mind could be one minute and how torn betwixt and between dark things the next.

At last they came out on high ground with only two more miles between them and the church. The mountains loomed along the eastern horizon in great sweeping ridges, the dark emerald of the Laurel meeting the sky, the lighter green of the Chestnut curving before it. In the valleys between, the bright sunlight picked out the white masses of dogwood and blossoming thorn; and overhead the sky was blue with high floating clouds. As though a sudden rapture had spread through the group, their spirits lightened. It was open country now down the long sloping hill and up the next to where the church stood waiting. Already they could glimpse other groups just ahead. A feeling of relative safety swept over them; they quickened their pace.

Martha's heart was full. Her lips moved in the familiar words:

> "I joy'd when to the house of God
>   Go up, they said to me. . . ."

They were approaching no white edifice with a heaven-pointing spire, such as she remembered on the village green of her girlhood. But it was still the house of God.

At last they reached the churchyard itself with its new grave plot already sprinkled with humble stones. The men tied their horses at the posts close to the building. There was a reason for having them so near. No seasoned scout among them could so unerringly detect the presence of an Indian as could a horse. By some strange, subtle reaction, whether from sight, smell, or hearing or from another sense unknown to man, a horse always knew when Indians were near and neighed its bitter uneasiness. So the hitching posts were close to the sanctuary.

The women went with ill concealed eagerness to speak to the friends they had not seen for months. There were Mrs. Proctor and Mrs. Lochry from near by; there was a large group from over Congruity way; there were those from the settlement along the Loyalhanna; the Guthries, the John Shieldses, and Mrs. Samuel Craig. Martha went first toward the latter. Only last November her husband had been riding toward Ligonier for salt when he was waylaid by the Indians and either killed or captured at the foot of the Chestnut Ridge. Some rangers had found

his beautiful mare dead with eight bullets in her, but
there had been no trace then or since of her rider.

"Mrs. Craig."

"Martha Murray!"

Their arms went about each other.

"It's a sore blow! Oh, but my heart's gone out to you."

"The Lord's will be done, Martha. I'm trying to bear
up. How's your family?"

"In health, I'm thankful to say. Sam's rheumatism
seems better this spring, but he's still lame. Where are
your children?"

"We left the young ones all in Shields' fort. We thought
it was safer. The older boys are well so far and write now
and then. Oh, I wish this war was over! I miss them so,
especially Sam with his jokes and his songs. I felt I just
had to come to hear the Blind Preacher today. It would
maybe bring a healing to my heart. Here are the
Shieldses!"

Martha turned to greet them. Colonel John Shields, a
tall, rugged man with broad forehead and dark, twinkling
eyes, was the only doctor in the whole countryside. Even
so he was not kept very busy doctoring, for the Back
Country women with their own anguish brought their
children into the world or served as midwives to their
sisters; and each cabin shelf had a whiskey and wild
cherry bottle upon it, with a bunch of boneset dangling
above. It was only when a lancet was needed, or a broken
bone had to be set, that everyone turned to Dr. Shields,
and on his gray horse he came as swiftly as he could.

He gave Martha's hand a strong grasp now and then

left the women together. Both Mrs. Shields and Mrs. Craig were eager for more news of the flight of the Tories, and both looked anxious as Martha repeated all she knew.

"The times were never so black," Mrs. Shields sighed. "They say ever so many families are going back east. Some say it's no use trying to hold out here any longer."

"We've got to put the fears out of our minds for this day at least," said Mrs. Craig. "It's something else we're here for. Oh, but my heart lifted when I saw you all coming up the hill! It seemed like the old tribes going up to Jerusalem itself."

"I've been watching for the MacRobertses. I hope naught will keep them away," Martha spoke, scanning the hill anxiously.

"There's Colonel Proctor at the door now. I doubt it'll be time to go in. We're to have preparatory prayer meeting since there was no preaching yesterday," Mrs. Shields said. "Why, here's Violet! How are you, child?"

"Bless you," Mrs. Craig smiled. "You've a May-time face and no mistake. Can that big fellow there be your Hugh, Martha? Why, he's man grown! And a handsome one at that. I doubt you'll be having *two* daughters before long!"

They all joined the general movement toward the door, entering as quietly as the stacking of rifles permitted, and then taking their places on the hard benches. In the space at the front before the pulpit, the plain board tables were spread with bleached linen cloths, which Mrs. Proctor own hands had spun from her own flax. Upon them, covered decently with smaller squares, were the sacred ele

ments themselves. The eyes of the congregation moved
anxiously past this, however, past the rude pulpit to the
figure seated behind it. It was the Blind Preacher.

He was an old man, tall and very spare, his head covered with a white linen cap, his sightless eyes closed, his
shriveled hands trembling with palsy.

There was something close to the supernatural in the
aspect, as though, instead of a body housing a living soul,
here was a soul clad thinly and fleetingly in a body.

A hush fell upon the congregation now as five young
men took up their watchful posts at the windows and
door—Hugh and Dave at the east side where their keen
gaze could sweep the farther hills and the near valley.
They held their rifles in their hands ready for instant use.
In Violet's heart as she watched Hugh's tall back, straight
as a candle, there was a startled pain. Mrs. Craig's chance
words had sent a new fear through her like an arrow. Just
when there seemed peace between her and Hugh and the
happy closeness they had always known before this winter! *What if he should marry?* In all the confusion of her
heart she had never once thought of this possibility.

Colonel Proctor had risen and was making his way to
the front to open the prayer meeting. His face looked old
with care and anxiety today.

"Let us raise our voices in praise to God with the use
of the Thirty-seventh Psalm. A part of Psalm Thirty-
seven: 'For evil doers fret thou not.'"

A lump rose in Martha's throat. Of all the Psalms of
David this one was the most appropriate for their times.
It was almost as though the Colonel had said to them:

"McKee and his minions have gone over to the British. Simon Girty is now on the side of the Indians. The times are the worst they've ever been, but still we'll sing out our faith."

James rose to take his place as precentor, one of the few copies of *Rouse's Version of the Psalms* in his hand. His clear voice lined the stanza and raised the tune:

> "For evil doers fret thou not
>   Thyself unquietly;
> Nor do thou envy bear to those
>   That work iniquity.
>
> "For even as the fading grass
>   Soon be cut down shall they;
> And like the green and tender herb
>   They wither shall away."

The voices gained confidence and strength with each line. The deep tones of the men joined the women's high treble:

> "Set thou thy trust upon the Lord
>   And be thou doing good;
> And so thou in the land shall dwell
>   And verily have food."

Had David and his people long ago warring against the Philistines known the same pains of want and danger and destruction? How else could he have put these words in his holy song, Martha's thoughts were running.

It was time for prayer. Colonel Shields was called upon

first. The phraseology of all the elders was stereotyped, but the voices bore the note of stark sincerity. The men, in so far as articulateness was possible to them, poured out the sorrows, the hopes, the fears of a pioneering people. Certain expressions, like old jewels, finely polished by the years and now fitted to their present need, were repeated over and over:

". . . And oh, Thou great Jehovah, lead us at last through all the perils of this wilderness of sin, into the Promised Land of Thy grace. . . ."

The prayer meeting was finally concluded. A breath of expectancy passed over the congregation. From his chair the Blind Preacher rose, his frailty even more apparent as he caught the pulpit for support. The palsy had spread now, until his whole body was racked with it. It would not be possible surely for him to preach a sermon and then address the communicants again at the sacrament as was the custom; so they were not surprised when he said: "Let us come now to the Lord's table during the singing of the One Hundred and Twenty-first Psalm."

The men and women rose to their feet; James standing at the front again read line by line and raised the tune. Slowly, almost as with reluctance, they all moved forward to the boards on which reposed the mystic elements—all but the sentinels, who still stood motionless at windows and door, their gaze fixed on the trees and vales beyond. Their voices, though, joined with the others in the psalm:

"I to the hills will lift mine eyes
From whence doth come mine aid."

The Blind Preacher stood now at the end of the long table at which most of the communicants were seated. The few who could not be accommodated there sat in the front rows of benches. There was in his air and manner a peculiar solemnity which sent a shiver through the frames of his listeners. Without further preface he began to draw a picture of the sufferings of the Savior: His trial before Pilate; His ascent to Calvary; His crucifixion and His death. Suddenly in the bare room the listeners were hearing the story as though for the first time. There was in the speaker a union of utter simplicity and majesty! It was clear to each one in his hearing that before them stood not only a saint of God, but a sublime orator and a man of profound intellectual attainments.

Slowly, with enunciation so deliberate that his voice trembled on every syllable, he went on. His peculiar phrases, colored by his own emotion, had such force of description that the scene appeared to be at that very moment enacted before the eyes of the congregation. They saw the hard Romans and the supercilious Jews; the faces bitter, indifferent, or distorted by malice and rage. A kindling flame of indignation swept over the listening men and women. Hands were involuntarily and convulsively clenched, lips set hard, throats tightened.

But when the orator came to touch upon the patience, the submissiveness, the gentle pardoning prayer of the life's ending—the trembling voice broke entirely. The Blind Preacher burst into tears.

The effect was inconceivable. The women sobbed openly. Groans and even tears came from the men. The had all known suffering in their own lives; and there were few who had not known bitter sorrow. But the necessity to shut it up in their hearts was like a law of the wilderness. The luxury of grief was for those back east who knew the ways of comfort, and who could take time for tears.

But now it was as though God himself were saying: "Weep, weep, my children, for the sorrows of your Savior. You who have had to make your hearts as stone over your own griefs, weep now and find easement with the Lord."

At last there came the prayer of consecration, and the elders rose to dispense the elements. The sweet unleavened bread, cut in small squares, was made from white flour, of which there was little enough anywhere. This had come from Mrs. Arch Lochry. The wine was always from Colonel Proctor's—a Madeira, thinned. The heavy pewter plate of bread passed slowly along the table. ". . . The body of the Lord which was broken for you. This do in remembrance of Him," ran the faltering voice.

The pewter cup followed, filled with the warm wine. Slowly it went from lip to lip. "The blood of the Lord which was poured out for you. Drink ye all of it."

Sam and four other men rose as soon as they had communed and took the places of the sentinels. The young men came to the table, and the plate and cup were passed to them.

It was all over too soon, Martha kept thinking: the beauty, the adoration of the Blind Preacher's words; the holy spell of the sacrament; the relieving tears that had loosed the tension of their hearts; the crying lift of the psalms; the peace of this hour with the May sunshine falling athwart the log walls and the faint scent of wild thorn blowing in at the door. How could she ever image it all to feed her spirit through the days to come? In her own musings she paused to regret that Hannah MacRoberts had missed it! They, of all the families usually in their place, were absent.

The Blind Preacher had risen again and seemed about to speak. The people leaned forward, scarcely breathing.

"My children," he began, "my strength is failing fast. The end of my earthly pilgrimage is at hand. And since it is not likely that any of you listening now will ever again hear the sound of my voice, I would leave with you if I could some word for your consolation."

He stretched out his shaking hands as though to gather them all to himself.

"My children, the times are dark for you. Dangers threaten to engulf you. Foes press in on every side. The blackness of fear encompasseth you."

He paused, as though craving from God the final word of comfort. Then he raised his sightless eyes, with a smile transfiguring his countenance.

"But remember this, that even as my own long night will soon give way to the brightness of heaven's morning, so for you too, some time, in some way, *the day must dawn!*"

There was only the sound of gentle breathing as though the hearts of the congregation had received a baptism of grace; while the Blind Preacher sank back again in his chair.

The closing psalm was announced, and James had read the first line when the sudden frightened neighing of the horses smote the air. In the instant every man sprang for his rifle. Hugh and Dave rushed to the doorway, their eyes strained upon the countryside. There was no outcry, only the low-voiced terror of the women.

From one sentinel to another there passed the quick word, "Nothing in sight." But still the sharp neighing continued.

Hugh and Dave spoke with each other, and then Hugh turned to the rest.

"Dave an' I'll go out and do some scoutin'. I'll take the upper side here, an' Dave the lower. If we find anything we'll give a signal. Keep sharp watch at the windows."

"Hugh!"

Violet did not know she had called out. The cry was wrung from her. "Oh, Brother, be careful!"

He looked at her, and smiled. Then they went out.

Violet crouched on a bench close to her mother. The women's faces had fallen into their old familiar lines of dread. Behind them, faltered the tones of the Blind Preacher praying. So they waited for the sound of a shot, for a bloodcurdling yell, for—they knew not what.

But all was still. Even the horses had grown quiet. From their vantage posts the men again reported, "Nothing in sight."

At the end of a half-hour Hugh and Dave returned.

They had scouted all around and found no trace of Indians. It was even possible that the horses had been frightened by something else. A bee sting might have set one off, and the rest taken fright from that. Or it might have been a rattler, or even a bear.

They talked the situation over with care from all angles. The men decided at last that the scouts' theory was probably correct. Something other than Indians might have startled the horses; but they must take all precautions on the way back, and leave at once.

They did not wait for the psalm. They bowed their heads for the benediction, said their good-byes with full hearts to the Blind Preacher and the groups each to the others, knowing well that some of them might never reach their homes alive; then, stealthily, watchfully, they left the church and gathered together for the return journey. Sam told Violet to ride behind Martha on the way back. In case of sudden attack they would have more chance on horseback. In the Hannastown delegation, the women were shielded by their menfolk in so far as the road permitted. Two men walked at the front and two at the rear of the procession. There was no talking. They moved in silence down the slope from the church, across the little valley, up the long hill and then through the deep woods.

It was when they had reached the point where a faint trail from the north joined the Forbes Road that the men at the front stopped short and raised their hands. The others drew near, the men with rifles ready, the women shivering with apprehension!

On the fresh green floor of the forest there were pools of blood and three prone bodies tomahawked and scalped! It was the MacRoberts family! The father and the boy lay near together as though they might have fallen first under sudden surprise blows. Hannah, the mother, lay a little apart near a tree, the trunk of which was covered with horrible spatterings. One of the men moved nearer and pointed now to the infant's brained body just beyond.

Martha, forcing back a terrible nausea, dismounted from her horse and walked across to her friend. She knelt down beside her and slipped her hand under the kerchief —doubtless like her own bleached with care for this day, but now white no longer. The heart was still beating faintly.

"Hannah," she spoke softly. "It's Martha Murray with you. Oh, Hannah!"

There was a faint twitching of the lips, and then under her hand the heart ceased to beat.

Martha struggled again with the nausea and with a mortal faintness as though death were touching her own body. She rose unsteadily and went back to Violet, whose face was hidden in her shaking hands. Most of the women, after the first glance, had averted their eyes; only Mrs. Kinkaid, Martha could see, was staring full at the ghastly scene, her face like iron.

The men conferred in low tones. They had examined the bodies of MacRoberts and the boy and found them already growing cold. It seemed likely that the Indians after doing their deadly work here had followed their own trail on toward the church. There, seeing from their hidden vantage points the number of the horses and reckoning that they were too far outnumbered by the whites to risk an attack, they had taken themselves off in another direction.

There remained now the sad work of burying the dead. Using their rifle ends, sharp sticks and their own hard hands, the men—all but James who was retching desperately behind a tree—managed to scoop out a shallow depression in the soft earth. In it they laid the bodies, the mangled infant on its mother's breast. They covered the grave as best they could, working fast, their eyes strained, their ears alert for the slightest sound that might mean a return of the foe.

Then in a silence that rose to heaven louder than any cry, they started on again toward Hannastown. They reached it in safety before sundown, parting, still in silence, at their own doors. Later on the women would talk their hearts out to one another; but now they were too stricken.

In the Murray cabin Martha set about getting the supper with Violet, her face drained of all color, putting the rude dishes on the table. Sam and Hugh ate, but mother and daughter could only make pretense. When the remains of the meal were cleared away, the Sabbath sun had dropped behind the hill. A warm, sweet breeze blew over the land. Martha and Sam sat down in the doorway with Hugh and Violet on the plank step below. Hugh's arm was stretched out behind her, and little by little she leaned against it, feeling his strength.

At intervals Martha sighed deeply as though indeed

each sigh were a drop of blood drawn from her heart.

They sat on till the darkness fell and from a near-by tree came the high echoing call of the whippoorwill—the death call, people said. Violet shuddered against Hugh's arm, seeing once more the scene in the forest.

From behind them, Martha spoke at last.

"Poor Hannah," she said. "Oh, poor Hannah! She didn't live to see the day dawn here, but belike she'll be seeing it yonder."

May 16 Had thought to set down all the account of the meeting and the Blind Preacher's sermon but I can't rightly think on it yet. Hannah MacRoberts and her husband and children were all massacreed yesterday on their way to the church. We found them as we came back. Hannah was scalped. Oh to think of her pretty brown hair. The baby was brained on the tree beside her. She must have seen it done for she was still alive when we found them. Died under my very hand. Oh Hannah my friend! She had wanted a little girl so and was so pleased when this one came. I doubt she meant to have the Blind Preacher baptize it today. I feel felled to earth by this. Poor Hannah. So proud and hopeful about their land. So pretty she was and young. I feel bitter over it and unreconciled. May God give me grace to bear with fortitude all that may be laid upon me. Even Sam is quiet. It brings other things back. . . . Just now as I write a strange thought has come over me. Maybe this is the way it is. There's some that must go before and some that must come after. There's some that must cut down the wilderness and break the rough ground and maybe wet it with their blood. And then there's some that will come after and live on the fat of the land. God must sort out which is which.

VII

The Rattlesnake

It was at noon the next day while they were eating dinner that the sound of shouting came from the tavern. Sam and Hugh sprang for their rifles; but in a minute they all realized that for once the news must be good, for though the voices were confused an occasional "Hurrah!" rent the air.

They hurried out into the street to find that the occupants of the other cabins were all doing the same.

"What's up? What's happened now?" passed from lip to lip.

Then from the tavern emerged Robert Hanna himself and John Irwin who kept the store. They stood on the narrow porch and shouted at the top of their lungs while the words ran together and yet flared out on the ear as though they had been painted in scarlet for the eye.

"The Eighth's been ordered home! *The Eighth's* been ordered home!"

For one second there was no voice but the echo; then such joy and relief swept the town as had never been felt there before. The men broke into yells as they tore forward to the tavern; the women all but split their lungs in the sudden jubilation. Over and over the glad news was repeated, one running back to tell another who had not yet heard.

"The Eighth's been ordered back! An express is just here with the word!"

"The Eighth's—coming—home!"

There was no thought of meat or drink or even of the work in the fields. The cabins were all but deserted while the whole town flocked to the tavern. They gathered about the porch, where Robert Hanna and the express rider between them gave out the details amidst the cheers of the men and women.

"It's God's truth," the express called, his weathered face beaming. "I'm on my way to Pittsburgh with the whole story. The request came last week from the Board of War that the Eighth Pennsylvania and the Thirteenth Virginia be ordered back for frontier duty—"

He couldn't go on for the shouting. Robert Hanna's round face was scarlet; the veins stood out on his temples; he was waving his arms, while his voice rose above the others.

"So at last they're paying some heed to the Back Country! God knows it's about time! Quiet now! Quiet, folks, while you hear the rest of it!"

After a little the express could go on:

"Congress accepted Hand's resignation on the 2nd of this month."

They all cheered again from sheer exuberance.

"The same day Washington appointed Brigadier General Lachlan McIntosh to the command at Fort Pitt."

"Is he any good?" John Kinkaid yelled.

"How would I know?" the express grinned. "He killed a fellah in a duel down in Georgia an' then got transferred up to Valley Forge. They say General Washington took a great shine to him. That's all I know about him."

Robert Hanna's voice rose again.

"The man he killed in the duel was Button Gwinnett, one of the signers of the Declaration."

"Shows he can shoot straight, anyhow," Sam put in.

"Never mind about McIntosh. Tell us when the Eighth's comin'," someone else called.

"That I can't rightly say," the express returned. "By next month most likely, they'll be settin' out. Well, folks, I'm glad for once to bring you good news instid of the kind you usually get back here."

They cheered the express; they cheered Robert Hanna; they cheered Michael Huffnagle who was Adjutant of the Eighth, while Mrs. Huffnagle wiped her eyes for joy and shook hands with everyone in reach; they cheered Captain Brownlee and Captain Sam Miller who lived just over the hill; they cheered Captain Matthew Jack, and even his horse, Matchit, the fastest in the whole countryside. They cheered Sam Craig, who had carried the Rattlesnake flag. They cheered everybody until their throats were hoarse, then slowly dispersed to attend to the duties of the day, but with what a lightening of the spirits! Such hope now in the heart!

There was small talk of anything that afternoon but the Eighth in the cabins or the fields; men and women told one another again the stories of the famous regiment as the news had come back by letter or by messenger through the intervening months.

That journey east for the soldiers had been a tragic one! They had received their orders to join Washington's army in January of '77. Though amazed at the command and loath to turn their backs on the duty for which they had enlisted, they had shown little hesitation. They had no uniforms and no tents; their blankets were scanty, their cooking utensils scarce enough. In spite of this they had prepared to go. The scouting parties were called in, the pack horses were collected, and the regiment had begun its desperate march in the very worst period of the Pennsylvania winter.

It was three hundred miles across the state, along the worst possible roads, tracks, and trails, through deep snow, over perilous mountain passes. There was never enough food; their clothes were in tatters; they slept in the lee of rocks with great fires going at night to fend off stark death from the cold in so far as was possible.

By the end of February, when they reached the outskirts of Philadelphia, one-third of the men who had survived the march were sick; and fifty died within the next two weeks, including Colonel Aeneas Mackay himself who was in command. Yes, a sad journey east it had been indeed, and many a mother and wife looked long for the letter that never came! As Mrs. Huffnagle had often said then to Martha: "If Michael's got to die, may it be in the fight and not starved or frozen by the roadside like a bear in a trap."

Washington, who by that time had won the victories of

Trenton and Princeton and so relieved Pennsylvania from the danger of immediate invasion, had taken post with his little army north of the Raritan River in New Jersey. So it was to this spot, after a brief rest, that the Eighth had gone to be placed in the second brigade of General Anthony Wayne's Pennsylvania Division.

But the news that had thrilled the folks back home in Kittanning and Ligonier, in Hannastown and Redstone and Pittsburgh and all the settlements between, was the story of Morgan's rifle corps. This organization had been formed by Washington the following June and was made up of the best sharpshooters in the whole American army. Five hundred dead shots! And for this corps more men had been chosen from the Eighth Pennsylvania than from any other command. Ah, when this word came back, here was proud rejoicing in the Back Country! Many a man caressed his rifle as though it were a live thing.

Sam Murray's pride in his countrymen had held one drop of bitterness.

"We'd 'a' been in it, Hugh, tane or tither of us, if we'd only got to go. Yessir, we'd 'a' made the corps, sure as there's a tail on a turkey."

The corps had been sent up north to General Gates and had done its full part at Stillwater and Saratoga, sharing in the triumph of Burgoyne's surrender. The rest of the Eighth had been busy meanwhile under Wayne at Brandywine and Germantown. But with the coming on of the winter they had all been joined again at Valley Forge. Now that winter of their suffering was ended. The men of the Eighth were coming home.

"If only they were *all* coming!" Martha said wistfully as she baked a pone that evening. "It's so cruel hard fo them that can't rejoice now. I saw Mrs. Beatty just pu her hand to her heart when the shout came, and then g back into the cabin."

"And the Kilgores!" Violet said. "They went alon; with the rest to the tavern, but Missus was white as deat] and said naught to anyone."

"I'll have a look-in on them tonight, I think," Marth decided. "It may be a bit of help to know someone feel for them. Aye, there'll be many a sad heart as well as . light one when the regiment gets back."

After supper Sam left for the tavern, and Martha o; her errands of sympathy. Hugh and Violet were alone i the cabin. Hugh took a knob of wood he was whittlin for a fancy noggin and sat down in the doorstep. Viole after a little hesitation, sat down beside him with he knitting. The May dusk was sweet about them with a ne moon over Gallows Hill. They each felt the other's nea ness as shoulder touched shoulder, and gradually, as th mystery of darkness came on from the forest and enfolde them, their work lay idle in their hands and they talke as they had never done before.

"It's strange-like what a difference a few hours ca make," Violet mused. "Here we sat last night with th sorrow for the MacRobertses so heavy on us, and no eas ment for our fears. And now all at once today we get th news about the Eighth and we can take heart again."

"Things happen sudden-like," Hugh answered slowl "A trouble may be lyin' heavy on you, an' the next mi

te it'll just whup off and be clean gone." He paused.
'An' sometimes it works the other way round. I've no-
iced that often."

"It's all been a strange-like day to me," Violet went on,
eeling for the words. "This morning Mother talked to
ne about something that fair gave me a startle. I guess it
vas what happened yesterday set her to it. But I never
aw her so anxious-like about anything before."

"What was it, then?" Hugh asked quickly.

"She said she wanted me to go back east to Phila-
elphia where things would be easy for me and I'd know
vays of living like gentlefolk. She said—I'm not rightly
ure what she meant—but she said maybe there might be
omeone else would want to go some time and—I wouldn't
e alone."

There was silence. They could feel each other breath-
ig. Then Violet spoke again with slow shyness.

"Would you ever favor going east for yourself, Brother?"

Hugh swallowed a deadly lump in his throat.

"I never thought to go, for a fact."

"Would you care, think you, for city ways?"

The fear of death was on him, but he had to answer
ue.

"I don't think I'd care rightly for livin' my life in a
wn, Sister. I always thought to have my own land under
y feet."

"Yes?" Violet prompted eagerly.

"It's in my mind to take up a big piece of acreage when
ings get settled more. I plan to girdle an' cut down all
e trees in a wide stretch an' plant more crops than we

have here an' build a big cabin—bigger than any in Han-nastown."

"Why—why, you've got it all thought out, haven't you?"

"It comes over me often. It's no more than natural for a man to want his own land. In a big country like this it's here for the takin' if you've got the will."

He stopped short.

"How do you look, then, on your mother's plan?"

"It was maybe just the MacRobertses that put her in mind of it. And me saying so often I'd like to eat off a flowered plate! It's maybe just a conceit of hers."

"You're not then—you don't rightly favor going?"

The eagerness in his voice set the air aquiver.

"It would seem strange-like to be long in a city. I'd miss the forest, I doubt."

"Things'll soon be better here. They're bound to!"

"When the war's ended some thinks there'll be no more trouble with the Indians even."

His voice was low.

"There's some traders might chancet to have a flowered plate. I didn't rightly know you fancied one so. I'll be watchin'."

The soft spring night flowed around them with sudden hope in it and boundless promise. Hugh's hard strong hand dropped to the step between them; Violet's crept into it. There was union then at the touch: a warmth so sweet, a strength so renewed! They sat on, speaking but seldom.

"It's fine land, this, once you get the trees off it."

"There won't be near so many snakes, Father says, when it's cleared more."

"An' with the savages beat back once for all—what's to fear?"

"What's to fear?" Violet echoed softly.

The next weeks were hot. A sudden curtain seemed to have been withdrawn from the springtime sun, and its rays poured vehemently down upon the wildness and the cleared land. In the last few days the flax plants had shot up, and now, Martha decided, the delicate matter of weeding should take place at once. They discussed the matter at breakfast. Sam and Hugh were going to work that day in the field next to the flax patch. This would be advantageous, for there had been more rattlers than usual abroad this summer. Up from their dens in the rocky places where great numbers of them slept through the winter, they had come now, fresh in their new skins, velvety black or brown-banded on sulphur yellow, their new rattles shaking their deadly warning, to sun themselves and hunt their food in the open fields.

It was nothing for the men to kill four or five of them in a day; but so far this summer no one had been bitten. There was developed in the frontiersmen a curious sharpening of all the senses. They could see an almost invisible speck of flying wings against the sky; they could hear a leaf fall in the forest; they could *smell* a rattlesnake, by the faint, peculiar vapor the scaly skins gave off in the warm sunlight.

"Mind you keep your eyes open now," Sam cautioned

the women as they all set out together. "Work with your faces to the wind so you can get a whiff of one if it's nigh-hand you. Keep a club close to you an' give the varmint a clout if it's even nip an' tuck with you; but if you've got time just give us a cry, and one of us will come."

"I'll run across often an' see how you're makin' out," Hugh said reassuringly. "Here's a good stick for each of you. Just look sharp an' you'll be all right."

But there was more on the men's minds than the fear of rattlers. Just over the northern hill the week before the Hart cabin had been found in ashes, with John and Sarah Hart's mutilated bodies near by and no trace of the children. That meant captivity for them. Down toward Redstone a young settler had come home to find his wife's head cleft by a tomahawk and their baby brained on the doorsill. Over Ligonier way two young girls had been caught as they were driving home the cow. One had been left tomahawked; the other captivated. Daily now the dark reports came.

But Violet was in high spirits in spite of everything that morning, for a lightness of heart often overcame her now—she could not tell why. Besides, the day was so fair. It was June, and the air was heavy with the rich perfume of chestnut tassels; while up from the little thicket beside the creek came the fragrance of wild grape, sweetest of all the scents of earth.

The weeding was tedious. The heavy nightly dews and the hot days produced a rank growth everywhere. Here among the slim flax stalks was no exception. With firm and cautious hands the women proceeded to pull the weeds, being careful never to dislodge the flax itself. They spoke little, for the sun was hot, backs grew cramped, the possibility of danger was always present, and it took all their strength and fortitude to keep steadily at work.

By noon one end of the patch shone out beautifully bare of undesirable growth, the flax plants spraying their delicate stalks untrammeled. Dinner was a cheerful meal, and they were all soon at their tasks again. Violet's mind was busy with many things. Her mother had not spoken to her again about the plan for her to go back east. It was likely then just a passing conceit. This was a relief, for how could she ever leave them all? Brother would never go, of that she was sure. He was made for the forest and for wide rolling lands. And maybe she was, too. If Mother ever spoke of it again she would tell her this. It was queer, she thought, how your wants and wishes could get so mixed up, like. Here was she, her breath coming quick even just to *hear* about Mother's old home and the polished tables, the garden full of lilacs, and the flowered plates for tea! She had dreamed about all this ever since she could remember, and now of a sudden, when her mother spoke as though she might actually go back east and see such houses, she felt strange and forlorn-like and kept thinking of the wilderness: the way the snowy petals of the wild serviceberry looked in the spring; the way the wild grape smelled right now; the witch hazel blooming in the fall as if it was a miracle; the brightness then of the sumac and the sugar maples; the inside of the chestnut burr that sent a little shiver through you because it was like an angel wing—the softness! So many things she got pleasure from that you wouldn't have back east in a city. And then to leave Mother and Father. No, she could never do that. . . . And Brother.

She bent lower, her cheeks flushed. There seemed so much to think of just this afternoon, like. The Eighth had left Valley Forge, so one of the late express riders said, and were on the march homeward. They would stop in Carlisle, and then start on across the mountains. There would be a throng time for sure when they got to Hannastown—everybody excited, with all the soldiers in and about the houses and the tavern, telling their stories and having a frolic even, if they were here long enough and the times were quiet.

She hoped by then Betsy would be herself again and not so dwiny and peevish-like. It wasn't that she was mad at Dave, as it appeared at first. There was something else bothering her, but when Violet questioned her she just said she couldn't abide so much noise as there was alway in their cabin. It fair set her head in a whir, she said. She'd had toothache too, cruel often. That was hard to thole, and no mistake. If she would only let her father borrow the "pullikins" from Ezra the blacksmith and jerk it out, she might be like herself again. She and Dave would like as not be married come fall. Then there would be a jollification! A wedding was the real time for pleasure, and that was a fact.

Violet stood up to stretch her stiff back. She looked toward her mother, who was working quite a little way ahead; then she turned toward the grain field. Hugh had apparently just paused also and was looking across at her

"Are you all right?" he called.

"We're fine," she answered.

They stood so for a moment watching each other in the bright sunshine. Violet drew a long breath of the air's sweetness.

"Can you smell the wild grapes?" she hallooed through her cupped hands.

She thought she could see him smile.

"We'd better get on with our work," he called back.

But the smile was in his voice. She knew he was smelling the perfume just as she was, and seeing the blue sky with its soft drifting mountains of cloudy snow.

She took another draught of the fragrant air, then moved forward to begin her weeding, for the moment unwary in her happiness.

There was instantly the hollow sound of rattles from the deep weeds. In her quick alarm she stepped the wrong way. Before she could scream even, she saw through her error the flashing loop of a black and yellow neck! She felt in her leg the ghastly sharpness of the poison fangs!

She stood still, frozen, rooted in a dead wonder. It could not be she, Violet, here with death's tooth in her veins! No—no! The bright, happy day was still all about her. No, it could not be—this horror. It was but a daily dread like to that of the Indians. But this had never happened to any of them. No, this had not happened to her!

But it had. The burning pain had already begun. She screamed then, the wild despair of her voice covering the flax patch and the grain field beyond. Martha came tearing back, her face like chalk, her lips shaking.

"Child, child, are you bit? Oh, child, are you bit?"

"My leg," Violet gasped.

The men were almost there, hurtling through the flax unmindful of the plants. Hugh outran Sam and flung himself down before her just as Martha had stripped of the stocking.

"Get out of the way!" he cried roughly.

His fingers held the flesh while he found the bright bloody red marks on the skin. He put his lips to them an sucked hard, spitting out vehemently. He could see th swelling starting already. Sam had run off to the hous for the whiskey bottle.

"Carry her, Hugh. I'll hurry on to fix up a poultice, Martha said trying to keep her voice from trembling.

Hugh gathered her up in his arms. She held around h neck, pressing her face against him.

"Will it kill me, Brother? Do you think I'll die lik Sally Bates and old Jake Turner and all the others?"

"No!" Hugh fairly shouted the word. "You'll get fir over it! Think no fear now. I got some of the pizen ou anyway."

But even in the little time it took to bear her to th cabin, the leg had swollen to almost twice its size. H placed her on the settle where Martha could work we with the poulticing. Sam's hand was not steady as he he the cup of whiskey to her lips.

"There's naught like whiskey to droon the pizen," mumbled.

From being his usual casual, assertive self, he had come weak as water. Violet, the apple of his eye, his prir treasure—Violet, who had scarce known a sick day in her life, was now suffering danger, and beyond his power to defend her.

Martha made the poultice swiftly of herbs and crumbled corn pone mixed with milk, and wrapped it carefully around the swollen leg. The other symptoms, known, alas, too well to all of them, were now developing rapidly: the dripping perspiration, the hard vomiting. It was as though nature was trying desperately, blindly, to rid the body of its deadly burden.

"You might fetch Mrs. Brison, Hugh. She's good at doctoring," Martha told him quietly.

She had scarce turned about when Mrs. Brison came running, and Mrs. Kinkaid with her. Hugh's pale, set face disappeared again from the doorway.

"I'll be back in a few minutes," he said over his shoulder. "Call sharp if you want me."

Martha's eyes met Sam's. They knew where Hugh had gone.

Mrs. Brison bent over Violet, smoothing the heavy beads of perspiration from her forehead with a large cable hand.

"Just rest as quiet as you can, child," she adjured. "Wet cloth, Martha, an' we'll wipe off this sweat. Where was the varmint?"

"In the flax patch," Martha told her, relieved a little by speech. "I was ahead an' didn't hear the rattle even. I don't know yet just how it happened."

Violet spoke with difficulty.

"I stepped on it. Just for the once I didn't look—"

"Well, the damage is done now," Mrs. Kinkaid broke in with her strong, uncompromising voice. "There's not much to do but wait the outcome. It won't be long though afore you'll know—"

Martha spoke quickly, for Violet's face was piteous. She forced her tone to assurance even while her heart was lead in her breast.

"Her blood's pure and clean, for she's never ailed in her life, even if she is delicate made. She can throw off the poison. Now let's change the poultice."

Other neighbors had come running by now, many of them with remedies in their hands. Robert Hanna left the tavern to hurry with new advice.

"Get chestnut bark, Sam, quick as you can for wrappin' round the leg. Just the other day I heard a man say that works wonders. Bring some of the leaves with you too for boilin'. Then you pour the water over the wound. Keep up heart, girl. There's lots of folks livin' now that's been snake-bit."

Sam, who was suffering for the first time in his life with a very paralysis of fear, stumbled out, glad of a definite errand. Betsy Kinkaid passed him in the doorway, her hands filled with plaintain leaves. She had been running and her breath was quick.

"Mrs. Huffnagle sent these an' says to boil them in milk an' then for Violet to drink it up as fast as she can. That's what they did when their Jake was bit."

Violet from the depths of her pain, fright, and nausea moaned that she could take nothing more.

"If she was my child I'd give her a good dose of nanny

tea," a voice from the steps said. "There's nothing better
to drive out any kind of poison."

At the very mention, Violet sickened again. She raised
pleading eyes to her mother's face between her retchings.

"Not 'nanny tea,' Mother. I can't. I can't stomach it."

"Tush!" Mrs. Kinkaid said sharply. "You can do what
you have to. What signifies a bit of sheep dung if it's going to save your life!"

"We'll make it a last resort, then," Martha said grimly.
"I've never favored nanny tea much myself. Here comes
the men with the chestnut bark. We'll try that. There's
like to be virtue in it."

Mrs. Hanna knelt down with difficulty and looked at
the leg when Martha removed the poultice. It was an ugly
sight. The skin was stretched tightly over the puffy flesh.
The wound itself with its two bright scarlet spots was
angrily inflamed; around it discoloration had set in.

Mr. Hanna carefully wrapped the limb in the freshly
peeled bark, asking for a clout to hold it on. Martha gave
him the tail of a hunting shirt, clean-washed. He tied it
round gently. Meanwhile Mrs. Brison and Mrs. Kinkaid
were busy over the fire, the one with the milk and plantain, the other with the chestnut leaves. Betsy stood close
to her friend, smoothing her hair with an awkwardly affectionate hand, while the tears stood in her eyes.

"Oh, Vi, if it had only been me!" she kept repeating
over and over. "If it had only been me."

Violet could keep down only a small portion of the
milk and plantain, but when they poured the water from
the boiled chestnut leaves over the wound she said it felt

good. Even this admission was enough to lighten the wait
ing hearts a little.

"We'll keep it up, then," Martha said eagerly. "We'l
keep it up steady. There must be virtue in it."

Sam and Mr. Hanna were standing just outside th
door when they saw Hugh returning. He was dragging
behind him a long, inert scaly rope of sulphur and black

Sam gritted his teeth.

"I knowed he'd get it," he said. And then as Hug
came closer, "Where was it?"

"Among the flax. Not so far from where it struck her.

He flung it down. The men stood looking at it.

"By God, it's a big one," Sam said. "Must be five fee
the damned dirty varmint. I wisht I could kill it twic
over!" His voice sounded unnatural. "It's the first thin
that's ever gone wrong with Vi'let. She's never ailed sinc
she was a little'n, not even bad with the whoopin' coug
Never run a splinter in her foot even! I sort of though
nothin' would ever hurt her noways. That's why I'm"
his voice broke—"a leetle upsot now."

"There's many a one gets over it, Sam," Robert Hann
said. And then they all stood there, silent, looking dow
at the snake. Neither Hugh nor Sam would say th
thought in their hearts: *And there's many a one that die*

At last Hugh spoke with a terrible abruptness.

"Will I be cuttin' it up?" he asked.

Even to the men, hardened by lifelong experiences
which they could neither ask nor give quarter, there w
something revolting in the thought. Yet it could not

ut aside. They must face it, for it was one of the reputed
ures.

"That's what the Dutch do. I've heard them talkin',"
Hugh went on. "Two-inch pieces, you cut it. Then you
ut them one by one on the bite an' burn them up sharp
fterwards. There was a fellah at the tavern once said that
ured him."

"I've heard tell of it often," Mr. Hanna said slowly,
though I never took much stock in it. What think you,
am?"

Sam's face looked gaunt and bleak.

"Could she thole sight or touch of it, think you?" he
sked.

"We'd fix it so she wouldn't know. She's mebbe never
eard tell about this much. She'd just feel it was another
oultice."

"It might stink in the fire. There's a smell to them,"
Mr. Hanna said.

"I'll make a fire out here, like, where we can burn the
eces." Hugh's tone was harsh. He kept swallowing
ften. "This fellah swore it was what cured him, an' he
id they did it for his brother when he was bit by a cop-
erhead, an' it fettled him too. There's words you say
hile the flesh burns. I mind some of them."

"We don't dast not to try it," Sam said. "Go ahead,
ugh. I dunno what your mother'll say. She's again all
e Dutch charms. She'll mebbe think it's like witchcraft,
rnin' it up an' all. But, by God, we'll try everything."

Hugh drew his hunting knife from his belt, a dark look

on his face. He picked the snake up by the horny rattle:
and started toward the stable.

"I'll do it out there," he said.

Robert Hanna went back to the tavern saying he o
Mrs. Hanna would be looking in later. Sam reentered the
cabin, his heart dead in his breast. They had Violet or
her bed now, and this somehow seemed to increase the
seriousness of the situation. Her cheeks were flushed, and
her lips hot and parted. Her curls, damp with sweat, la
unnaturally away from her face. To Sam it was as though
death were already upon her. Betsy sat beside her, fan
ning her with a sunbonnet, and the women moved from
fire to bed with the hot decoction made of the chestnu
leaves. Sam signed to Martha, and they both went outside

"Oh, Sam," Martha whispered, "I'm fair beside m
with fear!"

"Hugh got the varmint," he said grimly.

"I supposed he would. But oh, what does that signif
now? The harm's done."

"He's cuttin' it up."

"Sam!"

"When it starts gettin' dark, so Vi'let won't see o
know, we'll try puttin' it on. Hugh's goin' to build a fir
outside. We'll burn it there."

"Sam!" Martha's stricken eyes had new fright in then
"That's evil work. That's like calling the devil to aid. I'
have none of it. It's a dark charm, and you know it."

"Dark or light, we're tryin' it."

"You're not! I won't have it, Sam. I tell you, I won

countenance it. We'll live or die in the fear of God. I'll have no league with Satan."

"We're tryin' it, Martha."

"Please, Sam. I *beg* you not. I *beseech* you, don't do it!" Her voice was piteous.

"We got to, Martha. It's cured some. We dasn't *not* try it."

She knew the iron will of the man beside her; she saw, too, the anguish in his eyes.

"When it comes dark, we'll start. You'll have naught to do with it."

"It might even bring—a curse."

"It'll be on Hugh an' me, then. We'll take the chancet."

She turned without another word and went back into the cabin. The other women were making ready to leave to attend to their own duties at home.

"The fever's catchin' up with her," Mrs. Kinkaid said abruptly. "She's gettin' out of her head."

"Keep a cool cloth on it," Mrs. Brison advised. "There's some go out of their heads awful easy. James does, for one. Just a little brash of any kind will send him crazy as a loon. We'll be in again right after supper, Martha."

Suddenly Violet sat up, her eyes very bright and staring.

"Don't let him shoot, Brother! Don't you see? It's caught in the crust! Come on, Betsy, let's run! It's the Irishman after us!"

Betsy gave a smothered cry and started for the door, her face white as death.

Her mother intercepted her with a stout arm, eyeing her disgustedly.

"Well if you ain't a posy! A body'd think you never heard anyone out of their head before! Get back there now an' sit with Violet while her mother makes the supper. What ails you anyway?"

"It just give me a startle," Betsy muttered.

Violet was sobbing now.

"I never saw a fawn like it. Don't let him shoot, Mother!"

"Yes, yes, child," Martha said soothingly. "We'll stop him. It's all right."

"It's the Irisher, the one with the dirty mouth. You've got to stop him!"

"He's gone, child. Don't be afraid."

"But he shot me in the leg," Violet moaned. "Oh, it's paining cruel now."

"Run off to the spring, Betsy, will you?" Martha begged. "And fetch some fresh water. This is warm, like. Yes, yes, now"—turning to Violet—"we'll fettle it. We'll stop the pain."

"Where's Brother?"

"He'll be here soon, now." Martha tried to keep out of her voice the deep revulsion that overcame her at thought of what Hugh was doing.

"You ask him," Violet begged earnestly, "if he smelled the wild grapes."

"My, she's clean off an' no mistake," Mrs. Brison said. "Well, it's just the pizen working. Don't fret too much, Martha. I'll be back as soon as I can."

Sam had come in and now sat down by Violet, smoothing her curls and talking constantly in a low voice. Martha could hear the steady stream of words, the tenderness and profanity mingled. It brought to her eyes a quick mist. Sam's grief and fear seemed somehow more impossible to bear than her own.

". . . an' don't you fret, my dawtie, we'll have you cured up yet, damn my soul to hell if we don't. . . . Aw, my pretty, just you lie quiet now, an' take it easy. By God, we'll cure you or know the reason why. . . . That's the girl now. . . ."

Hugh came in, his lips set. He got a gourdful of water and washed off his hands at the door; then he walked over to the bed and stood looking down on Violet's flushed face.

"She's been out of her head," Sam said. "She was askin' for you."

Violet opened her eyes suddenly, saw Hugh, and smiled faintly.

"Did you smell the wild grapes?" she asked.

Hugh swallowed hard. "I did, for a fact. They're powerful sweet just now."

"You won't go away?" she said.

"I'll be nigh-hand."

"You set here," Sam said getting up. "She mebbe wants you."

Hugh sat down, his heart beating terribly. Violet caught his hand.

"My head feels so big and heavy," she said, very low, "and I'm cruel scared. How long is it before you—know?"

"I know now," Hugh said.

"You're sure, Brother?"

"I'm sure."

She gave a little moan of relief and turned her head on the pillow. In a few minutes she was sleeping heavily.

Martha came to peer at her and wet the wound again.

"Thank God she's dropped off. She'll forget it for a little while anyway. You'd better have a bite of supper now, Hugh. It's late as it is."

It was a poor attempt at eating for all of them. When they were finished, Sam and Hugh looked at each other and then started for the door.

"You must stay here, one of you, while I milk," Martha said desperately.

"I'll wait, Mother," Hugh replied.

She caught up the wooden pail and signed for Sam to go with her.

"I'm feared I'll come on—on what Hugh's done," she told Sam. "Where is it?"

"In the stable, belike."

"Get it out of my sight then. Are you still set, Sam? Can naught move you?"

"We've got to try."

There were no more words between them. Martha held back while Sam entered the stable and brought out firkin. He carried it to the side of the cabin and started building a fire there.

When she had finished the milking, she hurried back at the doorway she paused. Violet still slept, and Hugh was sitting close to her, his hand touching her hair. H was looking down at her with all the passion of his love and his fear written full upon his unguarded face. He jumped up quickly now from his post, fearful lest he had betrayed himself. But Martha had not noticed. Her eyes had seen only Violet.

"She's never waked," he said, "but she keeps mutterin' in her sleep. About that fawn still that the Irisher shot."

"I know. She was at it this afternoon. It's always lain on her mind, some way. Fix up the fire, Hugh. We'll have to heat up the chestnut leaves again. Surely there must be virtue in them when she's able to sleep."

"It ain't too good a sign when they sleep, I've heard say."

Martha sighed. "It's the heaviness of the poison, maybe. Well, we've got to hope and pray, Hugh. Don't forget that."

He didn't reply. Through the door came the drifting smell of smoke, then Sam's figure, carrying the firkin.

"Is she still dozin'? Then let's get this over with. I'll put the pieces on her, Hugh, and you can grab them when they come off an' run to the fire with them. Keep out the way, Martha, if you don't want to look at it."

"There'll be folks coming now it's evening. I'm shamed to have them know." Her voice still besought.

Sam did not answer, only set the firkin down at the foot of the bed, and began to remove the bark from the wound. Martha went to the fireplace and leaned her tortured head on the rough log mantel. The smoke from the low fire rose to smart her eyes. She was glad, for now she could let the tears come. Behind her she could hear the movements of the men. Sam would be taking from the firkin one of the horrible pieces of serpent flesh and laying it on the bite. Martha cringed at the thought.

Then she heard Hugh's quick "Give it sharp here," and his leap from the doorstep.

She found she could not stay in the cabin. She ran out. But this was even worse. A strange stench was on the air, and the low burden of Hugh's voice above the fire repeating the words of the dark charm. Once Violet cried out, and Sam could be heard to speak soothingly.

"Just lie still now, dawtie. We're tryin' a new kind of poultice. Just shut your eyes an' doze off again."

Martha walked back and forth wringing her hands. How could any prayer of hers rise now to heaven above the smell of the burning varmint flesh and Hugh's broken mutterings?

She caught sight of Mrs. Brison and James leaving their cabin, and started hurriedly to head them off. She wanted no one to see Sam and Hugh at their work. But even as she went she could see Mrs. Brison sniffing the air with its strange sweet stench.

"You don't need to tell me," she said to Martha as they met. "I know what the men are at."

"It was no will of mine," Martha said weakly. "Oh, it's the last straw to have to bear this. But there was no stopping Sam."

James' face looked white.

"How is she?"

"My mother always said no good comes of a *burnin'*

charm," Mrs. Brison broke in, "but we'll just have to bide our time an' see what befalls."

"She's been asleep now this while," Martha said to James. "See if you can keep the other neighbors back till this is over. I can't a-bear them all talking about it."

"Trust Mary Kinkaid to smell it out," Mrs. Brison said. "We'll keep on the lookout, though, an' be round a bit later. Better take a good swig of whiskey yourself, Martha. You look clean washed out, an' that's a fact."

The waiting seemed an endless time to Martha, watching the smoke of the fire. She walked back and forth, back and forth on the edge of the forest.

"It's the cold flesh," she muttered once, shuddering. "Cold blood burns slow."

But at long last, when the early dew began to fall, it was over. Hugh had carried the empty firkin from the door, and was now scattering the hot ashes and pouring water over them for safety. Martha went back to the cabin to find Violet tossing, hot and restless, and Sam putting fresh bark back on the leg.

"I'm going to try a flaxseed poultice," she said quietly. "It's not so much for drawing but it always soothes. We've got to give her some easement, or the fever will keep going up."

"Aye, you might try it," Sam returned, laying his large, horny hand on Violet's hot head. Neither spoke of what had just been done.

There was a precious gourdful of flaxseed on the shelf, which Martha had saved from her spring planting for the emergencies of sties and bealings. She used most of it now lavishly, mixing it with water and stirring it over the fire until it was a thick, mushy mixture. Then, tearing another piece from the old hunting shirt, she spread it on, and laid the whole warm, gelatinous mass on the wound. She felt Violet relax under it.

"Does your leg pain you so now?" she asked.

Violet shook her head. "Not a sharp pain. It just *stoons*. This feels good on it."

"Rest yourself then, and doze off if you can. . . . Ach," she added as she passed the door, "I'm afraid there's a boon of folks on the way here. They all mean it kindly, but I'd fain have you sleep quiet now if I could."

Not even to Martha, with her intuitive wisdom, did it occur to ask the neighbors to stay out of the cabin. No matter what the kind or degree of illness on the frontier, people went and came freely. The one-roomed houses gave the invalid no chance for privacy or silence. Even during the processes of childbirth, no one thought it strange for many neighbors to be present. Often women near death from the dreaded childbed fever, or young persons sinking fast from the "putrid sore throat," or consumption, had their last hours stifled, especially on a winter's day, by the heavy air from many pairs of lungs and half as many weed-burning pipes!

They all meant it kindly, Martha thought again now as the cabin filled. Mrs. Brison and James were back and the Shaws, the Hannas, and Mrs. Huffnagle. Colonel Lochry himself came to the door to inquire, and all the young people filed in slowly and stood awkwardly about, watching Violet and putting in a remark now and then with more honesty than tact. They were all deeply fond of her and were now anxious and shaken by what had happened; but their lips were as awkward as their hands.

"They say June's the worst month to get bit. The varmints are fuller of pizen then," Hen Wilson said. "Course I don't rightly know. I jist hear them talkin'."

"Old Jake Turner's the last one round here to die from snake bite, I guess," Dave said thoughtfully.

"That bound boy at Miller's was after him."

"Well, I just meant here in Hannastown."

"There was a woman over by Fort Ligonier found a copperhead in her bed one night this spring. She had consumption anyway, so she didn't have no chancet."

"Copperhead bite's worse than a rattler's."

"No, it ain't. It's just that you die quicker iffen—you're goin' to—"

Violet sat up, wild-eyed.

"Brother says I'm not going to die! He says I'll get over it!"

"Of course!" Martha put in quickly, bringing a fresh cloth for her head. "Lie back now, and rest easy. Where's Betsy, I wonder? We miss her fanning. She fair wore out a sunbonnet at it this afternoon."

The words were barely out of her mouth when Mrs. Kinkaid, her black eyes flashing fire, and her hair loosened as though from running, appeared in the doorway. She paused for a second, catching her breath, paying no heed to Violet. Instead she raked the cabin shadows with her piercing look.

"Is Dave Shaw here?" she called sharply.

Dave, who had been standing a little behind the others, came forward at once.

"Why here I be, Mrs. Kinkaid. Do you want me?"

The civil question seemed to sting her to greater anger.

"Do I want you? You've a brass, young man, to ask me that as mealy-mouthed as though butter wouldn't melt on your tongue! You know right well why I want you. It's took me a long time, I must say, to see how things stood, but my eyes is opened now! You come along here before John gets a gun to you."

There was a terrible silence in the cabin as Dave stood there, his face full of blank distress.

"I don't know what you're talkin' about, but I'll come with you."

There was still silence within as the high, hard tones of Mrs. Kinkaid's voice came back to them all from the path.

"Stop askin' me why, like a fool. If anybody knows, I guess you oughta. Why didn't you marry her like a man in the first place? If there was a preacher near I'd have the thing fixed up tonight, I'll tell you that."

"My God," said Sam with his usual candor, "so that's what's been ailin' Betsy! An' Martha here said it was consumption startin'."

There was a slow movement among the young people toward the door. The boys looked uneasy and embarrassed while the girls drew together, red-faced and shy their eyes avoiding those of their elders. There were murmured good-byes and hopes for Violet's recovery, and in a few moments they were all gone. James got up a though to follow them, and then sat down again. Martha's eyes dwelt upon his thin, troubled face. In the ways of life, she was thinking, he's younger than our Hugh.

"Well, *there's* a pretty kettle of fish," Mrs. Brison was remarking. "I've suspicioned something was wrong, but I wasn't goin' to be the first to start a report."

"Och," Mrs. Huffnagle said, "Mary Kinkaid ought to save her wind. They're not the first young ones to get the start of the preacher."

"She hates anybody to beat her out, Mary Kinkaid does. She'll want Dave up in court yet, you mark me, just to prove she's got the best of him," Mrs. Hanna observed. "I must say I'm surprised at Dave though."

Hugh suddenly strode out, without a word. There was something in the set of his jaw and the angry fling of his shoulders that sent the conversation back to Violet. She had dozed off again, tossing feverishly. There were more suggestions as to cures: What about soft soap and maple sugar mixed? That would draw like beeswax and was softer on the flesh. And were they giving her enough whiskey? There was a man once at the tavern, Mrs. Hanna said, who had rubbed salt and gunpowder in the wound and been cured. But maybe for soothing down the fever the slippery elm was best.

In spite of all this, Martha sensed that the callers would not prolong their stay, and she was glad of it. Surely the quiet would be better for Violet. She hoped the child had not really taken in what had been said. And yet if she had heard nothing it must be because she was far gone in the fever.

The neighbors offered every help, and at last took their leave. Martha could feel in them all the pulsing of a double excitement. There would be for them that night in their cabins not only the danger of Violet's condition to discuss, there would be also the sudden startling news of poor Betsy and Dave. In a few minutes the whole town would know what had lain secret for months. The hidden was always brought to light at last. Just as the serpent danger had threatened them for long and then had struck them in the end. She wondered now whether on this night she would rather have Mary Kinkaid's trouble or her own. "God be thanked I haven't to choose," she thought.

Sam had followed the neighbors out and stood now on the road in the dark, feeling rather than seeing Hugh's approaching figure.

"Did you see Dave?" he asked in a low tone as the boy came up.

"I seen him," Hugh said shortly.

"I'm surprised at Dave bein' up to dirty tricks."

"He wasn't. He's as clear of it as I am. Hasn't he been worryin' about why Betsy acted queer for months back now? He ain't a fool. If—if anything had happened between them, he'd 'a' known what was wrong."

"Who is it, then?"

"Damned if I know. Mrs. Kinkaid's still on her high horse an' Mr. says naught but just sits holdin' his rifle. He's like to take a shot, he is."

"What's Betsy say?"

"That's the trouble. She just says it wasn't Dave, an'

she won't marry him noway. Dave's clean beside himself, you can see."

"By God, it's a mixtery. Well, we got plenty trouble our own selves the night."

"That we have," Hugh agreed heavily as they started back to the cabin.

No one went to bed though Martha urged the men to rest a little.

After the ritual of family prayers, in which Sam's mumblings choked and became completely inaudible, he sat watchful as a hawk near Violet's bed; Hugh stayed at the doorway as though keeping guard against invaders; Martha moved about, making new poultices, smoothing the hot pillow, and wetting the cloth on the sufferer's head.

Outside, the sultry darkness deepened. There was no breath of the wild grapes now upon the air; only the faint ineradicable odor of the dark fire. Upon them all lay the burden of the hours. Life or death must win soon.

Toward midnight it was apparent to them all that Violet had taken a turn for the worse. She lay on her back, her eyes half open, her lips thick and dry with fever, moaning dully with the pain. Even as Sam and Martha saw the change, the call of the whippoorwill came from the forest, clear and insistent, sounding the note of near death.

By two o'clock they had done again and again all they knew to do. Again and again Hugh had hurried to the spring for fresh cool water; but nothing would stop the burning. Martha repeated all her ministrations and then suddenly turned to her husband.

"Keep close watch on her. Keep the cloth wet on her head and the poultice moist. If there's any change, call out for me. If not, leave me be."

"Where are you goin'?"

"Outside."

There was that in her tone which precluded further questioning. Sam watched her with haunted eyes as she passed Hugh and was lost in the night.

She skirted the spot where the fire had been lest she tread on the ashes, but she kept on to the forest edge itself. Here in the thick darkness she fell upon her knees. If indeed a curse had followed the charm there was but one way to lift it. The continuous petitions of her heart which had been rising from the moment of the accident were not enough. She must wrestle now with the Spirit even as Jacob had done. In solitude, with all the strength of her whole body and soul she must tear through the veil that intervened between her and the throne of God. She must pour out prayers of blood.

There was no human ear to hear, so out of her agony she spoke aloud, straining, beseeching, imploring, compelling the very heavens to bend to her need.

Sometimes there was a dangerous rustle in the woods about her; once there sounded the distant call of a wolf, and once the far, faint, bloodcurdling cry of a panther. Martha heard nothing; only her own voice pouring out resistlessly the burden of intense supplication.

At last as the limit of her strength was reached she

sank back against the tree trunk, her breath in gasps, her limbs exhausted. When she opened her eyes again upon the world about her, she saw that the blackness of the night had gone; the new day was breaking. Slowly, very slowly when she could, she dragged herself up and moved out of the forest shadow into the clearing. The first misty wonder of the dawn lay upon the world. Dim pinks and blues and pale gold were alive now in the east where only the dead darkness had been before. She hurried through the half-light toward the cabin, weaving unsteadily as a drunken man does. As she passed where the fire had been she drew a long, quivering breath. There was no odor now; nothing but the fresh air of the morning.

It was as she neared the threshold that she was struck by a sudden thought that gave strength to her limbs. Though at a glance she saw Violet's state was no better she did not falter.

"Hugh," she said with sharp haste to the boy as he worked over the fire, "get on Ranger and ride as fast as you can for Dr. Shields. Don't let a blade of grass grow under your feet. Tell him it's life or death, and Martha Murray bids him come."

Hugh straightened in surprise.

"Dr. Shields?"

"Martha, you can't send for him. This is nayther a sickness nor a broken bone. What could he do for snake bite we haven't done?"

"Get you gone, Hugh, and hurry," was her only reply. "You had your way yesterday, Sam. I'll have mine now."

Hugh needed no urging. He grabbed his rifle and

started for the stable on the run. In a moment they heard him tearing past and on out the road, regardless of Ranger's stiff joint.

A calmness had settled upon Martha, which neither Violet's stiff swollen lips nor Sam's bloodshot eyes could break. She bent over her child, speaking reassuringly, doing once more for her all her brain could think of. Then she made the breakfast and ate of it, forcing the food upon Sam, whose face showed gray now in the early light.

"Where was you?" he asked irritably. "Goin' off like that. What if—if she'd died an' you not here? What was you up to?"

"I had to do what I had to do. Same as you, Sam," she said quietly.

It was scarce over three miles to the Shields place on the Loyalhanna, but Martha's heart forced her to admit many possible delays. What if Colonel Shields had gone early to the mill? What if he had been called off to the eastward to a sickness? What if Hugh was waylaid by Indians as he went?

But she remained calm and steady, waiting.

It was barely seven when the sound of flying hooves came to their ears. Hugh reached the cabin first with Dr. Shields on his big gray horse close behind him. The Colonel, who was both soldier and blacksmith as well as physician, flung himself off, and greeted Martha at the doorway.

"Well, Mistress Murray, here I am at your service. I don't often get called for snake bite, but I've got a few idees I'd like to try out. How's the girl by now?"

For answer Martha only pressed his hand and then pointed to the bed. Sam too, for once, was speechless.

The Colonel bent over Violet, laid his ear on her heart, held his hand a long moment on her forehead, and then, with Martha's help, removed the poultice from the swollen leg and peered at the wound.

"Highty-tighty," he said through his teeth. "The varmint spilt it all, and no mistake. When did it happen?"

"About four yesterday."

"Um-h'm."

He was never a man of many words. Now they could only watch him breathlessly, forbearing to question, as he drew from the pockets of his long, shabby black coat the instruments of his profession. The three small boxes containing them he placed carefully on the end of the table. He fingered them for a moment as though uncertain in his own mind which to open first. Then he settled upon a little homemade two-inch wooden box fastened with a leather whang. His big fingers seemed awkward as they opened it, then became suddenly knowing and expert as they drew forth a tiny lancet of fine-worked black iron.

"The tother one," he said, tapping the leather box, "is all brass and cost me a fair price; but I sort of favor this one. Made it myself in my own shop."

He rubbed his finger testingly over the small end sharpened to blade thinness.

"Now, Mrs. Murray," he went on, addressing Martha as though she were alone, "you've done all you can, I take it, with poultices, whiskey, and such."

"Oh, that we have, Colonel."

"Sucked the bite at the first?"

"Hugh did."

"Then I'm going to try the lancet. I knew an old squaw years ago—good old crittur, she was, too. She said she'd never lost a case of snake bite and she always cut the wound to let the corruption out. I did it once on a boy near us, and he got well. I'll want you to hold her steady while I'm at work."

When all was ready, Martha took her place at Violet's head, holding the girl's hot, listless hands tightly in her own.

The Colonel polished the blade of his lancet carefully on his pant leg and then gripping the swollen flesh firmly between his fingers he made the incision. Violet roused up, screaming as the blood gushed from the wound.

"There, now," said her mother. "There now, this'll make you well, child."

The doctor was busy with the old linen and the water Martha had set for him. When he had finished, he sat down and took the girl's hand in his.

"Could you sup up some milk?" he asked her.

"Not with plantain leaves," she moaned.

"Not with anything. Just good fresh milk from the cow."

She nodded.

"Fetch her a noggin, Mrs. Murray. Give her plenty Keep these other devil brews away from her. Keep the cut there washed and open. Let the corruption drain out We'll see how it works."

He replaced the little iron lancet in its box, fastened the whang, and then put all three boxes back into his big pocket.

"I'll ride over again this afternoon," he said briefly, and started out the door. "I've got a woman in bad trouble along the Loyalhanna, or I'd just stay on now."

Sam followed him out. "Has she a chance, think you?" he asked.

"Everybody's got a chance till the ground's on top of them," the Colonel responded. "She's in a bad way, Sam, but she's young; and the young uns have a way of pulling through. She's been hearty enough, has she, before?"

"Never ailed in her life."

"Good. It'll stand her in good stead now. Well, luck to ye, Sam. You'll soon know."

The big gray horse was soon out of sight. Sam, looking after him, recalled again that the Colonel was the one man in the Back Country who carried no rifle. He had once cured an Indian chief, and because of that he bore a charmed life in the forest.

Through the long morning, Sam and Hugh tried to work in the field as though nothing had happened. Every hour Hugh loped back to the cabin, his heart thundering within him, to see how Violet did. By noon, however, they all felt a lightened tension. The wound was draining, the fever was down, Violet had taken more milk and asked her mother to comb out her curls. Her eyes, freed from their delirium, were now at peace as she looked at them.

When Dr. Shields came back about four o'clock he confirmed their hopes.

"That's the only good thing about snake bite," he said jovially. "Don't keep you long in suspense. You're either dead or gettin' well afore you know it! Now, child, you're one of the lucky ones!"

He examined her again, his big fingers tender. The heart was steady now and slower, the fever still down, the swelling abated. The little black iron lancet, he said proudly, had done its work well. The darkness and the fear were over. Violet would live.

Hugh, out in the corn patch, heard the glad news from Sam. He straightened on his hoe, his whole body as sore as though it had been tied to the whipping post. His heart had been so stunned, so beaten down with dread, that it was slow now to respond to joy. He had never known such strain before. He kept saying over and over to himself wonderingly, "She'll live! She'll live!"

Was it the charm after all that had cured her? He didn't dare speak of it even to Sam; certainly not to Martha, and least of all, ever, to Violet herself. Belike it was the doctor at the last that had fettled her with the lancet. But who could rightly tell? At least he had done all he could. And he'd do it again even if he were accursed for it.

If there was nothing else now hanging over them, how happy this evening would be! With Violet propped up in bed, her eyes safe and shining again; with Father giving a tune on the fiddle, mebbe, to please her, and Mother at the doorway with her knitting and himself back in the shadow where he could look his heart full and none to see.

But there was all kinds of sorrow in the world, and you had to bear your friends' as well as your own, like. A message had come to him while he was alone in the field. One of the little Kinkaid boys had brought it.

"Dave wants you to meet him by the big oak on Gallows Hill round sundown."

So now he would soon know what Dave had to fight against. Belike there were some troubles sharper even than the varmint's fang.

June 30, 1778 I love the Lord because he hath heard my voice and my supplications. Because he hath inclined his ear unto me therefore will I call upon him as long as I live. The sorrows of death compassed me and the pains of hell gat hold upon me; I found trouble and sorrow. Then called I upon the name of the Lord, O Lord I beseech Thee deliver my soul. Gracious is the Lord and righteous, yea our God is merciful. The Lord preserveth the simple. I was brought low and he helped me. Return unto thy rest O my soul, for the Lord hath dealt bountifully with thee. For Thou hast delivered my soul from death, mine eyes from tears, and my feet from falling. Amen. Psalm 116, verses 1 to 8. Yesterday about three while weeding flax Violet was bit by a rattler. The danger is now past.

VIII

The Weasel

Hugh walked toward Gallows Hill slowly as a man moves toward evil tidings. His heart was heavy for Dave, though what disclosure he was now about to hear, he could not guess.

It was a warm evening. The clouds, weighted with moisture, hung low above the earth; the early dew was already upon the grass. Hugh did not walk along the road but, skirting the cabins, went by a path the boys often used up the hill. The great oak tree which crowned the eminence was not so distinguishable in summer, when all the woods were green, as in winter when its dark, majestic frame towered and spread itself against the whiteness of the snows; but the path ran straight enough toward it, and in a few minutes Hugh was standing beneath its wide tent in the deep silence. Dave had not yet arrived, so with his back to the tree and his rifle at rest he waited.

He smelled the rich forest earth below him and the thunder in the air overhead. Only his eyes moved to catch the flight of a corbie or the early shifting shadows on the leaves. The hush, the suspense which precedes both dawn and twilight was upon the earth.

Suddenly on the green moss a couple of yards distant a small brownish form appeared. It was a young rabbit which had emerged from the thick grass beyond and now moved hunching and limping across the open stretch. Hugh watched it at first with curiosity; then a strange emotion seized him, as though he were witnessing a hidden drama of nature too intimate for the eyes of men. He had seen rabbits a thousand times running from their foes like a streak of light! But here was something different. The rabbit was uttering tiny screams; every hair had risen on end and yet it was not running. It moved, yet scarcely moved in its misery. All at once Hugh perceived that it was because of an abject and paralyzing terror that the rabbit was crouching there; and with the perception he saw the cause. Swiftly, with a flying leap, a weasel had darted from the grass and fallen upon the pursued creature. Its short arms were about the rabbit's neck, its face thrust down into the soft fur of the nape. The rabbit, still uttering its tiny screams of despair, threw back its head as the sharp teeth of the weasel punctured the spine. Then Hugh knew with a sick certainty that the aggressor was drinking the warm blood. The muscles of its neck and sides swelled and contracted while its face continued buried in the hollow behind the rabbit's ears.

At last the head of the victim fell forward limply; the weasel, satisfied from his draught, straightened, became aware of Hugh, bared its teeth in an angry grimace, then flowed like reddish brown water into the high grasses again. On the green moss lay the small, inert bunch of brown and white fur.

"So that's the way they do it," Hugh muttered. "The damned dirty bloodsuckers!"

Only now did it occur to him that he might have shot the weasel. Had he himself been paralyzed by fear, by surprise, by loathing? Familiar as he was with the hard and cruel ways of nature, this that he had witnessed for the first time was somehow intolerable. He stood there, unmoving, his eyes fixed on the body of the rabbit.

Dave was late. Dusk was descending when he appeared, breathless from his hurried climb. The boys did not greet each other as they ordinarily would. Hugh waited for his friend's first word.

"Got to talk to you, Hugh."

"Go ahead."

"What've you been thinkin'?"

"Nothin'."

" 'Bout me, I mean."

"Nothin' at all. Knowed you was clear."

"It would have been better if it had been me."

"Any idee who?"

"That's why I had to talk to you where no one could hear whisper of it. I got Betsy by herself last night just for a minute. I made her tell."

There was a low, frightful huskiness in Dave's voice.

"It was that Irisher."

Hugh's throat contracted. He could not speak for the sudden rage.

"You mind the day last winter when the girls went racing on the crust?"

"I mind."

"It was late. The rest had gone in. Betsy thought she'd take one more run. The Irisher had been lurkin' round. He got her at the sugar hut. She said she couldn't fight. She was struck dead, like, overcome. . . . I don't rightly see —how it could be."

"It—could—be," Hugh said slowly.

"Just paralyzed like with fright, she said."

"It could be."

"You think so?"

"I've—known of the like."

A terrible sound like a sob came from Dave.

"She'll have naught more to do with me now. She's queer-lookin' in the eyes. She's done for an' distraught. I'm goin' to kill him, Hugh."

"Yes."

"I may be needin' you, some way."

"I'll be ready."

"He's still in Pittsburgh. I found out accidental from Joe Irvine. I'm settin' off for there tomorrow."

"Thinkin' of—doin' it there?"

"Wherever I get up with him."

There was a long silence. Then Hugh spoke with a cold, calculating bitterness.

"He was awful keen to go huntin'."

"That's what they said."

"Out round here now in the woods, there ain't as many people lookin' on as would be right in Pittsburgh. Gun go off awful easy in the woods."

They stood again silent.

"No jury'd hang you, but you might be jailed if you was caught."

"I got to do it."

"I would myself if it had been—"

"I'll think about that huntin' plan. Well, guess we'd better be gettin' home. You'll back me up if I call on you?"

"Just say the word."

"An' keep your mouth shut about everything."

"Need you be tellin' me?"

On the way back the boys spoke only twice. Once Dave mentioned Violet's recovery, and once Hugh said he had seen a weasel kill a young rabbit; but Dave made no reply to that.

When Hugh got to the cabin he found things indeed as he had pictured them. Violet from the propped pillows smiled at him; Martha looked weary but full of happiness; and Sam, one leg outstretched, was playing the fiddle. So he could rest. Hugh thought to himself, from other sadness, here in the present joy, for this one night at least.

For a week he awaited word from Dave. There were plenty of winks and side remarks about his absence. Even the Shaws themselves, Hugh knew, were as unaware of his real purpose as any of the others. Peggy had run in to tell them with innocent pleasure that Dave was off to Pittsburgh, and what could have put him up to that *she* couldn't say when he'd always traded here before, only she *hoped* he'd find a bit of something nice for her in the stores there.

"If it was Hugh now, he'd be sure to bring back a mirror or a ribband or something fine, wouldn't he, Violet?"

"Oh, that he would!" Violet echoed.

Her leg was almost back to normal size again; and while she was weak there was nothing to fear, and she was enjoying her first experience as a convalescent. The neighbors still looked in often, and a bit of white bread or an unusually light square of pone often found its way to her. Because of Martha's iron regulation she had heard nothing yet of Betsy's trouble.

Hugh had finished weeding the flax patch himself in the evenings without a word from anyone. He was always doing things like that, Martha thought, to save her and Violet. More gentle-like than Sam had ever been. A good lad, Hugh.

One afternoon as Martha was coming back from the spring Mrs. Brison stopped her.

"You've heard tell of the Negleys over by Ligonier, haven't you?"

"Yes," Martha replied. "She was a friend of poor Hannah MacRoberts."

"Well, they're all at the tavern now for the night on their way to Pittsburgh, so James tells me. I just thought it might be neighborlike if we'd give Mrs. Negley a look-in. She had a narrow escape from the Injuns, they say, just before her baby was born."

"Why, I'd be very pleased to go," Martha said, with a touch of inner excitement. "When supper's out of the way, I'll stop by for you."

She was glad of the mirror that evening, for she combed

her hair with the greatest care and rearranged her kerchief twice over. It would be nice to have a little visit with a strange woman and hear her news!

She and Mrs. Brison found Mrs. Negley seated in the back room of the tavern house, nursing her baby, with Mrs. Hanna beside her holding a tiny girl on her lap, while two more young children played on the floor. The women drew their chairs close and made the most of their common pleasure in being together. They admired the children and exchanged remedies for colic and croup.

"And if you ever have trouble with worms, Mrs. Negley, let me tell you that there's nothing does away with them quicker than the scrapings of a pewter spoon," Mrs. Hanna said. "Many's the one I've told that to, and they always thanked me later."

"You don't say!" Mrs. Negley exclaimed. "I never heard that. I'll try it, you may be sure. Though I've heard it said if this war keeps up we may have to give up all our spoons for bullets."

"Ach, I don't believe a word of it," Mrs. Brison put in. "Surely the government can make shift without taking the very spoons out of our mouths."

"I'd give up the few I have, willingly enough, if it would bring peace any quicker," Martha said thoughtfully.

"Robert says Congress has bungled and boggled things so, that's why it's so hard to get supplies. He says if we ever got a real attack here he doubts there'd be enough ammunition in the town to withstand it."

"It's scarce enough over at Fort Ligonier, I know that,"

Mrs. Negley said, settling the sleeping baby more comfortably on her arm.

She was a small plump woman with pretty features and a firm mouth. Her eyes were deep-set and bright.

"I hear you had a bad experience yourself," Martha said to her.

"Tell them," Mrs. Hanna urged her guest. "It's enough to make your hair stand up. Tell them the way you told it to me."

Mrs. Negley smiled and sat quiet a moment. Then she told her story.

"Well, you see Alex, my man, joined up with Captain Sam Moorhead's Rangers when the war broke out, and this last winter they were stationed at Ligonier. About March he heard tell that the Injuns were on the rampage not far from our farm, so he rode as fast as he could and got to us one afternoon. It was just a month before little Johnny here was born, and I was awful heavy on my feet. I was stirring a pot of mush when Alex opened the door like he was crazy. 'Get your things on, Mary Ann,' he says. 'Wrap up the children. Jake, get your gun and help me get out the sled. And hurry in the name of God,' he says. Jake's twelve and a good strong boy. He did well for his age that day."

"He's a fine lad and no mistake," said Mrs. Hanna. "He's out in the taproom now, listening to the men."

Mrs. Negley in her low quiet voice went on with her story.

"I grabbed what I could to wrap up the three little

ones, and we put them in the sled. 'You drive as fast as you can go to the fort,' Alex says to me, 'an' Jake and I'll ride behind and keep them off you.'

"After we'd gone a few miles Alex decided the Injuns might find the tracks of the sled and the horses and try to go round in front and ambush us, so he told Jake to ride close behind the sled and shoot as soon as he saw an Injun and he'd hide in the thicket and maybe kill a few as they came along the trail."

"Don't forget about your petticoat," Mrs. Hanna put in eagerly.

"After while the shots came thick and fast and the sled horse took fright and run the sled up a bank. The shaft hit a rock and split clean in two. I didn't know what I was doing hardly, but I jerked off my petticoat and bit a hole in it so it would tear and then I pulled it to pieces and mended the shaft with them. You do things some way when you have to."

"Aye. That you do," Martha echoed slowly.

"Alex kept fighting the Injuns back from the thicket. He fired as fast as his hands would work to make them believe there was more men there, and this held them off us. Then when dusk come on he rode over to us and told us we'd have to make a dash for the fort. It was just a mile, but the Injuns were close. He got off his horse and told Jake to, then he shot both beasts to keep the Injuns from getting them. He and Jake could do better on foot then."

She stopped a minute, and Mrs. Hanna filled in for her.

"The horse the boy was riding was one she had raised from a colt. It was a real pet, she said. They called it Prince."

Mrs. Negley sighed quietly.

"They fought off the savages a'most hand to hand then that last mile. But God was with us. We got safe to the fort, and none of us harmed."

The women exclaimed together. It had taken small imagination on their part to live the story themselves.

"And when did you go back home?"

"I never went back," Mrs. Negley said quietly. "I'd had too big a scare. I just said to Alex, 'I won't go back to that farm, ever, so there's the end of it,' and he knew I meant it. We just stayed on at the fort till now. We're going to get a place round Pittsburgh. I think I'll like it there."

The women were watching Mrs. Negley as though fascinated. Martha seemed more moved by this last statement than by all the rest of the story.

"If that isn't wonderful!" she said softly. "To make up your mind like that and stick to it. You're right to do it, but if it had been me I doubt I'd have had to go back to that farm and fend it all off again till Sam got ready to move. He'd have given me no rest, and then there would have been my conscience to prod me, for I wouldn't have been sure what I ought to do. But you're *right*, Mrs. Negley. I can see it for you plain as day, and I'm glad you had the backbone to stick up for yourself and your children."

Martha's cheeks were flushed as she spoke.

"Men are different," Mrs. Brison said. "My Tom wouldn't have budged an inch from sheer contrariness

James now, my son, is as easy as a woman. He always says there's no sense to run out lookin' for trouble like some of the fellahs do round here."

"Robert's got a will of his own," Mrs. Hanna said, "but he's a good man to me, I must say. When we have a clash there's no telling which of us will come out on top, for I've got a temper myself. Ach me! It takes a deal of handling to manage a man."

The women all agreed and, drawing imperceptibly closer, settled to more and more intimate conversation.

When Martha and Mrs. Brison said good night at last and started back to their cabins, there was a note of quiet elation in their voices.

"I declare it does a body good to talk to a strange woman and get her views on things," Mrs. Brison remarked.

"That it does. Going up there tonight put me in mind of the way my mother used to dress up and go out to call on her friends when I was a girl! I'm surely obliged to you for letting me know about Mrs. Negley."

"There's one thing you can say for Hannastown," Mrs. Brison remarked as they parted. "There's never any lack to the news brought in!"

"If only most of it wasn't bad," Martha replied.

Before the week was out the town was stirred by a piece of good news. Daniel Boone had escaped! The story of his captivity and its climax was brought by a passing messenger and was repeated with relish in every cabin of the village. Boone, it seemed, had been taken first to Chillicothe, the chief Shawnee town, and then on to Detroit where Hamilton and the other Englishmen treated him well and wanted to ransom him for a hundred pounds sterling. But the Indians had grown fond of him because of his good nature and his amazing skill, so they refused the ransom and brought him back to Chillicothe. Here he had been for two months, biding his time.

When he saw a large war party gathering, ready to march against Boonesborough, Boone could stand it no longer. No matter what the odds were against him he decided to try to escape and warn his friends if he could. One morning before sunrise he managed to give his guard the slip and then made a straight dash for it through the woods. He got to Boonesborough in four days, having had but one meal during the whole incredible journey of a hundred and sixty miles!

"There's a man fur you!" Sam kept saying complacently. "There's a man fit fur a frontier an' no mistake. Straight as a crow, he come through the wilderness. An Injun couldn't have come no straighter. Yessir, I don't take my hat off to many men, I tell ye, but I'll take it off to Dan'l Boone. Kind of wisht we'd gone on down to Kentucky when we was movin'. They say the soil down there's a little easier worked than here. Not so many damned oak trees."

Martha looked up in quick alarm.

"We're not movin' again, Sam, mind. If this place just quietens down, this is to be our home for good."

"All right, all right," Sam said irritably. "You needn't get riled. I just said I *wisht* we'd gone."

But Martha felt disturbed. As a matter of fact she had

had a hard week. The reaction from the fright and strain of Violet's danger had left her body limp. It was all she could do to get through the heavy daily chores. In addition to this the whole distressing story of Betsy's trouble preyed upon her mind by day and would not let her sleep at night. There was a sinister tinge to the situation. Here in the Back Country with parsons scarce and conventions few, it was not too unusual for a young couple to "get ahead of the preacher," as Mrs. Brison had bluntly put it. But this did not seem to be such a case. Even Mary Kinkaid herself had gradually toned down her allegations, to the point of admitting that she *might* be wrong about Dave; so the fact that Betsy's lips were sealed as to the identity of the real culprit left every young man of the neighborhood under suspicion. All the mothers of sons lay staring those nights at their cabin rafters, wondering. Through it all was the dark fact whispered now cautiously from lip to lip that Betsy acted queer-like. It wasn't just the shamed look, woman told woman; it was the wildness in her eye. Of course it might pass when she was farther along.

Dave's absence was talked over from every angle.

"If Mary Kinkaid was as hot-foot after him as she was at the start I'd think he'd just cleared out, so I would," Mrs. Brison told Martha at the spring. "Here he's been gone ten days. What would keep him that long, an' work lyin' here in the fields? His father's gulderin' at everybody in reach, he's so put out. Do you think Dave's guilty?"

"Our Hugh's very close to him, and he told Sam that

Dave's clear of it. He's been worried for months over the way Betsy's been acting. Could it have been any of the stragglers round here at court week, think you?"

"The dear knows. If James kept his eyes open an' talked to people he might find out some news. But he's always got his nose in a book, even court week. Oh, well Betsy's made her bed now; she'll have to lie in it."

On the evening of July 7th two men, Al Harbison and Joe White, trembling and spent, ran out of the north woods and all but fell upon the tavern porch where a group of men were sitting. For a time neither could speak. Then, helping each other, they told their terrible story. Captain Samuel Miller from Miller's Station just a mile or so below, who had been sent back from the Eighth to provide a stock of forage and provisions at Hannastown for the returning regiment, had set out that morning with nine men to bring grain from a farm on the Kiskiminetas River. Around noon they had been attacked by Indians and all killed but the two bearers of the tidings.

The men on the porch waited only to hear the facts; then with the fewest words they hurried to their cabins, Sam and Hugh among them.

"Just one of us can go," Hugh said. "You'd better let it be me, Father. If there would be heavy walkin' to be done, by any chancet, you couldn't manage with your knee." In every small foray against the Indians there lay upon them all the possibility of captivity.

"The dirty devils is likely fur enough by this time,' Sam growled. "All you can do, belike, is find the bodies.

All right, Hugh, you go ahead, an' see you shoot straight if you get a clip at them."

A small band of men on horseback set out that night with Joe White to guide them. By sunset of the next day, however, they were all back. They had seen no trace of the Indians. Not so much as a feather had been found to show that the redskins had ever been near the place. Only their ghastly work was left behind them. The bodies of Captain Miller and his seven men were found along the bank of a little run, scalped and stripped. The men had buried them where they lay and come home with hard faces.

"This war's got to be fought to a finish," Hugh said that night after he had given the family the brief report of their sad and fruitless quest. "This here country has got to be free, an' it's got to be swept clean of savages so's a man can go about his work in peace. That's what!"

"Why, Brother!" Violet said in surprise. "I never heard you talk so. . . . I never saw you look so—so *serious*."

"It's serious business, this," he said.

Martha, watching him, realized more than ever that Hugh was a man now. He had reached nineteen. His shoulders had broadened these last months; the slight boyish slouch had disappeared. His face had taken on the look of early maturity which the wilderness gave its sons. In the dark eyes there were new depths. She saw a difference now in the way he sat, the way he leaned against the doorway, the way he got up swiftly from his place at the table and went out. The strong lithe legs, the long, hard-muscled arms had in them the sinews of manhood.

"It won't be long now, I doubt, till he'll get him a wife," Martha was thinking. "He'll just take up with someone sudden, belike. Someone we never think of. It will be a big miss for us to lose him, though. What would we ever do without Hugh!"

On a hot, sultry evening, Dave turned up suddenly at the stable and, when Sam wasn't looking, hitched his thumb toward the big oak. Hugh understood and nodded.

The two friends met as before, silently. When they had glanced sharply about on all sides Dave lowered his voice and told his news.

"I found him one night in Semple's Tavern. I made up to him. He was half drunk, so it was easy. He's a dirty devil, an' I think he's been there on Tory business, though he's sorta workin' when he feels like it round Smith's store. He said he'd always wanted to come back to Hannastown. Said he found the huntin' good out here."

Dave's voice was edged steel.

"Bragged about shootin' the fawn an' says he wants to learn to shoot a wild turkey on the wing. I told him I'd teach him. I played friendly with him. He talked an awful lot. He's a vile bugger. Worse than we ever thought. He's had Violet in his eye too. Described her to me even."

"When's he comin'?"

"He's here now."

Hugh swore beneath his breath.

"I told him to start off toward the south woods early in the morning an' I'd meet him there."

"Want me to come?"

THE DAY MUST DAWN 283

"Thought you might. Don't need to if you don't want to."

"I'll be there. Little after sunup."

"I got to do this, Hugh."

"I know."

In the pearly mists of the morning, Hugh fed Ranger and Reddy and the sheep, and then, telling Martha he thought he might scare up a little game before breakfast, he took his rifle and struck off toward the woods on the south, to a spot where the boys before had discovered turkeys roosting.

It was a good month, this, to shoot turkeys, for the young cocks were now well grown, their legs and wings strong and their breast tufts showing, while the young hens were purring and leaping and plump for the pot. The old cocks, too, were likely to be assembling in spots ready for their summer flight. Yes, Hugh thought as he pressed into the forest, they could find some turkeys. But that was not what they had come out to hunt. His throat was dry, and his eyes hot. He had not slept well the night before. But the necessity of this, which Dave was about to do, was unquestioned in his mind—like his killing the rattlesnake.

He felt strange and shaken, though, when he saw Dave and the Irishman approaching. The Irishman's red, flabby face, the color of his bright coat, had a leering grin upon it. He was speaking of unseemly things as he approached with Dave, pale and grim beside him.

"I don't know what you're after thinkin' of to let a stranger now get ahead of ye among these little petticoats round here, but belave me you'll have to hurry to beat me, you will, for I'll be makin' the most of me opporchunities—"

He stopped short, seeing Hugh. His mouth curled in anger.

"So it's you again, is it, you blasted—"

He looked quickly from one youth's set face to the other, and the red began to fade from his own. Fear spread slowly over it.

"What's this you're up to, the two of ye? Is this a trick you're leadin' me on to? The soft words of ye, tellin' me you'd teach me a thing or two with the gun—"

Suddenly the pallor on his face grew ashen as neither boy spoke or altered the still hatred of his countenance.

"Look ye now," he babbled, "I'm meanin' no harm to ye. I'd never have come back at all if this fellow here hadn't— Look ye, *what are you doin' there?*"

The last words were a scream, for Dave had slowly raised his rifle.

"Run, you damned weasel," he said through his teeth, "or shoot if you can. I'll give you that much chance. But you ruined my girl, an' you're goin' to pay for it."

The Irishman was shaking, paralyzed apparently with his terror (even, Hugh thought while he too kept him covered, as Betsy herself must have been). He tried to raise his own gun, failed, then casting it from him, still with strange, womanish screams, he started to run through the woods. Once he fell headlong over a spreading root, once he paused as though winded, then he went on again, his short legs wavering but still carrying him.

Hugh, tense, his finger strong upon the trigger, watched as he got farther and farther off between the trees. At one point he was lost to sight! What did Dave mean? Had he weakened? Had he changed his mind? He, himself, could do it with a right good conscience, but it was Dave's job.

Suddenly there was far ahead a last glimpse of the fleeing form. Dave's rifle blazed, and the red coat dropped.

The two boys slowly put down their guns. Their eyes met for the first time that morning.

"Good shot," Hugh said hoarsely.

They started back through the woods. After a dozen yards Hugh stopped.

"What about the gun?"

"Leave it lay. We want none of it."

They went on.

In a small open space Hugh stopped again, sighted carefully and brought down two wild turkeys from the top of a tall tree. The one was only winged so when it reached the ground it ran off with the dangling, straggling gait of its kind but still with a speed which could outstrip any other creature of the forest. The other turkey, however, was dead. Hugh went over to it, picked it up carelessly by its legs, and walked on.

At the road the two parted, still in silence. Dave went slowly toward the Shaw cabin, and Hugh, carrying the turkey, entered his own.

July 20, 1778 A strange like thing has happened and the town is full of it. There's been rain all day to keep the men from the fields so Sam's up to the tavern now with the rest to talk it over. That Irishman the one that shot the fawn in the crust that upset Violet so last winter, was found in the south woods this morning with a bullet in him. Dead a week or so the men say. Young Jake Huffnagle found the body. It seems he'd been in Pittsburgh ever since last February till the night of the tenth he turned up again at the tavern. The next day early he left and Mr. Hanna just thought he'd skipped his lodging bill for it seems he was a poor sort. But it's thought now he was trying for game in the woods maybe in the early morning for a gun was found some distance back. A stray Indian got him belike though he wasn't scalped. Poor Captain Miller. It's made me think again of him. I wish I could get over to see Mrs. Miller. I believe I always felt a little envious of her fine big house. Poor soul it won't bring her husband back to her now. I must try earnestly to be content with my own lot. To envy another might be to bring sorrow upon them. God help me to keep a pure heart and a righteous mind. One thing about this Irishman's death is that it shows no one should venture even a little way into the woods alone. The girls get careless with all my telling. But I'm going to see to it now. There's danger on every hand. Will we ever know the ways of peace and quietness? We are in God's hand though and must bide his time.

James Brison here last evening. Sat on step with Violet. When he talks I could think it was my father. He speaks and acts so like a gentleman. Repeated passages from Shakespeare. Violet appeared to enjoy it greatly. Just she and I here as Hugh was off somewhere with Dave and Sam at the tavern. Hugh moody of late. Glad of J. B.'s call last night for Violet has been brooding over Betsy's plight ever since she knew. I told her myself at the last. Poor Betsy seems distraught especially these last days. Violet trying to comfort her but there's small comfort in a case like hers. I can't riddle it out but it keeps waking me up nights. Hugh and Dave aren't like they used to be either. Joking and chaffing. They both act so quiet like lately. It sets me wondering. I've tried to talk to Sam but he won't listen. What if it was Violet in trouble I said, what then? I'd kill any man that laid evil finger on her, he said. And he would, soon enough. But he won't bother to think on Betsy. There's good news from the east. All the British have evacuated Philadelphia and our troops have moved in. General Benedict Arnold is in charge and the report is he is courting Peggy Shippen, the daughter of Edw. Shippen, one of Gov. Penn's Councilors. They say she's the beauty of the town and even the British officers all used to toast her. Oh if I could but put Violet in her place the belle of Philadelphia and a fine General in love with her! She could grace it all. And somehow it fair embitters me to think of all the happiness in store for ones like this Shippen girl and Violet as beautiful I'd take oath and as sweet behaved as ever girl could be and yet with no chance here in this awful wilderness. Oh what am I writing and who am I to wish her in another's place. That's like covetousness again and may God forgive me. But I am cheered a little about the future. J. B. stayed later than usual last night. I kept back in the cabin leaving them to themselves. Of course I could still hear all. This is the second time this week he's been here. Rain letting up now a little. Heavy thunder all afternoon and terrible sharp lightning. Watch back under bed. The poor beast can't thole a storm.

IX

The Return of the Eighth

On both its long marches across the state of Pennsylvania, the famous Eighth was unfortunate in having to endure all the pains of untoward physical elements. On its way east from Kittanning to Philadelphia it had traveled through the snows of a bitter winter; on its way back from Valley Forge to Fort Pitt it journeyed through a scorching midsummer heat.

The end of the first week of July found the men wearily entering the outskirts of Carlisle under the command of Colonel Brodhead. General McIntosh, the new Commander for Pittsburgh, was awaiting them there, ready, as they all supposed, to conduct them on west after a brief rest.

Instead, the General met them with one of the most tragic stories in the annals of pioneering. A few days before there had taken place the infamous "Wyoming Massacre," and the Eighth, being the only regiment then near the spot, was detailed to go at once up the North branch of the Susquehanna to where only a few days before a large band of Tories and Iroquois Indians from central New York had burst upon the inhabitants of the beautiful Wyoming Valley and killed and tortured without mercy.

It was more than a month before the regiment, after doing what it could to reestablish the few families left in the stricken settlement, was free to turn again toward home. Then once more it took up its slow march over the mountains. It was two weeks getting as far as Bedford; it was over a week more crossing the Laurel and Chestnut ridges, until on a late afternoon in September, footsore and weary, the men entered Hannastown.

It was poor, indentured Liz Smith that caught the first glimpse of them. She had been gathering boneset along the road edge to the east of town. She gave a wild yell which echoed along the dusty street.

"The rigiment's a-comin'! The rigiment's a-comin'! I seen the sodgers!"

Women dropped their iron skillets, girls stopped their spinning, men and boys let fall their implements or set down their rifles. The word was passed like wildfire. Everyone thronged into the road, peering along the way Liz was pointing.

There they came! The men of the Eighth at last. Trying to step up smartly now in spite of lame knees and blistered feet, to make a good showing for the town's welcome. On they came with Sam Craig carrying the flag, the officers riding ahead, dressed in their Continental blue, and the men in the hunting shirts, long leggings and broad-brimmed, looped-up hats they had received back east. These gave them that appearance of military strangeness which caught the fancy of the waiting citizens and threw an added zest into their shouts.

"Hooray! Hooray for the Eighth! Welcome back! Welcome to Hannastown!"

As the lines reached the middle of town, personal cries were raised above the general confusion.

"Michael!" called Mrs. Huffnagle with her hands outstretched. "Oh, Mike, are you safe back!"

"There's Hen! Look, next the tall fellow there. *Henry!*"

"Ezry! Ezry! God be praised, there's Ezry. He never wrote once. I thought him dead."

"There's Matthew Jack! Hey—Matthew! Nancy's as pretty as ever. Still waitin' for you!"

And Martha herself called out to Captain Brownlee as he passed:

"They're all well at home, Captain. Welcome back!"

So ran the happy shouts.

Before the tavern the order to fall out was given, and the local soldiers greeted their families and old friends. But here as along all the line of their march across Westmoreland there was grief mingled with the joy. There were those in the village who turned quietly back to their houses, lips set, eyes tortured. For nearly three hundred of the brave frontiersmen who had gone east to the aid of Washington did not return to their home borderland.

General McIntosh, a handsome, strong-featured, benevolent-looking Scot, and Colonel Brodhead, shorter, heavier, and keener of eye, entered the tavern and were welcomed by Robert Hanna in the privacy of the court room and served there to the best the house afforded;

while the common soldiery swarmed into the main tap-room and yelled lustily for Monongahela rye!

The men, under Colonel Brodhead, would stay for a few days' rest at Hannastown, for it was General McIntosh's wish to proceed to Fort Pitt alone and look over the situation there before the regiment arrived. Meanwhile the townspeople were asked to allow as many soldiers as possible to be quartered among them. The weather had grown frosty at night, and the men's summer equipment was light, so they would dispose themselves about in the stables and the cabins or wherever a bit of shelter was available. Behind the tavern a rough commissary department was set up, drawing upon the provisions for both men and horses that Captain Miller had paid his life to secure.

In every house, now, there was bustle and anticipation. Violet, her cheeks flushed and her eyes bright with excitement, stopped her work to comb her curls carefully before the mirror.

"Oh, I hope we get some real nice soldiers here," she remarked.

"You do, Sister?" Hugh asked in an odd voice.

"Why, yes. That I do. They'll have tales enough to tell, no fears, and we can coax them to sit up late telling them. Mother says we can sleep a dozen easy on the floor here and the cockloft, and more too in the stable. Oh, they'll all find places right enough. Aren't you excited, Brother?"

"Not special," Hugh replied. Martha busy at the fireplace turned suddenly and looked at him. He was watching Violet, whose eyes were still upon the mirror, with an

expression so strange, so intense that Martha's heart stood
still in surprise.

Then she shook herself with annoyance.

"I'm full of fancies and vapors, that's what's wrong,
and I'm always imagining things where Violet's con-
cerned."

"Give me a hand here, Hugh," she spoke aloud, almost
sharply. "I want these tubs set over close to the wall. Set
the churn back there and the extra bench. We'll make all
the space we can here, and then you can move things
round in the cockloft yourself, can't you? Come, Violet,
fetch more water right away. We want things clean and
tidy."

"I'll fetch the water," Hugh said, "an' do this when I
get back. There'll be a crowd at the spring."

"But that's why I want to go," Violet said eagerly.
"What's to hinder? Peggy and I'll go together." She
snatched the pails.

Hugh reached to take them from her, but Violet held
fast.

"Give them me, Sister," he said firmly. "The stockade's no place for you just now."

"Maybe Hugh's right, Violet," Martha put in. "I never
thought. The town's so full, and there'll be all sorts. I always keep thinking every soldier's a gentleman some
way."

"But I want to go," Violet persisted, holding on tightly.
"What's got into you, Hugh? When would we ever be
safe if it wasn't with the regiment here? Let go, I say!"

But Hugh did not let go. He loosed Violet's fingers by

the force of his own strong ones, took the pails and wer
toward the door.

The red slowly rose in Violet's cheeks until they wer
scarlet. Her anger was a rare thing. Indeed, her mothe
had never before seen her in a passion.

"You're mean, Brother! Oh, you're *mean* to me."

Hugh did not look back, and Violet burst into tear

"Why, my! Why, my!" Martha kept repeating. "Th
is no way to take on, Violet. Hugh meant it well. He
always watching over you."

"He hurt my fingers," Violet stormed, "and he didn
have to be so sour and so set about it. I'm just *mad* at hir
And I *did* want to go to the spring. Am I not to set foc
out of the house, then? Why, Mother, you *know* we'r
twice as safe with the soldiers here. Brother's just *cros*
that's what."

"He must have his reasons. Now you calm yoursel
child, and get on with your work. Think shame if som
one would come in and catch you crying."

When Hugh came back with the water he looked anx
iously at Violet, but she paid no heed to him. Her cheek
were still red, and her normally smiling lips set in
straight line. She was quiet at supper, too, her head ver
high, her eyes elaborately avoiding Hugh's.

"We're gettin' ten," Sam announced. "Poor feller
They all seem tickled to get inside a house again. Wel
we ought to hear some good yarns the night. Can you st
up a pot of mulled cider, think you, Martha? We'd ougl
to have something to wet their whistles fur them, an' ou
whiskey wouldn't be a patch fur that many."

"I just thought of that. We'll make them as welcome as we can, for they've been through plenty, poor lads."

"What's wrong with you, Vi'let?" Sam said suddenly. "You look like your nose'd touch the rafters most any minute. An' Hugh, here, glowerin' like a hoot owl. Have you had a fight, or somethin'?"

Sam spoke jocularly, quite secure in the belief that nothing could ever upset the steady devotion of his "young uns."

"Nothing's wrong," said Violet crisply. "I'm going to help Mother with the cider."

The guests arrived during the evening, some hesitant, some bold enough. The fire was bright, the candles were lit, and the door closed against the sharp September chill. Six of the men were in their thirties or forties with wives and families awaiting them over by Kittanning. Four of them were in their early twenties, and two of these were unattached and as dashing and handsome as maid could wish. John, the blond, hailed from the Redstone settlement, and Bill from Sewickley Creek. It was evident in a moment that they had eyes for Violet alone and were blessing the fate that had quartered them here.

Violet, on her part, began to play a new role as though she had been born to it. Martha, watching, was dumbounded, but, after the manner of all mothers everywhere, gratified. With the boys of Hannastown, and with James, too, Violet had always been serene, friendly, gay. But with these strangers whose eyes languished upon her, who vied with each other as to who would pick up her ball of yarn or reply to her questions, Violet drew sudden

knowledge from the bosom of Eve. She raised her dar
lashes slowly and lowered them with cruelly telling effec
She tapped Bill's fingers playfully with her knitting need
and made a small coy mouth at John. She hung upo
their words one minute, her blue eyes shining, and the
laughed them to scorn the next. In short, no city-bre
coquette could have wrought more deliberate havoc wit
her charms than did Violet that night in the log cabir

In the midst of her startled admiration Martha hap
pened to glance past the older men to where Hugh stoo
with his back to the far wall. He was watching Violet wit
such bitter stress on his dark face that Martha all bu
cried out. For his hidden thoughts were open now in thi
moment; his carefully guarded secret was written ther
in lines of jealousy and anger.

Hugh's in love with her!

The words seemed to rise from Martha's heart to strar
gle her. All at once the room was suffocating, and th
faces of the men seated on the benches or the floor blurre
before her. It was like a nausea, this feeling of shock-
almost as though Hugh were her born son who in hi
thoughts had desecrated his own sister.

Hugh loves Violet.

It was because of this, then, that he showed no interes
in any of the other girls of the village; that he neve
paired off like the other lads to walk to the spring or t
stand chaffing at the tavern or the store. She had though
him merely slow to develop, too young in his heart fo
the strength and stature of his body. And all the whil
great fires had been burning within him as the look o

his face now testified. No matter how much she might try, he could not construe those set lines of pain to be a brother's solicitude. They were the outward evidence of a man's strong love.

And what was to be done about it? While dangers for Violet pressed her on every side, this was indeed the greatest. For Hugh was as much a son of the wilderness as Sam himself, born to conquer and subdue the new country, to live by the skill of his rifle and the strength of his arm; to go before and fight the savages and break up the hard ground for those who might some day come after. This was Hugh. And because of this his love must never touch Violet. For even as Martha now knew Hugh's secret, she felt sure that she knew James' also. There had been lately a quickened expression on his thin, ascetic face, a light in his eye as he looked upon Violet. His calls at the cabin were becoming more and more frequent. She knew now for a certainty also that James' dream was to go back east when the times grew more settled. She never missed a chance to draw him out on this subject and to encourage him. It seemed as though all things pointed to the fulfillment of her plan. And now, this discovery that chilled her heart with fear!

Hugh! Did Violet guess?

Martha rose suddenly and went over to the iron pot where the cider was heating.

"Hugh?" she called.

"Yes, Mother."

With the word on his lips, her own heart eased a little. Something deeply intuitive told her that Hugh's secret

was still unavowed, and would remain so, perhaps forever. A new bond suddenly linked her to him, stronger
even than the love between them. It was their common
love for Violet. She knew she could count upon this as
she would rely upon Hugh's strength to defend them in
danger. She would find a way to show him that they must
both think only of Violet's good. Poor lad! Oh, poor lad!
Would life ever show mercy to them all? Must pain be
added to pain?

"We'll dish up the cider now, Hugh, if you'll give me
a hand with it."

Even under the influence of the hot spiced drink, the
guests proved a disappointment in one respect that night.
The anticipated stories of their experiences back east
were not forthcoming. Sam grew almost irritable as he
kept plying them with questions. But the men apparently
didn't want to talk war. Yes, it had been a hard trip there
and back. Sure, the Rifle Corps had done some nice work.
Pretty good shootin' if they did say it. Yes, Valley Forge
was pretty bad.

What they did tell in full detail was how Bob Bradley
got butted on the behind by an old billygoat over at Bedford and even the Gineral himself laughed, for Bob got
up cursing to beat Satan and said hell, that's the worst
crack he'd got in this war yet. Bill and John told how
they'd tamed a rat in their cabin back in Valley Forge.
You'd hardly believe it, but they'd done it. Even had it
doing tricks at the last. They'd hated to leave it behind
but some of the other fellows plead so for it. A big gray
rat it was with long whiskers. They'd named it *Tony* for

Anthony Wayne, and damned if the crittur didn't learn to come for it! You'd hardly credit it! The talk drifted into an animated discussion of rats in general, and even Sam finally gave up his questioning.

When Martha suggested that they all sing the new war song before they broke up for the night, the men gave each other half amused, half ashamed covert glances while Sam was getting his fiddle.

"We mebbe don't know the words so well that you sing to it," Bill said at last.

"Oh, do you have other words? Please sing them for us," Violet said innocently.

John's face was red with embarrassment.

"No, ma'am, I guess we'd better try the reg'lar verses."

There was a roar of laughter from the men as they suddenly in their shared looks were lost in their own soldiers' world again.

Sam swung into the tune, and they all finally raised their voices:

> "Father an' I went down to camp,
>   Along with Cap'n Goodwin . . ."

The room had grown hot, so Martha opened the door as they sang, and stood for a moment looking over the village. All the cabins were lighted, and from others came bursts of the same rollicking air:

> "Yankee Doodle, keep it up,
>   Yankee Doodle, dandy,
> Mind the music and the step,
>   And with the girls be handy."

She drew a long sigh and went back to spread blankets
on the floor and supervise the sleeping arrangements in
the cockloft and the stable.

Long after everything was quiet inside, drifting waves
of song, sporadic yells, and shouts of distant laughter
broke the low steady chorus of crickets in the deep grass
beside the door. Even these had changed to silence, however, before Martha's troubled heart found rest in sleep.

The next day Hugh had a long talk with Dave, after
which they went together to Colonel Brodhead. When
Hugh came back to the cabin he told the family quietly
of his plan.

"I'm thinkin' of goin' with the regiment for the winter
at least. General McIntosh is aimin' to get up an expedition right away to try to take Detroit. He needs extry men
for it, for of course a lot of the reg'lars will have to stay
round Fort Pitt. Dave wants to go, an' if you've no objec-
tions I'd like to sign up till spring. I could be back by
early plowin' time."

Sam agreed at once. Martha was anxious at the thought
but wondered wretchedly if this was the ordering of Providence to prevent the thing she had just begun to fear.
She knew, with a faint sense of relief, that nothing she
could say or leave unsaid would hold Hugh back.

Violet, meanwhile, was irritable and unlike herself.
John had fought it out privately with Bill, apparently,
for he now assumed a clear field, plying the girl with
small attentions and following her as long as she was in
sight with lovelorn eyes. There was something faintly

ludicrous in his mooning orbs. Hugh made no effort to conceal his scorn.

The evening before the regiment left, he picked up the wooden buckets to go to the spring.

"Want to come along, Sister?" he asked carelessly.

"Oh," Violet replied with attempted sarcasm, "so I can really go to the spring, can I?"

But she moved toward the doorway at once and started off with him.

When they had left the cabin behind Hugh hesitated. "We might go along the lower path," he suggested.

"Yes, we might."

The lower path struck off toward the fields and then kept close by the creek. They followed it slowly, conscious of the rich autumn fragrance of the earth and the first faint glory on bush and tree. Away over Gallows Hill the sunset lay in smoky red.

"I've sensed you were put out at me," Hugh began with difficulty, "but I couldn't rightly explain about the spring. I had a fear some way to see you go that first night."

He stopped, and Violet saw with surprise that his face was working with emotion.

"There's danger in these times for a girl. . . . I can't explain. Only *promise me* you won't go racing on the crust while I'm gone this winter!"

The explosive force of his voice along with the strangeness of his request made Violet look at him in amazement.

"Not go—racing?" she echoed.

"Only with a big crowd," he repeated, his voice stil
thick. "Never off by yourself like Betsy, even for a min
ute—"

He caught himself up sharply, and Violet stopped dead
in her tracks.

"Like Betsy!"

Hugh's face was scarlet. He swallowed painfully, and
was dumb.

"Like Betsy."

With sudden terror she saw again the scene on the
crust. She felt the weight on her heart, the sorrow, th
prescience. She saw the coarse, cruel face of the stranger
and Betsy's blithe rosy one near her own. There had been
tragedy bound up with that day, then, more than th
death of the fawn—more than the sharp strangeness which
had come between herself and Brother that night.

"It was the Irishman."

She hardly spoke the words, but Hugh heard them. I
shamed them both to be sharing the knowledge, but the
had gone too far now to go back. Hugh nodded, his hea
averted.

The whole weight of life fell upon them, and mor
also. A blacker shadow covered them, the blackness c
the shadow of Cain.

Violet's eyes were heavy with horror.

"It wasn't Injuns, then." Her lips were stiff on th
whisper. "It was the morning you went out for the wil
turkey. I saw you and Dave coming out of the wood
never speaking, never looking at each other. Was it—wa
it—your shot?"

Hugh shook his head. Then in a sort of frenzy he dropped the pails and caught her arms.

"Promise as there's a God in heaven you'll never say word of this to anyone! Swear by God himself you'll keep it. I don't know how I come to give it away to you like this. Mind it's serious enough. I'll be torturin' myself now for fear—"

"I swear it, Brother. It'll be a fell load to carry, but you may be sure I'll bear it. You know you can trust me."

"It's not as if it was all my own secret, mind."

"I know. Oh, poor Dave! It's awful for him. He was in love with Betsy, and she with him. It's so cruel, what's come to them."

"Cruel enough."

"Why do things have to happen like this?"

"There's none to tell us why."

Then, out of a silence, Hugh spoke, pausing between the words.

"There's something else I've got to ask, and I want you to tell me true. Do you—are you thinkin' of takin' up with this John chap?"

Violet gave him a level look.

"I don't care two pins for him. I only acted like I did to spite you for not letting me go to the spring. I've never seen anyone I liked as well as I do you—Brother. You ought to know that yourself."

"Will you kiss me good-bye, then?"

"What if someone would see."

"Back of this tree. We're hid from the town. There's only the woods below."

"If we're hid . . ."

He had her close in his arms, their lips clinging.

Hugh felt her tears against his cheek.

"If you're just kept safe, if no harm befalls you. It'll be long this time to wait, so much longer than the Squaw Campaign. *Must* you go, Brother?"

His young face, warm with its love, steeled to resolution again.

"Somebody's got to go. It might as well be me. I've been thinkin' a lot lately about things. The war's got to be fought for freedom, an' the savages cleared out. The country's got to be made safe. I want it safe for *you*, mind. So I must be doin' my part."

She raised her head.

"I'll keep a strong heart then, never fear. I'll be thinking of you every day, while I knit and spin or mind the cooking. Every hour I'll be wishing you safe and praying naught of harm will touch you. You'll come back."

They kissed again in sweet wonder, and then slowly went on to the spring.

The next morning the Eighth marched out of Hannastown to complete the last thirty miles of its long journey. With it marched Dave and Hugh. As long as there was sign of them on the road, before the great hill hid them from sight, the people of the village called and waved and called again; then, with an empty feeling in their hearts, they all turned to their several occupations—old Ezra to his blacksmith shop, Robert Hanna to his tavern, the women to their cabins, the other men to the fields. The Eighth had come, had tarried, and now had passed on in way again. Would the security they had dreamed of come with it? Time alone would tell.

Martha questioned Violet gently during the morning.

"Did John say anything about coming back some time?"

"Oh, yes. He's a blather."

"You don't—you don't set special store by him, then?"

"Him?" Violet replied as though the subject were already dismissed from her mind. "I'd care naught if I ever set eye on him again."

Martha drew what comfort she could from the statement.

During the next weeks news came back steadily from Pittsburgh. When Colonel Brodhead and his men had arrived there on September 10th, they had found the chiefs and the warriors of the Delaware Indians already camped along the shore of the Allegheny, waiting to confer with the new officers about a treaty. Of all the Indian tribes, the Delawares were the only ones who had maintained a neutrality between the Americans and the British. They had made their first treaty years ago with William Penn under the great elm at Shackamaxon and had ever since, as a tribe, been generally friendly to the white men. In addition to this, their head sachem, White Eyes, one of nature's own noblemen, had from the first been firm in his allegiance to the American cause. He believed in the struggle for liberty with a peculiar sympathy and understanding.

The council had begun at once with General McIntosh and his colonels and staff officers in what new uniforms they could muster, presiding; while White Eyes, Killbuck, and Captain Pipe, painted, feathered, and beaded in their best, represented their people with a brightly painted, gayly blanketed band of warriors to support them.

After assurance of friendship had been given and belts of wampum presented and accepted, General McIntosh's new project was explained to the Indians. This was the campaign against Detroit. While the government leaders back east who were urging it did not in the least realize the dangers involved in this undertaking, the Delawares understood only too well. They knew that it meant a march of three hundred miles through a wilderness where most of the Indians were hostile to the American cause; it meant carrying an army far from its base of supplies at Fort Pitt when the very base itself was precarious; it meant, most pertinently of all, that the Americans must have the permission of the Delawares for a free passage through their territory.

But White Eyes was undaunted. He promised that the army might pass in safety through the Delaware land and even be aided by a band of their own warriors. Pledges on both sides were given and taken. On September 17th the articles of confederation between the United States and the Delaware Indians were solemnly signed in triplicate, one copy for Congress, one for the Delawares and one for General McIntosh.

By October 1st the new army, consisting of thirteen hundred men, five hundred of whom were regulars and the rest militia and temporarily enlisted recruits like Hugh and Dave, together with White Eyes and his band

f Delaware warriors, started building a road along the
outhern bank of the river as they went, their ultimate
oal—Detroit.

So came the general news back to Hannastown.

One evening James entered the Murray cabin with a
ober expression on his face. He had seen Sam on his way
o the tavern first, so he knew he might speak his mind
eely to Martha and to Violet. His manner was plainly
oubled.

"I had to pour out my feelings to somebody," he began,
and there aren't many here who would listen."

"Why, what is it, James?" Martha asked kindly.

"It's this last Pittsburgh Treaty with the Delawares. It
ckens me. It makes me ashamed I'm a white man!"

He drew a paper from his pocket.

"I'm just back from Pittsburgh, and while I was there
talked with several men who were at the Treaty, and
ith Job Chilloway who interpreted. So I copied down
hat I could learn to put with our records here. It will do
o harm to have it."

"But what's troubling you, James?"

"It's White Eyes. I saw him once at Fort Pitt a few
ars ago just when he was back from a long trip down to
ew Orleans, round by boat to New York and then
rough Philadelphia and on back here on his way home.
e's as honest as daylight, you can see at a glance, and a
iend of the whites if they ever had one. Now he's bound
imself and the Delawares not only to friendship but to
tive help on this campaign, and while I wouldn't dare
y it in many places, I think he's made a sad bargain."

"But I thought the Treaty was all signed honorabl
and peaceably on both sides. That's the way the new
came here."

"It's signed rightly enough. But whose tongues wer
in their cheeks? Why, McIntosh's and Brodhead's an
William Crawford's and all the rest of them. All the
want from the Delawares is a chance to get through thei
territory safely. They'll promise anything to keep on th
good side of them."

Martha's face was intent, open as always with sympath
and intelligence.

"Have they promised aught they can't keep then?" sh
asked quietly.

"Well, what think you of this? It's the last provision
That the Delaware nation shall eventually have a repre
sentative in Congress, *provided nothing in the articl
shall be considered conclusive without the approbation o
Congress!* There's a neat little bit of deceptive wordin
for you! This idea of an Indian state with a representa
tive in Congress has been White Eyes' dream—so the
were telling me in Pittsburgh—ever since he made tha
big trip round the country to see how civilized folks liv
Now this thing isn't worth any more than the paper it
written on. Never was meant to be."

"They're hard put to it, James, those men at Fort Pi
and all in authority. I oftentimes think of that," Marth
said sadly as though weighing the evidence.

"But they needn't go out of their way to deceive a
Indian like White Eyes. He has *vision!* Even asked fc
'our wise brethren in Congress' to send a schoolmaste

out to his towns to instruct the children! I wish I could do that job myself for him. I'm very sure Congress won't pay heed or hap to the request just now."

"Oh, you'd make a fine schoolmaster, James," Violet said quickly. "Far better than old Dame Forest here. Did you never think of it?"

"And there's always need of good schoolmasters back east," Martha added eagerly.

James' pale cheeks colored at the praise. He looked at Violet as he spoke.

"I've got other plans," he said. "I hadn't meant to speak of them yet awhile, but to you . . . I know you'll both keep my secret. I'm reading law."

"Oh, James!"

The women cried out together in surprise and pleasure. There was even a little of awe in Violet's tone. Her eyes dwelt upon him with heightened interest.

"I've been often to Pittsburgh of late, as you know, and it's been to see Mr. John Culbertson, a lawyer, who is come there. He has been pleased to take an interest in my ambitions. Even without college schooling he thinks I can be admitted to practice. It will take some time—several years, he judges, the way I'll have to do it, but I'm willing to wait and work hard meanwhile. He's lending me books."

There was in Martha's heart such a sudden surge of glory she could scarcely keep her voice from trembling with it. She told him of her interest, of her pride in him and her confidence in his ultimate success; then listened while Violet questioned him excitedly.

"And is this why you're planning then to go east, James?"

"That's my hope. Mr. Culbertson says he knows plenty of influential barristers in Philadelphia. He'll recommend me when the time comes. For himself he likes the frontier. He aims to keep moving on westward if there's ever any big settlement beyond Pittsburgh. He thinks there will be some day. I told him my interest was all to get to the east if I could."

"Yes," Martha said. "That's right, James. You're suited for the other way of life, and you ought to have it." Her eyes swept over Violet too. "Those that are made for gentle living—oh, the east's the place for them. Not this cruel wilderness."

There was such strength, such determination in the quiet words that both James and Violet looked startled. Something seemed to catch their spirits up together and hold them with power. James' face flushed again deeply while Violet smiled nervously and picked up her knitting.

"You'll make such a wonderful lawyer, James. I can just see you. Maybe you'll be a judge some day. And rich. I'm glad you told us your secret, for we can be thinking of it and encouraging you, like. Won't you recite some Shakespeare for us now like you did before? It pleasures us to listen while we knit, doesn't it, Mother? And keep our minds off—other things."

James leaned back in the settle, one arm half raised, the long, slender hand against his scholar's face. Even the attitude, Martha was thinking, had a natural and unconscious elegance.

She watched every lineament of his countenance as he sat thus for a few moments, smiling into the fire. Then slowly, in a low voice, he began:

> "Let me not to the marriage of true minds
> Admit impediments. Love is not love
> Which alters when it alteration finds,
> Or bends with the remover to remove:
> O, no! it is an ever-fixèd mark,
> That looks on tempests, and is never shaken. . . ."

There was no sound for a little space when he had finished. James still sat gazing at the fire, while Violet looked wonderingly at him, and Martha, her heart pounding in her breast, watched them both.

"Is that from Shakespeare, James?" Violet asked at last.

"Yes. He wrote other poetry beside the plays. What I just recited is called a sonnet. They're all at the back of the book. There are many other beautiful ones: 'Shall I compare thee to a summer's day?' for instance."

His voice was steady, his face still averted; then he turned abruptly.

"But now for *your* favorites. What shall it be, Mrs. Murray? Hamlet again?"

It was Sam's entrance that broke the spell at last. By that time there had been long passages read, and much unaccountable laughter in between even as they discussed them. Never had James seemed in such high spirits.

"It's been a wonderful evening, Mrs. Murray," he said as he rose to go. "It has even taken my mind clear off White Eyes and his problems. After all, I suppose we have enough of our own. I'll bid you good night, Mr. Murray. Good night—Violet."

When he was gone, Sam mimicked him. *"Vi-o-let!* If he don't put on the airs! An' I'll bet he couldn't hit a rabbit if it was sittin' on his thumbnail."

"He's a scholar, Sam, and a gentleman."

"All right. All right. Them as wants scholars an' gentlemen can have 'em, but for me I'd ruther have a man that knows which end of a gun the shootin' comes out of."

Toward the end of October an event occurred in Hannastown which took the minds of all the women, at least, off dangers near and far. Betsy's baby was born, a little girl. Martha had been holding herself in readiness for the call every day and night for a week. But the request for neighborly help did not come. Instead, Mrs. Kinkaid herself brought them the news one mild morning when haze hung low upon the hills and the rich leafy smell of autumn filled the air.

"Never did I know of as easy a birth," she told them. "With every one of mine I've had to tear at the bedpost. Betsy's come as easy as spittin'. You never can tell."

There was a faint displeasure apparent in her recital, as though she felt Providence had let Betsy off too easily.

"It's a girl, an' no help it'll be to riddle the mystery, for it's the born image of Betsy herself. They're as like as two peas in a pod. Well, thank God it's over, though I must say we haven't much need of another mouth to fill at our house. Come in when you can."

The whole problem of Betsy seemed now to take on a new complexity, for when the neighbors went in to see her and say a kind word, they found to their amazement that the wild look was gone from her eyes. There was no shame there, either. Instead there was a shining joy. Close to her breast she clasped the tiny bundle, loath to give it up even for a moment. Her happiness held in it a sort of holy wonder. She would lie watching the little face—which so exactly resembled her own—with such deep, untouchable rapture that those who came prepared to cheer her with charitable words went away puzzled and in most cases disapproving.

Martha, as so frequently happened, divined the truth. "I believe," she said thoughtfully to Violet after one of their visits to the Kinkaid cabin, "that poor Betsy's been sort of starved for love all her life. Mrs. Kinkaid is—well, not just rightly affectionate with her children. Betsy's got something all her own now to pour out her feelings on. No matter what's gone before, she's got her baby."

"Maybe that's it," Violet answered slowly. "Only it's queer she can be so happy after—everything that's happened."

Violet was burdened these days. As she sat spinning she sighed often, deep saddening breaths that seemed to drain her heart. It was hard to keep the terrible secret of the Irishman's death locked in her bosom. Sometimes she felt if she could even run off alone into the deep woods and make her confession to the silent forest it would give her easement. But never must word of it pass her lips even in the depths of the wilderness. She had sworn to Hugh, and he trusted her. It was always, though, a sort of pain to keep the knowledge between her and her mother.

In addition to this there was the steady ache of anxiety for Hugh's safety. She did not dare imagine life without him. As resolutely as she drew the shutters of her mind against this possibility she closed them against acknowledgment of her real feelings for him. She rested on the familiar bonds of their family life together.

Each day she visited Betsy, and found herself temporarily lost in the strange world of her friend's new motherhood.

"She *is* pretty, isn't she?" Betsy would ask, fingering the baby's tiny hands.

"Oh, that she is, Betsy. What will you name her?"

Betsy lowered her voice.

"I'm going to call her after myself. Mebbe no one else would want the name, anyway. Mother says it's sort of shameful, but I'm going to do it. We can say, 'little Betsy.' "

"Why, that will be nice," Violet said, keeping surprise out of her voice.

"It's like this," Betsy went on. "I never had things the way I craved them, sort of. I can't rightly put it into words, but when I was little and got hurt there was no one ever to *gentle* me over it. I heard your mother and you laughing once together and singing like—like sisters almost. Well, I'm going to be like that with little Betsy. If she's afeard of things I'll never chide her. I'll just hold her close, like. And when she's hurt I'll comfort her. I'll sing to her and call her pet names, I will. No matter what folks say."

She looked upon the child, her pent-up love flooding her countenance.

"All I've never got I'm going to give to little Betsy."

Violet felt the quick tears in her eyes.

"As soon as ever you're able you must bring her down and sit an afternoon with us. Mother knows how to make dolls out of corncobs with faces and linen bonnets and all. She'll show you."

Betsy's face was alight.

"I didn't never have a doll," she said. "But I'll be always making them for *her*."

Meanwhile, on a high bluff overlooking the Ohio River at the point where the Beaver empties into it, the army of General McIntosh had been engaged in building a fort. It was well built of heavy logs filled in with earth on top of which six-pound cannon were mounted. Inside were barracks enough for a regiment, and space for munitions. The General's idea was that since this spot was the most western point to which supplies could easily be brought by water it should be an advance depot for provisions.

All the while they were building, the General was trying to get his stores forward from Fort Pitt ready for the march into the wilderness. But there were many delays. Everything went slowly, and the fine autumn days were relentlessly passing by. The Delaware warriors and White Eyes himself could not understand why so much time should be taken to build a fort which would not be needed when Detroit was captured, and most of the

American officers, while not sharing the same complete optimism as to the outcome of the campaign, still felt that the month spent at the mouth of the Beaver was wasted. The new depot, incidentally, had been called *Fort McIntosh.*

By November 3rd a herd of bareboned, lean cattle, driven over the mountains, had arrived, and two days later the army began its march westward to the Tuscarawas River. One provision of the treaty which General McIntosh had every intention of honoring was the building of a stockade in the Delawares' country to protect their women and children in case the other tribes, who were ranged on the side of the British, should now consider them enemies and attack them.

Night after night White Eyes sat in council with the American officers planning the details of this fort. The place was agreed upon. It was to be at the Delaware capital of Coshocton. White Eyes was indeed in the highest spirits these days in spite of a physical indisposition. He had all the appearance of a man whose greatest ambition had been realized. His devotion to the American cause was touchingly sincere. So, he constantly affirmed, was that of his sixty warriors. Even Dave and Hugh, with their inborn hatred of the savages, agreed that perhaps the old Injun was honest.

"First one *I'd* ever trust," Dave admitted grudgingly.

Hugh, still slower to impute any good to a redskin, added, "Course time'll tell."

But time had no chance to prove the integrity of White Eyes, which even Hugh in his own heart recognized. On a dull, foggy evening a terrible report moved swiftly among the men of the army. White Eyes was dead. In the manner of such reports no one seemed actually to tell it, and yet everyone knew. The men came of a tight-lipped breed so that their words now were few, but eye to eye spoke volumes. They knew that White Eyes had been shot by a Virginia militiaman who, half crazed by the recent tomahawking of his wife and child, felt that one Injun was like any other Injun and revenge was revenge. This was the fact. The statement given out by the officers to the warriors and sent back to the Delaware tribe was that White Eyes had died of smallpox. This had some claim to credence since the Indian had been suffering from a digestive disturbance which had caused a mild eruption on his face.

The warriors heard the news as McIntosh gave it to them. They said nothing, but the American officer watching their inscrutable faces could read the dismay in their eyes. It was matched, indeed, by that in his own soul. The sight of the still copper face wrapped in the vast dignity of death moved him more than anything had ever done before. White Eyes, with his noble plans for his people, his utter faith in the "buckskins" with whom he had courageously cast his lot; White Eyes pleading at the Treaty, triumphantly signing the papers which he thought would create a Delaware state; White Eyes eagerly conferring in these last days as a brother officer about the new fort and the campaign—this man now lay in the rude tent, slain by treachery.

This feeling passed among the men, too. The same

emotions which made McIntosh and Brodhead grave and
heavy-hearted caused a wave of uneasiness to spread
among the troops. Even those who failed to grasp the
full tragedy of the Indian chief's death, realized the dis-
astrous effects it would have upon the campaign. For,
without the strong, guiding hand of White Eyes upon
his people, how long would the Delawares remain
friendly? Might not his death turn them at once into
open enemies?

For a week this desperate uneasiness continued to ex-
ist, growing in degree as it became apparent that the
sixty warriors had, almost to a man, disappeared night
by night in the darkness and returned to their own town
of Coshocton.

By the last of November a different type of enemy had
attacked the army: a gentle, noiseless assailant that did
not strive nor cry. The snow. McIntosh and Brodhead
talked and argued and planned. The former had ambition; the latter had common sense. The fact that both
were determined men made the arguments more bitter.
But at last Brodhead—and the first snow—won. General
McIntosh announced sadly to his army that a winter
campaign through the land of the savages without the
aid of the Delawares was now out of the question. The
great attack upon Detroit must be postponed. Upon one
point he remained adamant. There must be some sort
of visible accomplishment to mark the adventure. He
would build a stockade fort here where the army was now
encamped to hold the place during the winter and serve
as a point of departure for a new expedition against De-

troit in the spring. It would fulfill the letter of the treaty
also in regard to building a place of refuge in the Delaware country.

Work began, therefore, on the fort. Hugh and Dave
labored together day after day, both disappointed and
glum.

"Looks like we ain't even goin' to shoot squaws this
time," Dave said once. "Why the hell can't these fellahs
plan ahead once? Hasn't McIntosh ever seen snow before? Didn't he know when we started we'd run into
winter if we didn't hurry up?"

"Wasted all the good weather back yonder," Hugh
agreed bitterly, "buildin' *Fort McIntosh*, that's what we
did."

"What're they goin' to call this rathole when we get
it built?"

"Fort Laurens, I heard them sayin'. Honorin' the
President of the Continental Congress!"

"Oh, my God!" groaned Dave.

The new fort was small, enclosing only about an acre
of ground, around which ran high embankments of earth
topped by pickets. By the time it was finished, the whole
situation was worse. The Virginia militia had enlisted
only till the end of the year. Their time was now out and
they wanted to go home. The killing of White Eyes by
one of their own number had not made their present
position any more comfortable. The weather, too, had
grown colder, and the poorly managed commissary had
failed to get the provisions forward. So, seeing no help
for it, General McIntosh recast his plans and divided up

his men. One hundred and fifty under the stout frontiersman, Colonel John Gibson, would remain to hold
Fort Laurens. A larger force under Colonel Brodhead
would form the winter garrison at Fort McIntosh, while
the General himself with the rest of the Eighth would
return to Fort Pitt, there to nurse his disappointment as
best he might.

Hugh and Dave were depressed the night before the
break-up, for they were to be separated. Dave was detailed to remain at Laurens, while Hugh was to go back
as far as McIntosh. The two boys, born scouts, expert
riflemen and strong young sons of the forest, had not
escaped the notice of the officers.

"I wanted to keep you both," Gibson told them, "but
Brodhead thought we'd divvy up on you Hannastown
lads."

Dave especially was low in his mind. "This is goin' to
be the devil's own hole this winter," he said despond-
ently. "If any news from home could get through, it
wouldn't be so bad."

"If I can manage any way at all, I'll get a line through
to Fort Pitt. From there it's easy. They can mebbe send
back word from home then. There'll be some messengers
through to Fort McIntosh."

"What good'll that do me?"

"The General is sendin' supplies here in January. I'll
get something through to you, no fears. Mebbe I'll be
comin' myself."

"If you're writin' home, ask about Betsy," Dave said,
very low.

"It was to be about October, wasn't it?"

Dave nodded.

"I'll find out, some way, for you. Don't fret yourself."

After a silence Dave spoke.

"Dream much, Hugh?"

"Not so much."

"I do. I keep seein' that damned red coat in amongst the trees. I don't like it, some way."

"Lie on your right side, they say. That'll keep you from dreamin'."

"He was a filthy beggar."

"That he was."

Dave drew a heavy breath. "Well, hope we all pull through this winter. Take care of yourself."

"I will. You do the same."

To their surprise they found themselves shaking hands.

For Hugh the next weeks back at Fort McIntosh were the longest he had ever spent. The futility and the tedium were intolerable to him. More than all, he had the gravest fears concerning the men at Fort Laurens. How was Dave faring?

By early January a messenger came from Fort Pitt bringing some letters for the men. One was for Hugh. His hands were not too steady as he opened the folded paper, for the fine, small hand writing was Violet's:

Dear Brother,

I take pleasure in writing you that we are all well and only hope you are safe and in good health yourself. Mother and I dipped candles today. Father's rheumatism is better. B- has a little girl born Oct. 28 and calls it little Betsy and seems

passing fond of it. It is very pretty and favors her and growing fast. Tell Dave Peggy seems to be really taking up with
Hen Wilson. She says she won't wed anyone that won't take
Jamsey too, though. We had a wedding last week Mary Duncan and Joe Sloan. It was a nice one and no mistake. Nancy
Wilson and Matthew Jack stood up with them. When all was
over the Captain lifted Nancy up on Matchit's back then
jumped in the saddle and away they went like the wind. I
suppose their wedding will be next. They say Matchit knew
him when he got back in September and followed him all
over the place. Ranger and the stock are all right. No sheep
gone yet though we've heard wolves at night. Mother says try
to keep your feet dry and if you get a cough chew a little
slippery elm bark. Watch is asleep at my feet now I think he
misses you. So do I.

Your affectionate sister

VIOLET

Hugh folded the paper and put it inside his shirt. He
would show it to Dave when he saw him, which he hoped
would be soon. He had already asked to be one of those
selected to take provisions back to Fort Laurens.

By the middle of the month they set out, Captain John
Clark of the Eighth with fifteen men, and six pack horses
laden with flour and meat. It was hard going, but they
reached the fort without mishap a week later.

Hugh was shocked at Dave's appearance. He was gaunt
and bearded and dirty. The men reported a hard time.
Early in the month the savages had begun to prowl about.
The building of the fort had greatly provoked the Wyandots and the Mingoes, who were now bent upon its
destruction.

"We haven't even been able to do any huntin'," Dave told his friend. "The minute we set foot outside the stockade an Injun draws a bead on us. Course we've picked off quite a few, but there's no end to 'em. I don't know how in thunder you folks got here safe."

He read Violet's letter over and over.

"It looks like *her*," he mused. "Thank God for that. You know I've been thinkin'. Mebbe things'll work out for us after all. She may feel different now, about me, that is."

"Belike she will."

"I wisht this winter was over. For all the good we're doin'."

"So do I."

After a two-day rest, Captain Clark and his men said good-bye to their friends at the fort, leaving them cheered with a temporary supply of food, and set out on their return journey. The men marched more warily now, for they had been well warned. For three miles there was no sign of life in the forest. Then suddenly in a little gully they found themselves ambushed. The shots from the Indians cracked through the frosty air. Five of the men dropped and Hugh felt a wretched burning hurt in his right arm. He managed to raise his rifle and take aim at the nearest visible foe. Suddenly he recognized him. It was Simon Girty!

In the same instant he heard Girty's voice calling.

"I told you, you were on the wrong side, lad. You should have come with me."

For answer Hugh fired, but his aim was poor. Even to

hold up the rifle required superhuman effort. Clark's voice came above the crack of bullets.

"Back to the fort as fast as you can make it! Bring the wounded along."

Two of the fallen men were dead. The other four, with help, got on their feet. Keeping behind trees, dragging the wounded men with them, firing whenever they glimpsed a feather, Clark's little band retreated. The three miles back to the stockade were far longer than the previous week's journey.

They reached it at last without more casualties and fell, weary and dismayed, within its shelter. Dave took immediate charge of Hugh, washing his wound and dressing it as well as he could. The bone was safe, they decided. The bullet had just grazed it, passing through the flesh.

"It's naught," Hugh kept repeating, but the distress seemed out of proportion to the hurt. It was indeed the first real pain he had ever known, and he felt a mingled glory and shame in it. He told the others about recognizing Girty, and the men's faces grew harder.

"Pity you missed him. No one outside the devil I'd rather hit," Gibson said.

At the end of three days Captain Clark said they must try it again. A longer stay would put a serious drain upon the newly brought provisions. Two of the wounded men were able to attempt the trip; but Hugh and three others were still so weak from loss of blood that they had no choice but to stay on at Fort Laurens. They all watched the little band out of sight from the front of the stockade, with sinking hearts. One thing Hugh hoped for. It was that Girty, with his reputation for loyalty to a friend, might not attack the group, supposing that he was with them. He had a shamed conviction that Girty liked him. Another hope was that the Indians had gone away since there was now no sign of them.

But what the winter would bring to themselves here at the post on the Tuscarawas was gloomy enough in prospect. And this soon became reality. By the middle of February the Indians had returned in greater numbers. Hugh could occasionally distinguish Girty's form among them and that of another white man, who Gibson said was Captain Bird, a Britisher. It looked as though they had come to stay.

A few days after the Indians were sighted, more fuel was needed in the fort. Early in the winter the men had cut a large quantity of firewood and stacked it in the forest near by. On this morning eighteen men, with a good deal of good-natured banter and chaffing back and forth, prepared to take the wagon out and return with a load of the logs. It was only a half-mile back in the woods and they were well armed. They set out in good spirits. Indeed there was some friendly rivalry as to which ones would go.

The morning passed, and the men did not return. Gibson's face was grave as the afternoon hours wore on.

"Either the red devils got them," he said, "or they're hiding till nightfall."

But the darkness did not bring them. Toward midnight, Gibson and two others left the fort. They made their way cautiously in the direction of the woodpile. There was a small moon and with the light of the snow they saw at last what in their hearts they had feared. In the lee of a large Indian mound lay sixteen men, dead and scalped. Two were missing—young Bill Miller and Joe Slade. It was captivity for them, then, or worse.

The men, sickened, turned and made their way back to the fort. It was a sorry night. No one pretended to sleep. They sat about the fires, talking little, their faces grim, their hearts like lead.

The next morning on the hill across from the stockade and in full view of it, the savages paraded in single file, shouting, waving their guns and battle axes and the newly taken scalps.

"Count them, men, count them!" Gibson called to his soldiers. "If there aren't too many, we'll make a sortie against them."

With eyes strained and faces hard the men at the fort counted. There were over six hundred by all tallies. Hugh, whose eyes were as good as a hawk's, made it six hundred and eighty.

A black despair seized upon the men. They were hopelessly outnumbered then. There was nothing for it but to endure and wait, since the plan of the Indians was evidently to starve them out. Day by day the savages kept up their taunting parade. Night by night their campfires lighted up the bleak woods.

Colonel Gibson, of a race which does not know the word "surrender," took stock of his resources. By sending out small groups at night, he managed to get enough wood brought in to keep the men fairly warm. By cutting down the daily ration to a quarter-pound of flour and the same weight of meat, he figured they could keep alive for another six weeks.

Hugh's wound was healing, but his arm was stiff and sore. He had dark moments of fear that it might remain so even if they ever did get out of this place. Every day he patiently worked it up and down, making light of the pain. He and Dave together read over Violet's letter as often as they could make excuse. Even to themselves they did not admit that it brought home and familiar things close and lifted the dark threat of the present for a moment at least.

"Let's have a look at that letter again," Dave would say with elaborate casualness.

Or, "What was that Violet was sayin' about wolves bein' round?"

Hugh, himself, sought for pretexts.

"So Matt Jack an' Nancy stood up with them." Out would come the letter. "She doesn't say how many were at the weddin'."

"Or if they had an infare. Let's have a look at it, Hugh."

The paper grew greasy, and the writing dim. Not even Dave suspected, of course, that Hugh in the darkness of the night sometimes held it to his lips.

One day an Indian was seen approaching the stockade under an improvised flag of truce.

"Let him come on," Gibson ordered. "I've been expecting this."

When he was close, Gibson opened the stockade gate, with his men behind him.

"Well, what do you want?" he asked.

"Cap'n Bird he say you surrender this fort, he give all soldier safe back to Fort McIntosh."

Gibson shook his fist under the Indian's nose. "You go back and tell Captain Bird to go to hell and that I'm not going to surrender. Do you understand? Repeat it now!"

The Indian mumbled.

"Tell Cap'n Bird go spirit land and not surrender."

"*No,*" Gibson shouted. "Go to *hell. Hell,* man. Say it."

"Cap'n Bird go hell, you not surrender."

Gibson grinned.

"Now you've got it straight. Get back there where you belong before we put a bullet through you."

The Indian turned and scuttled into the forest.

When another week had passed Gibson called his men together and told them plainly that unless help arrived there wasn't much hope for any of them.

"I've got to get word to Fort McIntosh. It's a hazardous trip. I needn't tell you the man who makes it will have a tough job on his hands. But if he gets through, it may save our lives. Is there a volunteer?"

"I'll try it, sir," Dave said instantly, while Hugh watched him with envy in his eye.

Gibson looked pleased.

"You're a good choice, lad. We'll all chip in, men, to fit him out as best we can. What about getting off to-night?"

"As good as any time, sir."

A quickening of hope ran through the fort. The chance was slim, but still it was a chance. The men tore tails off their hunting shirts, and took deer hair from their moccasins, to reinforce Dave's clothing. Hugh took off his own shoe packs and pressed them on his friend.

"You'll need an extry pair, and what do I want them for, sittin' here by the fire. Mind you keep bearin' east just a *shade* north'ard. Try to head for that patch of sycamores we struck about midway. You mind them? There's a rock shelf there on the side of the hill just beyond. You mind it? We said comin' that it would make a good shelter for a night. If you feel lost in the daytime wait an' get your bearin's from the stars. Hope the snow don't get any deeper."

They all gave advice, their thin faces doing the pleading for them. Every man pressed some of his own scant day's ration upon Dave. Hugh baked his flour pone for him and cooked his meat. Though starvation loomed within the fort, the scout must be fed, or there was no possibility of his standing the trip.

Dave ate before he left, a bigger meal than he had had for many weeks. He tried not to look at the others as he swallowed the meat and the flour cake. Then he stored his provisions and the extra shoe packs in his shirt, pulled his coonskin cap low over his ears, tested the blade of his hunting knife, secured it in his belt, picked up his rifle, and stood ready.

Colonel Gibson handed him a paper.

"Read it," he said, "so if you lose it you can give it to Brodhead or McIntosh by word of mouth."

Dave read:

Genl. McIntosh and Col. Brodhead, Sirs, We are sur-
rounded by a large force of Savages our supplies are well
nigh Exhausted. Send help for Gods sake Meanwhile I will
hold the Fort to the last Extremity Yrs respfly J. Gibson.

Dave put it carefully in his breast, gave a quick look
around, and, with a lift of his hand in reply to the men's
Godspeed, left the stockade and was lost in the darkness.

Hugh had never felt so alone as he felt that night.

During the next week the men huddled over their fires
and traced day by day the possible position of their messenger. Hugh, his heart thundering in his thin chest,
watched hourly those first days from the stockade gun
holes to see whether a new scalp would be triumphantly
waved from the warriors' hilltop. But there was no sign
of it. This meant that there was a likelihood at least that
Dave had evaded the besieging band. They were not the
only hostile Indians abroad, though. On every step of his
way, peril would face the lone runner.

In the second week the men's talk changed.

"If he got there safe, they'd ought to be startin' back
about tomorrow."

"What d'you mean? It'll take them two days or so anyway to collect supplies."

"It'll take a week."

"An' a week to come back."

"That's two weeks more."

"At the best. But how do we know he got there?"

"He'll make it," Hugh kept saying.

But the two weeks passed, and another. The men's eyes were sunken now, and their bones almost pierced the skin. They dragged themselves with effort about the stockade, or through the night to bring in the wood in weak armfuls. They could all see that there were left only a few barrels of food. But no man spoke of it.

One day the watchers at the gun holes reported a delegation approaching under a white flag. Colonel Gibson's mouth was set in a thin, grim line.

"Now what?" he muttered.

The snow was deep and the Indians advanced with running leaps like those of a hare. There were eight of them. They made a great show of waving their flag as they neared the gate. Gibson signed for some of his men to line up behind him, guns ready, then opened the gate and stepped out alone. The spokesman who had come the other time, now advanced.

"Cap'n Bird say can you give us food. Mebbe one barrel meat one barrel flour?"

"Why should I feed you damned Indians? Haven't you made trouble enough for us?" Gibson parried.

"Mebbe you not have much food I tell Cap'n Bird," the Indian shrugged, his sharp eyes on the Colonel's face.

"Of course we have food. Plenty of it." Gibson made a gesture indicating vast stores. "Much, many barrels. Can you take two back with you?"

A great surprise and pleasure spread over the Indian's face. He quickly translated. The others looked at each other and then made eager sounds of assent.

"All right," Gibson said. "Wait here, and I'll send

some out to you. And tell Captain Bird *and Girty* if he's there, that I hope they eat so much they die of the belly-ache."

He went inside, motioned the men back and then stood squarely before them. Their gaunt faces and sunken eyes were raised to his. They were beyond jesting now, but he knew by their expressions that they felt his words had been a master joke.

"Men," he said, "I'm going to do as I told them. Give them a barrel of meat and a barrel of flour. Help me roll them out."

For a second there was the silence of death, as though in their weakened state their minds were slow to understand the words they had just heard. Then a fury broke.

"Have ye gone mad?"

"You'll give them over my dead body, you will."

"The starvation's got you, man, you're gone crazy!"

They were no longer officer and subordinates; they were human beings facing death together.

"Why would you say such a damnable thing? To torture us?"

"You dasn't do that, Colonel, we'll not stand it. Look at us. Starvin' we are like bears in a trap. Would you take the last bite from our mouths? Where's your reason?"

A shaking voice came from the fringe of the group. It was Andy Peters. He had been running a fever now for a week. His rifle was raised and pointed at Gibson.

"We'll give you a reason, you damned traitor, but we'll keep our grub."

Gibson did not move.

"Put that gun down, Andy, and shut up, you men, and listen. There's little or no game about. Those Injuns are hungry too, I'll bet my pants on it. Captain Bird thinks we're about starved out."

"And by God he's right."

"But why tell him so? If we shove a couple of barrels out to them they'll be like to think we've got plenty. If they think that they may give up and go away. It's a chance, but we've got to take it. Men, I'm in command here. I've got to make the decision. I expect every one of you to obey and keep your mouths shut. Don't forget I'm as hungry as you are, and if we die we do it together. Hey, you fellahs there by the barrels, start a couple rollin'. I'll help you get them to the front."

The other men stood back, their lips sucked together. Poor Andy Peters let fall his rifle and sank down shivering, the tears of utter weakness dribbling down his beard.

They watched in a terrible silence as the barrels were rolled slowly to the gate. Gibson opened it himself. His voice was strong and assured, and the men within, hearing it, honored him even while despair seized them.

"All right, you damned Injuns, here's your barrels. We'll never miss them, so you might as well have a feed. Get on back now and tell Captain Bird what I told you."

The interpreter grinned admiringly.

"Cap'n Bird go hell."

"That's it. You're a smart Injun. You can all go to hell. Now clear out."

He barred the stockade himself, watched until the Injians with their booty had at last disappeared, then came slowly back to his men. There was nothing more to be said.

Through that afternoon and evening the sentinels could see evidences of feasting and revelry on the opposite hill. How many Indians were still there, the men had no way of telling. But on the next day and the ones following an excitement shook the soldiers in the fort; for there was no sign now of an Indian to be seen. At night the bleak woods were wrapped in darkness. Not a flicker of a campfire broke the gloom. It was evident, then, that Gibson had guessed rightly. The Indians and their leaders had given up the siege as hopeless and gone back where they came from.

But in spite of this great victory the shadow of death still lay upon the fort. Though the soldiers could venture out now in search of game, there was none to be seen. The weather was cold, the snow deep, and watch as their weary eyes might, there was no sign of marching men and laden pack horses approaching from the east.

On a fateful day the last grain of flour, the last scrap of meat was doled out. The men ate slowly and in silence. The gallant ribaldry which they had all known in other types of danger was not possible during this slow weakening of the body with its gnawing pains. A tortured stomach knows no jest. During the next week they dug feebly under the snow for what roots they could find and drank the water from boiled rawhides.

Hugh had a lightness of the head now which made him think strange things. He thought Violet was in danger and once he was sure he saw the Irishman's red coat be-

tween the trees. Sometimes there were happy thoughts.
He felt Violet's face close to his own and his lips on hers.
Once as something touched his knee he said, "Down,
Watch, old boy!" He was ashamed when he looked
around. But no one had paid any attention. All the men
did and said strange things in that last week.

They learned afterwards that the day of their deliver-
ance was the 23rd of March. Just as they had dreamed it
would be; just as their longing, bloodshot eyes had
strained to see, so there came into view on a late afternoon a train of marching men and laden pack horses over
the hill and down the slope toward the stockade. It was
a scream that first announced it, a scream of joy. The
words were barely articulate.

"They're here! They're here! They're here!"

The famished men, in a frenzy of happiness, ran out
of the fort with their rifles to meet the troops. Gibson,
his own eyes misty with relief, was still the only one who
kept his head.

"Take care, men. Don't scare the horses! My God,
men, watch out what you're doing."

But the yelling men did not even hear him. Dizzy with
hunger and beside themselves now with joy, they fired
volley after volley into the air, not even noticing in their
glad delirium what was happening. For the pack horses,
terrified at the sudden thunder of the rifles, had broken
away from their drivers and were stampeding through
the forest, hurling their priceless burdens to the ground,
trampling the food underfoot or leaving it buried in the
snow.

It was hours before the rescuing force got into the fort. Terrible hours. When the men of the garrison saw what they had done, many of them wept like children. They had scarcely the strength to watch the others retrieving what food they could. They stood about, shivering and despairing.

But little by little the first shock of horror at the accident passed. Some of the horses were still missing, but about half the food had been saved. More than this, the newcomers, having known no recent pangs of starvation were inclined to optimism. They had made a hard trip safely. They were here, now, in reach of warm fires There was enough food for all for the present and they had brought good news along with them!

"Buck up, you fellahs," they called. "Save your shootin for the Injuns next time. We've still got enough grub here to stick to your ribs. Come on, get the pot boilin'."

When they were all in the fort at last the starving men smelled the stew with a joy like to anguish itself, then ate what was judiciously doled out to them with promises o more on the morrow, and felt life returning both to their worn-out bodies and to their hearts. For all around them now was laughter and loud, strong swearing and a rough lustful gayety that made the blood run warm again.

The rescuers told their good news: George Roger Clark had captured Vincennes and old Hair-Buyer Hamilton himself on the 24th of February! Yes, sir! It was true. A runner had got through to Fort Pitt with the story. Takin' Hamilton down to Virginia, they were prisoner. No, there wasn't any mistake. He'd done it

Clark had, with not so many men either. He'd taken Vincennes *and Hamilton!* Now, whoop 'er up, boys!

Oh, it was a great night. A great night. All the adventures were retold: the thrilling story of Dave's trip back to Fort McIntosh, the regiment's difficulties in getting the supplies, then over and over the details of the last weeks here at the stockade; and back once more to Clark's capture of Vincennes and the *Hair-Buyer.*

Hugh and Dave did not talk much to each other. They sat close and grinned often, understandingly.

In a few days, with hearty stir and confusion, the reorganization of the men began. All the faithful defenders of Fort Laurens were to return to Fort Pitt. A hundred fresh men of the Eighth were to take their places as garrison at the wilderness post with promise of more supplies soon.

As though nature had suddenly determined to smile upon the dependent sons of men, a springtime sunshine bathed the earth on the homeward march. According, also, to the vagaries of Indian warfare, no trace of a redskin was seen on the return journey.

Once back again at Fort Pitt, Hugh and Dave received honorable discharge and started early one morning for Hannastown. They were both thinner than when they had left it, but youth was on their side. Steady rations again and the outdoors they loved had repaired most of the ravages of the winter. To the casual eye they were as they had been: two tall young men, one dark and one fair.

When they reached the top of Gallows Hill and saw

the little town below, shadowed by the first spring leaves, its tall chimneys smoking blue in the clear spring air, they quickened their steps.

"*You've* got a great story to tell them anyhow, Dave," Hugh said a little wistfully. "I wish I had more to show for the winter."

"We both did our best. What more is there?" Dave answered.

So, still together, the two friends descended the hill.

April 8, 1779 Hugh and Dave home safe and sound last night and what stories they have to tell is past believing. Poor lads what they've been through. Violet so excited couldn't go to bed and Sam and I little better. The boys seem a little older-like. Hugh thin but I have to say handsome. Must set to work at once on new shirt for him. Watch went nigh crazy when he came up the path. I kissed Hugh. Have not done that since he was a little lad. I was so taken aback when he appeared. Violet did too (kissed him) I suppose because she saw me. Then I felt worried but it's just sister-like I'm sure with her. Will be more careful in future. The men are all away at the tavern now to tell the tales and no wonder. Sam was over the moon anyway with General Clark's taking that Hamilton man. What a good job that was. Now Sam's fair beside himself with the boys home. Wonderful evening with new moon and young leaves. Oh it's good to have a light heart after heaviness. Violet up at the Hannas.

June 12, 1779 Last night I had the chance I've been waiting for but now I'm vexed in mind whether I did well to speak or let things bide a while longer. Have seen nought amiss between Hugh and Violet since he got back and half inclined to think it was all my fancy but felt I ought to make sure. He and I alone in cabin after sun down so I said how fine it was James seemed so bright and lively these times. Hugh said there was still room to go so I said then plain that I felt J. had a feeling for Violet. Hugh only laughed so I said Violet was too delicate made for a frontier woman's work and I'd die if I could to save her from the life I've led that it would be cruel for anyone to force it on her if there was a way out for her and I said I was sure J. B. was the way. Hugh never spoke only turned and went out. It wasn't natural his look and the quiet of him. All day I've watched him with his jaw set and nothing to say. My heart's torn between the two of them but feel he's young and will get over it. Yet how could anyone stop loving Violet I ask myself in the night watches. That's what makes it so cruel hard for me to see Hugh suffer. I'm sure I made it plain without him ever suspecting I knew how things stood with him. I said I loved Violet better than myself and when love was like that it thought only of what was best for the loved object. It was then Hugh just turned sudden-like and went out. I'm weighted down with the worry of it. I'm going to keep this journal in the chest now. I'm afeared it might reach the eye of another. McIntosh has left Fort Pitt we hear and Brodhead now in command. I declare they don't more than warm a bed there till they're up and off again. Hugh says Brodhead's a good man, though. This afternoon cloudy and very close. I pray constantly for guidance. This is Mother's birthday. She would be 71 if she'd been spared.

X

The Young Beaver Crying

And again May came. The forest was fresh with new leaves and beautiful with the amethyst of the mountain laurel and the creamy blooms of the serviceberry. It was full of new life, too. Running delicately like dancing shadows were the little fawns in their spotted coats; the winter sleepers had all come forth now with their young, the black bears and the raccoons, while the mother skunks, followed by their large families, walked with confidence and indifference along the wilderness ways, gonfalons high, secure in their powerful weapon against all enemies. The little weasels from their nests in the rocks, the little foxes from their burrows, the young martens from their hollow trees, and the small wolves from their lairs, all looked out with bright, busy eyes upon the new world.

Along the streams the Beaver People, as the Indians called them, were the busiest of all. Out from the lodge beside the dam the mother beaver led her kittens these days—out through the beaver pond into the stream itself. There was much to teach them: the delicate taste of poplar bush or bark from the aspen tree; the dam itself, now four feet high and six feet wide at the center, must be pointed out and explained; there must be warnings given against the otter, their greatest enemy, and lessons in swimming, of course. Then when the instruction was all over, the beaver kittens were allowed to climb on their mother's broad tail and, standing upright holding on to her thick fur with their tiny paws, ride back to the lodge in comfort.

Wise and kind little people, the Beavers. Builders not only of dams but also, unconsciously, of empire. For, even as ivory or gold, so their furry coats were forever luring men farther and farther across the frontiers of a new world.

Hugh and Dave, setting their traps with care, did not realize all this; but they did know and respect the beavers even while they hunted them. Sometimes in the daytime a peculiar, sharp sound like a shot came to their ears from the stream. They knew then that a father beaver was giving a danger signal by bringing down his hard flat tail sharply upon the water.

"An otter's after them, likely," Dave would remark.

Sometimes as the boys stole through the moonlight to place a new trap they would hear the sudden crash of a falling tree.

"They're hard at work the night," Hugh would say to his friend.

And once when they were near the creek a sound smote their ears which made them stop and look at each other as they listened.

"You could a'most swear that was little Betsy off somewhere, couldn't you?" Dave said.

"That you could. They sound awful human like, them kittens."

The boys crept cautiously nearer. The thin crying continued, growing more and more localized as they advanced toward the Beaver dam.

"Mother said once back in Cumberland County there was a woman had her baby killed by the Injuns an' after that she'd go nigh crazed if she heard a young beaver."

"They could give you a startle an' no mistake," Dave rejoined.

He was very ready these days to talk about little Betsy. Hugh, watching his friend closely, saw the heavy shadow lifting from his countenance. He felt that he knew why. Though Dave had not yet told him, he was sure that things were righting themselves between Dave and his girl. Since his return Betsy would talk to him shyly and smile in her old fashion. She looked like herself this spring, too. Her cheeks had got rosy again, and her eyes were always bright, especially when she had the baby with her. Of course it seemed odd-like to see her so pleased over little Betsy. People still talked behind her back and said what a thing it was for a girl to act so happy under the circumstances. But everyone agreed that the child was prettier than common.

Dave's attitude was odd too, in a way, yet Hugh respected him for it. Apparently he felt himself to be the logical protector for both Betsy and the baby. Though

the word "love" had, of course, never been named between the boys, Hugh knew the strength of Dave's feeling for Betsy. Sometimes he wondered if his friend had
guessed his own secret. He hoped not.

As in every other springtime, even the pressing danger
of the Indians could not entirely dispel that strange, delicate delight which is implicit in the rebirth of the year.
Hannastown was shaded now by a panoply of living
green, swept by scented airs, bathed in the sunshine's
tender glory. Even though the melting of the last snow
had meant the recurrence of watchfulness and strain,
there was still, especially among the young people, a
quickening of heart and hope.

Hugh and Violet went about their ways as usual, content for the moment in his safe return and their accustomed nearness. His arm was almost back to normal now.
Only on a rainy day did he feel the stiffness. He plowed
and planted their fields while Sam walked alongside, rifle
ready, eyes watching keenly for signs of trouble. No man
worked alone that spring. The danger was too great. And
report said that, back from the towns on the isolated
farms, the harried settlers did not get their grain planted
at all. A bad spring that, except for the beauty of the
weather.

James came often to the Murray cabin, usually when
Sam was not there; but when he started on Shakespeare,
to Violet's embarrassment Hugh always got up at once
and went out. She took him to task one evening when
they were alone. Hugh only laughed as he cleaned his
rifle.

"I'd listen to you or Mother right enough, but I can't swallow James an' his fine words. He's too slack in the twist some way to suit me."

"It would be a lot better for you if you'd pay a little attention to a scholar, once. All you and Dave know is just hunting and shooting and—and rough ways," Violet said severely.

But Hugh was not angry. He just continued to smile while his eyes looked full at Violet with such a light in them that she dropped her own.

"It takes rough ways for a rough country," he said.

Then he lowered his voice.

"Betsy told you anything special lately?"

Violet shook her head. "Only she seems awful bright and pleased these days."

"Mind you keep it to yourself now, but I've an idee she and Dave are going to finish things up right soon."

"Oh, *Hugh!* I'm so glad. What makes you think it? Did Dave tell you?"

She came over and dropped down on the little three-legged stool in front of him, her face shining up into his.

"Now mind you don't give it away till Betsy tells you. Belike she will soon. Dave let it leak out to me just today because he heard tell at the tavern that there's a young preacher on the way here an' he thought they could get the knot tied while he was in town."

"When's he coming?"

"In a couple of weeks. He's just through Princeton, so Mr. Hanna told Dave, an' he's preachin' all along the route. He's at Bedford now, they say."

"Oh, it's past believing, isn't it, how it's all come out! When it looked so black for them."

"It'll be a good job if they get married. Dave's thinkin' of puttin' up a cabin right back of the Shaws'. I'll help him evenings to finish it off. There'll be plenty to give a hand for the raisin'."

Hugh laid aside his rifle. His eyes were still fixed upon Violet.

"It's a fine thing for a man to marry and get him his own land and his own cabin and all."

"Would you—would you rightly fancy that for yourself, Brother?" Violet asked shyly. But there was a sweet compulsion in her voice.

"I'd give my right arm to have it so," he said.

"But you'd need both your arms then more than ever," Violet returned with a bit of laughter.

"That I would," he answered, his eyes burning upon her. "That I would. I only mean I've thought of it night and day now this year or more."

"Yes?" she whispered.

"Violet!" He leaned nearer, speaking her name, their faces almost touching.

Then there was the noise of voices, and they broke away. Hugh started up to hang his rifle on the peg, and Violet went to the door. It was Dave and Betsy. They were laughing in the old way, and Betsy was fair with blushes.

"Well, so here you are," said Dave in a proud, strong voice. "We just come to see if you'd stand up with us at our weddin'?"

"Why, Betsy!"

"Violet, it's wonderful, ain't it? There's to be a young preacher here week after next. We won't have a big fuss, just you folks and the Shaws and ourselves. Just quiet, like. But we want you an' Hugh to stand with us."

Out on the step in the sweet spring darkness they talked together. The shame and pain of the past seemed wiped out. Love had its way with all of them that night. Their cup ran over. Dave and Betsy, almost one at last, planning the wedding and the cabin and their future together; Hugh and Violet hearing below the voices the deep beating of their own hearts. They spoke as of Dave and Betsy, but they knew it was really of themselves. Such sudden lightness of the spirit filled them all! Such young, unreasoning joy!

Before Dave and Betsy left, Sam and Martha had returned. It was all told over again. As Sam cheerfully gave the young people his good wishes, Martha had time to think of his refusal to "fash" himself over Betsy's trouble, in contrast to the wretched sleepless nights she herself had experienced because of it. Now, all was well again. Perhaps Sam's attitude was best after all. If she could ever achieve it!

When they were gone, Martha had exciting news of her own to relate. Mr. Hanna had spoken to her of the coming of the young preacher and asked if the prayer meeting could be held in the Murray cabin when he came.

"He said," Martha repeated with pride in her voice, "that it wasn't just seemly to have the meeting at the tavern, for they never knew when stragglers would set up a din, else they would have it themselves. And then he said ours was the tidiest cabin and the nicest furnished, and would I let them meet here?"

"Mr. Hanna said that?"

"The very words. And I'll not deny I feel lifted by them. We'll start tomorrow and wash up the bedclothes so there's naught dirty in the house. We've plenty of candles, and I'll give the chairs and settle a rubdown with a bit of soft soap. I'll spare no pains to have things as nice as I can, after what Mr. Hanna said. And it will be wonderful to hear the Gospel from a young man fresh from his studies."

For a week the town was enfolded in its own happy affairs. Dave and Hugh started at once to stake out the cabin and fell the trees for it. The women went from door to door, or lingered at the spring, talking it all over with eagerness. Betsy was lucky, they all agreed, to have things turn out like this. Maybe, after all, Dave was the man. If he wasn't, then it was the biggest mystery the town had ever seen. They made their plans for a real celebration at the cabin raising. Out of their slender stores they set aside a little to help start the young bride and groom in their housekeeping. They had much to say to one another, too, about the coming of the young preacher. It had been many months now since there had been one in the town. If the weather kept fine and warm the men could stand about the door and the women could all be seated in the Murray cabin. The experience of *pleasant* anticipation was rare enough, and everyone made the most of it.

One night Martha woke suddenly with a knocking at the door.

"Mrs. Murray!"

She jumped from the bed and hurried to draw the bar. It was Betsy standing on the step, her eyes streaming.

"Child, what's the matter?"

"It's little Betsy. She can't get her breath. Oh, I'm so scared. Will you come quick an' help me?"

Martha caught up her moccasins and threw her dress on over her bedgown. She gathered up some cloths and the few simple remedies she possessed and hurried over the path to the Kinkaids'.

Sam had roused up and called out: "What is it? What's up?"

"It's Betsy's baby sick," Martha had answered briefly.

Sam had grunted disgustedly and turned over in bed. "Och! I thought it was Injuns."

He would be asleep again by now, Martha thought as she hurried on. Men shed some kinds of trouble so easily.

In the Kinkaid cabin as usual there was confusion. Mrs. Kinkaid in a loud voice was ordering her own small children back to their beds, and scolding Betsy at the same time.

"Such a fuss over a spell of croup I never did see! Bringin' you out of your bed, Mrs. Murray, at this hour of the night! I'm ashamed to lay eyes on you. Haven't I brought up seven childer myself? But no, I don't know anything. Betsy's got to rout the neighbors out for *her* young un."

Martha had gone quickly to the cradle where little Betsy lay. Her heart stood still as she saw the child.

"How long has she been sick, Betsy?"

"Since day before yesterday. Just quiet like and didn't want to eat. It seemed to hurt her when she swallowed. I didn't think much of it till tonight, then I *knew* she was worse; but Mother wouldn't hear to it. Oh, Mrs. Murray, tell me what to do for her! *Say* she'll get over it."

"We'll heat this oil as quick as we can, Betsy. Don't give way, child. You must be brave. We'll put a hot rag round her throat. That may ease the breathing. Make up the fire, will you, Mrs. Kinkaid? We'll try if she can take a spoonful of hot milk, too."

As Martha worked, trying to keep her voice calm, her own heart failed her. She had seen a baby once, strangling for breath like this. The uneven struggle had not lasted long.

The night wore on. Martha worked ceaselessly. Poor Betsy leaned above her baby, pouring her very heart out in her tears.

Martha knew she was beaten. There was only one hope. If they could get Dr. Shields he might do something, though her judgment doubted even that.

"Betsy," she said gently to the weeping girl, "would you want to run for Dave and ask him to ride fast for Dr. Shields?"

Betsy's lips went white.

"Is she as bad as that?"

"I'm afraid so."

Without another word Betsy flung herself out the door, Mrs. Kinkaid's critical voice still pursuing her. It was only a short time until they heard the hard hoofbeats of the horse along the road.

"He's gone," Betsy said breathlessly, as she came back. "Oh, Dave's good! He's gone as fast as he can ride."

She had hope on her face until she came back to the cradle. Even the brief time of her absence had left its mark upon the child.

Betsy did not cry out as she looked. She only lifted her face slowly to Martha, sealed in a white despair.

They worked together then, with the frenzy of desperation. But before the night was gone, there was no need to work longer. Martha took Betsy in her arms and held her close. There was a terrible stillness now in the cabin. The younger children slept on. So did Mr. Kinkaid in the farthest corner. Even Mrs. Kinkaid was quiet. There had been no death amongst her own healthy brood, so her voice had been sharp the night through, bidding Betsy save her tears and stop making a fuss. Now her own face was stricken and for once her tongue was silent.

Martha was alarmed for Betsy. For the tears that had rained from her eyes all night were now dried up at their source. The girl's body was rigid. When Martha gently released her, she looked about as in a daze. Out of all the room's strange quiet, Betsy's was the most terrible.

Martha spread one of the pieces of linen she had brought over little Betsy's small form. There was nothing more to do now, except heat some milk and bid Betsy drink it. The girl sipped it obediently, her face still graven, her eyes far away.

"Lie down awhile, Betsy dear. 'The Lord gave and the Lord has taken away.' Lie down and get some rest."

The familiar words had risen automatically to her lips. But was it the Lord who had given? Was the coming and the going of little Betsy part of the will of God?

Martha pondered on this as she went along the path back to the cabin. It was still dark, but a faint pink showed above the eastern hills. The crescent moon, clear-cut and golden, shone in the east, secure within its delicate shadow circle. It was a symbol, Martha thought as she looked up at it, of youth held within its destiny, growing to reach the round of its fulfillment. But for these young of the frontier—Violet and Hugh and Dave and Betsy and the rest—would the round of their lives be that of peace and plenty, or would it hold still the crimson threat of danger and war?

Poor Betsy! On the very eve of her wedding to have this happen to her! Just when she seemed happy and herself again! Of course there would be plenty to say it was all for the best and now Betsy and Dave could start their new life clear and free from the past. That did seem reasonable too, but Martha could not feel safe in the thought. She had watched Betsy these last months with interest and wonder. The very heart and passion of motherhood were in the girl's eyes. And now there was that stony gaze which only great sorrow brings.

Sam was already yawning and stretching in bed.

"Where've *you* been?" he asked in surprise.

"At the Kinkaids'. Sam, little Betsy just died."

"She did? Well, it ain't any great loss, I guess. Now Dave an' Betsy can go ahead."

"Don't!" Martha said sharply. "Don't say that as if it didn't matter."

"Well, it looks to me as if the Lord knew just what he was doin'. What are *you* so worked up for?"

Martha made no reply. She dressed wearily and started to prepare the breakfast.

They all saw Dr. Shields with Dave ride hard along the road about seven. Within the hour he rode by again, and Martha, watching, went out to speak to him.

"I'm sorry you had the trip, Dr. Shields. It was me sent for you, too."

"That's all right, Mistress Murray. The Grim Reaper often gets ahead of me. In this case I couldn't have done much anyway. This membranous croup takes the little ones. Well, well, a strange Providence, this, all around."

"That it is."

"The girl's heartbroke, you can see. Ah, well, young hearts mend easy. It's the older ones that stay cracked. At least that's what they say. How's your own girl?"

"She's well as ever. I can't thank you for what you did! How's your own family?"

"All right at the present. But the times are dark enough. We'll have to mind what the Blind Preacher told us, though, and keep up heart."

"Yes, I often think of that. It's a comfort and no mistake. Give my kind remembrances to Mrs. Shields and to Mrs. Craig too, when you see her."

"I'll do it with pleasure. Now I must be on my way. I'm busier blacksmithing just now than doctoring. Well, good day to you, Mistress Murray."

The big gray horse galloped out of sight.

Hugh and Dave, working together, made the small coffin. Martha laid deer hair in the bottom and covered it with a bit of old linen. It was Betsy's great desire that the baby be buried in the new Unity graveyard; but this would involve a difficult and dangerous journey just now. So the tiny grave was dug in the field on Gallows Hill just across the road from the big oak. There were a goodly number of other graves there, so little Betsy would not lie alone; but Betsy's heart was not satisfied. To Martha she confided her fears.

"The churchyard seems more holy, like. She'd mebbe be safer there. Oh, Mrs. Murray, she'll not be *lost,* will she? Never baptized or anything. I can't sleep for thought of it. If I could just be *sure,* some way."

Martha looked into the sheer terror of the eyes before her.

"Of course you can be sure, Betsy. There's mercy always in the love of God. Didn't Jesus say, 'Suffer the little children'? Now, you put such thoughts out of your head. You ought to be thinking of poor Dave these days, too. He's been so happy over the wedding. You mustn't cloud it over too much for him even if your own heart is torn."

"The wedding." Betsy said it blankly, and Martha felt chilled by the tone.

"Of course!" she went on, trying to make her voice bright. "The preacher comes in a few days now. Violet's been fixing up her dress, and I've made Hugh a new shirt to stand up in. Mind, dear child, that in life sometimes sorrow and joy tread close on each other's heels. We must take them as they come, and not question."

Betsy's eyes were still away. There was an unnatural hot flush on her cheeks. "I can't sleep," she said, "never even for an hour since little Betsy went."

But outwardly she was calm, and the simple wedding plans went on. Hugh and Violet were doubly solicitous; for Dave's face was pitiful, too, these days. Betsy's grief had stricken from it the gladness it had worn. It bore now a look of patience.

"Once we're married," he told Hugh, "an' get the cabin raised an' all, she'll have more to take up her mind. Mrs. Kinkaid's a wildcat if ever there was one. I think Betsy'll be all right if I just get her to myself."

"Belike she will," Hugh responded. "It's mebbe all for the best."

"I didn't mind the kid, some way. It favored her so, an' she set such store by it."

Hugh looked at his friend.

"There'll be another some day."

Dave flushed. "I hope so," he said.

Word came that the young preacher would arrive on the Wednesday from Fort Ligonier. It was arranged that the prayer meeting would be held that night and the marriage of Betsy and Dave the day following. Martha, busy with her last preparations in the cabin, realized as the hours wore on that she had not seen Betsy for two days. She questioned Violet carefully.

"Well," Violet said, "she looks queer, for her cheeks are so red in the mornings and then they're so white by afternoon. She's calm, like, and she can't wait for the preacher to get here. She says she thinks the days will never pass."

"I'm glad of that," Martha said heartily. "If she's got her mind so fixed on her wedding she'll be all right."

"I couldn't rightly tell whether it was the wedding she was thinking on or—something else. She won't talk much."

"It'll be that, of course," Martha returned. "Now I do believe we're nearly finished here. We've got about all the chairs and stools in the town. We'll make short shrift of supper and then tidy up the fireplace the last thing. If I can just get your father to clean himself up, then we'll be ready."

Martha's own cheeks were flushed with the excitement of entertaining the strange young minister and her towns-folk under her own roof. It was an experience of deep moment to her. It was not for nothing then that she had worked her fingers to the bone staining the rough raw wood of the settle and chairs, spinning and dyeing the curtain, making the cushions of deer hair! It was noticed then and commented upon. Even by Mr. Hanna himself.

She lighted the candles early, for the shadows fell soon in the cabin. She laid the Bible on the stand with a nog-gin of water beside it for the young preacher. The fire had been allowed to die down as much as possible, and the hearth was swept clean with a fresh turkey wing. There was nothing more now to be done but await the guests.

Mr. and Mrs. Hanna came first, bringing the young minister with them. He was tall and thin with dark hair and serious eyes. Even his greeting bore a touch of solemnity. His name was McAllister and his parents had come from Scotland. He had just finished at Princeton and had felt the call to make a missionary trip to the frontier. He was looking forward especially to his stay in Pittsburgh, for he had heard that the town was in great need of the saving grace of the Gospel. He counted it a privilege to be one of those who might offer the cup of salvation to dying souls there. He might even go farther into the wilderness to preach to the Indians. His dark eyes glowed with zeal as he spoke.

The audience gathered quickly. The cabin was soon filled with women and children, in their poor best, as clean as they had had opportunity to make themselves. The men and older boys stood about the door their rifles resting beside them.

Martha, busy with her greetings, did not see Betsy until the preacher rose to start the meeting. Then she caught her breath. The girl sat on the edge of the bed, her eyes riveted on the young preacher's face. There was a wildness in them that made Martha shiver. Suddenly she saw again the scene of the kissing-party, when Betsy screamed and threw the mirror from her. What had she seen, or fancied she saw, then? How was the terror of that night linked to this?

The young preacher was announcing the First Psalm and James rose to precent it:

"How blest and happy is the man
Who walketh not astray
In counsel of ungodly men,
Nor stands in sinners' way."

The sound of the voices met the silent wilderness and was lost within it.

There was next the reading of the Word, followed by prayer. Martha knew instantly as phrase followed phrase what sort of sermon they would hear. There would be in it none of the gentle benediction of the Blind Preacher. The young man had not lived long enough for that. Nor suffered. He was fresh from his books, so he would preach theology with the inexperienced fervor of youth. Well, it would do them no harm, she supposed.

He read his text over three times, raising his voice slightly each time: "How shall ye escape if ye neglect so great salvation."

His sermon, he said, would be divided into three parts: first, the Great Salvation; second, Acceptance or Neglect; third, Escape or Punishment.

Slowly, solemnly, he proceeded with the discourse: the lost and sinful state of man, the Plan of Atonement, then Predestination and the Doctrine of Free Will, reaching finally the peak of his oratory in a vivid description of heaven and hell.

His dark eyes glowed as he bent toward his listeners. He had reached his last sentence.

"Remember," he said, weighing each syllable, "that for those souls which are not among the elect there will be no escape year after year, century after century, eon after eon, to all eternity, from the burning fires of hell."

A sob broke the hush. It came from Betsy. A great uneasiness had fallen upon Martha during the last minutes, but she tried to shake it off. There were other sounds of emotion in the room. It was not only Betsy whose nerves had snapped under the strain of the sermon.

When the meeting was over, the men and women came forward, shook hands awkwardly with the preacher, nodded their good nights to Martha, and left quietly. Sam and Hugh with Dave and a few others stood talking on the path where Violet had just joined them. Martha saw then that Betsy was still in the far shadows of the cabin. She came forward slowly as the preacher was extending his hand.

"I've got to speak to him, Mrs. Murray. I've got to ask him about little Betsy. I can't ever sleep for thinkin' of it. Oh, you ask him, Mrs. Murray."

Betsy was shaking. The fever flush was high on her cheeks. Her eyes, like live coals, burned them both.

The young minister was at once all interest.

"You wish to consult me about someone's spiritual welfare?" he asked.

Martha started to explain, but Betsy broke in, her voice shaking like her poor hands which she kept twisting together.

"It's my baby. It's little Betsy. She died. An' I can't sleep for thinkin'—for bein' afraid. She wasn't baptized even. I wanted to take her up to Unity, an' Mother wouldn't have it. She was so pretty. Such a good baby. You're a preacher. You can tell me for sure. She's in heaven now, ain't she? She couldn't ever be *lost?*"

Her voice broke in its agony of entreaty. The young minister's face was touched.

"You yourself are a believer?"

"Yes—yes."

"And your husband?"

Betsy's eyes besought him. "It's us that's to be married tomorrow. Dave an' me."

Martha saw the preacher's young face stiffen.

Betsy caught his arm.

"Just say you're *sure*," she pleaded. "Just tell me you're *sure*. I can sleep then, mebbe, even if she's gone. Just so she's *safe*."

The young minister cleared his throat, hesitated, then cleared it again.

"We are all born into a state of sin and death, as you know. We are taught that elect infants, dying in infancy are by the grace of God saved. Of those not elect we can, of course, have no complete assurance—"

Betsy's eyes were wild sparks of light.

"You're not—sure?"

Martha tried to speak. "Oh think, Mr. McAllister, what this means to her!"

Betsy had caught his arm again. He winced at the grip.

"You can't tell me sure?"

He looked at her, but did not speak.

Betsy loosed her grip, still staring. She backed slowly away, her poor frenzied eyes filled with horror.

"I can see it in your face. You think she's lost. There in the fire like you said—"

Her voice rose to a scream.

"No! I'll not leave her by herself. If she's lost I am too. I'll go after her. I'll be with her, I will. An' don't you try to stop me!"

She sprang from the door, her screams cutting the night.

Martha brushed past the young man, whose own face now looked frightened enough. The men and Violet had come running back.

"It's Betsy!" Martha cried. "Hurry! She's going to do away with herself."

They could see in the pale moonlight a glimpse of her light colored dress back of the flax patch. They ran, all of them, Dave and Hugh ahead with Violet close behind.

"Which way? Which way?"

"There! That's her. She's makin' toward the creek!"

"Betsy—wait! Betsy! Betsy, come back!"

They all called, but she did not stop. Spurred by her desperate resolve, driven by her tortured fears, her feet knew no impediment. She ran like a thing possessed, over the fresh plowed field, never tripping over stumps, on through the devious woods to where the creek ran darkly.

Those ahead had gained on her. There might still be time. They could see her clearly now and hear her hard breathing.

"Catch her, Dave!" Hugh and Violet were a little behind him.

Then, suddenly, they all heard it. A thin wailing cry, riding pitifully on the still night air.

Betsy stopped for a second, and threw up her head.

"I'm comin', little Betsy," she called, "never you fear. I'm comin'."

With a last spurt she reached the creek bank and jumped far out into the depths of the beaver pond.

May 19, 1779 We laid Betsy away today on the hill beside the baby. She never came to after they got her out of the creek. It looked like she struck her head when she fell. The water there by the beaver dam is fairly deep but Dave was so quick jumping in he'd have saved her if it had been only the water to contend with. Poor child, it's been a sad sorry thing from first to last and she died with her secret still in her bosom. We're all bowed down with the sorrow of it. Violet can't eat and I don't wonder and poor Dave looks like a wraith. He and Hugh are off to the woods together now he seems like he couldn't face people. It's cruel hard to see the cabin staked out and the logs the boys had cut piled up there. I doubt Dave will join up with the regiment again if he can be spared. Oh it's a strange Providence. Mr. McAllister stayed to officiate at the funeral and he seemed softened. Well he might be. I hadn't the heart for argument or I would have had it out with him. That's a terrible like thing to think of God that he would punish a helpless babe I don't care what their theology books say. I think maybe a woman understands some things about God better than a man. There's plenty in town now that feel it's a question about Betsy's salvation too when all's considered. Mr. Brison spoke of it and several. I doubt I was sharp but I couldn't help it. I said why would you make God out worse than yourselves? That's sacrilege and for my part my Bible doesn't read that way. It seemed to quiet them for the time but there'll be plenty of talk at the tavern still and it wounds me to think of it. Poor young thing her life gone out like that. It's always hard for me to be reconciled when the young die. And yet who knows what they've been spared afterwards. That's something we can't see. I often think that about my own boys when I'm grieving that their lives were cut off. It's only if we could see all of life together that we could be sure about anything. This always comforts me. The ignorance of man is the wisdom of God, as my father used to say.

Scattered Entries from the Journal

June 20, 1779 J. B. here last night. Second call this week. Much talk of Arch Lochry's troubles with Col. Brodhead. It seems they can't get along. It's about the Rangers. Why would men bicker in times like these is what I can't fathom. Dave stopped in too so Hugh bided at home all evening. He's stayed in several times now when J. is here. Sits and listens but says nought. Eats as usual though and seems himself so I can't rightly judge if I was mistaken. Violet passing pretty these days with double row of curls all round her head. Makes them over a bit of cornstalk. Have felt constrained to warn her against pride. J. looks at her whenever he speaks. Told me in confidence his law work going well. Said to Violet yesterday what a fine man I thought J. to be and she said he *rightly was*. Am hard put to it to keep Sam civil to J. He's begun to gulder a little about calls being so frequent. I said it was me J. comes to talk to may God forgive me. It ain't you he looks at Sam says. I didn't think Sam noticed that much so I must have extra care how I handle him to keep him from upsetting everything. And here's another stab in my heart. If Violet goes east it would nigh kill Sam. Of course it would me too but I'd bear it for her sake but I don't know about him. Men are different.

July 8th, 1779 Court week. One poor fellow whipped at the post today for felony. 39 lashes well laid on. The law must take its course but oh I hate the sound of the lash. He was a youngish man James said from over Redstone way and stood an hour in the pillory too but no stones thrown. Long pack train in last night ten horses. Left this morning for Fort Pitt. Sam and Hugh busy hoeing corn. Flax growing unusual fast. How I've always set my heart on a scutching party and never a summer it seemed feasible. We've much to be thankful for and I shouldn't dwell on what can't be. Just our lives is a daily gift of God. Lord make me thankful and keep us in safety and most of all in Thy grace. Mrs. Hanna received a letter by express yesterday from Mrs. Negley. Says she fancies Pittsburgh greatly. They have purchased three hundred acres along the banks of the Allegheny river. It shows a woman does well to have a mind of her own I doubt at times I've been too yielding like and yet . . . Several stray beasts reported at court by Hempfield Twp overseer. What a loss to lose a horse.

July 27, 1779 Am still rightly perplexed about Hugh. He and Dave off in the woods all their spare time. Violet outwardly much as usual. Strange it is how a mother can't even read her own child. Every heart knoweth its own bitterness and not even our nearest can intermeddle with our joy. The wise man was right when he wrote that. J. still a steady caller. Talks of things that take us out of ourselves. His mother told me at the spring today J. so changed. Thinks all due to Pittsburgh trips. Kept my own counsel. Toothache again most desperate last night. Chewed calamus root and great relief today. Storm gathering now and air very close.

August 20, 1779 Well I had my scutching party and right
pleased I am I went ahead with it. After all as I said to Sam
what's the sense in talking about faith and then always expecting the worst? The times are bad enough but it was
borne in on me that a bit of frolic would ease the heart and
do us good. And if the Injuns were to come they'd come anyway. So I sent Violet round yesterday to bid the women and
right pleased they were. Never have I had such a crop of flax.
When it was retted and spread out to dry it covered the whole
patch and some here at the front. Hugh did the braking so
today all was ready. Mrs. Hanna, Mrs. Brison, Mrs. Steel,
Mrs. Shaw, Mrs. Guthrie, Mrs. Kinkaid, Mrs. Cook, Mrs.
Beatty, Mrs. Orr, Mrs. Scott guests. Men brought scutching
blocks over early. Ladies arrived nigh about eight with own
swingling knives. Violet, Peggy and the girls sorted stalks and
laid beside scutching blocks. Everyone worked with right
good will and to hear the laughing and the gossip none would
think there was a redskin within a hundred miles or a care
on a body's mind. It pleased me most mighty. I always like
a scutching. There's something rightly to my satisfaction to
see the stringy stalks falling away and the fibres and threads
all in a fluff like, lying in the grooves of the scutching blocks
Mrs. Hanna says scutching always pleasures her the same way
its not too hard yet shows up your work so. Peggy teased
much about Hen Wilson and believe there's something to it
Mrs. Cook says to use *new mown hay* to dye with it makes a
genteel black and a fast color. Will try as soon as I get my
linen spun. Who'd have thought it. Her sister wrote her and
generous it is in her to tell us all for she could have kept i
and none the wiser. Little reference to the war which was a
well. Some goings on here related not fit for the girls' ears.
put a stop to it when I could. But mostly pleasant talk and
plenty laughter which lifts the spirits. Ate at noon and man
compliments to my pone. Tried to turn them off but wa

pleased. Mrs. Hanna remarked very special on its quality. Asked my proportions of saleratus to buttermilk. Found many stirred into whole quantity of milk. All interested in way I do mine. I *do feel* without vanity that mine has finer texture than most. Mrs. Kinkaid quiet for her. Poor soul she maybe grieves more than we know. Mrs. Scott *got sick sudden* and had to lie down and we all looked at each other and said nought for a few minutes we were so taken aback. She's in her forties and it gave me a turn and no mistake. No one ever suspicioned how it was with her till today. Mrs. Guthrie is a clip she said God save us we'd better send all our men off to fight the Injuns if this keeps up. After dinner all set to hackle and by four were finished. Swingling tow in one big pile and linen fibre in the other. Women all seemed content and many compliments on the day. Feel lifted this evening. Full moon. Green corn moon as some call it.

September 29, 1779 The fall again. My how fast the years tread upon each other. Man's days are as grass. Teach us, O God to number them so we may apply our hearts unto wisdom. Good word from Pittsburgh about the last campaign again the Indians. Brodhead seems to have more gumption than any of the others. Raised a force of 600 and went north, raided the Senecas and Muncies and destroyed over 500 acres of their crops so the report goes and not a horse or a man lost. Poor Hugh I pity him to think he wasn't along this time when something was rightly accomplished. I still can't be sure what's going on in his mind and heart. Nor in Violet either for that matter. They act content to be nigh each other as always but it seems Hugh sees to it they're never alone together. I've noticed Violet even making excuse for it. There's a sadness in Hugh's eyes betimes too old for his years. But there's enough work and trouble to keep us all busy. Dipped candles this week and made soap yesterday. Always feel better when those two messy jobs are behind me. Oh but my heart does crave the pewter molds. Poor Watch full of fleas again they get in the house even the bedticks and I can't thole them. Will tidy up cockloft tomorrow. Sam and Hugh busy with the corn. Thankful am I to say we have a wee lock of white flour for the winter. Just a few gourds full. The men had it ground at John Cavet's mill when they were over. William Scotts have apprenticed his orphaned niece from down by Redstone until she be eighteen. James drew up the papers. He says the terms are to give her sufficient meat and raiment and cause her to be taught to read till her apprenticeship expires then to set her up with a new suit of wearing apparel a wheel a cow and a Bible which is fair and kindly. A pleasant child she seems and pretty spoken. Saw J. night before last move to settle to sit nigh to Violet. Hugh not here at the time. Weather clear and mild. At night from stable door stars most wonderful. When I consider thy heavens the work of thy fingers, what is man that thou art mindful of him. Sam restrung his fiddle and there's more tune to it now. He says the catgut much better than rabbit. Violet over at Peggy's with her knitting. She can beat me now on the turn of a sock. Oh may life be smooth beneath her feet. Governor Patrick Henry now out in Virginia so they say and a new man in Thos Jefferson his name. Well among them be it.

XI

The Lochry Expedition

The winter of 1779–80 was probably the severest in the history of the United States. In January the harbor of New York was frozen so solidly that the British drove their heavily loaded wagons on the ice from the city to Staten Island!

Back in western Pennsylvania the snow began to fall in early December, increasing at intervals until by early February it was four feet deep in the woods and over the mountains. No supply trains from the east could get through.

As the bitter cold continued the suffering grew. The garrison at Fort Pitt were short of both clothes and food; many of the soldiers had no shoes and the officers had neither money nor credit.

In Hannastown the pinch of cold and poverty bit deeply. It took all the men's strength merely to cut enough wood to run the fires and to attend to the stock. The cabins shook in the stormy blasts, the piercing wind entered at every crevice, and the bare business of daily living became an intolerable burden. There was no salt! And without it food was but a tasteless necessity. A sprinkling of hickory ashes was a poor enough substitute for the familiar savor.

In the deep wilderness even the wild things suffered for the snow was so deep they could find nothing to eat. When spring came at last the hunters discovered the dead bodies of deer and game and small desperate creatures scattered through the aisles of the forest.

"The Winter of the Great Snow," as it was to be called for a hundred years to come in those parts, took a toll of Indian life also. The destitution was especially great amongst the Senecas whose crops had been destroyed by Brodhead and his men the summer before. When scores of them died from starvation the desire for revenge against the Americans grew with every passing day.

But they were not able to renew their raids that spring. The necessity for planting their own ravaged fields lay upon them, and game was scarce and poor. So, with their hatred smoldering, they stayed in their own villages and the settlers of Westmoreland County, at least, knew a peaceful planting time after their hard winter.

Nothing in the long history of man is more startling, more significant, or more ironic than the effect of weather upon his destiny. A shower of rain may unseat a king; a snowstorm may send an empire crashing. Man with all his lordly powers must, at the very moment of his pride, pause and wait and be still while Nature moves about her own quiet providences. He must strip himself bare in his humility before such a simple thing as the fall of the evening dew or the gradual golden weaving of the dawn; and, most important of all, he must not question where there is no answer.

This was to Martha the hardest of all, that summer of '80. Not to question. Not to cry out, Why? Why? For the deeply penetrating cold of the winter had loosened the hard virgin soil so that the plows turned up richer furrows than ever before; there was no trouble from the Indians that spring, and so more crops were planted than had been in any other season. Not only corn but some *wheat,* with a prayer of hope for the precious white flour. And this grain grew and flourished and ripened to golden promise. All over Westmoreland County that summer there was little of the dreaded *sick wheat* which had been the farmer's curse before. Instead of the blackened ends there were the fresh, sun-filled awns.

Then came the drought! The hot sun blazed, the heavens were as brass, and the streams dried up at their sources. Not a mill turned. The corn and the wheat, in quantities that the hard-pressed pioneers had never possessed before, lay in heaps in the Hannastown fields or stables. Grown, cut, threshed with the flail—but not ground.

An entry in Martha's journal for that period runs as follows:

August 30, 1780 There must be no place in our hearts for bitterness as I said to Sam this morning, though it's cruel hard to bear. Sam is more crushed down than I've ever seen him yet. Bitterness he said—I can't write down all his words —I'm so mad he said I could amost grind all that grain with my teeth. Poor Sam I do pity him more than the rest of us,

him and Hugh for they toiled so hard and were so made up
over the big harvest. It is harder for them to submit to this
than have all the strain and work of it. God give us all grace.
They say the soldiers at Fort Pitt are all but starving. Brodhead can get no flour and he wants to buy cattle from the
farmers round here but what have they to spare. The whole
garrison of the fort paraded one morning in front of the
Colonel's house. James there that day and saw it. Says it was
a sight most pitiful. All in rags they are and gaunt. Brodhead
asked what did they want and they said they had been without bread for five days and were hungry. So are your officers
he said the same as you we are doing all we can. Men well
behaved and returned to barracks. Yesterday a few horse
loads of flour and a few head live cattle passed through clear
from the Cumberland Valley. That will help a little but
won't be a pinch for what they need. No special change here
at home since I wrote last. J. busy at his books making up
what he lost last winter. Have decided how it is with him.
He wont speak until he is ready to make final plans. It's
the way he's made, so must be patient. Comes regular. Some
notice of it now taken in town. Violet as usual though sometimes . . . Maybe it's my fancy and I must bide my time.

When the spring of '81 came round a new wave of
excitement swept the border—disturbing and dissentious.
General George Rogers Clark, who had captured Vincennes and Hair-Buyer Hamilton in the winter of '79,
was now zealously furthering another expedition against
Detroit. His plan was to raise a large force, float down the
Ohio to the Wabash, ascend that stream as far as possible
and then march overland to Detroit. He came up from
Virginia early in March to discuss the matter and made
his headquarters at the home of Colonel Crawford on the

Youghiogheny. It was only a few weeks before his plans
became the burning topic of conversation in Hannastown. At the tavern night after night the whole matter
was threshed over.

"I don't like it," Robert Hanna declared. "He's working for Virginia. Didn't she claim all the Illinois country
that he took before? What he's up to is to raise Pennsyl-
vanians to fight for his own state. He's a Virginia officer,
ain't he? What's he doing up here?"

"Course the boundary line isn't run yet," Captain Orr
put in. "There's still some folks round here think they're
Virginians. West of the Monongahela anyway."

Sam spat with vehemence and then delivered himself.

"I don't care a damned haet whether Clark's a Virginian or a Pennsylvanian. If he can clean out Detroit
and bust the hide off them red devils out there I'd enlist
under him myself if I had two good legs to carry me."

"Aye, aye, right you are, Sam," came from several of
the others.

Archibald Lochry was silent. He drummed on the table
and looked off over the heads of the others. He was a man
in his prime but he had aged the last year.

"What's your views, Colonel?" Robert Hanna asked.

"It's a problem," Lochry said, "any way you look at it.
Brodhead expected to make a new campaign against Detroit himself. Now he's jealous as the very devil. But
Congress favors Clark, and after what he's done already
you can't blame them. He's a great fighter. If he keeps
on asking for volunteers I'll feel it's my duty to support
him."

"You'll have tight work gettin' men to leave thei[r] homes now. The raids are breakin' out again all over," Mr. Brison declared.

Lochry looked discouraged. He knew better than th[e] others that there were sections of Westmoreland Count[y] right then almost depopulated. The settlers, wearied wit[h] their unending warfare against the Indians, had fled bac[k] over the mountains. On his rounds he had seen many [a] deserted cabin with perhaps a mute row of graves alon[g] the garden fence. This all spoke for itself.

He was anxious about ammunition for the militia—they would desert if it didn't come; he was harried b[y] constant bickerings with Brodhead; lately, he had eve[n] been criticized by President Reed himself, who had writ[-]ten, "We hear that when troops are raised for your pro[-]tection they are permitted to loiter away their time a[t] taverns." Lochry had wished grimly that the state officia[l] could come out to the frontier and wrestle with the prob[-]lems himself for a while. He'd learn a few things. No[w] there was this added responsibility of Clark's pressing ca[ll] for volunteers for the new expedition. Meanwhile h[e] hadn't yet given his neighbors the new piece of bad new[s] from the war itself.

"Let's have our usual toast, Robert," he said at length[.] "I'll stand it. There's no denying things seem to be goin[g] against us all along the line. I've just heard that Charles[-]ton has been captured with five thousand troops. Th[e] Carolinas are nigh overrun. But this is not the end, min[d.] It's the last surrender that counts."

There was excited outcry over the news, but Rober[t]

Hanna himself filled the noggins and motioned for quiet.

Lochry rose, his strong features grave and steady.

"To Liberty," he said, and drained his cup.

Sam and Hugh left the tavern soon after, walking back slowly.

"I dunno what's wrong with our ginerals," Sam growled. "Gettin' nowhere they are, fast, dammit."

"General St. Clair's done good," Hugh said. "The men in the Eighth were sayin' he was the one put it in Washington's head to attack Princeton that time they fell on the Hessians. They said they was all proud St. Clair was from these parts."

"Well, I wisht he'd put some more good idees in their heads, then. They need 'em right enough."

"About this campaign of Clark's," Hugh said. "I guess I'll be signin' up if it goes through."

"Belike you should, lad," Sam agreed gravely.

And so it was settled.

It was a busy summer in Hannastown, with more people going and coming than anyone could remember before. It was mostly recruits of one sort or another, of course, who rode or walked into the village, or maintained their temporary residence in the stockade or about the tavern. The Congress of Pennsylvania had voted that spring for extra companies of rangers to be formed, and Captain Thomas Stokely had raised one from Westmoreland County. These men were found to be congenial spirits by the people of Hannastown, for they were expert woodsmen all, and Captain Stokely a worthy leader.

By July the die had been cast. General Clark had the

promise of a fair-sized force from the Pennsylvania and Virginia border, and in spite of bitter opposition in some quarters and lukewarm agreement in others, Colonel Lochry had decided to raise a band to join him in the new campaign. His good friend Captain Orr volunteered to go and to urge some of his militiamen to enlist; and Captain Stokely's Rangers were also to join the company. Beyond these, Lochry set out to secure enough recruits to raise the number to a hundred. Hugh and Dave both joined up, as did most of the young men from Hannastown; some men from the Derry settlement enlisted too, including young Samuel Craig, while Fred Pershing represented the Fourteen Mile Run district.

It was decided that they would not set out until the harvest was finished but would all meet on August 1st at Carnahan's blockhouse about ten miles north of Hannastown.

Violet's heart was heavy with terrible foreboding those last days. It seemed to her as though she could not bear the weight of pain that lay upon it. For Hugh had been different in his attitude to her now these many months. His voice sounded almost rough betimes. He never looked at her now with the burning light in his dark eyes as he had done that evening when Dave and Betsy had come to the door to tell them their news. . . . Oh, how much of sadness had come their way since that happy night! Hugh never asked her now to go along to the spring with him. He would even make excuse to leave the cabin if they were left alone together. When she had once said

'Brother, is there aught come between us?" he had said,
'Naught," and gone out quickly.

Now he would soon be leaving, and with him would
go the sun from the skies. No morning and no night
would have meaning to her with him far away and pressed
by danger. She made up her mind she must talk to him
alone at any cost, even though she begged him on her
knees.

The chance came on the last evening but one. Martha
had gone over to see Mrs. Brison, who had not been well,
and Sam left for his usual trip to the tavern. Hugh was
starting hastily to follow him when Violet spoke.

"Wait, Brother." There was strength and purpose in
her tone.

Hugh paused at the door, his head lowered.

"I've got to talk with you." All at once her tears broke
as in a flood. "I'm heartsick, and you pay me no heed."

He took a swift step toward her and stopped.

"Don't," he cried out. "I've borne all I can. I'm tearin'
out my own heart. Don't try to stop me."

"But why, Hugh? What's come between us? It's killing
me. And now before you go I've got to have gentleness
from you, or I can't *live*."

She had gone close to him, catching his arms.

"What have I said or done to put you far away like
you've been? What is it, Brother?"

She could feel him stiffen. His face was white. His arms
hung at his sides.

"It's for you, Sister. I've always known you were too
delicate made for this life here. You ought to have easy

ways like gentlefolk. Even before Mother spoke to me I knew that."

Her hands gripped him the harder.

"What did Mother say to you?"

"I can't rightly speak of it."

"You must, Hugh. I'll give you no peace."

"She says you're—for—James. I can see myself he sets store by you. He'll take you east. You'll have ease there an' pleasant ways. Let go of me now! I'm tryin' to do my duty an' love you better than myself—"

But at the words Violet did not let go. Instead her arms reached up and circled his neck. She clung as though naught could loose her hold.

"You do love me then. Say it over, Hugh. Oh, say it so I'll rightly hear it from your own lips, and not just the hope of it to stay me."

And could he bear more? Not with the warm red blood of life within him and every drop of it aflame for her.

He held her to his breast like steel.

"I love you better than my life! I want to marry you. But it's been like a shame in my heart since everyone considers I'm brother to you. Tell me it's not as sister you love me."

"It's not as sister. I've deceived myself, but that's all past. Oh, Hugh, I tremble, like, just at the touch of you. I love you so. Is it that way with you?"

He held her closer. "You couldn't even understand."

"Kiss me."

His face was grave when he raised his head.

"I can't take you back east. I doubt it's the life here I'm made for."

"It doesn't matter, so we're together."

Then the black fact swept over them. Violet caught her breath in a sob.

"Don't go on this campaign, Hugh! I can't bear it, not now. There's others can go in your stead. Can't you bide at home and let us get married and build our cabin and—"

Her voice broke as she searched his face.

"You—have—to—go?"

He nodded, his eyes dark with the grief of it.

"I've signed up. I've give my word. I wouldn't honor myself if I broke it. They need men. Someone's got to go. We wouldn't be rightly happy thinkin' all the time I'd backed out of it."

The sighs of their hearts were drowned again in their kisses.

"We'll get married as soon as you get back. I'll pray God to keep you."

"I'll love you an' fend for you all the days of my life."

Suddenly he released her, smiling.

"I've got a present for you. I aimed to give it you just before I left. I'll get it now."

He was up the ladder to the cockloft in a flash and back with a flat package wrapped in a bit of dirty brown paper.

"I've been on the lookout for this for a good spell now. Joe Irvine just told me the other day he'd got a one for me from a trader."

He handed it over and watched as Violet opened it wonderingly.

It was a small flowered plate.

She turned it around and around in her hands, saying nothing.

"Is it not what you was wantin'?" Hugh asked anxiously.

Then she raised her eyes with a look of such beauty in them!

"I never really thought to own one. It was just sort of a dream, like. With little roses and leaves and all! I never had as pretty a thing in all my life. It's far more even than the mirror to me. It'll be for our own cabin, Hugh."

They fingered it together, their hands touching. The little twining wreath was like their love, fresh and fair and endless.

When Sam and Martha returned together, there was no need to speak the secret. The young people sat on the settle enfolded in each other's arms and looked up at them with shining wonder in their eyes.

Martha sat down quickly as though felled by a blow, but Sam looked at them and looked again and then threw back his head and roared with delighted laughter.

"Well, damn me for an old turkey buzzard if this ain't the surprise of my life! Why, you young rascals! Why, you little varmints! How long's this thing been goin' on?"

"I never meant to speak, Mother," Hugh said quickly. "It just happened sudden, like."

"I made him," Violet said with shy pride. "And now we'll get married when he gets back from the expedition.

That is, if you're not against it," she added, laughing.

"Fornenst it!" Sam shouted. "Why, anybody could see you two was made for each other. Well, there's no other man I'd give Violet to, my boy, without some backspangs, but you're a lad after my own heart. I feel as if I'd fathered you myself. Yes, sir, we've been blind as moles, not to see this afore!"

"I tried, Mother, like you said." Hugh's anxious voice still pleaded with her.

"I know," Martha spoke, a wan smile touching her lips. "I know, lad. You couldn't help but speak."

"An' why wouldn't he speak?" Sam asked in amazement. "He's a man now, ain't you, Hugh? No need for him to stand back like a bound boy at a huskin'. No, sir. He's the best shot in Hannastown after meself, an' he's handsome as they come, with as well turned a pair of legs as ever bore breeks!"

He slapped Hugh on the shoulder. "Eh, lad, you're a'most fit for our girl here, damn me if you ain't! An' that's the best thing I can say fur you!"

They all saw then the whiteness of Martha's face. The sickness which fear always brought her was near the mastery. Violet went to her.

"You're that surprised! I feel queer like, myself, with the true knowing of it. Lie down till you feel better. We were so mortal happy we never thought what a startle we'd give you."

"You're so—happy then, child?"

"Oh, past the telling. If only he didn't have to go on the campaign it would just be heaven come down to me!"

Before they all went to bed, Hugh told them he was enlisting under his own name of McConnell.

"I hope you won't think strange of it," he said. "But you see if—when I get back an' we're gettin' married an' all I'll be needin' my own name like, for Violet."

"Violet McConnell I'll be then!"

"*Mistress* McConnell," Hugh corrected with a look that seemed to set the whole cabin alight.

At long last when the rest were all asleep, Martha still lay rigid. For once, she could not even pray.

On the early morning of August 1st Archibald Lochry's contingent left Hannastown. Captain Robert Orr with his riflemen—many of whom he supplied at his own expense—and Captain Stokely with his Rangers went staunchly with their old friend.

Hugh had said his last good-bye to Violet in the breaking dawn. As the sun rose red, they had stood on the edge of the forest, lost in each other's arms. They spoke few words, and for his sake Violet held back the tears. Only her love she poured out upon him, leaving, and a smile as she finally waved him out of sight. He turned back as long as he could, with no shame now upon him, to wave and look and wave again.

Dave watched his friend in deep surprise.

"What's struck you? I never saw you act this way afore."

"I'm gettin' married to Violet when I get back," Hugh said simply. He knew the sorrow still in Dave's heart, so he felt more closely knit to him than ever as Dave exclaimed and questioned and planned with him about the future as they continued their march.

At Carnahan's blockhouse, a few more men on foot joined them, and a company of horse under Captain William Campbell. Lochry then outlined to them all the plan of advance. General Clark was now at Fort Henry (Wheeling), Virginia. They would go across the country as rapidly as possible to join him there. From then on, their forces strong, their leadership the best for frontier fighting which the country had ever had, they ought to get results. So Lochry cheered his men. There was no need to tell them that they represented the pick of the county's young riflemen. Without vanity they all knew that. This, indeed, was why they were there at all. What they did grumble about in true soldier fashion as they started their journey, was that many of them were poorly clad and provisions were none too plentiful. But once they got to Clark things would be all right, for he had provisions intended for them.

The little band did not go by way of Fort Pitt. Lochry thought it would be quicker to cross the Youghiogheny River, then the Monongahela at Devore's Ferry and proceed across the country, hugging the southern bank of the Ohio until they reached Fort Henry. By supreme exertion and good luck they might make it in a week; most of the men counted on ten days.

It was with a feeling of triumph then and hope riding high that they found themselves nearing the fort on the evening of the 8th.

"Pretty good traveling, I must say," Colonel Lochry told his men. "I knew I could count on this crowd."

As they entered the little settlement they were struck by its deserted look. If any large force of men were quartered here, they were keeping well out of sight.

"Must all go to bed with the chickens," Dave said to Hugh.

"Something wrong here, I doubt," Hugh returned anxiously.

Colonel Lochry went to speak to the officer in charge of the rude fort and then, with a puzzled air, returned to his men. He looked into their tired, hungry faces.

"It seems," he began calmly, "that General Clark had trouble with desertions while waiting here. He felt he had to keep moving. Just this morning he set out with his force in boats. He left a message saying he'd wait for us downstream about twelve miles at a point called the Three Islands. We're to follow and join him there."

"What about provisions?" a voice called.

"He left some. And one boat."

"Which of us is goin' to swim, then?"

There was an attempt at laughter but a poor one. They felt cheated if not betrayed. By those few hours between morning and evening, they had missed their chance.

Colonel Lochry drew Captain Orr and Captain Stokely aside. They talked long and earnestly while the men lounged about, resting, cursing their bad luck, eating a bit of leftover flapjack stored in their hunting shirts or prophesying bitterly of the future.

Lochry spoke to them at last. They had no choice, he said, but to follow on and this would demand boats. Clark had no more than he needed, so they must build their own, working harder than any of them had ever worked before, for every day, every hour was precious.

"It'll take a miracle, lads," he said, "but I'll bet we can do it."

And they did it. Straining, sweating, chopping, lugging logs and splitting them, building crudely from nothing by sheer determined man power, they finished seven boats in four days. With every joint and muscle sore and aching, but with hope now strong again, they embarked in their rough craft on the 13th and started slowly downstream, the horses and their riders keeping close to shore. Since at this time the Ohio River was the dividing line between the white man's country and the Indians, they were careful to keep to the left bank.

They poled and sculled slowly along, as silently as might be, not quite reaching the Three Islands the first day. They camped safely, though, being able to beach the boats, and set off again early in the morning. There was no difficulty in recognizing the location of the Three Islands as they approached. The geographical contours stood out distinctly. As the men strained their eyes they could see a large flatboat moored there and the figure of a man apparently on the lookout for them.

Sore backs and legs were forgotten. They had accomplished the impossible, and here they were at the appointed place ready for the union of the forces. There was some subdued shouting back and forth between the boats and a general lightening of spirits. As they drew nearer, however, they could see only seven men awaiting them. There was an oppressive silence over all the landscape as they reached the shore. The great woods were ominously still; so was the river. So were the few men ready to receive them.

Lochry sprang to land first and hurried to the bearded man who advanced from the little group.

"Well, here we are." Lochry spoke with quick heartiness. If he felt premonition he kept it out of his voice. "I'm Archibald Lochry from Westmoreland County reporting here with my men. Where is General Clark?"

The bearded man cleared his throat. It was evident that he had small taste for his mission.

"I'm Major Crascroft," he said as he shook hands. "I'm afraid I have news you won't care to hear. The General moved on yesterday. The men were getting restless. He felt he had to start. But he left this horse boat here for your animals and says to come on. He'll wait sure for you at the mouth of the Kanawha. You can't miss it. First stream of any size coming in from the left."

"How far down?" Lochry's tone was cold and even.

The Major hesitated. "Well, I'd say it was close to a hundred miles," he answered. "You've got the current with you, though, and with your horses afloat too, you ought to make twenty-five miles a day."

"We're low on ammunition and supplies both," Lochry said quietly.

They stood silent, looking at each other. Without speech they read each other's minds.

"We'll do our best," Lochry said at last. "Just tell General Clark we've *got* to catch up with him and we'll expect to join him at the Kanawha."

The Major reached his hand.

"Good luck," he said. "I needn't tell you to keep your eyes open. I've got a skiff here, so I'll take these men and push off. No point in us waiting any longer. Well, we'll see you at the Kanawha then."

Lochry nodded. The same silence brooded over the place as the seven men hurried to their lighter, speedier boat, shoved off, and waved good-bye.

The Westmorelanders watched them go with heavy faces. The ones near enough to have heard the conversation relayed it to the others. Then an anger, fierce and devastating, seized them. Their curses against General Clark, against the deserters, against the whole race of Indians who were responsible for their plight were bitter and terrible.

Lochry made no move to check them. When he had conferred again with the other officers, he signed to the men at last to gather close on the shore. The horses and their riders had just come up. Quietly, steadily, Lochry put the facts before them.

"We can't go back, men. We've got to go ahead. With the horse boat we can make time. It's bad, I know, but it isn't hopeless. We'll cook a meal here and then set out as fast as we can. Save your wind now for the work before us."

As Hugh ate the coarse pone, he found a difficulty in swallowing. Not even at Fort Laurens had he felt the same sense of coming evil. Dave was gloomy too. Their limbs still ached from the building of the boats; their stomachs were still half empty, and their hearts were heavy.

But they put out the fire carefully, got the horses loaded on the big raft, took their places, all of them, in the smaller craft they had built with unspeakable toil, and pushed off down the stream in the shortest possible time.

As the day wore on, Hugh and Dave, their keen eyes fixed on the wooded shores, their rifles ready, began to feel with their woodsman's sixth sense that the great silence around them was not that of isolation. The other men were feeling it too. You could tell by their sudden quick movements; their drawn brows shadowing their peering eyes; their tense, listening attitudes. They were all as keen as forest animals to detect the presence of danger. Like a sudden darkening of the sky, like a sudden thickening of the air, they all began to feel now that they were being watched—that other eyes, keener even than their own, were peering from the heavy leafy shadows of the banks.

The horse boat was of enormous help; the current was strong yet not dangerous. As the hours passed they all knew they were making unexpectedly good time. They kept going at night also, stopping only once a day to cook enough merely to stay their hunger, for their flour was nearly gone.

The night travel was difficult. The men took turns, those of one group poling and watching while the others lost themselves in uneasy and uncomfortable sleep. The greatest caution had to be exercised, for long sand bars projected here and there into the water and once the boats had scraped rock. So in the darkness they proceeded slowly. The night hours were oppressive even without the danger which menaced them. The air was hot and sticky and filled with gnats and mosquitoes. Worst of all to Hugh were the bats which kept flying about their heads. He could not forget Martha's abhorrence to them. "I can't thole bats," she was always saying. "I feel they bring bad luck."

At the end of the fourth day, the clear waters of the river were bright with color from a rich sunset. The men, always sharply on the lookout, saw before them clearly to the left the waters of a large stream emptying into the Ohio. This must be the Kanawha! Once again there was excitement and a great lifting of all hearts. So far, against tremendous odds, they had fulfilled every requirement. They were here now at this rendezvous even sooner than Major Crascroft had predicted. There was no smoke rising from the bank and no signs of life about, but this was not in itself ominous. The woods were deep. The General and his men might be on the other side of the Kanawha.

They poled the boats closer while Lochry and Orr standing, hands shading eyes, strained to see signs of the waiting army.

Suddenly Hugh caught sight of a tree near the water's

edge, with its bark freshly stripped from its trunk. He called the attention of Colonel Lochry to it.

"I've been eyeing it," he said. "Do you see a bit of white against it?"

"I do, sir. It looks to me like a bit of paper."

Lochry told the men to get the boat to shore. Hugh was close behind him as they all scrambled out. Lochry walked straight to the tree, the others following. The spot of white was indeed a paper, secured to the trunk of the tree by whittled wooden pegs. Lochry's face was as white as the paper when he took it down and opened it. He read it first to himself, his lips, drained of color, moving stiffly on the words. Then, as they all waited, he read it aloud.

Col Lochry Sir I regret to inform you I have had to move on. My men are deserting and I cannot delay longer. Follow hard after and meet us if possible farther down stream. Will be on the look out for you.

Respy
G. R. CLARK

At first there was no sound at all except a faint wind blowing the thick leaves overhead. Even the deep low coursing of the river was audible in the awful stillness. Then the storm broke from their pent hearts. A deer crashed through the brush behind them, a white headed eagle rose screaming, both frightened by the noise of the men's bitter cursing.

For now their condition was desperate. They had set out from home with only provision and ammunition enough to last them to Fort Henry. The small amount of foodstuffs left there for them by Clark was now consumed. Desolate, betrayed, and despairing, the men stood on this strange shore, far from home, with hope drowned in the waters of the river before them, which would bear them farther on its current, but could not take them back.

"We could strike off by land, Colonel, an' make a try for gettin' home through the forest."

"Just livin' on game's a chancy business!"

"Well, ain't it what we have to do now no matter which way we go?"

"Do you think there's a haet of a chance of us ever catchin' up to Clark, Colonel?"

"The damned rat! I hope he drowns before we get there!"

The storm rose and fell. Through it all Lochry was silent. When the men flung themselves down at last exhausted, he spoke to them.

"General Clark's got his own problems, lads. From the looks of this paper he only left here a day or so past. He's waited for us every place as long as he could. It won't do us any good to keep cursing him."

"Damn his tough hide, it does *me* good," one fellow called out.

There was faint laughter, and then Lochry went on.

"We'll keep on going. There's more chance of catching up with him than of trying to make our way back by land. Besides we set out to do a job. The main thing right now is grub."

"Aye, is it!"

"Captain Shannon, you're a pretty smart navigator. Will you take a few men with you in the best boat we've got and see if you can overtake Clark? Ask him to leave provisions for us and guard them till we catch up to you."

"We'll get started at once. Can I pick me own men?"

"Go ahead."

Hugh listened eagerly for his name and Dave's. But Shannon chose men he knew from the other end of the county, seven of them, then he selected the boat Clark had left behind at Fort Henry. While the last of the flour was being made into pone for them, Lochry wrote a message to General Clark which he read aloud to his men before he handed it over to Captain Shannon.

General Clark, Sir, We are now at the Kanawha and in sore straits to find you gone on ahead. We are bare a hundred men and the last of our provision is gone. Leave some behind we beg you with bearer of this note and tarry if you can till we get up with you.

Yours respectfully,

A. LOCHRY

The men listened and gave their assent. Already out of their despair, a new, faint hope was beginning to rise. Shannon might overtake Clark and get the provisions. . . . At least there was something being attempted.

They watched the eight push off and start downstream in the late sunset.

The men had some game that night, though not

enough. The problem of the horses' food had also become acute. While they snatched at low-hanging leaves and nuzzled about the ground during their brief stays on land, there was no proper herbage for them in the heavy woods or upon the sand bars which seemed jointly to cover the whole left bank of the river. The animals had grown thin, and one or two were definitely sick. Captain Campbell was anxious.

"These beasts can't go on too much longer, Colonel," he warned.

"I've been watching them," Lochry answered. "All we can do is hope."

The journey continued, with every eye fixed to catch sight of Captain Shannon's little band or of General Clark's force, or both. But the first day passed and the second, and there was only the transparent, shining, indifferent river beneath them and the woods, heavy and hostile, alongside. The August sun blazed down, and the low, steady, gnawing hunger made the men distressed and irritable. Always, too, there was upon them that weight of uneasiness as though they were being watched by hidden eyes.

On the late afternoon of the third day the men in the foremost boat gave a sharp signal, and pointed to the water's edge a half-mile downstream. Two figures stood there, waving their arms feebly. As the boats drew nearer it was apparent that the men's faces were scratched and bleeding and dirty almost beyond recognition; their clothing hung in shreds, and they seemed scarcely able to stand up.

"They're from Shannon's party," went from lip to lip. Lochry's boat moved as near shore as possible for the rocks. The two men stumbled out to meet it and were lifted on board. They had to rest a little before they could even tell their story. Then it came.

The day before they had landed to get food. Captain Shannon and the others had busied themselves building a fire close to shore while Kane and Jones had volunteered to go farther into the forest for game. At the end of an hour they heard shooting in the direction of their camp. They had gone close enough to see Captain Shannon and the other men dead by the fire and several Indians engaged in their horrible work. The two had crept back, and when out of reach had run for their lives through thick briers and undergrowth along shore, never stopping for food or rest until they had sighted the boats. They sank back now, utterly fordone, and slept.

Not only Colonel Lochry and his officers, but every mother's son of them as he heard this news, knew that the greatest loss to the company was not the death of the Captain and the five men, tragic as this was; it was the *loss of the letter*. For now in the hands of their enemies would be the information that they—the Westmoreland boys—were alone, separated from Clark, with scant ammunition and with no food.

Hugh drew close to Dave until their arms touched.

"Don't look so good for us, now," he managed to say, though his throat was dry.

"It looks pretty damn bad. Pity you come, Hugh. Don't matter so much fur me."

"Had to do my part. Same as you. Anyhow, we might fool 'em yet. We've been in tight spots before this."

Dave did not reply.

Later on, in the darkness, Hugh touched Dave's arm. "Sleepin'?" he said very low.

"Nuh."

"If you'd happen to get back an' I don't, you might tell Violet . . ."

He could go no further. There was no message that other lips could convey. He felt ashamed to have made the attempt.

"Aw, shut up. You'll get back," Dave said.

The night was long. It seemed as though the dawn would never break as the small flotilla floated on slowly down the stream.

XII

The Buffalo

The morning of the 24th of August was clear, cool, and bright. As the boats rounded a sharp curve of the river, there was spread out before the weary men a scene of such amazing natural beauty that even their hardened, fear-harried eyes softened as they looked upon it.

The river was low at this point, and a long sand bar, projecting from the Kentucky shore, compelled them to pass close to the opposite side. Here stretched a level, grassy meadow at the mouth of a little creek. Behind it a wooded bank rose protectingly. The bright, quiet freshness of the green mead after the dark and forbidding forest growth which they had watched for days was enough in itself to tempt the men to land.

But there was more than this. Standing at the edge of the lush grass, black-brown and shaggy against the green, was a *buffalo!* Its great bearded head leaned to drink from the river and then rose again, looking at the oncoming boats with large, deep-holed, considering eyes.

With an instinct as involuntary as breathing every man in the first boat drew his rifle. Dave was the nearest and the quickest. The report rang out sharply and the great creature quivered, threw up its massive hairy head and then crumpled forward, its heavy forequarters bent, its light spindling hind legs digging the earth. Then it fell over on its side and lay dark and still amidst the bright green of the grass.

"Good shot!" Hugh said to his friend, forgetting until the words were out when and where he had last used them. But Dave was so pleased he did not notice.

A tremendous excitement now filled the men. Even Lochry himself called across to Orr and Campbell in a hurried voice of elation. They all realized that a landing on the right bank was much more dangerous than on the left; but here before them, as though Heaven-sent, was meat a plenty for the famished men and fresh herbage for the horses. The officers spoke back and forth briefly. Even as they did so, the men were deciding for themselves. Each boat was nearing shore. It would have been beyond human endurance to pass on downstream leaving this spot of beauty and sustenance behind them! Lochry said to the men beside him that it was too much to ask, and waved his arms, giving the definite signal to land.

The hungry men poled and sculled like mad, a low rumbling sound of eagerness and satisfaction coming from their throats. In an incredibly short time every boat was safely beached, the horses were unloaded, and the men were hurrying through the deep grass, their strained faces relaxed and smiling. There was subdued talk again and even laughter. Relief and delight lay upon them all even as the blue sky lay upon this fair spot of earth.

"Who's a good skinner?" Colonel Lochry said. "Come on, Hugh, I know you can handle a knife. Dave too, for he shot the beast. Get to work, boys, we're all hungry. The rest of you get the wood together and the fires going. We got the water right here in the run, thank Heaven, clear as a bell. We'll have a good feed and rest a bit. You've all earned it, God knows."

Suddenly, like cracks of doom, a rain of bullets poured from the hill overshadowing them! The men, paralyzed for a moment, snatched up their rifles and turned to face the wooded bluff. Even through the hail of lead they could discern some of their enemies clinging like vampires to the tall trees that overlooked the meadow. They returned the fire as well as they could, the brief joy that had lighted up their eyes now stricken into desperation and despair. For their comrades were falling around them and the clear water of the little stream was stained now with more than the buffalo's blood.

"Get back to the boats. Fend 'em off if you can!" Lochry shouted.

With a furious rush the men pushed off the unwieldy boats and managed to get into them, their faces gray as they saw the fair meadow covered with their own dead.

Hugh, who had been picking off the sharpshooters from the trees, gave a groan.

"I've got no more shot!"

"Neither has anybody else," Dave answered grimly.

Suddenly, before the boats were a half-dozen yards from land, a large force of painted Indians swarmed down from the bluff to the very water's edge, covering them completely with their fire. At the same time a fleet of canoes, filled with other savages, shot out from the Kentucky shore. The Westmoreland boys knew then that the end had come. There could be no escape.

Lochry's voice, still controlled, called out above the bullets: "It's no use, lads. We've got to surrender."

He waved his arms as a sign to the Indians, and the men, with the rough oars like lead in their hands, pulled back again to the shore.

Hugh and Dave stuck close together, knowing it could not be for long. The men dropped down on the grass awaiting their fate. Lochry himself sat on a log by the little stream.

The Indian force was large, some of them Shawnees and some Wyandots by their dress, under command of a white man. The other leader was a strong, powerful chief who shouted an order now and then in English. From man to man on the grass there passed the word, "It's Brant and the Mohawks!"

"God help us," Hugh muttered.

Even as he spoke he felt Dave grip his arm. He looked up and the blood froze in his veins. A big Shawnee warrior had come up behind Lochry and with one stroke of the tomahawk had cleft his skull. The act seemed to be a signal. With whoops and yells, the Indians fell upon their captives. When the first of their fury was spent, the chieftain, Brant, seemed to be ordering the Mohawks to stop the massacre. The white man, too, was arguing with the Shawnees.

At last with fiendish blows of their rifle butts and

clubs, the Indians rounded up the survivors and started to drive them into the wilderness. Hugh and Dave were still among the living. So was young Samuel Craig. Captain Orr with one arm broken and limp from a bullet, and Captain Stokely still unscathed, walked beside them. How many more were now captive they could not tell, but it was a goodly number. They stumbled in complete despair through the rough forest, waiting for worse than mere death.

"The ones behind are the lucky ones, I doubt," Hugh said once under his breath.

"I wisht it was all over," Dave returned.

They marched all day. The Indians had apparently eaten well that morning before the attack, for they had made no move to use the buffalo and did not stop for forage now.

As they slowed to cross a stream Hugh found himself near the white man. He determined to take a chance.

"Do you know Simon Girty?" he asked.

The man looked surprised. "I'm his brother, George. What's that to you?"

Hugh opened his shirt and revealed the panther claw.

"Simon Girty gave me this once," he said. "Told me to keep it. Said it might come in useful some time." Hugh gave him a long, level glance.

Girty looked intently at the claw, then shrugged.

"I can't be lookin' out for his friends," he said roughly. "You got to take your chances with the rest of 'em."

When they had crossed the stream the men were divided into small groups which were led off in different directions, each under a band of Indians. Hugh felt the faintest hope stir in his breast as he found himself with Dave, Sam Craig, and six strange lads, still in Girty's company. It was short-lived, however, for after they had gone another five miles or so, the Indians stopped in a small clearing. The captives were seated on fallen logs while a large fire was built. Then Hugh saw with a cold sickness of the heart that the savages were preparing to blacken the faces of their prisoners. This meant death by torture.

When they had finished, the Indians sat down around the fire leaving guards beside their captives. They talked together then, gesticulating and laughing, Girty joining them in their mirth. One warrior rose with great dignity and executed a dance. Others apparently told tales of their recent exploits, illustrating with tomahawk or rifle or scalping knife. It was the hour of entertainment leading up to the chief play of all—the torturing of the prisoners.

All of a sudden through the forest a voice rang out clear and strong with a high lilt of melody. Hugh shivered for a second at the strangeness of it. Then he saw it was Sam Craig who was singing. His head was thrown back and his blackened face raised to the late afternoon sun. Hugh had often heard his voice rising above the rest at Unity church or at a neighborhood corn husking in the years before the war. But he had never heard him sing as he sang now.

He's doing it for his life, Hugh thought.

The savages had stopped and were now watching and listening intently. Higher rose the clear tenor, a gay note in it as though the singer had not a care in the world:

> "O lead me to some lofty shade,
>   Where grows the myrtle vine;
>   'Tis there my love will plight her troth,
>   'Tis there I'll give her mine.
>   For oh, the spring has come again,
>   The bloom is on the thorn,
>   The lark is high upon the wing,
>   And rosy is the morn."

There were several more verses of the song. He sang them all over and over, improvising, Hugh could tell, upon the already sweet melody with additional runs and trills. The Indians still listened, then looked at one another and, at last, began consulting in low voices. Sam sang on.

Finally one Wyandot rose from his place and came over to the singer. With his hands he roughly wiped off the black from Sam's face and then gave a sharp order.

"He wants another tune," Girty interpreted.

Sam began again instantly. As he did so, Hugh felt the hot tears rise to scald his eyes. Through the aisles of the lonely forest echoed the familiar words:

> "Oh, Sister Phoebe, how merry were we
>   The night we sat under the juniper-tree,
>   The juniper tree, I, oh!"

With an overwhelming passion that made his whole body tremble, he thought of Violet.

"I want to live," he muttered to himself. *"I've got to live."*

It was near the end of the song that he saw for the first time that Dave was gone! From the tail of his eye, without turning his head, he saw it. Dave had been on the end of the log, two men below him. He was not there now. He couldn't have been killed, for there had not been a sound except for the song. That was it! While all eyes had been set upon the singer, Dave had slid from the log and made a dash for it.

Hugh's heart thudded in his very throat. Which direction? Not behind them, for the Indians around the fire were facing that way. Not to the front, for the guards commanded the woods there. It would be to the side, straight out from where he sat. While the guards were watching the Wyandot rub the black off Sam's face, Dave had crawled like a snake from his place. If anybody could do it, Dave could. . . .

Still without turning his head or moving a muscle, Hugh looked as far to the right as his eyes would vision. He saw him! Just for a second between trees. He was weaving back and forth as though running in weakness. But every instant put him farther away. Hugh's breathing all but stopped. Any hope even in escape was scant enough. Yet he understood well the desperation that had made Dave try it. If the least chance came he'd do it himself. . . . Oh, go it, Dave—go it—go it . . .

There was a sharp growl from the guard behind him, and a shout from the other. Dave was barely visible now in the late sunlight. Then there was a quick report and he dropped. Hugh knew by the way he fell that he was dead. Dave. His friend. Dave, who was as his brother. Dave was dead.

Suddenly he found himself standing up, screaming out his rage and his pain, shaking his fists at the savages, cursing and calling upon Heaven for vengeance.

Then a great weight on his head forced him to the ground, and a blanket of darkness, cool and quiet, covered him over.

September 28, 1781 No word yet. Talked to Robert Hanna this morning on way to the spring. He says report is true the men set off safe from Fort Henry. A man from there was in Pittsburgh and told it. Had to make their own boats he said as Clark had gone on ahead. I'm fearful for Violet she just sits quiet in the doorway of an evening. Says her heart bodes evil and so does mine I don't know why. How strange is life. Was thinking today its just a year gone this month since news of General Arnolds treason. And in my heart I once wished Violet could be in that Peggy Shippen's place the one he married. Oh may God forgive my wandering thoughts and work His own will in all of us. Cannot rightly judge if J. knows about Hugh and Violet. I made Sam promise to keep still about it for a while at least. Some say Mrs. Lochry had a visitation in her sleep saw her husband dead on a greensward. I take little stock in such like things but have *great* heaviness of spirit. Full moon last night. Terrible sound of a bull-moose bellowing. Looking for a mate. Queer it takes them like this in the fall instead of spring the way it is with most animals. I feel clean flaxed out these days. As though I couldn't keep going. May God give me strength. Edward Cook been made county lieutenant in place of Arch Lochry since he's away. Cook a fine man all say. Has a plantation of 300 acres along the Monongahela. But though wealthy is not high headed, an elder in the church and much given to hospitality. Weather warm and dry.

October 18, 1781 Still no word. The men say theres messengers up and down the river betimes and if our boys had got to Clark there ought to be news of it someway after this long. Two months Tuesday week since they left. I can't sleep nights with the worry and a pain in my chest fear it is the heart but may pass away. Violet pale and eats little. Peggy over today and Jennie Hanna. Will try to have them back often to chirk her up. Sam a bundle of nerves, and gulders at the least thing. But I pay no heed he's anxious too and that's the way it takes him. J. comes as usual and if he knows he never lets on. Will be all through his studies come spring. Told me in private this Mr. John Culbertson praised him and is writing to a barrister in Philadelphia to take him in as a pardner. Tries to cheer Violet and take her mind up with reading. It seems to pleasure her too for the time at least. How passing strange are the ways of the heart. There is this I've thought out though and it comforts me. If Hugh gets safe home and they're married by the time the war ends things may be quiet here and the savages driven clear back and with crops better she will have more to do with than I ever had. It will be easier for her here than to break wilderness as Sam and I did at first and Hannastown may be a nicer place some day with a church even. It could be. I plan like this at night and it comforts me. She might get a set of real dishes too some day and a piece or so of furniture from the east when the roads get better. It could be. First hard frost last night. Black haws will soon be ripe.

November 19, 1781 Still no word. It looks very bad. There's a gloom over the whole town and country side. Poor Violet goes like a ghost. I said to her last night we must all mind the words of the blind preacher that the dawn will come. She just shook her head. I doubt this night will never end for me she said. It wrung my heart for it was too old a thing for her years. We are all bowed down with the dread but I try hard to keep up for sake of the others. Sam won't play his fiddle any more which is a bad sign he just sits looking at the fire. It seems every one had a premonition about this campaign even Sam now confesses to it. But felt they had to go. Oh I keep wondering often in the watches of the night if them that come after will know and care and think on all that we've gone through. It would make it easier-like if we knew they would. But who can tell. It's all bound up some way though even if it's beyond our knowledge in the plans of God. Of that I'm sure. Went up to cockloft today for extra corn and the sight of Hugh's bed just made me weak, like. Sat down till I was over it so Violet wouldn't know. Oh God in mercy watch over our lad. There's good news about the war in the east. A British General surrendered at a place in Virginia called Yorktown. This ought to help us some. If we just didn't have so much else to fend against out here. Of course Sam and the men folk are all set up over this victory. It just seems far away-like to me. Had a piece of woolen back from the weaver yesterday and think to try to dye it red for Violet. Would take no chances on spoiling if it weren't to take up her mind. Oh what will be the end of this suspense. Sam said last night he'd rather know the worst now and be done with it. His voice shook as he said it. But a woman always would rather hope on as long as she can. Pain in chest still troublesome. Have said naught of it. It may be only the weight on my heart. A new man this month at Fort Pitt Brigadeer general William Irvine. Brodhead gone like all the rest. None of them stay long. This Irvine is 40 years old we're told and Scotch Irish. Well we'll see what he can do. Sharp north wind today and first light skift of snow. Poor lads what will the weather be like where they are.

XIII

The Wedding

James was in the courtroom with Robert Hanna the bleak day in December when Colonel John Proctor rode into Hannastown, tied his horse to a stump, and then came stiffly up the tavern steps. His face was stricken, and the hand that held out the bit of paper trembled.

Robert Hanna took the letter without a word, smoothed it out, and he and James read it together:

"Colonel Proctor, Sir,

"I am pained to inform you that your county and all the frontier has suffered a severe stroke in the loss of Colonel Archibald Lochry and his entire expedition. I have delayed to send you this intelligence until there seemed no reasonable doubt of its accuracy. Now from all reports it would seem to be certain. Word from General Clark himself states that Lochry and his men never caught up to him. More than this a band of deserters from Clark's force have made their way back to Fort Pitt. They state that not far from the mouth of the Miami river they came upon a level stretch where a large number of men had been killed they could not rightly judge after the passage of time how many but it was Indian work. The carcass of a large animal, perhaps a buffalo was there amongst them as though they had been seeking food when attacked. Three other reports have reached me recently all bearing out this testimony. We must conclude the force were all killed or taken, chiefly killed. I have so written the President of the state. Keep your settlers from fleeing back east if it is possible though my sympathies for them are ardently excited. We are all in a perilous condition. Command me at any time if I can serve you.

"I am your obedient servant,

"WM. IRVINE

"Fort Pitt December 3"

It was James' voice that continued to the end. Robert Hanna's broke and stopped. He blew his nose hard now and set a chair for Colonel Proctor. His face was drawn.

"I've feared this. Everybody's feared it. Now it's come. Now we know. This is a blow we'll be long rising from."

Colonel Proctor cleared his throat.

"There's this we've got to face along with the sorrow of it. The ablest men have been taken from us as well as the best rifles about the town. What's to become of us if the Injuns ever attack us here? Now with the rest of the militia all deserting?"

"God help us!"

"Lochry was my neighbor and my friend," the Colonel said heavily.

Then they sat on in silence, their heads bowed, as James left. They did not see him go.

James himself felt dizzy as he went down the tavern steps. His feelings were so entangled that it was like many hands pulling him in different directions. With all his sensitive soul he was feeling the weight of grief and shock which the news of the letter had brought.

With that quick play of imagination which is at once a blessing and a curse, he saw the ghastly sight on the far-off Ohio shore. He saw the scenes which followed the Indian capture. In his own body he felt the fire of the stake. He sickened and felt faint.

He walked along back of the cabins, drawing deep, quivering breaths of the cold air, trying to gain control of himself, fearful, almost terrified at the thought which rose steadily, irresistibly above all the others. He tried to circumvent it with his own honest grief, with the fact of the community's desolation, and the added danger to the whole frontier.

At last he gave up. He leaned, still sick, against a tree and let the knowledge take full possession of him. Hugh was dead. Fate, destiny, providence, the cruel fortunes of Indian warfare—let the responsibility rest upon any or all of them. It was not upon him. Clean were his hands and truly also the thoughts of his heart up to this moment. Even that night when Violet had told him simply that she loved Hugh not as a brother, and would marry him on his return—even then he had never wished death upon him.

So now, might he not let the full import of this new fact fill his heart? Hugh would never come back. And Violet was young and gentle. With persistent tenderness and sympathy, with constant bright pictures of life in the east, might he not woo her grief away and win her at last when the time was right, for his wife?

He caught his breath suddenly in a startled recognition. He knew now what he had not realized before. He had never really expected Hugh to come back. As upon the rest of the town there had lain upon him too, though unconsciously, the heavy foreboding of disaster, the deadly certainty that the Westmoreland boys had gone on their last campaign. This, then, was the reason he had not given way to despair after Violet's confession. This was why he had been able to go to the Murray cabin as usual, week after week, and feast upon her beauty and feel the strange new warmth flooding his veins. But there had been no guilt in this to becloud his soul now. He had never *wished* Hugh dead. Not consciously. . . .

He shook himself. He, too, was caught up in the shaping of destiny. Why should he not accept the overruling hand of Providence and his own place in the juxtaposition of events? Hugh was dead. The true son of the forest now lay slain in its far depths along the distant river. He, James, who could not battle with the wilderness, whose finger always trembled on the trigger, was still alive with love and hope warm within him. He did not have to question and torture himself with pangs. He need but accept what fate had laid at his feet.

He stood up strongly. The sickness had passed, his head felt clear; he walked steadily to his own cabin and told his mother the tidings.

"Should we break it to the Murrays," he asked anxiously, "or wait till they hear it for themselves?"

Mrs. Brison's tears were flowing fast, and she was not one to weep easily.

"Hugh gone, and Dave. I can't believe it. And Ben

Wilson and Sam Craig and Billy Kane and the McFall boys, and Arch Lochry and Captain Orr! And John Scott and Peter McHarge! Oh, it can't be!"

Her moan continued.

"The Rangers and all the militia boys and Captain Stokely, too! But oh, it's Hugh and Dave that breaks my heart. Was Sam Murray round the tavern, or any of the Shaws?"

"Not a one. There were some travelers in the tap-room, but none of the townsfolk. I was with Mr. Hanna in the courtroom, and Colonel Proctor brought the letter there."

"You think it's true?"

"I fear there's no doubt of it."

"Then we'll go up to the Murrays'. They'll hear it soon enough, and at least we'll be there with them in their sorrow."

She threw a shawl over her head, and they started to-gether up the road. Even as they went, however, the news, like a dark wave of pain, was spreading from cabin to cabin. Other people were out now, running, wringing their hands, calling to one another.

"They're all lost—they're all lost. . . . The word's come at last—they're all lost."

When James and his mother reached the Murrays' they saw that the tragic news had preceded them. Sam sat by the fire, his head in his hands. He did not look up or give a sign as they entered. Violet lay face downward on her bed, her slim body shaken by terrible sobs.

Martha, her eyes sunk in her head, her face set, met them quietly. Mary Brison put her arms around her.

"Well, it's come," she said to her friend. "I guess we all expected it, but the blow's no easier now."

The two women wept together, but Martha still could not speak.

At last she straightened and begged them to sit down. Mrs. Brison accepted the chair, but James did a strange thing, a bold thing for him. He went over to the bed, sat down beside Violet and very gently laid his hand on her head.

That night, under the wailing winter wind, Hannastown lay stricken. The forest seemed vocal with pain as though it, too, mourned for its sons. Over and over through the sad, dark hours the bloodcurdling cry of a panther echoed from the hills. It seemed part of the common grief. For those who had been sorest stricken there was to be found no balm in Gilead. No reasonable hope was left now. As Martha said brokenly, it would even have been a comfort if a preacher had been near enough to bring them the consolation of the church. But Reverend James Power, now stated pastor of the Sewickley and Mount Pleasant churches, had not been in Hannastown since summer, and there was no regular preacher at Unity. In the Murray cabin at least the usual ceremony of family worship itself was dispensed with.

"I can't do it," Sam said that first night when Martha lifted down the Book from its shelf. He drew a sharp, shuddering sigh. "I loved the lad," he muttered.

It was the first time Martha had heard the word "love" on his lips since the days of their courtship.

Violet was still now. She sobbed no longer, but she had no power to rise. She lay prostrate, her face white and graven as though Death's wings were shadowing her also.

When Martha stretched out on her own bed at last, she fell at once into that exhausted slumber which a grievous certainty sometimes allows after long suspense. But Sam sat up all night by the fire, his face in his hands.

As the weeks passed, the town girded itself to bear what had been laid upon it. As Colonel Proctor had pointed out, there was more to this tragedy than personal grief. There was increased danger to the town itself with its best men and arms lost. News was already filtering in that Guyasoota, who had long been their most dreaded enemy, was now urging his Senecas to an uprising.

"I'll bet there ain't more than nine good rifles in this town," Sam said one evening in February. "An' I don't like this weather. It's set for trouble, that's sartin."

"It's surely mild for this time of year," Martha agreed. "I think I'll make a little call on Mrs. Hanna tonight and take her a bit of the fresh sugar sap. She's had such a cold in the chest. Are you—is James coming in tonight, Violet?"

"He said he'd be down," she answered.

"Then I'll wait till he comes. So's you won't be alone. We daresn't take chances these days."

Sam glowered. "Seems like I'm allays trippin' over that fellah. Is he here every night now, or what?"

"He does drop in often," Violet said. But there was no light on her face.

"I never took to him much," Sam said, eyeing his daughter narrowly. "But I s'pose book larnin's all right for them that wants it."

"Oh, he's smart enough," Violet replied. "He'll be a real lawyer by summer, ready to go back east. He's all made up about it."

"Well, see you don't get in too deep with him," Sam warned.

He was watching Violet anxiously these days, for her naturally bright spirit had not returned to her. She could not be described as melancholy, nor was she ill. Yet she was changed. It was as though the bright up-springing flame had gone from the fire, leaving only the dull level of heat to keep life in the log. That was the way it seemed to Sam as he studied her day by day. He understood, too, for his own spirit had departed from him now that Hugh was gone.

He tweaked her curls as he passed, with an effort at his old teasing, and went out. Martha swept up the hearth carefully, pulled the settle around at right angles to the fireplace, lighted two extra candles, and waited nervously for the knock on the door. It came soon, and James, more distinguished-looking now, more assured with his new profession upon him, entered.

"You'll be here a little while, I doubt," Martha said to him smiling. "I want to go to Mrs. Hanna's, and I don't like Violet to be alone."

"I'll stay till you get back, *willingly*," he said. His laughter came with readiness.

"Good-bye, then," Martha said, sweeping them together with her glance. "There's a bit of mulled cider keeping hot for you."

When she had gone Violet picked up her knitting, her eyes on her quick-flying needles.

"Well, James. Is it to be Shakespeare?"

"Not tonight." The words were so decisive, so full of feeling, that Violet looked up unaware and met his gaze. It frightened her.

James sat down close to her upon the settle. He took the knitting from her hands and laid it aside.

"I want you to listen to me," he said. "It's not of a lover in a play that I would speak to you now. Violet, it's of myself."

"No," she murmured, drawing back a little.

"Yes. It is time that I told you what lies in my heart. I love you. It has been long now. Longer than I ever knew. But year by year the love has grown stronger until now it fills my whole being."

"No, James." She shrank away, but he leaned nearer.

"I am not asking for all your heart. Not yet. You are still in the midst of your grief. I only ask you to let me bring what happiness I can to you. Let me love you now and later care for you, and perhaps some day bring you comfort and honor."

"But how could I, James?" Her voice was piteous.

He sat silent for a few moments as though considering what was the best way to answer. Then slowly, carefully, he went on.

"It must seem to you now as though your very heart were dead. But slowly, as time passes, it will wake again as the springtime succeeds the winter. You are very young. It would be a sad fate indeed, for you to live in sorrow all through the years to come."

Violet made no reply.

"I am no stranger to you. And in all gentleness I would await your will. In all things. Moreover, I have found at last that there is something I can do well. Perhaps exceedingly well. I feel that in time I may achieve some of this world's goods and perhaps even a modicum of fame. These I would hope to secure for your sake. To lay at your feet."

He paused again, but Violet still sat silent, looking at the fire.

"I am speaking now that you may know what lies in my heart. That you may ponder upon it and perhaps speak of it with your mother. By spring my law studies will be completed. I am making arrangements even now to go then to Philadelphia. I want to take you with me as my wife."

Still Violet was silent. At last, slowly and hesitantly, she put a strange question.

"Would—would—you—kiss me, James?"

"My darling!" His arms went out to her, but she held him gently at bay.

"No, please, you must understand first. I can't rightly

answer you now. I'm so heartbroke, so confused, like. All my love is for Hugh. But I meant, would you still— kiss me?"

For answer he held her to his breast. His lips were long on hers before she could release herself.

She crouched at the end of the settle then, her face averted so he would not see the tears.

"I just wondered," she said so low that he barely caught the words. "I had to know, like."

When Martha returned, she felt the air of the cabin charged with emotion. Violet was too still, and James too animated. There was an air of triumph about him, which seemed to add breadth to his shoulders and strength to his face. He left soon after, but as he said his good night to her he bowed over her hand.

"I have asked Violet to share a confidence with you," he said. "I need not beg you to give it your deepest consideration."

Martha was so overcome that she could not answer him.

As soon as he was gone she sat down opposite Violet.

"Has he *spoken,* child?" she asked breathlessly.

Violet nodded.

"Did you give him answer?"

Violet raised her eyes and looked sorrowfully at her mother.

"What answer is there to give?"

For once Martha was embarrassed before her daughter. Then, even as James had done, she began slowly and carefully to speak.

"It's not belittling your love for Hugh, my child, to consider well what James is offering you. Every girl must marry whether she carry a sadness to her bridal or not."

Violet drew a quivering sigh.

"In these times what woman can fend for herself? Look at Mrs. Miller. Captain Miller was not long dead when she married Mr. Cruikshank. It's part of life—on the frontier anyway. You can't get away from it. So, if you have to marry somebody, mightn't it better be James?"

"I suppose so," Violet agreed heavily.

"And it's more than just marriage James has to offer you. It's the life back east I've always coveted for you. It's life like I knew it when I was a girl."

Martha's eyes were wide with the intensity of her dream.

"You know how always from the time you were a little thing you've wanted to hear about the way things were back there. The house with papered walls and real stairs and polished furniture and *dishes*. And the gardens in bloom and the safety of it all. No Injuns or serpents, and the watchman's voice at night calling 'All's well,' so you can sleep in peace."

She stopped breathless, a high color rising in her thin cheeks.

"If you can see your way to marry James, all that will be yours, just as you've heard about. He'll be a great lawyer some day, or I miss my guess. And he's a good man, Violet. Else I'd never urge you. You'd need have no fears of him, ever."

Violet sat twisting her hands nervously together, an inexpressible sadness on her young face.

"It would mean leaving you and Father for good and all, like."

Martha's courage never wavered.

"Your new life would take up your mind so. Then we'd write letters by every express! Even with the awful miss of you I'd be content to think you were safe and fixed well for life. And maybe even—"

She stopped as though ashamed.

"What, Mother?"

"Oh, it's a fancy just come to me. Just a foolish thought, like."

"What is it?"

"It just come to me all of the sudden that if you were settled in Philadelphia your father and I might even go for a visit later on, in the years to come maybe, when the roads get fixed better. There might be wagoners passing through— Oh, I doubt it would never be possible, but the thought just come . . ."

Violet stared into the fire. When she raised her head at last her eyes were soft as they gazed at her mother.

"You'd be content then to see me marry James."

"If you could ever see your way clear, I'd be most mighty content, for your sake."

Violet sighed again as though the breath were beyond all control.

"I know I'll have to marry some time. It wouldn't rightly matter who. Not now. But when *you're* content and all, and he's no stranger to me, I suppose it might as well be James."

The tears were running down Martha's face. Tears of relief. Out of the depths had she cried, and her prayer was to be answered. Out from bitterness and grief there would yet come joy for Violet.

"But what will Father say?"

Martha wiped her eyes.

"We must gentle him into it. You can do it best yourself. If he knows it's for your happiness—"

"I couldn't truly say *happiness.*"

"Your wish then. Your decision. And mind, child, happiness is a strange-like thing in a marriage. There's many's the time when kindness means more to a woman than what folks call love, especially as the years go on."

"I'd have had it all with Hugh."

"Belike you would, but you must try and put your grief aside now and fix your affections as well as you can on James." Then her voice faltered. "Poor child," she said. "Dear child!"

It was not Violet's slow, quiet telling of her decision to Sam, however, that won him even to a loath consideration of it. At first he was wild, tempestuous, more profane than they had ever heard him. He scanted his words to James to the point of rudeness; but on the women he let the full force of them fall. Violet marry that thin-blooded, white-livered briggle? That book-readin', psalm-precentin', pukin' *sheep?* Never, while he could help it! Go back east where they'd never lay eyes on her more? With a man that didn't know which end of a gun went on his shoulder? He'd be double-damned if he'd let her throw herself away on a poetry-readin', pen-writin' slack-in-the-poop, who hadn't any more muscle to him than a *rabbit!*

Behind all his tirades Martha saw the dread and the sorrow in his eyes. He still mourned bitterly for Hugh; to see Violet go would be to tear out his heart. And her own. But she would draw comfort from deep wells that Sam knew not of. Poor Sam. Her heart ached for him these days.

So James came and went almost clandestinely. His heart was high, though, and he moved in the town now as a man set apart from his fellows by a great and overwhelming joy. Even though Violet had told him in all honesty again that she bore him no love, he was satisfied for the present. He would have her for his wife, and in the east under the spell of new scenes and his own growing success he would at last win her heart. It was strange that he, of all men, should be so confident. He pondered upon this mystery. All his young years he had known the humiliation of being unlike his fellows. He had felt the secret disappointment of his parents. To have but one child and him a weakling! In his own soul he had felt their pangs and cringed alike beneath their reproofs and their conscientious kindness. He was a misfit, a child born out of due season and into the wrong surroundings.

Now, at last, he knew where his strength lay. He felt his own peculiar power. Under the tutelage of John Culbertson he had grown up to his full stature.

"What a mind!" Culbertson kept repeating. "Great heavens, man, what a mind you've got!"

For some time now he had been in correspondence with a Mr. Wainwright in Philadelphia. He was a lawyer in high repute there. He would take James as his associate with a view to full partnership later on if such was mutually agreeable. Their letters each to the other had been highly satisfactory. There remained now only to finish up some intensive study of briefs which Culbertson had outlined for him. By April he would be ready to set out to conquer his new world if suitable arrangements could be made for the travel east. *And if Violet were ready for the wedding.*

All these thoughts of confidence, of ambition, of personal worthiness so new to him—as well as the ecstasy of his lover's dreams—surged through James' mind these weeks and made him a different man. Even his neighbors, last of all to admit a change in viewpoint, discussed him with interest and approval.

"Well, James has certainly spunked up this while back," Robert Hanna said one day over a bowl of rum to Mr. Brison. He spoke with the frankness of an old friend. "I think he's set now to make something of himself. I never thought he had so much gumption."

Mr. Brison beamed. "Yes, looks like he's found what he's fitten for at last. Goin' east this spring, he says, or summer."

"So I hear. How old would be he now?"

"Guess he'll be about in his airly thirties."

Robert Hanna leaned nearer.

"Good deal of talk about him and Violet Murray."

"Yes, I guess there is some. Mebbe just talk, I dunno."

"Where there's so much smoke there's bound to be some fire."

Mr. Brison laughed, pleased.

"I dunno. He don't say much. Closemouthed, I guess, like me."

"Goes courtin' pretty regular, they all say. Well, Violet's as sweet as they make 'em. Been sort of quiet like since the news come though. They say she and Hugh were going to make a match. Come as a shock to me when I heard it, for I always thought of him as her brother. Well, she's young. She'll get over it. James caught her at a good time, I dare say."

"Might be."

"Well, you can be glad your son took to a book instead of a gun. Otherwise he'd have been with the rest of them. Oh, that's the sorest stroke we've had yet. I can't seem to rise above it."

"Aye, it's sore enough."

"It's going to be a bad spring. The signs are all rising. They tell me a power of families have set off back east already. Sometimes I wish to God I could send mine there—or take them."

"Guess all we can do's wait an' take what comes."

"That's all. Have another tot?"

Violet felt those weeks as though another spirit were inhabiting her body. Certainly it was not her old self that went with Peggy or Jenny to the spring, that sat spinning or knitting in the cabin, or that lay with open

eyes at night watching the firelight throw shapes like
dancing Indians on the walls. It was a stranger now that
dwelt in the familiar flesh. This stranger listened to
James' eloquent love-making, submitted to his embrace,
heard Martha's eager planning and Sam's irritable opposition all with the same dead level of apathy. Her
heart could not be wrenched away from Hugh. Even
now she knew she was still forever his. The dearness of
his very presence in the room; his slow smile, the burning light of his eyes, the touch—the touch of his hands
and his lips . . .

Having known the shuddering sweetness of the reality,
could she now call upon her heart to embrace the
shadow?

But she knew she would marry James. The pressure
of circumstances was upon her, even the weight of love
itself. Not her own love, but that of her mother and of
James. Beneath this resistless force was the docility of her
own indifference. She thought it all over day after day.
If she could live out her life unwed, then she would refuse James absolutely. But, as her mother had pointed
out, she must marry before long as every girl must. She
was nineteen now, and that was old. And many a girl
had to take up with just anyone at all for sake to have a
man to fend for her. She knew too sadly well—as her
mother had kept saying so often lately—that no girl had
her parents forever. She had to get her a husband to protect herself against the time she'd be left alone. It was
the way of life, her mother had said, leastwise the way
of the frontier.

But the thought of living out here in the Back Country with another man than Hugh was intolerable. Every blow of his ax as he would split logs for their cabin, every time he would take down his rifle and set out for game, every time he would sit by the fire of an evening making moccasins, she would be seeing Hugh; and that could not be borne.

No, there was no other way out. It would be best to marry James and go east where all about her would be new and strange.

Sometimes she even had brief moments of a lighter spirit. As her mother told her again and again of city life, of ladies coming to tea of a winter's afternoon or sitting in the garden in the summer; of a church with a steeple where you could go Sabbath by Sabbath; of the silk dresses to be had in the shops and the comfort of rooms plastered and papered, with real glass windows— sometimes her face held a transient brightness.

"You'll have money in your hand, I doubt not, child," Martha said once. "And what a feeling of dignity and assurance it gives you! Not like this everlasting bartering out here. You'll go to market like a lady with your basket on your arm." She stopped, as though the full force of a new idea had even then just struck her. "Violet, child! You may have *servants* as time goes on! Think of it! Another pair of hands to lift the load off you when you're weary, and to serve you when you want to dress and sit nicely in your parlor waiting for your husband to come home to his tea!"

"Oh, Mother, do you think ever that!"

"I do indeed. James was talking to me last night before you came back from Peggy's. He's finished now with his work. And he says this Mr. Culbertson said to him, 'Your sails are all set now, young man. You can command your own ship into the wind with the best of them, and my guess is you'll go far!' Those were his very words. James tells me these things because he knows it contents me so to hear them."

"But, Mother, what are we going to do about Father? How can I go on with the marriage when he's so against it?"

Martha's face was grave.

"It's a fair worry to me. He's so grulchy all the time now, I can't get a quiet word in edgeways with him. We must be patient and see if something may just happen sudden like, to turn him."

It happened in March. The news came as always to the tavern and then spread quickly through the town. A force of 160 young men from Washington County had set out on horseback against the Indians, eager to avenge the many deaths of settlers in their section. They had finally reached the little settlement of Christianized Moravians at Gnadenhutten on the Tuscarawas. The fact that the redskins seemed peaceable and made no resistance gave them pause. Then Jim Wallace, one of the men of the party, discovered an Indian woman wearing the dress of his wife who had been slain along with their three little children a short time before. Her mutilated body, indeed, and that of the baby, had been found on their line of march. The men had stopped to bury them, swearing their vengeance to Heaven. It was not likely now that Wallace would counsel moderation.

In addition to this, there were discovered a few men with war paint still upon their faces. It was too much. Though the settlers knew that *most* of their prisoners were harmless mission Indians they knew, too, that there were some who were not. The fierce fires of revenge for bitter grievance overcame them. They savagely killed all of them, ninety-four, men, women, and children alike.

So, the news. There were many in Hannastown who rejoiced unqualifiedly over it. Sam was one. There were some who said killing fighting warriors was one thing but killing the mission Indians—and women and children at that—was quite another. Of this latter group James was the most outspoken. In his new self-confidence he even took sharp issue with Sam as they talked it over at the Murrays'.

"It's a dark blot on the history of the frontier," he said, "this brutal murder of harmless women and children. *Christian,* at that!"

Sam's thin face was dark with his hate.

"Why kill the lice an' let the nits live?" he asked. "Harmless women an' children! What about Mrs. Wallace an' *her* children an' hundreds like her? Ain't they 'harmless *Christian* women an' children' too? My God, how'd you feel to find Violet's body here stuck through a pointed stake in the woods an' then find an' old Injun bitch wearin' her very dress? Answer me that!"

James had jumped to his feet.

"All right," he shouted. "I'll answer you! Do you

think this Gnadenhutten massacre isn't going to be re-
venged? I tell you the Back Country will pay for it! And
you've brought Violet's name up. Very well, I've this to
say to you. I want to marry her and take her east out of
all this danger—where she can live in peace and comfort
and safety. She is willing. Her mother is willing. It's just
you, Sam Murray, that's holding her back. And if the
Indians ever raid this town as they well may do, and if
Violet falls a prey to them, her blood will be on your
head and *yours alone!*"

James stood over Sam, a tall, accusing figure, his long
finger pointing as to doom.

The change in Sam was startling. He stared at James,
his mouth open in amazement, then he shrank back in
his chair with his head on his breast. He looked like an
old man, crushed and beaten. Martha, watching in hope
and fear, was sure that there was moisture in his eyes.

At last he spoke huskily.

"You're set to marry James here, then, are you, dawtie?"

"I'm willing," she said quietly.

"You're set on it, Martha?"

"I think it's for Violet's best good."

He drew a long breath.

"Then I ain't got nothin' more to say again it!"

The blood rushed to James' face.

"Thank you, Mr. Murray, with all my heart and soul.
And I swear to you that as Violet's husband I shall de-
vote my life to bringing her happiness and comfort."

Sam looked up at him curiously.

"Lord love a duck!" he said with slow awe in his

voice. "I didn't know you'd that much guts in you, James."

So, with this dubious compliment, the matter was settled. With the high spirits which were now his daily portion, James pleaded for an early wedding. At the same time, Violet pleaded for a little delay, and Martha seconded her. There must be some preparations. Besides, her mother-heart now prayed for a few weeks more before the final separation.

Violet's reason, she confided to no one. Though she had no hope, she still felt that she could not leave the wilderness in the spring.

Once she said to Sam when they sat alone, "It's not as if there was any chance that Hugh might still be alive."

Sam shook his head. "There ain't a chancet. Not one."

"I didn't think there could be."

He fumbled for words.

"You'll get on, all right, with James, think you?" he brought out at last.

"James is a pleasant-like person and no stranger to me," she answered slowly. "I'll try to pleasure myself as best I can in the east. If it just wasn't so far away!"

"That's it," said Sam heavily. "God help us."

The time for the wedding was first set for early May. But as April began, Violet spoke one night, hesitantly, to her betrothed.

"If we could wait another month I'd rather. I'd like to see the woods turn green again, and the serviceberries blossom and smell the wild grapes—before I go."

James' eyes were tender. He cupped her face in his hands and looked into her eyes.

"Shall I compare thee to a summer's day,
Thou art more lovely and more temperate: . . .
But thy eternal summer shall not fade.

"You see? I'll be taking my spring and summer with me whenever we go. My darling, you are very beautiful. Sometimes I say to myself, 'Am I really James, the old bachelor, who feared even to look at a girl?' I'm changed, my darling! Metamorphosed! I'm a lover at last!"

"Could we wait then?" she pleaded.

His face fell a little.

"June, if you wish it. The weeks will go fast."

Strangely enough it was Sam who finally urged haste. James' bitter words of warning had sunk deep into his heart. He kept watching Violet now anxiously, especially on the days when there had been bad news of the Indians. And at last, early in June, there came direful word, indeed.

A new expedition chiefly from Washington County under Colonel William Crawford had set out in May to attack the Indian towns on the upper Sandusky. Perhaps a wish to wipe out the memory of Gnadenhutten by more virile victories prompted it; in any case a big force of Scotch farmers had volunteered. General Irvine at Fort Pitt gave them some gun flints and powder though he had little enough to spare. He could give no soldiers, for the remnant of the old Eighth was scattered now among the various small forts, while many of them had returned to their homes in order to protect their own families. He did send Surgeon John Knight of the Seventh Virginia and one of his own aides, Lieutenant Rose, a Russian nobleman who had been serving the American cause. So the force set out.

On a night march through the deep forest, one of the strange panics which sometimes descended upon white men during Indian warfare, seized the troops. They scattered suddenly in all directions. Many were captured and killed at once; others wandered home after incredible escapes. A goodly body of the men under Lieutenant Rose were finally brought together and fought the savages with success before they returned. But Colonel Crawford himself had been one of those captured on that night of the panic as he was searching for his sons who were also on the expedition.

Dr. Knight and one of the guides who had been with him through it all, had for some unaccountable reason been spared, and had finally reached Fort Pitt with the details.

The express who had heard them there, and who told it all in the Hannastown tavern, said Dr. Knight still shook and trembled like the ague when he talked. All the captives had been put to death by squaws, he said. That was for Gnadenhutten. Crawford had been burned at the stake after four hours' torture. It was the Delawares that had done it, and Simon Girty and Matt Elliott had been with them, sitting on a log watching it all. In his agony Crawford had kept calling, "Girty, shoot me!

Oh, Girty, for God's sake, shoot me." And Girty had just sat there smiling and said, "I ain't got a gun, Colonel."

The news of the Lochry expedition had not shaken the town in the same manner as this. Then, there had been the quietness of despairing grief; now there was a fury of revengeful rage that swept like fire. Most of the men had known Crawford to some extent. He had served as justice there some years back at Court Sessions. And they all hated Girty, the renegade, with implacable bitterness.

Sam was beside himself. His eyes glittered.

"It all fits in with what Hugh told us about Girty, do ye mind? He said he hated Crawford like pizen. I always said Girty was an Injun himself. If I could string him up an' *slowly* shoot holes through him startin' at his feet an' goin' up, I'd die happy, I would, the son of hell!"

"Oh, Sam, keep still! We've heard enough without you adding to it. We've got to fix our minds on other things to save our reason. Now there's to be no more mention of Crawford or Girty either in this cabin tonight. I can't stand it, and neither can Violet."

It was quite true. It made them see Hugh and imagine unspeakable things. Sam looked at Violet's white face, then suddenly left. He went straight to the Brisons' and called James outside.

"James," he said, "since you an' Violet are gettin' married, I wisht you'd do it in a hurry an' get off east. I don't care much for the look of things."

"You know I'll marry her tomorrow if she's willing. We can't leave till round the end of the month, though, on account of the pack train going back then. There's a group of about fifteen people going from Pittsburgh. It's the best way I've heard of to go, and the safest."

"All right," Sam said. "Get on with it as soon as you can though. They say Guyasooter's up on his damned hind legs this time fur sartin. He's gettin' the Senecas stirred up fur some divilment, that's the report."

"I'll see Mr. Culbertson this week, and find out for sure about the pack train. It ought to be through here any day now. That express yesterday said he passed it back beyond Bedford. My impression is it will stay in Pittsburgh around a week or ten days at least before starting back. Don't tell Violet for fear it may not happen, but I have hopes that Mr. Culbertson will be going east himself with his wife. She's homesick, and, besides, he wants to get her out of danger until the Indian troubles clear up."

Sam nodded. "Another woman fur company—someone she knowed of—would be nice fur Violet."

The next day the pack train passed through. James, returning later in the week from Pittsburgh, brought the word that it would start for the east again on July 2nd, leaving Hannastown the 3rd.

They talked it all over then, planning each detail. Martha and Violet had already been busy over new linen dresses, both bleached and dyed. There would be as nice a wedding as Martha could make it, with the neighbors as guests. Once again the cabin would be cleaned with unremitting zeal; once again there would be wild turkey and her best and lightest pone to go with it.

The date was set for July 2nd if they could get a preacher. Then the young couple were to go to the Brisons' for supper on their wedding evening and stay there that night before joining the pack train when it left Hannastown the following day.

The silk dress was brought out from the chest under the bed and smoothed with loving hands. It was hung up carefully for a few minutes each day in the air to allow the wrinkles to blow out. It fitted Violet perfectly, and in it she looked like the great lady her mother was sure she would one day be. Martha tried to make little teasing remarks to awaken a response in her daughter's eyes.

"Mrs. Judge Brison will have a few select ladies to tea at her home tomorrow afternoon! She will wear mauve silk sprigged with pink roses, with black velvet at the neck and wrists!"

Violet would smile a little, perhaps, but the shadow never left. When Martha suggested they bring pine boughs in to decorate the cabin for the wedding, she cried out sharply against it.

"Not that, Mother. No, I'd rather not. It's—it's too much trouble," she added lamely.

James had grown more and more boyishly excited. He came in one evening, his face beaming.

"Know all men by these presents that the services of the Reverend James Power have been secured for the nuptial ceremony of Violet Murray and James Brison, of Hannastown, Pennsylvania, on the second day of July in the year of grace one thousand seven hundred and eighty-two!"

"Well, that's a load off our minds then," Martha exclaimed. "I thought he'd likely come now it's summer if you could get word to him in time. I think Violet will have two bundles, James, instead of one as we thought at first. Look at the big stroud the Hannas have given her! And Mrs. Lochry, dear soul, brought this fine linen with the tears in her eyes as she gave it. And Mrs. Proctor sent in six pewter spoons! I thought it was most wonderful of her!"

As the time drew nearer, Sam kept to the cabin both day and evening. The tavern never saw him, and the fields were left to themselves. His face was piteous. He followed Violet about or sat watching her until Martha felt she could not endure it. She knew that for her the time of emotional reckoning would surely come, but just now there was so much for her hands to do and for her mind to plan that she held the excitement and the gallant hopes of it all to her heart and sternly bade sorrow stand aside for the present. Violet, she was glad to see, was calm and quiet. When the girls came in every day to look at the silk dress and talk over enviously all the details of the wedding and the great trip east, Violet seemed a little like her old self. Only occasionally she showed what was beneath the surface.

One night she put the little flowered plate in her mother's hands.

"I want you to keep this," she said in a strange voice. "I'll have others belike, and it's best maybe I shouldn't be always minded of—things that are past. I must try to be a good wife."

Then she turned quickly and went out and was gone a long time. Martha's heart bled for her. But the new scenes will help her, she reasoned to herself. And James is ever gentle with her and kind. O God, be merciful to her and lift up the light of his countenance upon her and give her peace!

When the day before the wedding arrived, all was in readiness. Sam had shot enough game to feed the town for a week, Martha told him. Some of it was already cooked; the rest would be done early in the morning. It was Martha's sudden suggestion that the ceremony itself should take place under the big oak tree in front of the house if the morrow was fine. When she broached it, James was enthusiastic.

" 'Under the greenwood tree!' Now it was like you to think of that, Mrs. Murray. What could be finer, eh, Violet?"

She tried to smile. "It will be all right," she said.

"And, ladies, wait till you see my new suit! A present from Mr. Culbertson. I couldn't say nay to him, he was so fain to give it in spite of all else he's done. He says I must land in Philadelphia clad like a gentleman or they'll pack me off to the Back Country again before I have a chance to show my mettle. Besides, with a wife clad in *silk,* what sort of a figure would I cut in hunting breeches?"

So gay was James, that morning!

In the afternoon about three o'clock Violet dropped down in the doorway to rest. Sam, who couldn't bear to be far from her even for a moment, sat on the log step below her, nervously whittling out another noggin from a knot of wood to add to the pile he had already made against the needs of the wedding dinner. Martha was busy inside the cabin, scrubbing the table and giving the settle and chairs another wipe-down. There had been a constant stream of neighborly calls these last days. Never before had she realized how much Violet was beloved. And James, they all said, had changed so, this while back. There were plenty of reports from Pittsburgh now about what this Mr. Culbertson had said of him. The smartest young lawyer he had ever known, he'd told Colonel Proctor. Well, it was a fine match after all, they agreed, and Violet deserved a gentleman if ever a girl did. In Martha's heart the pride still warded off the coming pain.

Suddenly a shouting up by the tavern cut the quiet, heavy summer air. At the first sound Sam leaped into the cabin for his rifle.

"Get inside quick!" he ordered Violet. "It's Injuns!"

But the shouts were changing. They had become yells of joy. "Hooray! Hooray! Hooray!"

"What in hell's up now," Sam said, puzzled, still keeping his rifle ready.

There was a little group collected, they could see, up by the store steps. Women were running now, and the thin voices of younger children joined the heavier shouting. Then the crowd began to move along the road, slowly, and with continued cries of joy.

The Murrays watching, puzzled and wondering, from their doorway, saw that two men were being carried on the shoulders of the others. It was Violet that knew first. She gave a scream that echoed above all the rest.

"It's Hugh!"

Then her strength failed her. Her feet refused to carry her. Sam was the one who, forgetting his stiff knee, tore like a wild man along the road to meet them.

For it *was* Hugh and Sam Craig, dirty, bearded, their clothes in tatters, who were being borne on the shoulders of their old neighbors and were set down in front of the Murray cabin at last. It was there Violet ran into Hugh's arms. It was there in the eyes of them all that their lips joined. After the long grief and pain, they were lost now to all the world, lost in each other. And a hush fell upon the shouting crowd, for none that saw that kiss could doubt that here was love, true love, that could never be denied.

James, coming late, saw it and, having seen it, turned, white and sick, back to his own cabin.

They seated the wanderers on the steps, and all the neighbors crowded about eager to serve them, beside themselves to hear their story and to ask for hope for the others who had been thought dead. Violet brought a cloth wet in cool water and wiped their faces. Sam brought them whiskey, and Martha food, while all the time the sad, desperate questions were beseeching them.

"Oh, Hugh, is our Billy alive?"

"Sam, Sam, tell us! What about Peter? Is he safe?"

"And Dave. Where's Dave?"

It was then Hugh could not speak.

There were tears of new joy and tears of old sorrow renewed as the truth was told. Then when they could, Sam and Hugh gave them all the story of the expedition: the terrible trip down the Ohio with all its disappointments; the shooting of the buffalo, the landing on the green meadow; the Indians' attack, and that dark scene in the forest when the sign of death was on their own faces.

"Hugh had showed his panther claw to this George Girty, who was with them, an' told him his brother Simon give it to him, and I think after that he meant to save Hugh all the time."

"But it was Sam's song got him off," Hugh put in eagerly. "You should have seen the savages listenin'! He sung like he was happy as a bird. You never heard anything to beat it."

The neighbors pressed nearer.

"What did you sing, Sam?"

"Oh, just the first thing come into my head."

"Sing it. Let's hear how it goes. Aw, go on, Sam!"

They wouldn't take no for an answer. They had to hear the song to complete the picture of that desperate hour. So Sam good-humoredly granted their request. His strong voice rose above the tree tops. Even James, leaning weakly at his cabin door, heard the words.

> "O lead me to some lofty shade,
>   Where grows the myrtle vine;
>   'Tis there my love will plight her troth,
>   'Tis there I'll give her mine."

"No wonder they let him off," Robert Hanna said, blowing his nose, when Sam had done.

Hugh couldn't tell about Dave's death. Sam had to do that. He went on then with their saga. How Hugh had been hit on the head when he cried out, but how Girty had spoken up for him; how the Indians had taken them first to Detroit, where they found twenty more of the Westmoreland boys including Captain Orr and Captain Stokely, who had been conducted there by the Mohawks under Brant. The rest had either been left behind on the green meadow or dispersed and killed later by the other savages. After a short stay in Detroit they had all been transferred to a prison in Montreal, where the others were yet.

The wonder of it all spread over the group. "How'd you two get out? How'd you ever escape?"

Hugh and Sam looked at each other. There were marks of dark things upon them. There were experiences of which they could not speak. Yet.

Sam threw up his head and smiled, showing his wide teeth.

"Well, I'll tell you. This here fellah, Hugh, couldn't be held noway. What's a few stone walls to him. He was hell-bent to get back home here, so I just thought I might as well come along—for the trip!"

There was laughter and confusion of exclaiming, then Sam spoke with no smile. His eyes were solemn as those of a man taking oath.

"But I'll tell you one thing. If you ever have to go through a tight place with death nippin' your heels all the while, you can't have a better man with you than Hugh here. He saved my skin more than once. Yes, you did, Hugh Murray—or I guess it's Hugh McConnell now."

"That's right," Hugh said, with his eyes upon Violet. "McConnell's the name."

They told a little of the trip back. They'd cut across New York State to the Genesee River and then struck the headwaters of the Allegheny. From then on it wasn't so bad. They'd picked up a couple of good rifles from a passle of sleepin' Injuns one night. Best luck they'd had, pretty near. They'd got a good rest and feed at Kittanning and another at Chartiers, so they made out. Anyway, here they were.

No one wanted to go home. People hung about the cabin steps, plying them over and over with questions, looking at them with wonderment and affection. Even those whose grief had been confirmed seemed to find strange comfort in the presence of these two who had been as dead and now were alive and home again. The Shaws especially stayed close to Hugh. It was almost like Dave himself come back.

At last Sam Craig stood up.

"I've had a bit rest and helped Hugh here with the news of us, now I've got to get on and give my own folks a surprise."

There were a dozen offers at once. It was finally settled that Robert Hanna and Joe Irvine would take two horses and conduct Sam to his home on the Loyalhanna. The whole town stood in the roadway till they were out of sight.

Then Hugh turned swiftly to Martha.

"Is there plenty hot water?" he asked. "I'm not fit to be near folks till I've had a wash-off. I've been in some bad spots."

She hurried to lay out a clean hunting shirt and the pair of breeches he had left behind him. Sam brought new moccasins. When all was ready Martha and Violet went out again to the steps as Hugh, smiling, closed the door. They could hear his voice and Sam's talking steadily, most of the time in low tones. Once there was a great burst of laughter.

It went through Martha strangely: the joy, the grief, the happiness, and the pain, all bound up together in this day. Violet was clinging to her, all the long tension gone. She was clinging now, relaxed, the loveliness of her soft flesh pressing against Martha's own body. She was weeping with joy.

"He's back! He's alive! My Hugh! Oh, Mother, Mother, he's back."

At last the door opened and Hugh came out. Even Martha's own heart was quick at the sight of him. What must Violet's be? For he stood before them tall and straight and handsome, the fresh shirt and breeches molded to his body, his face clean-shaved, his dark hair shining-wet. All that he had been through was written in strength upon him. He stood there before them a man, seasoned by danger and suffering; powerful now in his victory over them.

And Violet was suddenly again in his arms; and then they were walking to the edge of the forest.

They could not speak at first, not with words. Sam had told Hugh, though, of what had been set for the morrow, and Violet spoke of it at last out of her wounded heart. Hugh listened gravely, understandingly.

"It's that must have fetched me through everything," he said. "It was laid on me some way that I had to get back."

Violet shuddered. "If you'd come too late—"

"But I didn't," he answered her. Then he added, "I must go now an' speak with James. It's me has to do that. It's only honorable."

"I'm so grieved for him," she said, "but what can we do?"

When he came back he told them that James had acted like a real gentleman. He had said his best wishes were ever with Violet, and while he couldn't rightly see his way to come down to the cabin again he sent his kind respects to them all. He would go on to the east as he had planned, and he understood that Violet could not do other than follow the leadings of her heart.

Martha felt the slow tears gather as she stirred the fire.

"An' so," Hugh went on, "I was thinkin' when the preacher will be in town tomorrow Violet an' I could get married ourselves an' no more delay."

"The very ticket!" Sam shouted. His joy now rampant. "We'll have the weddin' jist as planned only the right man in it. What say, Vi'let?"

She blushed like a wild rose.

"It would be wonderful-like, since there's no telling when another preacher will be here."

"But we couldn't have all the neighbors and the big dinner and the celebration," Martha cried in distress.

Hugh and Violet both spoke up quickly.

"Not that. Oh, we wouldn't have that!"

"Just the preacher an' us," Hugh said, "and all quiet-like."

"Just after supper tomorrow maybe, and no one need ever know till—till after the pack train leaves."

So it was arranged.

Never was a fairer day than the one that dawned for the lovers. Martha quietly sent portions of the game to her neighbors, saving only what they could use for their own supper. The minister was told all the story in confidence and promised to respect it. So no one in town knew that it was to be a wedding day after all. The word was passed around, though, that James sat all day long, locked in the empty courtroom. Those that made bold to peer in the window at intervals said he had the record book open before him and wrote now and then on a blank page. He was very white, they said, and never looked up.

In the late afternoon Hugh and Violet went to the forest for pine.

"It'll be nice to remember, like," Violet had said, her eyes like stars, "and it's no trouble!"

While they were gone Martha hastened to attend to the last arrangements. In her perplexity she consulted Sam.

"Would we let them have our bed for the night?" she asked him in a low voice. "It's a little nicer like, than sending them up to the cockloft."

"Naw, naw," Sam said, "let them get away up there off by themselves. They'd like it better."

So Martha opened the bundle that was ready for the pack train and took out the bleached linen sheets and pillow slips that were to have been a part of Violet's slender dowry, and with these over her arm she climbed the ladder and made the rude place above as fair as she could.

When the minister came, the cabin was sweet with the pine boughs and bright with many candles. Violet wore the precious silk dress, and her beauty made even the preacher stop for a moment and take breath again for the ceremony. Hugh was fine and handsome in the new shirt Martha had made for him to stand up with Dave and Betsy. No one must think of that now, though, or of aught that was past. Only of the present, this night, this throbbing hour when the true lovers were being made one.

When the benediction was over and Hugh had kissed his bride there was a sound of voices on the path, and there came some of the neighbors to hear the strange story of the escape all over again. They looked at the green-decked cabin, at Violet in the rose-sprigged dress, at the preacher—and they knew.

So there was a celebration after all with laughter and rejoicing and even a few tunes on the fiddle, for Sam was fair beside himself.

At last, when they were all gone, Violet kissed her mother and her father, and Hugh shook hands with them both. Then he quickly climbed the ladder to the cockloft and waited as Violet, holding up the silk skirt, shyly climbed after him. When she was near the top he reached down and lifted her up, holding her for a minute in his arms. Martha, watching, could see the shine in his eyes brighter than many candles.

In spite of his excitement Sam went quickly to sleep; but Martha, too weary and too full of thoughts yet for slumber, lay quietly upon her bed. She could hear the soft, low murmurs from above. Violet was a wife now. Hugh's wife. She would never see the east and know its comforts and its honors. But, oh, this *must* be the will of God moving upon them, for else how should Hugh have gotten here just in time, like a miracle?

And the way they looked as they stood there taking their vows! The love that lay upon them would have made the very angels weep for tenderness. Oh, it was wrong belike and tempting Providence to try to plan people's lives for them. Even that of your own child.

But James. The tears slowly wet her pillow. Poor, poor James! If there was only aught she could do or say to comfort him! Mayhap it was kindness, though, to let him go away in silence. God bring him solace! She wondered what he had written on the paper during his long day's vigil in the courtroom.

At last the turn of the night came. The wide wings of darkness brooded more closely over the town and this, the last and farthest cabin in it. The light summer wind blew from the forest bringing the last perfume of the wild grapes. It would be blowing in at the little window overhead. And Martha knew that, in spite of all her long and ardent hopes and the bitter blow dealt them, her heart must learn to be at rest for her two children in the cockloft.

The little wind sighed and died away. The stars looked down in peace and all was still.

John Culbertson

I will
Comand your Ship unto the Wind Bay
I
Ship unto the I Wind

Carl John
John Culbertson Command you meay your

Come Lead me to some Lofty shade where
Tor the hnawrn there Love tat shadows
Those Lines Comes to Let you know

when I was a yong man I luke i loue I pes my
mind al
Known allalt min By thef
Know all men by these Presents That I James Law Decerese

Philadelphia

THE ORIGINAL PAGE OF WHICH THIS IS A FACSIMILE IS IN ONE OF THE
OLD VOLUMES OF HANNASTOWN COURT RECORDS NOW IN THE WESTMORELAND
COUNTY COURT HOUSE, GREENSBURG, PA.

July 13, 1782 Haven't had time to set a line since all the excitement till today. Sam and Hugh gone off early with a few of the other men to help Michael Huffnagle harvest. A pity too the way it fell out for there's to be Communion at Unity tomorrow Rev. Power preacher and Preparatory meeting today. Colonel Proctor sent the word round but before that our men had promised Mike to help harvest today. Huffnagles being Lutherans they wouldn't be going. Sam said he'd stick to his word for the grain might spoil so they're away at it with their sickles. Violet gone to spring with Watch at her heels. Never have I seen such happiness. It warms my heart in spite of everything and its come over me how much easier her life will be after all than mine was. We plan every night now sitting at the door in the dusk. So much more to Hugh than I ever even dreamed and his feeling for Violet most wonderful. Deep calleth unto deep where there's true love. As soon as harvesting is past he'll start the new cabin and he says its to have two big rooms and a loft besides. Oh what a comfort to have an extra room in time of child birth or a sickness. The big war's about finished up, all but the treatys the men say so things may soon quieten down all through the Back Country. That's my great hope. Am going to have big flax crop again so will make plenty linen to fix up Violet's cabin extry nice. Hugh already set to get dishes from the east if possible. Maybe one at a time he says. Their love beautiful to see. Hugh working from supper to dark every night on their furniture. Has great knack of it. Making bed now. Will get feathers together soon for tick. Jane Brison giving all hers which I think most kindly of her. She bears no ill will but grieves sore for James. We caught sight of him leaving that morning with the pack train but he looked neither to left nor right. Poor fellow my heart aches for him but daily now I find I can rejoice in the children's happiness and see their years lived out here in peace. Sam says the town will grow as is most important on whole frontier next to Pittsburgh. I try to see it all in the best light for Violet's sake. They're to have a bit pleasure tonight and right pleased I am for them. The youngest Gourley girl over by Miller's was married last night to a Duncan lad and they're having a big infare at the Millers' blockhouse, this afternoon and evening. Mrs. Cruikshank she that was Mrs. Miller sent word over. It's less than four mile and Hugh says he and Violet can ride Ranger. It will be nice for them and no mistake. Violet all made up over it. Mrs. Hanna and the girls already gone. Sam and I bidden too but still bothered with that pain and Sam said he'd be a posy to start after a day harvesting so thought to let the young ones go by themselves. Will try to be ready for Communion tomorrow. Hope naught prevents. Court on this week with Edward Cook on bench. Several felonies they say and one case of bastardy. One whipping yesterday very bad. A man from northwards. Poor fellow but guess he deserved it. Matthew Jack Sheriff now and in town today for court riding like Jehu on Matchit. A noble beast. Did some tricks for the girls riding this morning, picked hat off ground as he tore down the road. A brave man he is with plenty dash to him. Says Nancy is over at her mother's for a little visit. They were just married in February and now they say she's expecting. Well, that's the way it goes. Wonder how it will be with Violet. At least I'll be near by to help her and see that

XIV

The Burning of Hannastown

A sound made Martha put down her quill. It was the thud of quick-running feet and subdued cries of alarm. She hurried to the door, unconsciously keeping her journal in her hand. Hugh was tearing toward the cabin. The other harvesters, she could see, were scattering through the town.

"Injuns!" Hugh panted as soon as he was near enough. "They're coming. Where's Violet? Run for the stockade. Don't wait for anything! Where's Violet?"

"There," Martha pointed. "There she is now, coming from the spring."

Hugh clutched her arm. "Hurry," he said. "Run."

She ran with him toward Violet who dropped her water buckets at sight of them. Hugh caught her arm too, with his other hand, and urged them on by his strength. Sam was coming now, they saw, straining across from the northern field.

Hugh called to the neighbors as they passed, though the other men were all arousing their own families. Sarah Shaw was washing clothes in front of the cabin. She ran after them, shaking the suds from her hands. Mrs. Kinkaid was stirring soap. She ran, still clutching the stirrer, pressing her children ahead of her.

"Don't wait for anything," the men kept calling. "They're close! Get to the stockade. Quick! The stockade! Warn everybody!"

Martha's heart was thudding in her breast. For years they had lived in fear of this. Now, on this calm summer morning it had come. No amount of dread or expectancy beforehand made the reality of the moment seem less unreal.

They reached the stockade from every side and poured into the fort. Peggy came, shepherding some of the younger children as she always did, with Jamsey clutching her hand. The men in court had been warned. Robert Hanna and Edward Cook came running with the record books and papers; the others, whatever their opposing status had been a few minutes ago, were now one in the common danger.

"Open the jail. There's two fellahs in there," someone yelled.

Robert Hanna rushed over to the log door of the jail and turned the key.

"Where are they? Where's the Injuns?" came from every hand.

The harvesters, breathless from their chase, pieced out the story quickly. They had all stopped to eat their lunch under the trees in one corner of a field. Hugh had been suspicious of a movement across on the other side. He had sneaked along the edge of the woods near enough to

see a band of Indians, stripped and painted for war, peering through the underbrush.

Crawling back again he had warned the rest. They had
clutched their guns and escaped toward the town. It
looked like a real attack at last.

Matthew Jack heard the story, and in a flash was on
Matchit's back.

"I'll ride round the edge of the fields and see what sort
of a force they've got."

Hugh and Bill Guthrie and Henry Wilson looked to
their rifles, and then looked at each other. Hugh spoke
in a low tone.

"We three'll do a little scoutin'. You folks keep safe
in the fort and see the gate's well barred. How many
rifles have you got inside?"

There was a hasty count.

"Six!"

"Hold your bullets as long as you can," Hugh said to
Sam. "We'll need 'em later."

"*Hugh!*"

It was Violet's cry.

There was no time for word or kiss. But his eyes met
hers.

"We'll see that everybody's out of the cabins before
we start," he said. "Come on, boys."

The cabins were empty. All the townsfolk, trained
to quick action, familiar with dread and disaster, had
obeyed the warning instantly, the men from the near-by
fields and truck patches, the women from their household work, the children from their play. They were all

there now except the scouts and Matthew Jack, who had taken their lives in their hands to reconnoiter.

The men hunted about to see what the deserting militia had left behind them. They found a few bullets and two more rusty rifles.

"The damned red devils," Sam growled. "They knowed all about us here. Knowed we was weaker now than we'd ever been. It's that Guyasooter, you mark my words."

It was not much more than an hour when the watchers in the stockade saw the scouts returning, running for their lives. They barely got to the gate and inside when the whole pack of redskins could be seen coming across the field back of the town. They were approaching quietly as yet, evidently under the impression that they could take the place by surprise.

"There must be a hundred an' fifty of them," Hugh panted. "A few whites among 'em. We come on them in that thick woods across the Crabtree. They almost got us. Matt Jack's rode on to warn the countryside an' to tell them over at Miller's at the infare. Get to the loopholes, an' for God's sake don't waste the bullets. Pick 'em off if they come too close—but we've got to save ammunition till help comes."

It seemed natural for Hugh to take command. Even Michael Huffnagle and Edward Cook listened to him. The men ranged themselves, tense and watching, rifles fixed.

The Indians, still apparently hoping to surprise the settlers, did not shoot or make a sound until they had closed in among the cabins. Then at sight of the desertion, showing they had been cheated of their prey, a yell of rage arose from them so indescribable in its terror that the women in the fort crouched white and shivering, their arms around the children, their blood frozen in their veins.

There was a rain of quick shots at the stockade then, but the men at the loopholes held their fire. Sam was desperate to shoot, but Hugh kept him back.

"Go easy," he said. "Just pick 'em off when you have to. Mind they've got a hundred and fifty men an' plenty bullets."

The Indians after their first desperate fit of rage began to see at least the chance of pillage left them. They swarmed into the cabins, throwing the rude furniture and utensils out in heaps before the doors. They jumped upon them, hacking them to pieces; they looted the clothing, showing one another their trophies, laughing, yelling in grotesque delight. Violet, her eyes ever on Hugh's face, saw it suddenly stiffen in such a look of anger as she had never seen before. She heard him cursing terrible oaths, and then with careful aim he fired a shot. A yell of pain and fury answered it.

"You got him," Sam gritted.

Violet knew later that from their cabin one warrior had torn out the chest and strewed its contents on the dusty road. He had picked up the precious silk dress—the wedding dress—and with shouts of glee had attempted to put his foot through the sleeve. It was then Hugh shot him.

The other men, with care and dispatch, followed

Hugh's example. When the provocation was past bearing or the danger too great, they picked off one of the invaders.

No one saw the tragedy among their own number in time to prevent it. The women and children for the most part had remained huddled together in the fort proper; a few intrepid ones such as Mrs. Kinkaid would go out at intervals to peer between the pickets of the stockade and report upon the destruction outside. Suddenly Jamsey, now a little chap of six, darted out from the safety of the fort, past the men at the loopholes, to pick up a bit of string that had caught his eye. Quick as thought Peggy ran to snatch him back. As she did so, an Indian bullet came through a broken picket and lodged in her breast.

The men carried her back with tender hands and grim faces. The women now, indeed, had work for themselves. They laid her on an old cot and staunched the blood with their kerchiefs. Thank God the spring was there, so they had clear, cool water to bathe her head and give her to drink while her terrified eyes implored them. There was little more they could do, except try to comfort her.

"It's lodged in her lung, belike," Martha whispered to Jane Brison. "Her breathing's so heavy."

Poor Mrs. Shaw bent above her, helpless and despairing. Her father came over once and patted Peggy's hand while Henry Wilson merely looked back from his loophole, his face white and set.

When the savages had finished looting the cabins they

turned to the stables. The oaths from the men at the loopholes increased. They could see. The women could only hear the confusion of the terrified death cries of the animals. The sheep, the quiet sheep, the faithful cows, the horses . . . These were a close part of each family life. Now there were the cruel, wanton shots and the poor dumb cries. The women's faces sickened over. Violet crept close to her mother.

"Do you s'pose they've got Ranger and Reddy?"

"I've been thinking of Watch, too, poor faithful beast. The look in his eyes when he came up to the stockade with us and was shut out. Oh, is there no mercy left for us all!"

The long, hot afternoon wore on. There was the spring at their very feet and everyone drank often from it. There was no food, for no one had taken time to bring any with them. The women found some stale meal and mixed a gruel. It satisfied the children and softened the hunger pangs for everyone. The men kept up their careful sniping. When an Indian approached too near the fort he was warned by a bullet. But they all knew that unless help from the outside reached them before morning they could not hold out. Death and captivity pressed close upon the women as they crouched together through the hours.

Just at dusk there was a strange quiet. The animals were all either dead or driven to the woods; the noisy shouts of the Indians had died down. Within the stockade there was the tension of extremest fear. What next?

Then a groan came from the men.

"They're firin' the town."

"No! It can't be!" Martha's voice rose, piteous, above the rest.

They all rushed, heedless of danger, to peer between the pickets. Already the red flames were rising, the black smoke like hearse feathers waved above the cabins. The savages, with whoops and yells, tore in and out between the doomed houses, tossing firebrands and brandishing their tomahawks. Sam suddenly recognized Guyasoota himself, but couldn't get a shot at him. The eerie light fell only for a moment upon his gleaming copper body and tuft of hair swaying in the wind.

For there was a wind with a promise of rain in it, blowing from the north.

"It'll keep the fire off the fort anyway," Robert Hanna said, scanning the heavens.

But oh, the sickening smell of the smoke and the hard heavy crackle of the logs that had been cut and hewn by those who now watched them burn! Poor and rude though the cabins were, they had been built by toil and sacrifice, they had housed love and birth and death; darkness and dawn, joy and sorrow had visited them; they had been homes.

"This is the end, then," Jane Brison said heavily. She swayed as she went back to the fort and sat down there. "This is the end."

Martha felt a great weakness swallowing her up. She went back too, and sank down beside her friend on the hard earth floor.

The wind still blew, but though there was thunder

there was no rain. The men announced at last, however, that the fort was safe. So was Robert Hanna's house in the lee of it. All the rest were burning except . . .

Hugh came back once to speak to Violet.

"I can't rightly tell. There's too many between. But it looks like just the end of ours is charred. It's off by itself, an' mebbe they didn't get it fired at the start. Don't count on it, though, for it might flare up any minute."

"Hugh, what's to come, think you?"

He took her in his arms in the darkness.

"I don't know. Can you be brave?"

"I'll try. If it's the end that comes, Hugh, and you can, I'd rather it was your bullet than—"

His lips were white as he kissed her.

"Will you promise?"

He whispered it, held her close to him for a long moment, and then went back to his post.

Toward midnight the savages withdrew beyond the Crabtree Creek to make camp, evidently waiting for morning to conduct the big attack. This, the men all knew, was in keeping with Indian character. Like children they would stop for rest and grotesque play with their new trophies, while they delighted themselves in the anticipation of greater and bloodier conquests soon to come. The sound of their loud revelings was borne back on the wind. Tensely now every man in the stockade kept peering out for a sign of coming help. If Matthew Jack had got through to warn the neighbors at George's and Miller's especially, surely, surely now under cover of darkness they would rally to the aid of the beleaguered fort. If not, all hope was lost.

About one o'clock there was the sound of hoofs falling softly from the south. Every ear was strained, every eye pierced the gloom. No one breathed or spoke.

At last from the lower side of the stockade the men could detect in the occasional gleams from the burning logs, a little company of horsemen approaching.

"There's Matt Jack at the head of them," Sam said. "I knowed he'd stir somethin' up."

The riders came cautiously toward the back of the fort. Hugh crept out to meet them. In a few moments they were all safely inside the stockade. Matthew Jack's face was grave. They all knew he brought evil tidings. Robert Hanna came up to him and tried to speak.

"Were the Injuns at Miller's too?"

Jack nodded.

"I only got as far as the yard. The Injuns were swarmin' all over the place. They saw me an' shot at me. It was tich an' go. Look at my bridle rein. It's shot in two. I galloped as fast as I could over to George's and got these men together. It's all I could raise."

Robert Hanna's lips were stiff.

"You saw naught of—my folks?"

"I didn't see anybody, only the Injuns. Now, what's to be done here?"

The Hannastown men did not need to tell what had happened. The burning logs spoke for themselves. So did the shouts and fiendish laughter that still came from across the Crabtree.

"There's over a hundred of them," Hugh said. "Most of them's Injuns though they've got some whites along too."

"An' that he-devil of a Guyasooter's in the lead, for I seen him myself," Sam put in bitterly. "If I could jist have got him!"

"How many guns here?" Jack asked. "Only nine? The devil! I thought we might make some kind of an attack. Well, we've got to do something. We can't just sit here an' let them shoot holes through us come morning. Is there any way we could scare the livers out of them? Put your brains in steep, men. We've got to figure out something."

The women had gathered around, all but those who watched over Peggy. Little Billy Kinkaid, still awake, was quietly handling an old drum he had dragged from a corner—relic of bygone musters.

Suddenly Matthew Jack grabbed it from the child.

"I've got an idee," he said. "There's the plank bridge down in the meadow there over the run. We fellahs on horseback will go down there an' ride back an' forth like there was about a thousand of us. One of you men come along an' beat this drum like hell while we're doin' it, an' all the rest of you here yell an' sing out like you was rejoicin' over reenforcements come. The trick might work."

"It's a good idee. It's got to work," Hugh said grimly. The men all agreed.

Hugh picked up the drum. "I can beat this," he said. "I'll go with you."

In a few minutes they were all ready.

"Don't drown out the hoofbeats," Jack cautioned, as the horsemen went out. "But whoop 'er up between times."

It was the sound of the drum that first broke clearly on the night air. Those in the stockade could hear the shouts beyond the Crabtree die down. The Indians, then, were listening. With no feeling of acting the women's voices suddenly rose high.

"They've come!" they yelled. "Here's help come! Thank God, we're saved! We're saved!"

The men's heavy voices joined them in whoops and hurrahs. Then came the sharp clatter of quick hoofs over the plank bridge. Over and over and over and yet again and again, while Hugh beat the drum.

Even those in the stockade, knowing all, found themselves suddenly swept away by the seeming reality of it. They called, they shouted, they yelled their victory and their derision in the ears of the foe.

At last the horsemen came back.

"By God," Sam told them, "you done that good! You had even me fooled there for a while."

"Let's keep quiet now. Not a sound," Jack advised. "That'll keep 'em wondering. We'll see what the day brings."

For the rest of the night they all waited, tense and sleepless, the inescapable sorrow crowded down by the continuing suspense of what greater disaster might yet befall.

There was a light rain just before dawn, but it was too

late to do any good. When the gray Sabbath broke, the sickening desolation of the ruined town was seen completely for the first time. But there was no sign of returning Indians. Even as the slow hours of the morning passed there was no sound, no movement coming from the direction of the last night's encampment. It looked as though the trick had worked.

Toward noon the men ventured out of the stockade, some of them to look over the ruins, some to ride back to Miller's to learn the full story of the destruction there, and others to dare the dangerous direction beyond the Crabtree to find out certainly which way the Indians had gone. These latter came back about three o'clock with good news, the only light in the blackness of that day. They found that the enemy had indeed slipped away, convinced evidently that great reenforcements had reached the fort. Guyasoota and his raiders had left a plain trail north toward the Kiskiminetas. There were the marks of horses' feet, the stolen ones, and scattered articles of household goods here and there. Yes, the Indians had actually gone, but they had left devastation and despair behind them.

It was when the word came back from Miller's that the women broke down utterly. Even Mrs. Kinkaid sat sobbing. Eleven people had been killed there, including Captain Brownlee and his youngest child. And among those carried off captive were Mrs. Brownlee and her other children, and *Mrs. Hanna and both the girls.* Robert Hanna put his trembling hands to his head as though the news had crazed him. He could not speak.

Matt Jack told it all briefly. They had found a few of the survivors when they went back. Miller's big blockhouse was burned to the ground, though several other near-by cabins were still standing. Mrs. Cruikshank herself had escaped. She had told him that the infare was in full swing when the Indians surprised them. There had been no chance to fight. The savages had killed Captain Brownlee as soon as they recognized him, for his name as an Indian fighter was known and hated among them. Jack and his men had followed on to the point where they found Brownlee's body with several others. They had given them burial there, according to pioneer custom, where they had fallen, and then returned to Hannastown with the bitter news.

It was Martha of all the women who first dried her tears, and braced herself.

"We've got to rummage round and find something to cook for supper," she said. "Everyone's weak and starved. Some hot food will help to stay us. Besides, we mustn't give way altogether. Our own lives have been spared. We'll pray Peggy's wound mends. And Robert," she added, turning to Mr. Hanna, addressing him by his Christian name for the first time in her life, "don't you despair, either. Mrs. Hanna and the girls weren't slain with the rest. That's one thing. Maybe the Injuns will continue to spare them. And they never ravage a woman, that's another thing to comfort you. We'll pray for their safety day and night, and that they'll be restored to you and to all of us. Look at our Hugh, and his escape, and never despair."

"Thank ye, Martha," Robert Hanna said weakly, then could say no more.

It was late sunset when the women emerged from the stockade to hunt about in the bitter gray ashes of the cabins for kettles and pots while the men brought what they could find from the truck patches. The sight of the slain animals was cruel hard to see. The women's tears flowed afresh.

"Oh, Mother," Violet cried out suddenly. "There lies Reddy! Down there by the run."

"And there's our Pet," Mrs. Guthrie lamented. "We drove her clear over the mountains ahead of us! The best cow ever was and just about to calve."

"And the sheep. The poor, innocent sheep—look at them . . ."

"And never a horse to be seen."

"Oh, it's the land of our desolation."

Martha, raising her eyes from her searching, saw again her own cabin. To her it was a more eerie sight than the heaps of rubble and charred logs that represented the other dwellings. It was like a skull. It stood alone, wrecked and forsaken. The end nearest the rest of the town was burned away. You could see through this gaping hole the shadowy outlines of the blank emptiness beyond. Like a skull, she thought again.

The men built fires and set the kettles of water over them. Someone brought hunks of fresh-skinned meat. No one asked from whence it came. They boiled the stew and hardened their hearts that they might eat.

Even now—so quickly must a pioneering people adjust

themselves to disaster and change—plans were being formulated. Many families from Westmoreland had already gone back east in the last two years. Now there would be more to follow. What was the use of struggling longer, asked some.

But there were others, Sam among them, who set their teeth and said they'd keep to the new land, by God, and fight the redskins to the end.

The Kinkaids would move at once down to the Redstone settlement, where they had relatives; the Brisons would go over Sewickley way; others to Chartiers. The Guthries spoke of Pittsburgh. And as she listened, a new hope rose in Martha's heart. Pittsburgh. It was far from being Philadelphia, but it was a step nearer civilization than ever Hannastown had been. And hadn't Violet often wished to walk in the King's Artillery Gardens and hear the band concerts at the Fort or ferry over to Coal Hill? Suppose they took up land on the edge of Pittsburgh as the Negleys had done? Even a little. Oh, it would be a better life than here. More likelihood of comfort for Violet in the days to come. If it worked out this way, then she would make never a moan over the loss they had borne. She would speak to Sam and to Hugh when she got them by themselves. For of course there would be no thought of rebuilding. There was a deeply ingrained feeling against that. "If they burn you out, move on." That's what Sam had often said back in the Cumberland Valley. He was saying it now, and so were the other men.

Michael Huffnagle, who was clever with the pen, took

Robert Hanna with him over to the courtroom while it was still daylight. When they returned they had a letter composed to the President of Pennsylvania. Michael read it aloud to them all in the quiet, slow-gathering dusk, while Robert Hanna for the first time since the dire news of his family had come, seemed to be gaining control of himself:

"Sir,—I am sorry to inform your Excellency, that last Saturday at two o'clock in the afternoon, Hanna's Town was attack'd by about one hundred Whites and Blacks. We found several Jackets, the buttons marked with the King's Eighth Regiment. At the same time this Town was attack'd another party attack'd Fort Miller about four miles from this Place. Hanna's Town and Fort Miller in a short time were reduced to Ashes, about twenty of the Inhabitants killed and taken, about one hundred head of Cattle, a number of horses and hogs killed. Such wanton destruction I never beheld, burning and destroying as they went. The People of this Place behaved brave, retired to the Fort, left their all a prey to the Enemy, and with twenty men only, and nine guns in good order, we stood the attack till dark. At first some of the Enemy came close to the Pickets but were soon obliged to retire farther off. I cannot inform you what Number of the Enemy may be killed, as we see them from the fort carrying off severals.

"The situation of the Inhabitants is deplorable, a number of them not having a Blanket to lye on, nor a Second suit to put on their Back. Affairs are strangely managed here; where the fault lies I will not presume to say. This Place being of the greatest consequence to the Frontiers, to be left destitute of Men, Arms, and ammunition is surprising to me, although frequent applications have been made. Your Excellency, I hope, will not be offended my mentioning that I think it would not be amiss that proper inquiry should be made about the management of the Public affairs in this County, and also to recommend to the Legislative Body to have some provision made for the Poor distressed People here. Your known humanity convinces me that you will do everything in your power to assist us in our distress'd condition.

"I have the Honor to be your Excellency's
"Most obt. Hbe. Servt.,
"MICH. HUFFNAGLE"

There was general approval of the letter, though plenty of doubt too as to its efficacy.

"What can you get from the government? They're a brigglin', bunglin' passle of nincompoops. Arch Loughry was wore out askin' for ammunition for here, wasn't he?"

"An' the militia wouldn't never have deserted if they'd got any supplies. What do they care in them Congresses what happens to the Back Country?"

"But it's a good letter, Mike. It's worth sendin' on, soon's you can get an express."

"And if they've got any bowels of mercies—"

"They haven't, damn 'em!"

After the reading of the letter, Martha went over again to look at Peggy. She was sleeping fitfully. Her cheeks looked hot, and she moaned with pain every few minutes. Her breathing seemed a bit easier, though. Martha took off her petticoat and, folding it, placed it gently under the girl's side.

"It'll maybe ease her up a bit," she said to Mrs. Shaw. "Call me if you need me, Sarah. I'm going to snatch a little rest."

In fact she found she could no longer stand up. The strange feeling in her chest was frightening, and her legs gave way under her. She lay down in the corner on an old cast-off coat. As she did so a paper rustled in her bosom. She felt of it in surprise. It was her journal! She had had it in her hand when Hugh came to warn them; she had thrust it into her dress as she ran and never until this moment remembered it. The little book was not very large—though the entries covered a number of years —for her writing was delicately fine. Strange that it should have been saved. She was glad, however, that it was so. A little warmth crept into her heart. The journal represented one continuous thread of her life which had not been severed.

She watched Hugh and Violet standing close to each other across the stockade. Her face was white, but her eyes were raised to his; and he was smiling down upon her. Neither flame nor war nor desolation could destroy that love, Martha felt sure. And if they settled again near Pittsburgh they might all even live to bless this day.

I'm a great one for hoping, she thought to herself with a sigh, *but after all, there's little else left me, now.*

XV

The Whippoorwill

In the morning there was stir in the stockade even before daybreak. The few strangers among them who had been there for court said an early good-bye and scattered for their own homes, convinced by now that there was no more danger from the Indians. Edward Cook left to try to raise a new body of militia for the fort, though some of the men said it was no use locking the door after the horse was stolen.

The rest, who were bound together by their years as neighbors, and now bound more closely by their common disaster, talked their plans over again in the morning light. The first concern was for Peggy, whose condition they all realized was serious. Mr. Shaw had already started on foot for Dr. Shields, and at Robert Hanna's suggestion they carried her over to his house. It was Hen Wilson's strong arms that bore her. There was room there for more than one family, so the Guthries and the Shaws moved in for the present. The women made shakedowns in the courtroom, too, so that more people could be comfortable at night. The Kinkaids, with the dispatch natural to Mrs. Kinkaid at least, got their children to-

gether and set out for the Redstone settlement that very
morning. They said their good-byes calmly enough, but
Martha saw her stopping for a last look toward the graveyard on the hill.

She feels more than she ever let on, she thought, and
then went after her to say another farewell.

Sam and Hugh went back to the remains of their own
cabin at the break of day. Hugh returned to the fort
before noon.

"We've got things fixed up a little," he said in a low
tone to Martha and Violet. "It'll be better than stayin'
here anyway. Father says to come on an' we'll make what
shift we can."

It was a relief to leave the crowded, noisy fort. The
inevitable reaction to all that had passed was setting in
already. There was bitter distress, physical discomfort,
and weary, discouraged family bickerings. Martha leaned
heavily upon Hugh as they walked slowly up the road.
At one place she stopped short. Torn, half burnt, tram-
pled in the earth was the Shakespeare. She tried to pick
it up, but her strength failed her. Violet stooped and
gathered the few remains tenderly in her hands.

"Just a bit of 'Hamlet,' " she said, "and a page or so
from the Sonnets. That's all. And you can hardly read
them."

The cabin itself looked strange enough. The fireplace
and chimney were intact but all else was changed. The
men had found the hacked and broken furniture and
brought inside the few pieces that could be made to hold
together. The feather tick from the big bed had been

rent, and the feathers tossed to the winds. The Bible was gone and "Pilgrim's Progress"! The mirror, and the candlesticks, and the fiddle! All those little softening features with which Martha by patient sacrifice had tried to ameliorate the roughness of the wilderness were wiped out as though they had never been. Only the three rude walls were left and the wide gaping space.

Martha sat down on what had been the settle.

"I'm afraid, Violet, you'll have to see about the dinner. I feel queer-like, as if—as if . . ."

She was dimly conscious of supporting arms and of water put to her lips. She could hear their voices faintly:

"Did the Injuns get up in the cockloft, Hugh?"

"No."

"Fetch down our tick, then, and the sheets. Hurry, Hugh. Hurry, Father. We must fix a bed for her."

Martha could make no move to help, to speak, to reassure them. When she lay down at last, she could not question or even look up. She lay, with her eyes closed, in complete, unreasoning exhaustion.

When she woke up, she felt better. Violet was beside her, her face pale and anxious, but at Martha's smile she became herself again.

"Oh, Mother, what a startle you gave us! Are you all right?"

"Just tired, dear. I'll be in fine fettle soon."

"I've got some dinner keeping hot for you. We've found a lot more things! The crane and the big pot and the spoons Mrs. Proctor gave me, and the noggin with the salt in it, and *my little flowered plate!* It's not broken!

They never went up in the cockloft at all, so that's something. Hugh brought our tick down for you, and he's out getting balsam boughs now for our bed. We'll get along some way, Mother. Don't worry. We're so much better off than the others."

Martha watched her lovely, eager face. What a thing was youth! How free from fear, how confident in its love, how unmarred by yesterday, how expectant of tomorrow!

She had better speak at once about getting to Pittsburgh. There was no time to waste. She ate a little of the stew Violet brought her and felt still stronger.

Suddenly a whimpering sound came from the doorway. Violet turned and then gave a great cry of joy.

"It's Watch! *It's Watch back!*"

The men came running at the sound and Martha raised herself up in bed that she might see. Watch was there, thinner from his two-day fast, his eyes still frightened, his coat torn, his ears full of briers, but his tail wagging in ecstasy. He could not tell his story, where he had been hiding or what sights he had seen; but here he was, whining with relief and happiness, rubbing against them, offering again and again his muddy, thorn-torn paw.

"Poor faithful beast. Poor old Watch," Martha kept saying with the tears in her eyes, while Sam blew his nose and Hugh laid his head against the dog's shaggy coat. Violet hurried to get him some food, and as they watched him eat, turning often to look at them for reassurance, a familiar tenderness caught their hearts.

"It seems happier, like, now, with Watch back," Violet

said. "And when Mother's just well again, we'll be all ready to start in the new."

"That was a funny turn I had, and no mistake," Martha said apologetically when the men came over to the bed to see how she was. "But I'm better now and ready to talk a little about our own plans. I've been thinking of the Guthries going nigh-hand to Pittsburgh to settle. You know the Negleys took up land there and are rightly pleased with it. We could surely find enough acreage there, and to be within reach of the town, like, would be nice for Violet and Hugh—"

She broke off, a dark foreboding heavy upon her. No one spoke for a moment, and then Sam cleared his throat.

"Hugh here's got the itch to go on into the Ohio country. Suits me all right. I've been ready to move on this good while."

Hugh spoke up quickly then, his eyes pleading with her, as they had pleaded once before.

"It's great country that. You see, I went through it when they was takin' us prisoners up to Detroit. An' there's so few settlers there now we could have our pick of acreage. I aim to take up enough to make us rich some day, Violet an' me. An' if we all go out together, it would be good—wouldn't it?"

Martha's lips were stone-white.

"The—Ohio—country! Why, it's *real wilderness!*"

"But it won't be wilderness always. Somebody's got to break it, an' it might as well be me. I'd rather clear my own land than take what some other man's done. An' Violet's willing. I've talked it over with her."

"Some says after this war's all fixed up, there's goin' to be folks from the east crowdin' round out here," Sam spoke. "I'm like Hugh. It's better to move on where you got plenty room."

"An' it's fine land, Mother. The finest I've ever seen. I've been tellin' Violet about it."

Martha turned her face slowly upon her daughter.

"You'd be willing to go?" she asked.

"If Hugh wants it. I'll go anywhere with him."

"Your mind's made up, Hugh?"

"I guess it is, Mother."

Martha turned to the wall.

"I'm a little tired. If you'll just all let me alone a bit, I'll—I'll rest . . ."

She heard their voices planning as the three sat on the steps. Sam was as eager as a boy.

"Course it'll take awhile to get things ready," Hugh said. "We'll have to have a horse for one thing. I won't start without a horse for Violet."

"Oh, poor old Ranger! I wonder where he is now?"

They were all silent for a minute, then Hugh spoke again.

"The Craigs have an extry colt. I might go over an' talk with Sam about it. Sam might even think of goin' along."

The voices rose and fell. Sometimes the words did not penetrate Martha's brain. She could not think. She could only lie there, quiet, helpless. The bruised reed was broken. The smoking flax was quenched.

It was nearly two weeks before the others realized that Martha would not be going with them to the Ohio country, though she had known it from the first.

"Sure you'll be able. We ain't startin' yet awhile," Sam kept saying those first days. "You've just got a little donsie spell from the excitement, that's all. You'll get rested up. Take plenty boneset tea. It'll fettle you."

Martha's eyes rested patiently upon him.

"It's not that I wouldn't try to go along with the rest of you, Sam. I just haven't the list, some way."

One day Violet spoke anxiously. "Hadn't we better get Dr. Shields over, Mother? Maybe if he bled you . . ."

Martha smiled gently.

"He could do me no good, dear. I guess I'm just worn out, like."

It was a sad enough day when the truth was finally borne in upon them all, for Peggy died in the early morning. There had been nothing anyone could do for her, either, not even Dr. Shields. The bullet remained in her breast, and the days had been slow, wasting ones. Naught but skin and bone she was at the last, dear Peggy! Hen Wilson was beside her till the end, and she spoke to him often and held on to his hand. She wanted Jamsey near her, too. Violet had been over daily to help in whatever way she could, and when there was no more now for loving hands to do, she came sadly back to tell Martha all that had passed. It was at that moment, as she wept for her friend, that her eyes were opened. She looked long in her mother's face and then sank on her knees beside the bed.

Martha's hand caressed her hair. "I'm glad you know, child. I haven't had the heart to tell you. But don't grieve so. We've much to say these last days. Don't grieve. You have Hugh. And your father will go along. That will be a part of the old home in the new. Look up, child."

Violet slowly raised her stricken face.

"I want to tell you something. In all the years you've never given me a frown or a harsh word. You've been naught but a joy to me since the day you were born. Some time—later on—it may pleasure you to remember this."

"Mother! Mother!"

"And I'll never be really far away from you. It's been like that with my own mother. A dozen times a day, like, it's always come to me, 'That's the way Mother did,' or 'I can just hear Mother saying that.' You never really lose your mother, child. Not when you love her. So don't grieve."

They held each other close, Violet sobbing still, Martha's eyes looking far away.

"Will it be—soon, think you?" the girl asked brokenly.

"I can't rightly tell. But there's many things on my mind to say to you, so we'll talk as much as I've strength for, tomorrow."

That night out at the forest edge, Violet told Sam and Hugh. At first Sam scoffed and would scarcely allow her to speak.

"Aw, your mother's as tough as a hickory knot. She'll be all right, I tell you. Now don't get idees in your head about her just because Peggy's died." His tone was angry.

But Hugh was grave.

"I've been wonderin', myself," he said slowly. "There's a look on her face."

"I know," Violet sobbed, clinging to him. "It's not of earth, like."

"Fiddlesticks!" Sam scolded. "You're both borrowin' trouble. You'll kill us all if you keep talkin' this way. Now stop broodin' an' vaporin', Vi'let, an' behave yourself!"

He stamped off, cursing heavily under his breath.

"I think he knows too, but he just won't face it," Violet whispered. "Oh, Hugh, hold me tight."

The next day Martha gave Violet the little journal. "I've always kept it, secret-like, but I want you to have it. If you get lonesome sometimes, it might bring things back to you to read it. And don't worry about all the plans for you I wrote down. I've just been thinking, lying here, it'll be *your* child, maybe, yours and Hugh's, that will have the nice house some day and the papered walls and the flowered dishes—"

"And the pewter candle molds!"

Martha smiled faintly. "When you get discouraged you must keep thinking of that. It'll bear you up."

Violet pressed the journal to her heart. "This will be like your own self speaking to me, Mother."

"And mind, Violet, get a Bible before you start for the Ohio country. Whatever you may lack, be sure you have that. And cherish those few pages of Shakespeare, too. It'll lift your mind. And when your children come, be

sure to watch out for the fire and for soap-making days.
A burn's an awful-like thing. Bear grease is good for it,
and if you have myrrh growing near you, always keep
the bark on hand. A brew of that is healing. And mind
for earache, fill a bladder with hot milk and hold to it.
I've used a drop of warm bear oil, too. And for a croup,
soak a rag in hot oil, and wrap it round the neck . . ."

She hadn't strength to say more then; but in the evening she motioned Hugh to come to her. She looked at
him as though she were fastening in her mind every
lineament of his strong, dark face. His troubled eyes
answered her.

"You know, Hugh, this was never my plan for Violet."

"I know it, Mother, but I'll take care of her. An' with
the town here burnt an' all, it seems the best thing
to do—"

She raised her finger.

"I've been thinking over again how there's those that
go before and those that come after. There's some that
must cut down the wilderness and break the rough
ground, and there's some that come after and live on the
fat of the land. God sorts out which is which. Maybe he's
sorted you and Violet to go before, the way Sam and I
did. Be good to her, Hugh, be good to her."

The next morning they could all see that she was very
weak. Even Sam, his hands shaking, his mouth twisted,
went over to stand helplessly by the bed, asking awkward
questions.

Martha touched his hand. "It's all right, Sam," she
said gently. "Don't fash yourself."

He went out then, to sit on the steps with his head low upon his knees.

Martha tossed back and forth with pitiful unrest. Her breath came quickly and there were long-drawn sighs between.

"I've got more things I must say, Violet. Just sit close here." She touched the soft curls.

"Don't kick against the pricks, child, when life gets hard for you. I doubt I've always done that too much. Take it all as it comes to you, the good and the bad, and do your best with it. Then try not to fret. Never doubt there's reason to it somehow, though you can't riddle it out yourself. You'll mind, child?"

"I'll mind, Mother."

"It's to ease you over some day to come, I'm telling you this."

Violet put her arms around the thin form on the bed, but she could not speak.

In the late afternoon Martha grew more restless. Violet had scarcely left her bedside all the day. Now her mother motioned weakly for her to go out.

"I want to speak to Hugh by himself," she whispered.

Hugh came quickly.

Martha signed for him to shut the door.

He closed it, wonderingly.

"Hugh, lad, this is hard to do, but I have to, for Violet's sake. When her time comes—I mean in childbirth—there may be no other woman near. I have to tell you things—hard things. I want you to bear them and mind them for her sake."

She stopped, breathing hard.

"I'm ready, Mother."

"Put your head down close. Don't ever tell her till you need to."

Her whispers came with a great effort, but she kept on. Hugh's face flushed scarlet, but he did not flinch. Sometimes he would ask a hesitant question. Sometimes Martha would slowly repeat what she had said.

"You understand, Hugh? You must get it right, lad."

"I've got it, Mother."

"Then there's some things, Hugh, you must never do. You mustn't mind me telling you now I'm at death's door. I want your word."

When she had finished, his strong hand grasped her thin one.

"I give you my word, Mother. I love her better than my life. I'll take care of her and fend for her always."

Martha smiled at him then.

"I know you'll do your best, lad. God bless you."

The slow, gradual evening drew on. Martha's breathing became more and more faint. Sam still crouched on the step with his head buried. Sometimes Violet saw him shiver as though from cold. She sat close to the bed, holding Martha's hand, the tears running unstaunched down her cheeks. Hugh stood beside her, his eyes fixed on the woman who had been mother both to him and to his beloved. Watch would not move from under the bed.

With the first darkness Martha seemed to lose consciousness; her breath now came like a small candle flame blown in the wind.

"Mother, *Mother,*" Violet called.

For answer her lips moved feebly. Hugh bent close to listen.

"It's something about the dawn," he whispered.

"I know what she means," Violet sobbed.

Martha did not speak again.

The moon rose above the eastern ranges, round and golden. Then at last there came the sound for which they all waited. Not sadly but with a clear, sweet finality there echoed from the treetops the call of the whippoorwill.